BLOODLINES

A HORSE RACING ANTHOLOGY

MAGGIE ESTEP grew up moving throughout the country with her nomadic horse trainer parents. She placed her first-ever bet at Delaware Park, where her mother worked as a trainer. The horse she bet on, who looked exceptional in the paddock, won at eighty to one. Maggie has published six books, most recently *Flamethrower,* the third in a trilogy of crime novels set at the New York racetracks. Her work has appeared in numerous magazines, newspapers, and anthologies including *The KGB Bar Reader, The Best American Erotica, Brooklyn Noir, Hard Boiled Brooklyn,* and the forthcoming *Bad Girls Anthology.* Maggie is currently working on a novel entitled *Girls & Horses.* She lives in Brooklyn, New York.

JASON STARR skipped his high school graduation to go to Belmont Park with his friends and has been hanging out at racetracks and Off-Track Betting parlors in the New York City area for years. One of the world's top handicappers—in his own mind—Starr hasn't picked a Kentucky Derby winner since Genuine Risk. Naturally, horse racing plots and references have appeared in several of his crime novels, in particular *Nothing Personal* (1998), about a compulsive gambler who hatches a kidnapping plot to pay off his debts, and *Fake I.D.* (2000), about a Manhattan bouncer whose attempt to join a horse-owning syndicate has devastating consequences. Starr's other crime novels include 2004 Barry Award winner *Tough Luck* and 2005 Anthony Award winner *Twisted City*. His latest crime novel, due in 2006 is *Lights Out*. His novels have been translated into ten languages, and he lives with his wife and daughter in New York. He dedicates his story in *Bloodlines* to the memory of William Murray, who was unable to contribute to this book, but who was as enthusiastic about it as the editors themselves.

BLOODLINES

A HORSE RACING ANTHOLOGY

BLOODLINES

A HORSE RACING ANTHOLOGY

EDITED BY **Maggie Estep**

AND **Jason Starr**

VINTAGE BOOKS   A Division of Random House, Inc.   New York

A VINTAGE BOOKS ORIGINAL, SEPTEMBER 2006

Vintage and colophon are registered trademarks of Random
House, Inc.

An extension of the copyright page appears on page 371.

Cataloging-in-Publication Data for *Bloodlines* is on file at the Library
of Congress.

Vintage ISBN-10: 1-4000-9695-2
Vintage ISBN-13: 978-1-4000-9695-4

Book design by Mia Risberg

www.vintagebooks.com

Printed in the United States of America
10   9   8   7   6   5   4   3   2   1

CONTENTS

THE .50 SOLUTION   Lee Child   3

BLACK-EYED SUSAN   Laura Lippman   14

THE SMARTY JONES BUBBLE   Steven Crist   29

HIPPOMANCY   Scott Phillips   48

BEAST   Maggie Estep   57

WISE CROWDS AND FOOLISH BETTORS:
   Why It's Hard to Beat the Track   James Surowiecki   82

GURRIERS   Bill Barich   90

THE HORSE IN OUR HISTORY   Daniel Woodrell   104

HEART   Wallace Stroby   114

ALL HORSES HAVE BEAUTIFUL
    EYES AND A BIG COCK   Jonathan Ames   136

THE CYNICAL BREED   Charlie Stella   145

THE DERBY   Laura Hillenbrand   165

WHITE MULE, SPOTTED PIG   Joe R. Lansdale   184

AUGUST OF 1959   William Nack   240

THE SELECTOR   Jerry Stahl   265

RACING GODS AND WILD THINGS   John Schaefer   283

THE GRAVEYARD OF JIMMY FONTAINE   Jason Starr   302

WHAT I LEARNED FROM THEM AFTER THEY
    CAME HOME FROM THE TRACK   Jane Smiley   324

HORSE OF A DIFFERENT COLOR   Ken Bruen   340

MY LIFE AS A CHILDHOOD
    RACING JUNKIE   Meghan O'Rourke   352

THE CONTRIBUTORS   365

BLOODLINES

A HORSE RACING ANTHOLOGY

THE .50 SOLUTION

Lee Child

MOST TIMES I ASSESS THE CLIENT and then the target and only afterward do I set the price. It's about common sense and variables. If the client is rich, I ask for more. If the target is tough, I ask for more. If there are major expenses involved, I ask for more. So if I'm working overseas on behalf of a billionaire against a guy in a remote hideout with a competent protection team on his side, I'm going to ask for maybe a hundred times what I would want from some local chick looking to solve her marital problems in a quick and messy manner. Variables, and common sense.

But this time the negotiation started differently.

The guy who came to see me was rich. That was clear. His wealth was pore-deep. Not just his clothes. Not just his car. This was a guy who had been rich forever. Maybe for generations. He was tall and gray and silvery and self-assured. He was a patrician. It was all right there in the way he held himself, the way he spoke, the way he took charge.

First thing he talked about was the choice of weapon.

He said, "I hear you've used a Barrett Model Ninety on more than one occasion."

I said, "You hear right."

"You like that piece?"

"It's a fine rifle."

"So you'll use it for me."

"I choose the weapon," I said.

"Based on what?"

"Need."

"You'll need it."

I asked, "Why? Long range?"

"Maybe two hundred yards."

"I don't need a Barrett Ninety for two hundred yards."

"It's what I want."

"Will the target be wearing body armor?"

"No."

"Inside a vehicle?"

"Open air."

"Then I'll use a three-oh-eight. Or something European."

"I want that fifty-caliber shell."

"A three-oh-eight or a NATO round will get him just as dead from two hundred yards."

"Maybe not."

Looking at him I was pretty sure this was a guy who had never fired a .50 Barrett in his life. Or a .308 Remington. Or an M16, or an FN, or an H&K. Or any kind of a rifle. He had probably never fired anything at all, except maybe a BB gun as a kid and workers as a adult.

I said, "The Barrett is an awkward weapon. It's four feet long and it doesn't break down. It weighs twenty-two pounds. It's got bipod legs, for Christ's sake. It's like an artillery piece. Hard to conceal. And it's very loud. Maybe the loudest rifle in the history of the world."

He said, "I like that fifty-caliber shell."

"I'll give you one," I said. "You can plate it with gold and put it on a chain and wear it around your neck."

"I want you to use it."

Then I started thinking maybe this guy was some kind of a sadist. A caliber of .50 is a decimal fraction, just another way of saying half an inch. A lead bullet a half inch across is a big thing. It weighs about two ounces, and any kind of a decent load fires it close to two thousand miles an hour. It could catch a supersonic jet fighter and bring it down. Against a person two hundred yards away, it's going to cut him in two. Like making the guy swallow a bomb, and then setting it off.

I said, "You want a spectacle, I could do it close with a knife. You know, if you want to send a message."

He said, "That's not the issue. This is not about a message. This is about the result."

"Can't be," I said. "From two hundred yards I can get a result with anything. Something short with a folding stock, I can walk away afterward with it under my coat. Or I could throw a rock."

"I want you to use the Barrett."

"Expensive," I said. "I'd have to leave it behind. Which means paying through the nose to make it untraceable. It'll cost more than a foreign car for the ordnance alone. Before we even talk about my fee."

"Okay," he said, no hesitation.

I said, "It's ridiculous."

He said nothing. I thought: *Two hundred yards, no body armor, in the open air. Makes no sense.* So I asked.

I said, "Who's the target?"

He said, "A horse."

I was quiet for a long moment. "What kind of a horse?"

"A Thoroughbred racehorse."

I asked, "You own racehorses?"

He said, "Dozens of them."

"Good ones?"

"Some of the very best."

"So the target is what, a rival?"

"A thorn in my side."

After that, it made a lot more sense. The guy said, "I'm not an idiot. I've thought about it very carefully. It's got to look accidental. We can't just shoot the horse in the head. That's too obvious. It's got to look like the real target was the owner, but your aim was off and the horse is collateral damage. So the shot can't look placed. It's got to look random. Neck, shoulder, whatever. But I need death or permanent disability."

I said, "Which explains your preference for the Barrett."

He nodded. I nodded back. A Thoroughbred racehorse weighs about half a ton. A .308 or a NATO round fired randomly into its center mass might not do the job. Not in terms of death or permanent disability. But a big .50 shell almost certainly would. Even if you weigh half a ton, it's pretty hard to struggle along with a hole the size of a garbage can blown through any part of you.

I asked, "Who's the owner? Is he a plausible target in himself?"

The guy told me who the owner was, and we agreed he was a plausible target. Rumors, shady connections.

Then I said, "What about you? Are you two enemies, personally?"

"You mean, will I be suspected of ordering the hit that misses?"

"Exactly."

"Not a chance," my guy said. "We don't know each other."

"Except as rival owners."

"There are hundreds of rival owners."

"Is a horse of yours going to win if this guy's doesn't?"

"I certainly hope so."

"So they'll look at you."

"Not if it looks like the man was the target, instead of the horse."

I asked, "When?"

He told me anytime within the next four days.

I asked, "Where?"

He told me the horse was in a facility some ways south. Horse country, obviously, grand fields, lush grass, white fences, rolling hills. He told me about long routes through the countryside, called gallops, where the horses worked out just after dawn. He told me about the silence and the early mists. He told me how in the week before a big race the owner would be there every morning to assess his horse's form, to revel in its power and speed and grace and appetite. He told me about the stands of trees that were everywhere and would provide excellent cover.

Then he stopped talking. I felt a little foolish, but I asked him anyway: "Do you have a photograph? Of the target?"

He took an envelope from his inside jacket pocket. Gave it to me. In it was a glossy color picture of a horse. It looked posed, like a promotional item. Like an actor or an actress has headshots made, for publicity. This particular horse was a magnificent animal. Tall, shiny, muscular, almost jet-black, with a white blaze on its face. Quite beautiful.

"Okay," I said.

Then my guy asked me his own question.

He asked me, "How much?"

It was an interesting issue. Technically we were only conspiring to shoot a horse. In most states that's a property crime. A long way from homicide. And I already had an untraceable Barrett Ninety. As a matter of fact, I had three. Their serial numbers stopped dead with the Israeli army. One of them was well used. It was about ready for a new barrel anyway. It would make a fine throw-down gun. Firing cold through a worn barrel wasn't something I would risk against a human, but against something the size of a horse from two hundred yards it wouldn't be a problem. If I aimed at the fattest part of the animal I could afford to miss by up to a foot.

I didn't tell the guy any of that, of course. Instead I banged on for a while about the price of the rifle and the premium I would have to pay for dead-ended paperwork. Then I talked about risk, and waited to see if he stopped me. But he didn't. I could tell he was obsessed. He had a goal. He wanted his own horse to win, and that fact was blinding him to reality just the same way some people get all wound up about betrayal and adultery and business partnerships.

I looked at the photograph again.

"One hundred thousand dollars," I said.

He said nothing.

"In cash," I said.

He said nothing.

"Up front," I said.

He nodded.

"One condition," he said. "I want to be there. I want to see it happen."

I looked at him and I looked at the photograph and I thought about a hundred grand in cash.

"Okay," I said. "You can be there."

He opened the briefcase he had down by his leg and took out a brick of money. It looked okay, smelled okay, and felt okay. There was probably more in the case, but I didn't care. A hundred grand was enough, in the circumstances.

"Day after tomorrow," I said.

We agreed on a place to meet, down south, down in horse country, and he left.

I HID THE MONEY where I always do, which is in a metal trunk in my storage unit. Inside the trunk the first thing you see is a human skull inside a Hefty One Zip bag. On the white panel where you're supposed to write what you're freezing is lettered: *This Man Tried to Rip Me Off.* It isn't true, of course. The skull came from an antique shop. Probably an old medical school specimen from the Indian subcontinent.

Next to the money trunk was the gun trunk. I took out the worn Barrett and checked it over. Disassembled it, cleaned it, oiled it, wiped it clean, and then put it back together wearing latex gloves. I loaded a fresh magazine, still with the gloves on. Then I loaded the magazine into the rifle and slid the rifle end-on into an old shoulder-borne golf bag. Then I put the golf bag into the trunk of my car and left it there.

In my house I propped the racehorse photograph on my mantel. I spent a lot of time staring at it.

I MET THE GUY at the time and place we had agreed. It was a lonely crossroad, close to a cross-country track that led to a distant stand of trees, an hour before dawn. The weather was cold. My guy had a coat and gloves on, and binoculars around his neck. I had gloves on too. Latex. But no binoculars. I had a Leupold & Stevens scope on the Barrett, in the golf bag.

I was relaxed, feeling what I always feel when I'm about to kill something, which is to say nothing very much at all. But my client was unrelaxed. He was shivering with an anticipation that was almost pornographic in its intensity. Like a pedophile on a plane to Thailand. I didn't like it much.

We walked side by side through the dew. The ground was hard and pocked by footprints. Lots of them, coming and going.

"Who's been here?" I asked.

"Racetrack touts," my guy said. "Sports journalists, gamblers looking for inside dope."

"Looks like Times Square," I said. "I don't like it."

"It'll be okay today. Nobody scouts here anymore. They all know this horse. They all know it can win in its sleep."

We walked on in silence. Reached the stand of trees. It was oval-shaped, thin at the northern end. We stepped back and forth until we had a clear line of sight through the trunks. Dawn light was in the sky. Two hundred yards away and slightly downhill was a broad grass clearing with plenty of tire tracks showing. A thin gray mist hung in the air.

"This is it?" I said.

My guy nodded. "The horses come in from the south. The cars come in from the west. They meet right there."

"Why?"

"No real reason. Ritual, mostly. Backslapping and bullshitting. The pride of ownership."

I took the Barrett out of the golf bag. I had already decided how I was going to set up the shot. No bipod. I wanted the gun low and free. I knelt on one knee and rested the muzzle in the crook of a branch. Sighted through the scope. Racked the bolt and felt the first mighty .50 shell smack home into the chamber.

"Now we wait," my guy said. He stood at my shoulder, maybe a yard to my right and a yard behind me.

THE CARS ARRIVED FIRST. They were SUVs, really. Working machines, old and muddy and dented. A Jeep, and two Land Rovers. Five guys climbed out. Four looked poor and one looked rich.

"Trainer and stable lads and the owner," my guy said. "The owner is the one in the long coat."

The five of them stamped and shuffled and their breath pooled around their heads.

"Listen," my guy said.

I heard something way off to my left. To the south. A low drumming, and a sound like giant bellows coughing and pumping. Hooves, and huge equine lungs cycling gallons of sweet fresh morning air.

I rocked backward until I was sitting right down on the ground.

"Get ready," my guy said, from above and behind me.

There were altogether ten horses. They came up in a ragged arrowhead formation, slowing, drifting off-line, tossing their heads, their hard breathing blowing violent yard-long trumpet-shaped plumes of steam ahead of them.

"What is this?" I asked. "The whole roster?"

"String," my guy said. "That's what we call it. This is his whole first string."

In the gray dawn light and under the steam all the horses looked exactly the same to me.

But that didn't matter.

"Ready?" my guy said. "They won't be here long."

"Open your mouth," I said.

"What?"

"Open your mouth, real wide. Like you're yawning."

"Why?"

"To equalize the pressure. Like on a plane. I told you, this is a loud gun. It's going to blow your eardrums otherwise. You'll be deaf for a month."

I glanced around and checked. He had opened his mouth, but halfheartedly, like a guy waiting for the dentist to get back from looking at a chart.

"No, like this," I said. I showed him. I opened my mouth as wide as it would go and pulled my chin back into my neck until the tendons hurt in the hinge of my jaw.

He did the same thing.

I whipped the Barrett's barrel way up and around, fast and smooth, like a duck hunter tracking a flushed bird. Then I pulled the trigger. Shot my guy through the roof of his mouth. The giant rifle boomed and kicked and the top of my guy's head came off like a hard-boiled egg. His body came down in a heap and sprawled. I dropped the rifle on top of him and pulled his right shoe off. Tossed it on the ground. Then I ran. Two minutes later I was back in my car. Four minutes later I was a mile away.

I WAS UP AN EASY HUNDRED GRAND, but the world was down an industrialist, a philanthropist, and a racehorse owner. That's what the Sunday papers said. He had committed suicide. The way the cops had pieced it together, he had tormented himself over the fact that his best horse always came in second. He had spied on his rival's workout, maybe hoping for some sign of fallibility. None had been forthcoming. So he had somehow obtained a sniper rifle, last legally owned by the Israel Defense Force. Maybe he had planned to shoot the rival horse, but at the last minute he hadn't been able to go through with it. So, depressed and tormented, he had reversed the rifle, put the muzzle in his mouth, kicked off his shoe, and used his toe on the trigger. A police officer of roughly the same height had taken part in a simulation to prove that such a thing was physically possible, even with a gun as long as the Barrett.

Near the back of the paper were the racing results. The big black horse had won by seven lengths. My guy's runner had been scratched.

I kept the photograph on my mantel for a long time afterward. A girl I met much later noticed that it was the only picture I had in the house. She asked me if I liked animals better than people. I told her that I did, mostly. She liked me for it. But not enough to stick around.

BLACK-EYED SUSAN

Laura Lippman

THE MELVILLE FAMILY HAD PREAKNESS coming and going, as Dontay's Granny M liked to say. From their row house south of Pimlico, the loose assemblage of three generations—sometimes as many as twelve people in the three-bedroom house, never fewer than eight—squeezed every coin they could from the third Saturday in May, and they were always looking for new ways to make money. Revenue streams, as Dontay had learned to call them in Pimlico Middle's stock-picking club. Last year, for example, the Melvilles had tried a barbecue stand, selling racegoers hamburgers and hot dogs, but the city health people had shut them down before noon. So they were going to try bottled water this year, maybe some sodas, although sly-like, because they could bust you for not charging sales tax, too. The Melvilles had considered bags of salted nuts as well, but that was more of a Camden Yards thing. People going to the track didn't seem to want nuts as much, not even pistachios. Candy melted no matter how cool the day, and it was hard to be competitive on chips unless you went off-brand, and Baltimore was an Utz city.

Parking was the big moneymaker. Over the years, the Melvilles had figured they could make exactly six spaces in their front yard, plus two in the driveway. Discouraged any serious gardening efforts the other 364 days out of the year, but that was pure bonus as far as the kids were concerned. No beds to weed, no flowers to tend, no worrying about what got trampled. The rate was thirty dollars a spot, which was a fair price, close as they were to the entrance, and that thirty dollars included true *vigilance,* as Uncle Marcus liked to say to the people who tried to negotiate. These days, most of their business was repeat customers, old-timers who had figured out that the houses south of the racetrack were much closer to the entrance than the places on the other side of Northern Parkway. The first-timers, now, they were a little nervous about coming south of the track, but once they made that long, long trek back to the Northern Parkway side, they started looking south.

So, eight vehicles times thirty—that was $240. But they weren't done yet. All the young ones ran shopping carts, not just for the Melvilles' own parkers, but for the on-the-street ones who couldn't make it the whole way with their coolers and grocery sacks. Dontay and his cousins couldn't charge as much as the north-side boys, given the shorter distance, but they made more trips, so it came out about the same. Most of the folks gave you at least ten dollars to haul a cooler, although there was always some woe-is-me motherfucker—that's what Uncle Marcus called them, outside Granny M's hearing—who tried to find a reason to short you at the gate.

The money didn't end just because the race did. On the day after Preakness, the older Melvilles all signed up for cleanup duty in the infield, and there wasn't a year that went by that someone didn't find a winning ticket in the debris. Never anything big, wasn't like hitting a Pick Four or even a Pick Three, but often good for twenty bucks or so. People got drunk, threw the wrong tickets down. You just had to keep the *Sunpapers* in your back pocket, familiarize yourself with the race results. This was going to be Dontay's first year on cleanup, and he couldn't help hoping that he would find a winning ticket. His uncle had lied about his age to get him a spot on the crew, so he'd make the minimum wage up front. But the real draw was what you might find—not just tickets, but perfectly good cartons of soda and beer, maybe even jewelry and wallets without ID. Or so Dontay had heard.

But Preakness itself was the best day, the biggest haul. The night before, Dontay greased his cart's wheels and polished his pitch. There was a right way to do it, bold but not too much so. People didn't like to feel hustled. He also pondered the downside to Preakness: No one needed the carts to carry stuff away because the coolers were always empty by day's end, light enough for the weakest, most sissified men to heave onto their shoulders or drag on the pavement behind them. Which was a shame, because people were looser by the end of the day, wavy with liquor and their winnings. Dontay was still thinking on how to develop a service that people needed when the race was over. The main thing everyone wanted was a fast getaway, another virtue of the Melvilles' location, which had several ways out of the neighborhood. What would people pay to ride a helicopter, though? There had to be other possibilities. Dontay thought on it. Besides, more and more people were bringing in wheeled coolers, a troubling development. The shopping-cart concession was getting hit hard by those coolers with wheels.

Dontay was a Melville, and all the Melvilles were industrious by nature. True, some had focused their energies on less legal businesses, which was why the number of people in the house tended to fluctuate. They were at the high end right now, with Uncle Stevie home from Hagerstown and Delia's twins staying with them, while Delia was spending time on the west side, in that place that Granny M called "thereabouts." *When's our mama coming?* the twins asked late at night, when they were sleepy and forgetful. *Where's our mama?* "Thereabouts," Granny M said. "She'll be coming home shortly." Granny M pledged that her house was open to all her children and her children's children and, when the time came, and it was coming, her children's children's children, but she had rules. Church was optional if you were over twelve. Sobriety was not. That was why she had squashed Uncle Marcus's plan to buy some cheap tallboys and Heinekens, layer them beneath the bottled waters and sodas, in case some folks had second thoughts about paying track prices for beer, or decided they hadn't brought enough beer of their own.

The track didn't open its doors until nine, but the Melvilles' Preakness Day started at seven A.M., with Uncle Marcus and Ronnie Moe, a shirttail relation, taking the two cars over to the Wabash Metro stop, then cabbing back before traffic started peaking. Weather for Preakness was seldom fine—it either fell short of its potential and ended up rainy and cool, or it overshot spring altogether, delivering a full-blown Baltimore scorcher with air that felt like feathers. Today was a chilly one, and Dontay was on a roll, ferrying coolers faster than he ever had before, his money piling up in the Tupperware container that Granny M had marked with his name. He would have liked to keep his bills in his pocket, a fat roll to stroke from time to time, but he knew better. Even with the streets as crowded as they were today, with uniformed police officers everywhere, the bigger boys, the lazy ones who didn't like to extend themselves, wouldn't hesitate to knock him down and take his money.

In his head, he tried to add up what he had made so far. Granny M took a cut for her church, or so she said, but he'd still have enough for the new version of *Grand Theft Auto.* Or should he buy some new Nikes? But Granny M would buy him shoes, no matter how much she bitched and moaned and threatened to get him no-brands at the outlets. Beneath her complaints, she knew that shoes mattered. Even when Uncle Marcus was a kid, so long ago that there weren't any Nikes, it had been death to come to school in no-brands. Fishheads, they called them then. Granny M wouldn't do that to him, as long as he passed all his classes, which he had more than done. Dontay not only had almost all *B*s going into the final grading period; his stock-picking club had come in third in the state for all middle schools. And Dontay deserved most of the credit for that, because he had said they should buy Apple before Christmas, then drop it quick, all those people buying iPods and shit.

An iPod—now wouldn't that be something to have, although the Melvilles had only one computer and it was hard to get any time on it, even for homework. Plus, the big kids in the neighborhood knew to look for those white wires and they would smack a dude down for them, kick him harder if it turned out to be some knockoff player. Dontay counted up in his head again, but naw, he was nowhere close. And here it was going on three P.M., the meaty part of the day gone. Unless he found a winning ticket at the cleanup, he wasn't going to be buying anything like that. His own CD player, though, or maybe a little DVD player. That was within reach.

The big race was only ninety minutes away, and the neighborhood had pretty much gone quiet when a man and a woman in a huge-ass Escalade inquired about the final space at the Melvilles', which had opened up unexpectedly after some couple had a fight earlier in the afternoon. At least, that was what Dontay thought had happened. He had escorted two people in, a man and a woman, bickering a little but nothing out of hand. Then, not even an hour later, the woman had shown up back at the Melvilles, so impatient to leave that she had barreled right over the curb, no thought to the shocks on her Cabriolet. The Melvilles were wondering what would happen at day's end, if the man returned for the car that wasn't there. Maybe they could offer to take him home, undercut the local cabbies.

"How much to park here?" asked the latecomer, the woman behind the wheel of the Escalade.

Uncle Marcus hesitated. This late in the day, she would be within her rights to bargain for a discount. Before he could answer, she jumped in: "Forty dollars?"

"Sure," he said. "Back it in."

"I admit I can't maneuver this thing into such a tight space," she said. "It's new and I'm still not used to it. Would you do it for me?"

She hopped out and let Uncle Marcus take her place, her dude still sitting stone-faced in the passenger seat. Dontay thought that was cold, making a man look weak that way, but the man in the Escalade didn't seem to care. Uncle Marcus showed off a little, whipping the SUV back into the space and cutting it a lot closer than he should have, but he pulled it off. The woman counted two twenties into his hand, then added a ten.

"For the extra service," she said. Her man still didn't say anything.

Oh, how Dontay prayed they would have a cooler, but they didn't look to be cooler people. She looked like a clubhouse type—yellow halter dress with big black dots, big hat and dark glasses, high-heeled shoes in the same yellow as the dress. The man had a blazer and a tie and light-colored pants. Those types usually didn't have coolers. In fact, those types didn't usually park in the yards, but it was late. Maybe the lots at the track were full.

Still, it never hurt to ask.

"You need help? I mean, you got any things you need carried in?" He indicated his shopping cart. It had been in the Melville family for years, taken from a Giant Foods that wasn't even in business anymore. The wheels were a bit cranky, but it moved pretty fast.

"What's the going rate?" the woman asked. She seemed to be in charge.

"Depends on what needs transporting," Dontay said. After seeing how things had worked out with Uncle Marcus, he wanted to see what she would offer to pay before he named a price.

"We have three large coolers." She opened the back of the

Escalade, showed them off. Red-and-white Igloos, they looked brand-new, the price tags still on their sides.

"That's a big job," Dontay said. "They'll be piled so high in my cart, I'll have to go real slow so they don't tumble."

"Twenty dollars?"

Twice the going rate. But before he could nod, the woman quickly added. "Each, I mean. Per cooler."

"Sure." He loaded them up, one on top of the other. "But you know I can only take you up to the gate. You got to get them to your seats by yourselves. How you gonna do that?"

"We'll figure it out," she said. The man had yet to say a word.

The three coolers fit into the shopping cart, just, and rose so high that Dontay could not keep a quick pace. What did it matter? Sixty dollars, the equivalent of six trips. They must be rich people, the kind who brought champagne and . . . well, Dontay wasn't clear what else rich people ate. Steak, but you wouldn't bring steak to the Preakness. Steak sandwiches, maybe.

"You do this every year?" the woman asked.

Usually, people walked ahead or behind, a little embarrassed by the transaction. But this woman kept abreast of him, her yellow high heels striking the ground with a loud clackety-clack, almost as loud as the wheels on the shopping cart.

"Yes, ma'am."

"You ever think about going to the race?"

"No'm. I make too much money working it." He wished he could take that back. It wasn't good manners, much less good business, to draw attention to how much a person was paying you. No one wanted to feel like a mark, Uncle Marcus always said.

"Want me to place a bet for you?" she asked. She was white-white, her skin so fair it had a blue tint to it, with red hair like a blaze beneath her black straw hat.

"Naw, that's okay. I wouldn't know what horse to bet for."

"The favorite in the Derby often comes through in the Preakness. That's a safe bet."

Dontay liked talking to the woman, liked the way she treated him, but he couldn't think of anything to say back. He tried nodding, as if he were very smart in the ways of the world, and all he accomplished was hitting a pothole, almost upsetting the whole load.

"But you probably don't like safe bets." The woman laughed. "Me either."

The man, who was walking behind them, still hadn't said anything.

"I'm going to bet a long shot, a horse coming out of the twelve post. Know how I picked it?" She didn't wait for Dontay to reply. "Horse bit his rider during a workout this week. Now, that's my kind of horse."

He finally had something to contribute. "What's its name?"

"Diablo del Valle. Devil of the Valley. It's a local horse, too. That's also in its favor. A local horse with a great name who bit his jockey. And I live in the valley. How can I lose?"

"I don't know," Dontay said. "But based on what I see, a lot of people do."

She seemed to like that, laughing long and hard. Dontay hadn't been trying to be funny, but now he wished he might do it again.

"I'll probably be one of them," the woman said. "But you know, I don't gamble to win. I consider the track interactive entertainment, theater in which I hold a financial stake in the outcome."

"Like a stock-picking club?"

"Yes. Exactly. If I ever found myself *too* invested, I'd have to stop. Don't you think? It's awful to care too much about something. Anything."

Dontay wasn't sure he followed that, but he nodded as if he did. He was wondering if the woman was cold, her shoulders and back as bare as they were. With her yellow dress with the black dots, yellow heels, and big black hat, she looked like something.

"You a black-eyed Susan," he said.

She seemed to start, or catch a chill, but then nodded. "That I am. But they're fake, you know."

"Ma'am?"

"The black-eyed Susans at the race. They're not in season until late August, so they buy these yellow daisies from South America and color the centers with a Magic Marker. Can you imagine?"

"How much that pay?" It hadn't occurred to Dontay that there was a single opportunity in Preakness that his family had missed. Coloring in flowers sounded easy, like something Delia's twins could do.

"Oh, I don't know. Not enough. Nothing is ever enough, is it? Doesn't everyone want more?"

The question seemed like a test. Did she think him ungrateful or greedy, taking sixty dollars?

"I'm fine, ma'am."

"Well, you're a rare one, then."

They had reached the entrance to the grandstand, but to Dontay's amazement, the woman didn't stop there. "We're in the infield," she said. The infield? She was paying almost as much to bring her stuff as she was paying for the tickets. The infield was mud and trash. This woman would get messed up in the infield, where no one would care that she had taken the time to look like a flower. Dontay looked for the man, but he had disappeared. The woman didn't seem to mind that at all.

"You'll just have to let this young man help me," she told the ticket taker, but not in a bossy way. She had the ability to say things directly without sounding mean. When she said things, they sounded like the logical thing to do.

"Not unless he pays admission, too. And he can't bring that shopping cart in."

She peeled more money from her wallet, bought Dontay a ticket.

"And ma'am?"

"Yes?"

"We need to inspect them, make sure there's no glass, nothing else that's forbidden." The Preakness ticket had a whole long list of things you couldn't bring in, and Dontay always stuck close to his clients, in case they needed to send things back with him. The Melvilles already had a glass bottle of rum, which Uncle Marcus had said he would hide from Granny M.

"Why, they're just sandwiches." The woman opened the top cooler, pulled out a paper-wrapped sub. "Muffulettas. Muffies, we call them. We make them every year with that special tapenade from the Central Grocery down in New Orleans, so they're practically authentic."

She unwrapped one. It was an okay sandwich, although a little strong-smelling for Dontay. He didn't much care for cheese and olives.

The man quickly looked inside each cooler, saw that there

was nothing but other paper-wrapped subs, and waved her through.

It took Dontay and the woman three trips to carry in each cooler. It seemed like a math problem to him—how could they protect the unattended coolers at either end?—but the woman found a man in the infield to keep watch. She had that way about her. They stacked each one just inside the entrance. The people there looked nasty to Dontay, and he worried about leaving the woman there in her pretty dress. Where would she sit? Already, her heels were sinking in the mud.

"Diablo del Valle," she said, handing him four twenties. "You heard it here first."

"Yes, ma'am," he said. "But that's extra—"

"I'll lose more than that today. At least you'll still have the money when all is said and done. Unless you want me to place a bet for you?"

"No'm. I'm fine." He looked at the tote board, calculated the odds. Twenty to win at twenty to one—four hundred dollars. And it was an extra twenty, wasn't it? He wouldn't really be losing anything. But his thrifty soul could not bear the risk.

She took off her hat, fanned herself with it, and Dontay realized with a start that one of the shadows on her face was still there—a purplish bruise at the temple, visible at the edge of her oversize glasses.

He pushed the empty cart back quickly, flying along, wondering if he might catch one more trip, then wondering how it mattered. Eighty dollars! Still not enough for an iPod or even one of those runner-up MP3 players, not even when it was added to what he had already earned today. He wondered briefly if he had the discipline to save it all, but he knew he didn't. The woman was right. Nothing was ever enough.

Back at the house, the Escalade was gone. "Man came back and said he forgot something," Uncle Marcus said. Dontay worried that something was wrong between the man and the woman, that he had abandoned her to the infield and she had no protector. He thought of her again in her yellow dress and high heels, big black hat—and that bruise, near her eye. But he couldn't see the man in the jacket hitting her. He couldn't see anyone hitting that woman, sure as she was about things.

THE DAY-AFTER CLEANUP STARTED EARLY, even earlier than school. Just the sight of the garbage took Dontay's breath away, not to mention the smell. He had known there was a reason this job paid. But it seemed impossible that this patch of ground would ever be clean again. A bandanna around his face, Granny M's kitchen gloves shielding his hands, he picked up cans and wrappers and cigarettes, examining the tickets he found along the way, comparing them to the results page in his back pocket. But he hadn't noticed the three red-and-white coolers stacked in a column near the gates until another worker ran toward them, said, "These mine."

"How you figure?" Uncle Marcus asked.

"Called 'em, didn't I? They're in good shape. Hell, they're so new the price tags are still on them. I can use some coolers like that."

He opened the drain on the side and the water ran out, the ice long melted.

"If there're sodas in there, they still be cold," one woman said hopefully. "You'd share those, wouldn't you?"

"Why not?" the man said, happy with his claim. He popped the lid—and started screaming. Well, not screaming, but kind of snorting and gagging, like he wanted to be sick and couldn't figure out how.

Uncle Marcus tried to hold Dontay back, but he got pretty close. Overnight the water had soaked through the paper-wrapped sandwiches, loosening the packaging, so the sandwiches floated free. Only a lot of them weren't sandwiches. There were pieces of a person, cut into sub-size portions, cut so small that it was hard to see what some of them had been. Part of a forearm, he was pretty sure. A piece of leg.

"Well, it's definitely a dude," said one kid who got even closer than Dontay did, and Dontay decided to take his word for it.

Police came, sealed off that part of the infield, even stopped the cleanup for a while, but quickly saw how useless that would be. There weren't enough officers in all of Baltimore to sift through the debris of the infield, looking for clues. Besides, it wasn't as if the crime had been committed there. The coolers were the only evidence. The coolers and the things within them.

Dontay watched the police talking to grown-ups—the man who had claimed the coolers, folks from Pimlico, even Uncle Marcus. No one asked to talk to him, however. No one asked, even generally, if anyone had anything they wanted to volunteer. That didn't play in northwest Baltimore. Dontay just kept working.

LATER, WALKING HOME, Uncle Marcus said: "Them coolers look familiar to you?"

"Looked like any other I ever seen."

"Just that there were three and they was brand-new. Like—"

"Yeah."

"What you thinking, Dontay?"

He was thinking about the woman's face beneath her hat, her observation that nothing was ever enough. She had a nice car, a wallet thick with money, a man who seemed to do her bidding. She was going to bet on a horse that bit its rider, the Devil of the Valley, because she lived in the valley, wherever that was. She admired its spirit, but admitted it wouldn't win in the end.

"Doesn't seem like any business of ours, does it?"

"No, I s'pose not. I s'pose not."

The Melvilles had Preakness coming and going. You could park your car on their lawn, buy a cold drink from them, get help ferrying your supplies into the track, and know that your vehicle would be safe no matter how long you stayed or how quickly you left. Thirty dollars bought you *true* vigilance, as Uncle Marcus always said. Over the years, the Melvilles had their share of regulars, people who came back again and again. The woman in the hat, the woman with the Escalade, the woman who had dressed up like a black-eyed Susan—she wasn't one of them.

THE SMARTY JONES BUBBLE

Steven Crist

FUTURE HISTORIANS, at least those specializing in early twenty-first-century Nielsen ratings, may someday note with bewilderment that the most-watched television program for the week of May 29 through June 4, 2004, was not a reality show, a medical drama, or a situation comedy. It was, instead, a ninety-minute telecast of a two-and-a-half-minute horse race. The 2004 Belmont Stakes drew twice as many viewers as that race usually does, making it not only the most popular sports program of the week but also the highest-rated telecast of any kind, handily beating a new episode of the sitcom *Everybody Loves Raymond.*

It was not, as racing's promoters had hoped, the beginning of a resurgence in horse racing's popularity or prominence in American sports and entertainment. A year later, the Belmont would draw its usual audience, with both the ratings and track attendance nearly half of what they had been in 2004. Racing had reverted to its usual status, an eccentric passion among enthusiastic insiders. Its fifteen or ninety minutes of fame were over.

The 2004 Belmont, where a horse named Smarty Jones unsuccessfully bid to complete a sweep of racing's Triple Crown, had been the end rather than the beginning of a phenomenon, one that had little to do with horses or racing and everything to do with a twenty-first-century popular culture marked by cynically manufactured story lines and disposable heroes. The moment when Smarty Jones lost the Belmont was to racing what the dot-com implosion was to the stock market: the sudden end to a fevered madness during which truth, accuracy, and reason had all been abandoned.

IT WAS SOMEHOW APPROPRIATE that a high Nielsen rating was the most celebrated aspect of the 2004 Belmont, because television had played such a decisive role in the modern history of the racing business at two different junctures.

The first was in the early days of television, when racing was still the nation's best-attended spectator sport and the glowing tube beginning to dominate American living rooms figured only to increase its popularity. Print advertisements for new televisions often featured close-ups of horses racing neck and neck.

Racetrack operators of the time, a collection of dynastic land barons who enjoyed a virtual monopoly on legal gambling outside of Las Vegas, saw the new medium as a threat rather than a partner. Early television programmers, desperate for daytime content, thought it would be natural to broadcast the afternoon's races from the local track, but track owners, fearing a loss of on-site betting and frankfurter revenue, declined the opportunity for unprecedented marketing and exposure.

This shortsighted decision, and the ascendance of television as the decisive medium in exposing and promoting all sports, began racing's long slide from major to minor to "other" status on the nation's sports pages and in the public consciousness. By the time the industry facilitated legal off-track betting in an attempt to recapture its declining live audience, it was unable to get television exposure beyond the three Triple Crown races each spring. An entire generation of both viewers and decision makers grew up in a world where the presence of sports on television determined their prominence in the popular culture, and horse racing simply did not exist beyond the Derby, Preakness, and Belmont.

At the same time, racing was losing its once leonine share of the legal-gambling market, thanks to the implementation of lotteries and casinos by revenue-starved state legislatures across the country. Racetracks, like most monopoly businesses, had never been bastions of superior customer service. The fringe customers who had once been happy to lose two dollars a race on names and numbers now chose to do their random gambling amid free drinks, flashing lights, and the possibility of million-dollar payoffs. Racing still had its core enthusiasts, but between televised sports and jackpot gambling competitors, its casual fans were slipping away.

Racing found no way to lure them back, and survived the 1990s only through a very specific kind of television that had nothing to do with greater broadcast exposure. Simulcasting, the importation of televised racing signals from around the country into tracks, OTB facilities, and eventually homes, kept the game alive and even booming as it continued to disappear from wider view. Regulars who had once been limited to playing only the eight or nine live races at their local tracks could suddenly choose from fifty or a hundred races a day. Thanks solely to simulcasting, more money was bet on racing in 2001—over $12 billion—than when the sport had been at its peak of general interest and popularity.

That $12 billion annual handle, though, was more of a boon to bet takers than to the tracks and the horsemen putting on the show because of the different way the money was carved up. The lords of racing had been just as shortsighted about the potential of simulcasting as they had been about the usefulness of broadcast-television exposure, and set the initial fees for the signals of their races and access to their betting pools at absurdly low levels. Total betting was up, but tracks and horse owners were now getting only three cents out of each dollar on a simulcast bet, where they had once received as much as twelve cents on the dollar on a live bet. Once track operators realized that simulcasting was becoming the driving force, it was too late to raise the rates because of antitrust concerns and a lack of industry unity that would keep tracks from undercutting one another.

As the new century began, the economics of racing had been utterly flip-flopped. Whereas the game had once attracted 90 percent of its business from people at racetracks betting on live races, now more than 80 percent of that $12 billion a year was being wagered on races being run somewhere else or by people betting somewhere other than a racetrack.

THIS TRANSFORMATION WAS KNOWN to everyone in the business, but it was poorly reported in the occasional looks at the industry from the general media, which as usual recognized the sport only during the five weeks of the Triple Crown season each spring. The Triple Crown remained the one time of year that racing still got the attention it once routinely did, for at least the two weeks including the first and third Saturdays in May.

It is almost entirely random each year whether there will be a Triple Crown bid. Obviously someone has to win the Derby every year, and if that horse can win the Preakness two weeks later, racing gets another three weeks in the spotlight until the Belmont Stakes. So nearly everyone in the industry roots for the Derby winner in the Preakness.

At this writing, no horse has won the Triple Crown since Affirmed in 1978, a stretch during which ten horses have won the Derby and Preakness but then failed in the Belmont. It is the longest such drought in the history of the series, but both successful and unsuccessful bids come in clumps. There were three Crowns in the 1930s, four in the 1940s, then none between Citation's in 1948 and Secretariat's in 1973, the first of three in the 1970s. In a similar gap, there were no Triple Crown bids between 1989 and 1997, but then there were six in the next eight years.

The unsuccessful Triple Crown bids by Silver Charm, Real Quiet, and Charismatic from 1997 through 1999 and then by War Emblem in 2002 each bought racing that additional three weeks of sunshine. Each was accompanied by a spate of media accounts where news outlets ordered some general-assignment reporter to produce the obligatory "racing in decline" story as a sidebar to their Triple Crown–bid coverage. The people writing such articles never quite understood what simulcasting had done to racing and almost uniformly linked the declines in live attendance and media coverage to a bizarre new premise: Racing was not as popular as it had been because of the lack of a Triple Crown winner. Thus was born the enduring myth of the Horse Who Will Save Racing: Racing is on life support and its only hope is a Triple Crown winner to lead it back to its glory days.

The whole idea was nonsense. Racing had never been more popular than in the 1950s and 1960s, a time of no Triple Crowns and few transcendent star horses. Nor was racing in any danger of folding its tent, with annual handle at a record $12 billion and rising. But it made for a tidy story for both print reporters who had no idea how to link empty grandstands on a Thursday with the Triple Crown, and for television networks trying to surround the races they were broadcasting with sociological import.

Changes in both forms of racing journalism had set the stage for the wholesale adoption of such gibberish. On the print side, more and more racing stories were being written by people with little knowledge of the business because the job of horse racing writer had become extinct at many a big-city daily. As racing had slipped below so many other beats on the television-driven barometer, papers had allowed their racing writers to retire without replacing them.

The television networks had forsaken their traditional straightforward reporting of racing, and other nonmainstream sports in general, in favor of a more entertainment-based model. This stemmed from the formula they had come up with for covering the Olympics in a way designed to maximize ratings and broaden demographics: Rather than getting inside the somewhat esoteric athletic events and explaining them with any particular expertise, they now routinely produced featurettes, scored with sadly tinkling piano music, about "perseverance in the face of all odds" and "the triumph of the human spirit" and the like.

Just as Olympics coverage had become one story after another about sick grandmothers and cancer survivors, racing coverage was becoming keyed to exploiting any such afflictions among the human caretakers, while imbuing racehorses with bogus attributes—with the added zinger that if today's plucky, courageous underdog hero could prevail, he would not only affirm virtue but rescue a dying sport to boot.

This story line was repeated year after year, burning its way into the public consciousness and growing stronger as one bid for the Crown after another went down in flames. The perfect storm for Smarty Jones was almost in place; then came Funny Cide and *Seabiscuit*.

AFTER THE TWO-YEAR ABSENCE of Crown bids in 2000 and 2001, War Emblem led all the way to win the Derby and Preakness in 2002, but he was a tough sell as a savior. The horse had emerged from utter obscurity just a month before the Derby with a smashing victory in a minor prep race, after which he was sold privately to a Saudi Arabian prince. Seven months after 9/11, the American public found little to root for given the colt's ownership or backstory, and racing fans considered him to be a one-dimensional front-runner unworthy of joining the pantheon of Triple Crown winners. There was less than widespread mourning when he stumbled at the start of the Belmont and finished a dismal eighth.

The following year, there was a very worthy early favorite with similarly unlovable connections—another Arab owner, and a trainer, Bobby Frankel, whose achievements were legendary but whose confidence in his own horse, Empire Maker, was matched only by his bluntness about the shortcomings of others. Empire Maker was a regally bred, highly talented, and long-winded colt who blew through his Derby preps with contemptuous ease. In his final tune-up, the Wood Memorial, jockey Jerry Bailey didn't even fully extend Empire Maker, wanting to save something for the races ahead, and rode him to a carefully measured victory over a popular local gelding named Funny Cide, who was losing his third straight start.

A few days before the Derby, though, Empire Maker developed a minor foot problem that forced him to miss some training and left him at less than his best on Derby day. Funny Cide took the lead in deep stretch and Empire Maker was unable to catch him, settling for second to a horse he had toyed with when at full strength.

That was not quite the way the story was reported. Instead, it was a stirring triumph of the human spirit by a plucky underdog and a comeuppance for the rich owner and mouthy trainer of the now clearly overrated beaten favorite.

Empire Maker, his chance at the Triple Crown gone, was withheld from the Preakness to recover in time for the Belmont, a sensible act that was widely construed as cowardice. In the absence of Empire Maker and Ten Most Wanted, who hurt his back in the Derby and was also being freshened for the Belmont, Funny Cide ran against a wafer-thin Preakness lineup and romped, winning by a record nine lengths.

Funny Cide was a legitimately nice story. Several upstate New York friends had chipped in for the modestly bred gelding and ridden to the Derby in a yellow school bus. That, of course, was not enough. Funny Cide was now a patriotic symbol, and his owners, successful local businessmen, were portrayed as working stiffs who had done something brave and heroic.

Funny Cide had won the Derby over injured key rivals and the Preakness against weak competition, but was heavily favored to win the Belmont by a record crowd of 108,000 that had been whipped into a fervor by a sappy tall tale. More than twice as much was bet on Funny Cide as on Empire Maker, and even after Empire Maker won the race with Funny Cide a tired third behind Ten Most Wanted, nobody seemed to like or believe it. The headline on the back page of the next day's *New York Daily News:* "Evil Empire."

Funny Cide and Empire Maker never met again, but at season's end Funny Cide was voted the year's champion three-year-old by sportswriters and racing officials, in clear contradiction of the fact that Empire Maker had won two of their three meetings, losing only when injured.

Two months after the Belmont, the movie version of Laura Hillenbrand's runaway bestseller *Seabiscuit* was released, providing a variation on the Horse Who Will Save Racing theme. Much of the book's subtlety and detail was entirely lost in the Hollywood rendition, whose climactic scene was a fraudulent distortion of actual racing history.

When Seabiscuit won the 1940 Santa Anita Handicap, he raced close to the lead and just held off a stablemate who may or may not have been less than fully encouraged to win at his popular mate's expense. The movie did not have to get into that particular bit of intramural intrigue, but it also did not have to turn the race into an absurd fiction better suited to a Saturday-morning superhero cartoon. In the movie, Seabiscuit drops a football field behind the others, his jockey has a long conversation with another rider during the race, and then he makes up about thirty lengths to win in a performance that defies both the historical record and the laws of physics.

If someone had made a movie of Babe Ruth's career that ended with the Bambino jumping fifty feet in the air and hitting a ball that traveled seven miles, it would have been derided by every sportswriter in America. But this was horse racing, so no one seemed to mind, and those who noted the discrepancies were dismissed as cranky purists, the same sort of killjoys who might think Empire Maker was a better horse than Funny Cide or that racing's prosperity was not dependent on a Triple Crown winner.

Seabiscuit was now the Movie That Will Save Racing. The sport's promoters embraced it as being key to the industry's growth, and several writers predicted that the film would drive throngs of newcomers to the nation's racetracks. As it turned out, *Seabiscuit* did no more for racetrack turnout or betting than *Spider-Man* did for interest in radioactive spiders. It did reinforce the idea that with enough heart and pluck, a horse could leap tall buildings in a single bound or at least solve any sadness a nation might be feeling about war or the economy. The following spring, as if on cue, such a horse came along.

Smarty Jones, like Funny Cide, had some very likable attributes that made him a nice story if not a great racehorse. He was a good-looking chestnut-colored colt, he had survived a grisly starting-gate injury before his career began, and he ran his first two races at Philadelphia Park rather than at a fancier track in New York, California, or Kentucky. He came into the Kentucky Derby undefeated in six starts, against

mostly second-rate opposition, but looked as good as anyone in a mediocre year where no one had distinguished
himself.

While every later recounting of his Triple Crown campaign routinely referred to him as an unlikely long shot, he
was the betting favorite at the Kentucky Derby, as incon-
venient a fact as the reason why: It had been raining heavily
on Derby day, the track was a sea of goo, and bettors know
that such footing favors horses who go right to the front while
hampering those who get mud kicked back at them. Smarty
Jones was better than the other speedballs in the field, dis-
posed of them on the far turn, and splashed home a clear winner, while almost no one else ran anything remotely like his
best race.

Whereas winning the Kentucky Derby had earned Funny
Cide $800,200, Smarty Jones collected seven times as much,
thanks to a bizarre bonus that had been put up as a promotional stunt by Oaklawn Park, the track in Hot Springs,
Arkansas, where Smarty Jones had spent most of the winter.
Oaklawn was celebrating its one hundredth anniversary, and
its eccentric owner publicized the occasion by contracting
with an insurance company to offer $5 million if any three-
year-old could win the track's two Derby preps, the Rebel
Handicap and Arkansas Derby, and then the Kentucky Derby
itself. This had been done just once, and it seemed safe that
it wouldn't happen again in 2004, without any of the previous
year's leading two-year-olds scheduled to spend the winter
there.

Now, though, Smarty Jones had won the bonus and earned
more than $6 million overall, twice as much as any Triple
Crown winner had made in an entire career, putting him in

the top ten in American racing history. He had won only a single race against top company, and had done it on a sloppy track, yet had earned more than Secretariat and Seattle Slew combined. Victories in the Preakness and Belmont could win him another $5 million bonus, this one from Visa, the Triple Crown sponsor, and vault him past Cigar's $9.9 million American record.

As with Funny Cide a year earlier, the Preakness was a cakewalk in which most of the well-regarded Derby horses were absent. Smarty Jones broke Funny Cide's fresh record for largest winning margin, winning off by eleven lengths over two horses who had been excluded from the Derby field for lack of earnings. That was only two more lengths than Funny Cide had won by, and Smarty Jones had now accomplished nothing more than Funny Cide had at that point in his career, but it was enough to make the world decide that the rightful heir to Affirmed had arrived after twenty-six years and that Smarty Jones was a stone-cold certainty to win the Belmont.

No one had learned anything from what had happened with Funny Cide the year before, not to mention all the other and mostly better horses who had won the Derby and Preakness and come up short in the Belmont—nine of them in a row. The "Smarty Party" had begun, and the Belmont would be merely a coronation.

Funny Cide had lost six of his next eight starts since being proclaimed an immortal after his Preakness victory. His owners had teamed up with Lance Armstrong's ghostwriter to produce a book, and it had seemed like a good idea to release it during the following year's Triple Crown season. The book had a massive first printing but glacial sales. Instaheroes were disposable, and now that the Smarty Party was under way, no one wanted to hear about last year's failure.

This time there were no superior horses such as Empire Maker, or even Ten Most Wanted, waiting to tackle the Derby-Preakness winner at Belmont. On the other hand, Smarty Jones had glaring vulnerabilities. He was a pure front-runner who had never rationed his early speed, finished strongly, or passed a quality opponent. He also had a jockey, Stewart Elliott, who did not ride regularly at major tracks or in one-and-a-half-mile races.

Perhaps most compelling, Smarty Jones was trying to do something all nine Derby-Preakness winners since Affirmed—Spectacular Bid, Pleasant Colony, Alysheba, Sunday Silence, Silver Charm, Real Quiet, Charismatic, War Emblem, and Funny Cide—had tried and failed to do. By any objective measure, many of those horses had brought more raw talent and stronger credentials into the race.

Against that backdrop, and the overall record that only eleven of twenty-five horses in Smarty's position had gone on to win the Belmont, what were his real chances of becoming the twelfth Triple Crown winner? When a Philadelphia radio host called to ask me that question, I said it was probably somewhere around 40 percent, an answer that apparently was 59 percent too low for his liking and prompted a quick end to the interview. *USA Today* polled twenty sportswriters and nineteen of them said Smarty Jones would win. Smarty Jones was popular because everyone said he was popular. He was invincible because it would have spoiled the story for him not to be.

Of course, he did have the Catholic Church on his side. Approvingly featured on the Preakness and Belmont telecasts were tales of how the colt had the support of a group of Philadelphia nuns, and had raced with a religious medal under his saddle on Derby and Preakness day. Just for insurance, a local parish priest was applying holy water to the horse and asking for divine intervention in the Belmont.

Others close to Smarty Jones, and some of the people covering the story, had less holy reasons to root for him. Even $5 million bonuses were a pittance next to what the colt would be worth as a stallion if he won the Triple Crown. Every blue-blooded nursery in the world was already bidding to stand him at stud when his career was over, promising that the owners could syndicate him for at least $50 million, maybe more, if he won the Belmont by daylight and went on to further glories.

Book and movie deals were in the works, all contingent on a Belmont victory. This was the next *Seabiscuit*. The premise that a banged-up racehorse had lifted a nation's spirits out of the Great Depression was replaced by the far-fetched notion that Smarty Jones was relieving Americans of any worries about the war in Iraq.

The myths multiplied regardless of the facts. He was an "underdog" despite having been favored in the Derby and Preakness. He was a "blue-collar hero," even though his owners were wealthy from their chain of car dealerships even before their $5.8 million Derby payday. His trainer was constantly depicted as a hardscrabble rube and a stranger in paradise at the highest level of the sport, despite his actually having trained good horses in major events before. Even when jockey Elliott was found to have been convicted for assault for beating a "friend" with a pool cue a few years earlier, he was portrayed as a transformed alcoholic who had turned his life around, yet another triumph of the human spirit as the piano music tinkled on.

These heartwarming stories, and the repeated assertions that Smarty Jones could not lose, drew the largest crowd in the ninety-nine-year history of Belmont Park to the track on June 4, 2004, to witness what they had been promised would be the first Triple Crown in twenty-six years. The official crowd count was 120,139, about 110,000 more than the turn-out on an average Saturday at Belmont, and over 18,000 more than had come out in the rain to see Funny Cide a year earlier.

The place was unbearably crowded, and it is difficult to imagine that many of the extra attendees had a particularly enjoyable afternoon milling around and waiting for the big race. Traffic had been a nightmare, the fifteen thousand re-served seats had been gone for weeks, betting and food lines were long and slow. You wanted to tell any newcomer to go home, watch the race on television, and come back on a quiet Thursday when the beautiful old track could actually be enjoyed.

An astonishing number of people in the crowd being interviewed on television, or just overheard talking among themselves, kept invoking Secretariat's 1973 Belmont, con-sidered the single greatest performance in racing history. Those who had seen that race wanted to be present for an event that was supposed to rival that one, and those who had missed it thought this was a second chance to say, "I was there," when great moments in sports history were recalled.

There was no reason to expect such a moment. Secretariat, who won the Belmont by thirty-one lengths in track-record time, had already repeatedly shown true greatness. He had raced in the most important events since the start of his career, been so impressive a two-year-old that he had been named Horse of the Year, and gone on to run the fastest Kentucky Derby ever and win the Preakness with a breathtaking last-to-first move on the clubhouse turn. Smarty Jones was obviously a good racehorse but had done nothing similarly historic or spectacular, at least not yet.

As it turned out, Smarty Jones ran the bravest race of his brief career losing the Belmont. Concerns about Elliott's lack of familiarity with the Belmont surface and distance proved well founded, as the rider got caught up in two needless early duels while his colt was running some of the fastest middle fractions in the history of the race. Smarty Jones was sufficiently better than those early challengers to shake them off by the top of the stretch, and there was a moment when it looked as if he might draw away to a lopsided victory, the way Secretariat did after facing even stronger early pressure. The stands literally shook as the masses thought they were getting what they were promised.

But only for a few moments. Smarty Jones was tired, and a fresh horse was suddenly running at him, and it was just as suddenly obvious that the favorite was going to get caught. Birdstone was gaining with every stride, drew even long before the wire, ran right past him, and won by a length and a half. Never has a racetrack gone from pandemonium to silence so quickly. Someone had let all the air out of Belmont Park.

Birdstone's camp acted as if they might be stoned to death. His jockey, Edgar Prado, apologized for beating Smarty Jones as soon as someone put a microphone in his face. Marylou Whitney, the winning owner and breeder, a pillar of racing whose family had been trying to win a Belmont for a half century, had to act as if she were at a wake instead of enjoying what should have been the happiest moment of her racing career. Fans who had been waiting all day to witness history, some of them buying tickets on Smarty Jones in the hopes of making a killing on eBay after he won the Triple Crown, now had pockets filled with worthless losing tickets instead of cash, and began to boo.

The winner had been a highly promising two-year-old the previous season who simply could not get his feet under him on wet tracks, like the one he caught in his final Derby prep and then in the Derby itself, where he had floundered in the slop behind Smarty Jones. Interestingly, a storm system passed through New York City an hour before the Belmont, missing the track by less than a mile. Had it rained even a little, Birdstone's handlers would have scratched him, and it's more than likely that Smarty Jones would have indeed won the Triple Crown.

The quality of his Belmont performance would have made that an easier pill to swallow, but he would have been deified out of all proportion to reality. Either way, it was to be his final race. After repeatedly saying the colt would have a full career on the track, his owners quickly syndicated him for $37 million, and two months after the Belmont he was retired to stud so as not to lower his value or risk an injury that would keep him from his $100,000-a-pop matings the next winter. The owners tried to characterize it as a retirement forced by the rigors of racing, but there was no medical evidence the colt could not have recovered completely from the Triple Crown and raced again.

The quick retirement struck an especially sour note with the public, who had been told so often that Smarty's owners were ordinary folk who just wanted to invite the world to enjoy their Smarty Party. By season's end, the colt who was supposed to be Secretariat was not even considered the best racehorse of 2004. A faster older runner named Ghostzapper made just four starts from July through October, but they were so impressive that he was a runaway winner of the Horse of the Year title, getting twice as many votes as Smarty Jones.

Smarty's connections had lobbied for their colt as Horse of the Year, arguing not that they had the better horse, but that they had caused so much excitement and created so much publicity that the industry should honor them for that alone. It was a fitting argument to summarize the arc of both Smarty Jones's shooting-star campaign and what the Triple Crown and racing had become in the pop culture of the twenty-first century. Attention trumped achievement. If enough people said a horse was great, even if they were saying so only to sell commercials or movie scripts or stallion shares, he was great. Quality was merely a matter of how white-hot you were at the peak of a media frenzy.

The bursting of the Smarty bubble seemed to bring some sobriety and reason to the game, at least in the short term. The following year, a mediocre colt named Giacomo won a slow and chaotic Derby at odds of fifty to one, and only the most desperate promoters tried to pretend he was a good horse with any chance of winning the Triple Crown. He was properly dismissed at five to one in the Preakness and was beaten nearly ten lengths, ending the string of Triple Crown bids by War Emblem, Funny Cide, and Smarty Jones.

Perhaps the next time a Derby winner comes back to take the Preakness, there will be more caution and thoughtful analysis of whether we are witnessing the next Secretariat or just another War Emblem. Perhaps the public won't assume that something that hasn't been done for over twenty-seven years, something that ten straight horses were two and a half minutes away from accomplishing, is a cinch to happen this time just because people who don't know any better say it will. Perhaps the horse will be judged and enjoyed as a racehorse and not promoted as a distraction from international affairs, a plucky and heroic underdog carrying the dreams of a breathless and battered nation.

But I wouldn't bet on it.

HIPPOMANCY

Scott Phillips

I PULL UP HONKING in my cousin Noel's driveway twenty minutes later than planned, and he sprints out the front door and across the yard like he's late for childbirth, a tattered *Racing Form* in hand. "Sorry," I tell him. "We may miss the first race."

"I don't care if you don't care," Noel says, wheezing from the door-to-door dash. He's got on an old Pretenders T-shirt, worn-out cargo shorts and black loafers with white socks. "Six is enough for me."

I pull out of the driveway, too slowly to suit Noel. His big round face is so taut with the anxiety of the compulsively punctual that I almost regret having to tell him.

"Here's the other thing, though, I gotta stop at the bank and get some cash."

His hair is short but sticking out in all directions, and he's freshly shaved after skipping several days; tiny, fugitive black patches of beard remain under his chin and right on the border where his upper lip meets his nostrils. He calculates the likelihood of offending me by stating the obvious, then does it anyway. "There's ATMs at the track, you know."

"I gotta take care of some business at my branch," I tell him. We hit the 405 north toward the 101; it's Tuesday, and in another three or four hours the average speed here will have slowed to twenty or twenty-five miles an hour. For the moment, though, it's gloriously, miraculously fluid and we enjoy it in silence until we merge onto the 101 heading east.

"What's Terri have to say about you taking the day off to go to the horses?" Noel asks. He has a long-standing crush on my wife, and my failure to properly appreciate my great good fortune—as he sees it—is a sore point.

"Terri doesn't need to know about it."

He makes no comment other than sighing and folding his arms across his chest. For her part, Terri appreciates his boyish, uncritical adoration, even encourages it in her quiet way. More than once it's occurred to me that she ought to seduce him; for her it would conveniently serve as a combination grudge/mercy fuck and much-needed ego boost. It would certainly be the highlight of Noel's life, at least until it ended, and give him something to obsess over for the rest of his days.

MY BANK BRANCH is on Ventura Boulevard east of Coldwater. Before cashing my check the teller calls over a supervisor, and as the three of us confer gravely I glance over at Noel, his arms crossed again, sitting in a stuffed chair and wondering why the fuck I can't do my banking when we're not late for the ponies. I stuff the envelope full of cash into the inside pocket of my sport jacket and motion to him.

"We're a couple blocks from Jerry's, let's get a sandwich so we don't have to eat at the track."

"I have a bet I want to place in the third. Jesus, Tate. I could be at home working." I'm pleased—proud, almost—to see Noel's dander finally up. He takes his racing seriously and rightly considers me a dilettante, barely worthy of the benefits of his tutelage. This is the first time we've been to the track together in a year or more.

"We'll make the third race, unless we stand here arguing about it."

Pink spreads across his cheeks and he stares at the carpeting. Noel is four years older than I am, but for reasons neither of us can name, I've ended up in charge when we're together, which bothers him and delights me. We head down the sidewalk to Jerry's Deli.

AT JERRY'S HE SULKS with his nose in his *Racing Form*, illuminating the relevant pages like a monk with a series of pen-and-ink sketches of horses running and standing. He draws comic books for a living, and the fact that he has some sort of artistic talent is another point in his favor with Terri, who has said to me on several recent occasions that if I were a deadbeat engaged in some sort of creative enterprise she'd be happy to drag my ass along behind her. Alongside the drawings are scribbled notes and columns of figures, which he recalculates as he embellishes the drawings, contentedly oblivious to me and his surroundings.

I order a turkey sandwich on wheat, and since it feels like

a day for an indulgence I get fries instead of coleslaw. Noel orders a hamburger and an iced tea, and when I soak my fries in ketchup and eat them with my fingers he scowls. "You'd think working in a nice place you'd pick up some better table manners."

"You would, but you'd be wrong." I tend bar weekday afternoons at Chez Kiki, a once-trendy restaurant not half a mile west of Jerry's, and contrary to the expectations of most of my customers I'm neither a budding actor nor screenwriter nor musician nor puppeteer. I have no show business–related ambitions at all. I have no well-defined ambitions of any kind, in fact, which probably explains why I'm the worst-tipped bartender the restaurant employs. People are happy to underwrite a dreamer, even—especially—if they think his chances for success are nil, but they resent a man who's satisfied working ten to six watching terminally alcoholic second bananas from long-canceled sitcoms hit on grizzled ex-Bond girls with collagen lips like inner tubes.

My wife's not too keen on the situation, either. My disinterest in returning to grad school after she passed the bar provoked at first mild consternation which eventually progressed via serious concern to outright discord, occasioning a brief interlude with a family therapist. The therapist took my side and managed to make Terri feel like the guilty party, which bought me a couple of years' free ride. It's been that long since she brought up grad school, anyway.

Recently, though, things having gotten a little chilly around the house. I started thinking maybe I should take her up on it after all. Gingerly I chose a quiet moment after a pleasant Sunday dinner to mention it.

"How are you planning to pay for it?" she asked without

lifting her eyes from her book; I spent a minute or two staring at the tiny stray tendrils of hair curling on the back of her
neck and the scattered freckles on her shoulders. It was about
an hour afterward that I called Noel and suggested today's
trip to Santa Anita.

AFTER LUNCH MY DRIVING is aggressive enough to get
us through the turnstiles for the start of the third race, if
not in time to actually place bets. Noel's mood is sour, and
he mentions for the seventh or eighth time how much he
wishes I hadn't insisted on driving. He cheers perceptibly
upon the purchase of a pretzel and a large Pepsi; lunch
or not, it's not a trip to the track without them, and we settle
in the grandstand with his illuminated copy of the *Racing
Form.*

"You got any ideas about the fourth?"

I have none. "I'll stake a twenty on a long shot."

"Figures," he says, and goes back to his columns of numbers.

This is a typical betting strategy for me and one that Noel,
a dedicated scientific handicapper, reviles. I've often coun-
tered that he, in placing his scrupulously researched, relent-
lessly logical bets, always ends up agreeing with every other
oddsmaker in the pool. When he wins, which to be fair he
often does, it's usually two, maybe three to one, never a life-
changing sum. When I do, which almost never happens, it's a
bundle—less, granted, than the wife brings down in a week
after taxes, but it's cash and mine to spend as I please.

Noel makes a show of ignoring me as he scribbles in the
margins. "You know what'd be a great name for a racehorse?"
I ask him.

The left-hand corner of his upper lip lifts in a show of disdain. "What?" he asks, and I wait until he's siphoned up a whole mouthful of Pepsi before I answer.

"Vaginapants."

Noel laughs, snapping his mouth shut in a moment of panic so that the Pepsi in his mouth shoots bubbling out his nostrils and onto the bench in front of us, fortunately unoccupied at the moment.

"Fucker," he laughs.

"How about Whoretoilet?"

"Peebiscuit."

"Hobotaint."

Just then an enormously muscular couple in matching canary Day-Glo tank tops and black spandex bicycle pants scoots into the aisle in front of us and, without looking down, sit. The woman, a blonde who looks like she might be a professional bodybuilder, lowers her rippling, rock-hard ass right on the puddle of Pepsi.

"For Christ's sake, Stu, the seat's wet."

"Disgusting fuckers," Stu says. His muscles are even better defined than hers, his sideburns arch noseward to join up with his mustache, and behind his shades I feel certain that his eyes are cold, dead things that would register no guilt or remorse as he casually executed a couple of fucking wisenheimers who'd soiled his lady's titanium glutes. Before they take note of us, Noel and I slip over to the next section.

THE FOURTH IS A PHOTO FINISH between my long shot, Spincaster, and Noel's favorite, Cortnee's Minion. When the decision is in his favor he chides me for not betting Spincaster to place. "Or a quinella. That's where those long shots of yours come in once in a while."

"I'm out twenty bucks is all," I tell him. "My big bet's the sixth."

The next twenty-five minutes are spent reeducating me in some of the finer points of his handicapping method, with a conciliatory nod to my preference for the longer end of the probability spectrum. In the fifth we end up each putting down fifty dollars on favorite Osonafarias with third choice Hurry Skeezix; Noel plays it safe with a quinella and I put mine on an exacta with Hurry Skeezix on top. When it's over I've got four hundred–odd extra bucks in my wallet.

"How does that feel, buddy?" Noel says. "See what happens when you listen to your old cousin?"

"Feels okay," I allow. "That's the most money I've won at the track, except for once when I hit a trifecta in Wichita."

"Dog track doesn't count," he says.

"What's the matter with greyhounds?" I ask. I know perfectly well what's wrong with them, and he knows I know, but he rises to it and strikes. After listening for a minute I give him my dad's old dog-versus-horse theory.

"What I like about the dogs is there's no jockey factor. Little fuckers always screw up my handicapping."

No matter how many times we have this same debate—which Noel has to know means nil to me—he still always gets close to frothing when this part comes up, stammering and repeating himself on the paramount importance of the jockey to the serious handicapper, and finishing with the story of the greatest day of racing he ever saw.

"In Paris, maybe 'eighty-nine or 'ninety, I saw Cash Asmussen take six races on a seven-race card at Longchamp, and the only reason he didn't take all seven was the other jockeys deliberately ganged up and crowded him out in the sixth. Cash was the greatest athlete I ever saw, right up there with Michael Jordan." He goes on in that heroic vein for a while until I concede his point, at which point he softens and pats his wallet. "Hey, how about you and me take Terri out for a nice dinner tonight? It's a Tuesday, we could get in someplace really nice probably."

"I think Terri's working late. Besides, I don't know if I'll have the dough."

"What about the dough you just won?"

"I'm letting it ride."

He looks blank, then leans in close to see if I'm shitting him or not. "All of it?"

"Sure." I pull the envelope of cash from inside my jacket and add the four hundred, putting the remaining thirty-odd from the exacta in my wallet.

"What are you so dead-set on betting your wad on? It's the sixth, right?"

"Right. Wadana-Wadana."

There's apprehension in his eyes before they get to Wadana-Wadana on the roster, and horror when they find it. "Jesus. You're putting down the whole wad you just won?"

"Plus what I took out of the bank."

Without asking me just how much that might be, he walks away muttering, and I make for the hundred-dollar windows.

WHEN I FIND HIM AGAIN he's got another pretzel and a big Pepsi and the horses are at the gate. "I wish I could have convinced you that this was a mistake."

"You did. I spread it way, way out. Trifectas, quinellas, exactas, win, place, show. I boxed the shit out of that motherfucker."

He still disapproves, but not as heartily as before. "Well,

you're still setting yourself up for a loss, but not as brutally as the other way."

I'm examining my tickets as the bell rings, the gates open, and the horses burst out onto the track. We stand for a better look. "On the other hand if one of these trifectas hits I can buy a house in the fucking Palisades."

I hold the sheaf of tickets out to him. He looks away from the track at them, annoyed at the distraction, but troubled enough to take one. Now he's staring, his mouth gone slack. "You didn't put a whole grand on a trifecta?" He reaches for the other tickets, which I gladly surrender. "How much money is this?" I can barely hear him over the noise of the race.

"Twelve thousand two hundred dollars, plus the four hundred I won in the last race."

"Weeping Jesus, Tate. Does Terri know you took this out?"

"She will when she goes to the ATM."

There's a catch in his voice, as though the marriage in question were his own. "What the fuck are you trying to do?"

Instead of answering him I look up at the monitor to see Wadana-Wadana just starting to fall back from third to fourth place. The race is at that point where everyone's shrieking at his horse to run faster, goddamn it, and beside me Noel screams with tears streaking his face, begging the long shot to bring it in, bring it in, bring it in. I sit down again, lean back and let him yell for the both of us.

BEAST

Maggie Estep

HARRY LOCKED SAMANTHA IN THE BATHROOM and turned on channel 71. They were only showing the tote board just then, but any second, the redheaded commentator would come on, talking up each horse's chances in the first race at Aqueduct. Harry liked watching the redhead hold the microphone in front of her face awkwardly, like a drunk with an oversize lollipop. The way her speech was always a little off and her eyes drooped like upside-down parachutes, Harry figured the woman had to have a drinking problem. Just not as bad as Samantha's. Samantha was still having DT-induced pink elephants and cold sweats. Which was why Harry'd had to lock her in the bathroom. He couldn't take it anymore. She'd started shrieking every few minutes. The kind of banshee shriek that was a nice thing in the bedroom but not particularly pleasant anywhere else. Locking her in the bathroom was an act of mercy really, since it lessened the chances of her running around the apartment trying to slice her wrists with a dinner knife or stab herself with the carpet scissors one of Harry's exes had left behind.

Harry sank deeply into his favorite chair as the redhead came onto the TV screen. She looked less than interested in the state-bred maiden fillies being saddled to run seven-eighths of a mile on a cold March afternoon. Harry couldn't blame her. He wouldn't even be watching the race if he didn't desperately need to clear his mind. Where some folks went in for massages, yoga, or Valium to steady themselves, Harry looked at racehorses. It rendered him capable of great things. And he needed to be capable just then. He'd been hired by a gentleman collector to steal President Grover Cleveland's jaw tumor from the Mütter Museum in Philadelphia. Harry had never burglarized a museum, and while the Mütter, a museum of medical curiosities, didn't have a traditional museum's level of security, it was still a lot trickier than a common house. Harry had agreed to the job because the collector, who'd gotten Harry's number from Harry's lone friend, Nick, had offered $20K. Harry planned to use the money to send Samantha to a posh rehab. He didn't want her drinking herself to death or getting stabbed in one of the barroom cat-fights she was fond of starting while under the influence.

On the TV screen, a bay filly caught Harry's eye. She was on her toes and, Harry saw from glancing at his *Racing Form,* decently bred. Fourteen to one seemed like a nice price on a first-timer in a wide-open race.

Harry was about to call in a small bet on the filly when he

noticed that his feet were wet. He looked down and saw water on the floor. His cat, Flipper, had hopped up on the couch and was licking her paws. Harry craned his neck to look back toward the bathroom. Water was flooding out from under the door.

"Samantha!" Harry ran to the door and jiggled the knob.

Samantha had locked it from the inside and she wasn't answering. Harry imagined the worst as he rammed his shoulder into the door, trying to get it open. It took him three tries before the door suddenly surrendered and Harry fell through, landing on his stomach in a swirl of water.

It took Harry a few moments to absorb that Samantha hadn't drowned. She wasn't even there. Above the toilet, the narrow bathroom window was open. Harry stood atop the toilet seat and looked out. It was two stories down to the quiet street where Harry and Sam lived, a few blocks off Coney Island Avenue. Harry half expected to see Sam in a heap down there on Argyle Road, but there wasn't any trace of her. He couldn't quite believe she had crawled through the window. She was a bordering-on-strapping 130-pound girl. How she'd gotten through there, Harry had no idea. Nor did he know why she'd had to flood the bathroom to do it. As Harry puzzled over this, he had his first brilliant idea of the month. He suddenly knew, with incredible clarity, how he'd get President Cleveland's jaw tumor out of the Mütter Museum.

As Harry stood, by turns reveling in his own craftiness and worrying about his girlfriend, the clogged bathtub started gurgling horribly. Against his better judgment, Harry dialed McCormick Two, the plumber brother of his onetime associate McCormick, to come over and tend to the problem.

MCCORMICK TWO WAS EVEN less likable than McCormick the First, an ill-tempered thief Harry had occasionally worked with until McCormick One had turned on him. Like his brother, McCormick Two was of medium weight and medium height with medium brown hair. His teeth were pointy.

"This is a mess. What the fuck is wrong with you, Harry?" McCormick Two was wielding a wrench and looking at Harry like Harry was a complete and total imbecile.

Harry shrugged. Truth was, he didn't know what was wrong with him. It wasn't that he'd set out to have such an absurd life. His parents were decent people who had squirreled away enough money to send both Harry and his sister, Ava, to college. Harry had attended Hunter College, where he'd majored in architecture even though he had little or no desire to build things. Pretty early on, Harry had gotten tangled up with difficult women. These women had drinking problems, eating disorders, nymphomania, or all of the above. In his fourth year of undergraduate, Harry had taken up with Lorna, a diminutive vixen ten years his senior. Lorna was a thief. To Harry, this was a significant move up the mating food chain. Lorna didn't drink, starve herself, or masturbate on doorknobs. She just stole things. Harry had never broken a law in his life, but hearing about Lorna's adventures made something inside him stir. Lorna taught Harry the trade, which he took to, quickly moving up from shoplifting to burglary. When he proved gifted in the art of breaking and entering, Lorna got jealous and left him. Harry was devastated and swore off women for three months.

Harry was thirty-six now. He'd been arrested three times and jailed twice. He'd grown more cautious lately. Earned less money, but that was okay. His fondness for staring at horses had taught him a lot about a racehorse's appearance before a race. Now and then, it would be blindingly obvious to Harry that a forty-to-one shot was going to win, and Harry occasionally cashed obscenely lucrative tickets.

"How bad is it?" Harry asked McCormick Two, who was wading around in Harry's bathtub.

McCormick Two just grunted.

An hour later, as Harry watched a chalky favorite hit the wire first in a claiming race, McCormick Two emerged from the bathroom. He was dripping muck and he didn't smell good. He announced that the flood was fixed, then asked who'd won the nightcap at Aqueduct.

"Napoleon Solo. Three to five," Harry said. He knew that McCormick Two fancied himself a gifted horseplayer.

McCormick Two apparently hadn't bet on Napoleon Solo. He grimaced at this news. "You got a beer?" he asked, leaning against the wall.

"No, sorry, McCormick," Harry said.

McCormick then asked Harry for $300 for the plumbing call.

Harry was about to protest this fee when there was a knock at the door.

"Who is it?" Harry called out.

"Who do you think?" came Samantha's low voice.

Harry opened up and in walked his girlfriend, not only unscathed from jumping out the window three hours earlier, but suddenly wearing a short bright yellow dress under a red fake-fur coat.

"Look what the cat dragged in," McCormick Two drawled.

"Hi, McCormick," Samantha said, smiling up at the creep as she settled onto the couch.

There wasn't any rhyme or reason to whom Samantha would and wouldn't flirt with. At least, not that Harry could see.

"Where have you been?" Harry asked his girlfriend, "and where'd you get that dress?"

"I went to Lisa's."

"Oh," Harry said. Samantha's older sister, Lisa, was a big, tough blonde who didn't think any man was good enough for her sister. As it happened, she was also a teetotaler. At least she wouldn't have given Sam a drink. But just the idea of Lisa frightened Harry, mostly because she made him wonder if Samantha would eventually become as hardened as her.

Sam had seemed like a gentle girl when Harry had first seen her at the paddock at Aqueduct a year earlier. Harry hadn't been able to think of an opening line, so he'd bummed a cigarette from her even though he didn't smoke. When she handed him the Marlboro Light, Harry saw she had tears in her eyes. He lit his cigarette, tried not to cough, then asked her what was wrong.

"My horse got dropped to claiming $35K," she said, pointing down into the paddock at Sherpa Guide, a six-year-old bay gelding who was the second favorite.

"Sorry about that," Harry said.

"Not your fault," the girl said. She smiled then. She had a lovely, crooked smile.

It was only that night, after Sam had agreed to let Harry buy her dinner, that she told him she didn't actually own the horse. She just liked him. He wasn't the greatest racer, not even the prettiest. But he always tried. Sam didn't go to the track much but went to all Sherpa Guide's races, making sure to be there at the paddock every time he ran. Though Sherpa Guide had won a few state-bred stakes, lately he'd been dropping through the claiming ranks. On the afternoon that Harry met Sam, the horse looked so bad Sam had tears in her eyes. This was one of the things that made Harry like Samantha.

And it didn't hurt that she was a banshee in bed.

Sam moved in with Harry after two weeks. A month after that, Sherpa Guide ran last in claiming $25K. Sam, who tended to drink a little too much, went out on a bender. Came home two days later, stinking and scratched up. Never told Harry where she'd gone, and when Harry asked, she looked at him with a mixture of hurt and tenderness, then took off her clothes.

SAMANTHA WAS STILL ON THE COUCH, asking McCormick Two questions about his dull little life. He had tucked his wrench into his back pocket and grown a few inches taller. Samantha, who'd evidently been miraculously cured of the DTs, was all smiles.

Harry couldn't stand looking at McCormick Two anymore but didn't want to hustle him out too quickly because he was slightly afraid of him, same as he was afraid of McCormick the First, Samantha's sister Lisa, and more than 90 percent of the human population if you got right down to it. It was a scary world out there.

Harry left Sam and McCormick gabbing and went out to get some food. When he came back, the greaseball was finally gone and Sam was in the shower. Harry put some vegetable dumplings on a plate for her and waited.

She emerged with dripping hair and sullenly sat down at the table. She was wearing a ratty pink bathrobe.

"How do you feel?" Harry asked.

"Like shit."

"You seemed fine while McCormick was here."

"What's that supposed to mean?"

"Why do you flirt with the weirdest people possible?"

"What, and you're not a weirdo?"

"How am I a weirdo?"

"You're a fucking weirdo."

"Define weirdo."

"All you do all day is stare at that horse racing channel."

This was an unlikely thing for Sam to focus on, considering she had lost her paralegal job the third time she'd suddenly left work to go to the track to watch Sherpa Guide run.

"It's my living," Harry protested. This was what he'd told her. He had briefly held a real job as a handicapper for a tip sheet, so he'd told Sam this was what he did now. Just a minor stretching of the truth.

"Still," Sam pouted, "you could get out more. Get a hobby."

"I go to the track."

"You know what I mean."

"I go out." Harry protested. And he did go out. At least two nights a month, to burglarize houses. Sam didn't know this. Half the time she was asleep while Harry was gone. If he had to strike earlier in the evening, he drummed up an excuse of going to have a beer with the boys. Harry didn't have any "boys," just his one friend, Nick, and Nick didn't even like beer.

"I know you're angry about me locking you in the bathroom," Harry said, trying to get Sam to look him in the eyes.

"I don't want to talk about that," Sam said, abruptly getting up from the table.

"Sam," Harry said, following her into the bedroom.

Samantha lay down on the bed. Harry touched her arm.

"I don't want to be touched right now," she said.

Harry felt nauseous.

WHEN HARRY GOT UP THE NEXT MORNING, Samantha was sound asleep, naked, with one hand tucked between her upper thighs. Harry brushed a piece of hair off her forehead and kissed her. She didn't stir. Even in sleep she was tired of Harry. He figured by the time he got home, she'd be drunk or gone for good. Probably both.

Harry fed Flipper and left the apartment. He took the F train to Thirty-Fourth Street, where he got out and walked over to Penn Station, springing for a ticket on the all-reserved Metroliner to Philadelphia. It was eight A.M. on a Thursday. Men in business suits worked on laptops. Harry was dressed for his own business. Simple clean clothing. A pair of creased pants baggy enough to conceal the lined plastic container Harry had strapped to his left calf. Harry's roomy pockets held the few tools he would need. The wig and the glued-on full beard were itchy but necessary. The museum staff would get several good looks at him.

Harry sat by the window, staring out as New Jersey unfolded under a bulletproof sky.

HARRY TOOK A CAB from the Thirtieth Street station to the building housing the Mütter Museum. Ferdinand Hollow, the collector who had hired Harry, had told him over the phone that the presidential tumor was kept in a glass cabinet without an alarm. Hollow seemed to know so much about the tumor and its location that Harry had almost asked him why he didn't just steal the tumor himself. But Harry didn't want to screw himself out of an easy $20K.

As Harry walked into the lobby, he saw that the restrooms were, as he remembered, directly behind the security desk. This was slightly problematic. But only slightly.

There were few museum visitors. Two young girls with facial piercings, and what appeared to be a small class trip, a dozen boys about ten years old.

Harry ambled through the museum, stopping for a moment in front of the wall of eye trauma, an enormous glass case containing all manner of violated eyeballs. As Harry got a feel for the place, he took in a few more curiosities. The skeleton of twins conjoined at the head, the wax replica of Madame Dimanche's horned head, all of it encased in elegant glass. It was a lovely little museum. But Harry wasn't there to browse.

President Cleveland's tumor was in a jar inside a glass case on the lower level, resting next to the cheek retractor that had been used in the presidential surgery. Grover Cleveland hadn't wanted his enemies to know about his jaw cancer. A covert hospital had been set up aboard his yacht, and the tumor removed in great secrecy. Later, the president was fitted with a rubber jaw prosthesis and the public was none the wiser until well after his death.

It wasn't much to look at, this tumor. Desiccated flesh vaguely resembling the top of a chrysanthemum. Harry had no idea what Ferdinand Hollow wanted it for or how one would verify the authenticity of a presidential tumor but, Harry supposed, it was all information he could live without.

Harry headed past the security desk and into the bathroom to get to work. He went into a stall, put his gloves on, and took out the exquisite microblowtorch he'd bought while visiting Switzerland with an ex-girlfriend, Yvonne, a Swiss-German pianist.

Within four minutes Harry had torched a hole into the pipes behind two of the toilets. Water started pouring out. He waited until the floor was soaked, then emerged from the bathroom.

He saw that the pierced girls and the schoolboys were there on the upper level, gazing at curiosities. Harry went back to the deserted downstairs area, waited till he heard commotion in the lobby, then turned to the case containing the tumor. He took the tiny glass cutter from his pocket and cut a fist-sized hole. He was about to reach into the case when he felt someone nearby. He turned and saw the pierced girls standing just behind him like twin apparitions. Both were petite with dyed black hair and matching black clothing.

"Hello," Harry said, standing directly in front of the hole he'd cut in the glass.

"There's a mess upstairs. I think they want us out of here," one of the girls said. She was slightly taller than her friend. Her brown eyes were sad.

"Oh?" Harry asked. His heart was drumming. He imagined admitting what he was up to to the girls. Getting them to help execute the burglary. Cutting them in on the money Ferdinand Hollow had promised. Possibly even using them as accomplices in the future. He'd have to make them blend in better. Wear innocuous-looking clothing, get rid of the jet-black hair. He imagined this might depress them. They might feel naked and worthless without the uniform of alienation. He decided the whole thing was an incredibly bad idea.

"Yeah," the shorter girl said, "they want us out. They got a flood up there. They'll probably come looking for you in a minute."

Harry wondered if they knew. Decided they didn't.

"Thank you; I'll be up in a second," Harry said. The taller girl shrugged and turned to walk back up the stairs. The shorter girl followed.

As soon as they were out of sight, Harry delicately reached into the hole he'd made and retrieved the tumor's jar. He opened the jar, extracted the tumor, and put the dead flesh into the plastic container he had strapped under his pants leg.

Harry went back upstairs. He could see the schoolboys and the pierced girls standing outside. The security guards were hovering by the bathroom door, watching a janitor desperately mopping at the water that was pouring over the floors. It was only a matter of minutes before someone noticed the holes in the toilet pipes.

Harry felt bad about the mess. It wasn't his style. Nor was it his style to do something as splashy as steal a presidential tumor, a thing that might even generate news stories. But that he was slightly proud of.

Harry smiled at the pierced girls as he strolled out the front door of the museum. The taller one smiled back.

FERDINAND HOLLOW LIVED IN A LAVISH brownstone facing Prospect Park West. A butler showed Harry in. Harry hadn't realized there were still butlers in Brooklyn in 2006.

Harry was led down a dark hallway lined with glass cases similar to those in the Mütter Museum. There were bones and skulls and jars containing fetuses in formaldehyde.

"This way, sir." The butler showed Harry into a study with

book-lined walls and a chandelier. Ferdinand Hollow was seated at an immense mahogany desk.

"Mr. Sparrow." Ferdinand Hollow stood up.

The collector was as Harry had pictured him: tall but old and slightly stooped. He still had all his hair, and its long white strands were swept back off his forehead.

"Mr. Hollow," Harry shook Ferdinand Hollow's extended hand.

"Success?" Ferdinand asked.

"Of course," Harry said.

Ferdinand Hollow motioned for Harry to take a seat as he himself sat back down. Harry put his briefcase in his lap and opened it. Harry watched Ferdinand Hollow's eyes shine as he took the plastic container out and opened it, revealing the tumor.

"Yes," Ferdinand Hollow said, gazing at the flesh fondly, "this is wonderful."

As he waited for Hollow to finish admiring the tumor and get on with the business of paying him, Harry idly thought of White Deer Run, the rehab he planned on sending Samantha to. It seemed like a nice place. Harry half wished he could go stay there too.

"You've made me a very happy man," said Ferdinand Hollow.

Harry smiled pleasantly.

"You needn't worry about repercussions," Hollow said then.

"Repercussions?"

"With this." Hollow motioned at the tumor. "The board of the museum won't let this get out; you can be sure of that. They've always been concerned about their lackluster security, and I have an associate who strongly advised them to beef things up. They didn't listen to him."

Ferdinand Hollow was smiling a glinty mischievous smile.

"Oh," Harry said. He'd been looking forward to clipping the news stories and worrying about the FBI. He'd even wondered what the pierced girls would do when they saw the stories and maybe put two and two together. He'd had a crazy fantasy about the girls contacting him somehow. He would beg them not to report him, in exchange regaling them with his adventures as a burglar. Their sad eyes would round in amazement as he recounted close calls. Maybe he would even take the girls in while Sam was in rehab. He liked the idea of having them around. Companionship. Sam never gave him any.

"Well, then," Hollow said, "let's conclude our business." He opened a desk drawer and took out several stacks of cash.

"A pleasure doing business with you," Harry said.

"The pleasure was mine, of course." Ferdinand Hollow rose from his chair. "Hector will see you out," he added, motioning toward the butler, who had magically appeared.

It occurred to Harry that Hector was a lousy name for a butler.

HARRY ALMOST FELL OVER FROM SHOCK when he let himself into the apartment. Sam was at the stove, stirring something.

"You're cooking?" Harry asked, setting down his briefcase.

"Tofu surprise," Sam said, waving a wooden spoon.

"Ah," said Harry.

Sam was wearing a dress again. Royal blue this time. Shimmery synthetic fabric that could have been hideous but looked nice on Sam.

"I haven't had a drink," she announced.

"Oh, yeah?"

"Nope."

Harry tried to look like he believed her.

"You at the track all day?" Sam asked.

"Yes," Harry lied.

He kissed Sam's bare shoulder, felt her recoil slightly, then told her he was going to shower before dinner.

Harry went into the bedroom, closed the door, and stashed the money in the special compartment built into the wall behind the bed. He then showered and put on his flannel pajamas even though it was early. His pajamas relaxed him.

When Harry went back into the kitchen, Sam had served dinner. A steaming pile of muck, viscous cubes of tofu on top.

"This looks great, babe."

Harry ate as much as he could. Sam just picked. It looked to Harry like she had something on her mind, but she wasn't coming out with it, and Harry wasn't in the mood for prying it from her. In the background, channel 71 was on. Showing trotters. Later it would show racing from places like Australia. Harry had never been to Australia.

"Sherpa Guide's running tomorrow," Sam announced.

"Oh," Harry said, feeling dread in his stomach. Or maybe it was just the food. "You gonna go out there?"

"Of course."

"That's good," Harry said, even though it wasn't. If the horse looked unhappy, Sam would drink.

"Do you want to come?" Sam asked.

This surprised Harry. They never did things together. The fact was, they had nothing in common other than liking to look at horses. And they didn't even tend to do that together. They were just two lonely people who'd landed on top of each other and hadn't bothered getting up.

"I'd like to, Sam, but I can't. Nick needs me to drive him upstate, remember?"

Harry's lone friend, Nick, the only citizen who knew what Harry really did for a living, was a bicycle racer and a bicycle activist. Nick hated cars and refused to drive one. Since he was scheduled to race his bicycle upstate the next day, he'd rented a car so Harry could drive him.

"Oh," Sam said.

"Some other time," Harry said.

Sam shrugged.

HARRY WOKE AT THE UNREASONABLE HOUR of four A.M. to pick up the rental car and drive Nick to the bike race upstate. It was cold, and persistent rain made for cautious driving. Nick immediately started talking about Angela, the category-2 female racer he wanted to bed. She had monstrous quads and a cute smile. Nick seemed to have completely forgotten about President Cleveland's tumor in spite of the fact that he had set the whole thing up after meeting Hollow at a Brooklyn Historical Society soiree.

"I got the tumor," Harry said about an hour into the ride, when Nick finally stopped talking.

"Oh, shit, I forgot, Harry; I'm an idiot."

"You're not an idiot," Harry said.

"How'd it go?"

"Great. Fine," Harry said.

"Great and fine?"

"Well, there were these girls," Harry said. "I felt like they knew what I was up to."

Harry recounted the incident with the pierced girls, even

went so far as to tell Nick how he'd entertained the idea of making them accomplices.

"Harry, that's nuts."

"I know," Harry said. "I know. I guess I'm getting bored."

"Bored?" Nick was the kind of law-abiding citizen who wished he broke laws. He lived vicariously through Harry's career, just as Harry got vicarious rushes watching Nick race his bike.

"Maybe not bored. But something's not right. Something's missing."

"How's Sam?"

"I'm gonna send her to rehab."

"You think that'll help?"

"Sure," Harry lied.

HARRY WAS GLAD TO SIT in the car blasting the heat while Nick abused himself racing sixty miles in the driving rain. In the past, Harry had watched some of Nick's races more closely, stood on the sidelines, cheering Nick as he flew by, scraping him off the road when he crashed. Not today. Today Harry sat in the car, wondering how Sam and Sherpa Guide were doing.

Harry roused himself from the car long enough to stand at the finish line, watching Nick come in third, one bike length behind the winner. Nick was so depressed over losing a race he could have won that he didn't even go chat with Angela, the category-2 racer, who was standing under a tent with some other women racers in tight, brightly colored bike clothes. Harry wouldn't have minded talking to them himself. But Nick was too low. He didn't cheer up until a half hour into the ride home, when Harry recounted the tumor burglary for him again, in more detail this time.

Harry got home at three P.M. and went straight into the bedroom to take a nap. Which was when he saw that Sam had not only taken the money out of Harry's secret compartment, but hadn't even tried to disguise that she'd done it. She'd left the bed pulled away from the wall and the compartment wide open.

Harry sat down on the bed. He'd been left by a lot of women. But none had robbed him before going.

Eventually, Harry napped.

HARRY WAS MORE THAN SURPRISED when Samantha shook him awake just after seven P.M.

"Harry, get up; I need you."

Harry opened one eye and peered at her. She was sitting at the edge of the bed, hair loose, eyes big. She was wearing a navy business skirt suit left over from her days as a paralegal.

Harry sat up.

"What are you doing here?"

"I'm sorry about the money," Sam said, tucking a loose strand of hair behind her ear.

"Ah," Harry said.

"I need your help," Sam said. Her mouth was slightly open and Harry could see the tip of her pale pink tongue. It matched the absurd turtleneck she was wearing under the suit jacket. Harry hated turtlenecks. Even the name *turtleneck* gave him hives.

"What did you do now?" Harry asked.

"Sherpa Guide," she said, looking down at her lap.

"What happened to him?" Harry asked.

"I claimed him," Samantha said.

"You what?"

"I claimed Sherpa Guide. That's what I took the money for. He was in for $20K. I knew you were doing a job and would put the money in the hiding place. I'm sorry."

"How did you know?"

"Oh, I always knew. But this is the first time I've taken any money from you."

"Ah," Harry said.

"I called up a trainer I know, got him to claim Sherpa Guide; then I just gave the trainer the money. He helped me ship him and everything."

"Ship him? Where to?"

Sam seemed to think this was an absurd question. "To Windsor Stables, where else?"

"You put Sherpa Guide in that hole-in-the-wall stable by Prospect Park?"

"Where else am I gonna keep him?"

"Keep him?"

"He doesn't want to race anymore." She said it matter-of-factly, like stealing your boyfriend's take from a burglary and using it to buy a cranky racehorse were the most natural things in the world.

Harry stared at Samantha. She really was a pretty girl. Unconventional-looking, but Harry liked that.

"What do you want from me now?"

"I don't have any money for board." Samantha offered Harry a small smile. Harry didn't take it.

"Woody, the guy at Windsor Stables," Sam added, "he wants five hundred dollars. Like, now."

"Ah," was all Harry could say.

"Please, Harry?" Sam's face was a prayer.

"But you took all my cash." Harry motioned behind the bed to the now-empty compartment.

"Can we go to the ATM?" Samantha asked, making her blue eyes big.

THEY HAD TO USE AN ATM in a convenience store with a hundred-dollar limit per withdrawal. In order to get $500, Harry had to pay an additional $7.50 in fees. Harry wasn't a cheap bastard; he just didn't like paying pointless fees.

They walked along Coney Island Avenue toward Caton Place. It was only eight P.M., but the avenue was quiet in spite of its being a warmish night, spiced by a slice of yellow moon. Sam walked at Harry's side, her hand resting lightly against his upper arm. Harry had mixed feelings about that hand.

The stable was a squat old brick building with a big door facing out onto Caton Place. Across the street was a rash of hideous new condos, and just down the block, where the stable's annex barn had once been, more condos were coming. It wasn't the prettiest place in the world, but there were worse.

Sam led Harry up a ramp, inside the stable's low-ceilinged entrails. There were stalls as far as the eye could see, horses of all shapes and sizes poking their noses out.

A compact man with a pitchfork emerged from a side door. He had a big ginger beard not unlike the fake beard Harry had worn while committing the tumor burglary. He glared at Harry and Sam.

"Can I help you?"

"It's me, Woody. Samantha. With the racehorse," Sam said.

"Oh, right," said the man, "I put that hoss in the back till we see what's what." He gestured for Sam and Harry to follow him.

The back of the building was a row of small box stalls and, toward the end of the row, Sherpa Guide stood. He looked incongruous there with a big chestnut draft horse on one side and a mean-looking black pony on the other. He lifted his head at the sight of the humans but, as they came to the stall door, he pinned his ears back and waved his head threateningly.

"No one's gonna make you do anything," Sam said softly, standing at a safe distance.

Harry studied the gelding. Sherpa Guide's medium bay coat wasn't as lustrous as it had been the last time Harry had seen the horse in the paddock at Aqueduct, but it still looked good. His head was sculpted, almost delicate. His eyes were mischievous and intelligent. He was, Harry decided, a magnificent beast.

Harry gave Woody the $500 in cash.

"You're gonna want the vet to check him over. That knee looks funny to me," Woody said, indicating the horse's left knee.

As Harry nodded, Woody turned and walked away.

Sam and Harry stood there for a good twenty minutes staring at the horse. Now and then, Sherpa Guide would make threatening faces at them, but Harry had the feeling the horse was actually pleased to have people admiring him. Harry could have stayed longer, but Samantha started yawning.

"I need sleep," she announced.

AS THEY WALKED HOME, Sam seemed almost cheerful. She talked about the various vet and farrier appointments she'd be making for the horse. Harry didn't ask where she was getting the money for the appointments. He was just glad to see her cheerful without being drunk. Even if that cheer had nothing to do with him.

They went to bed. Sam didn't kiss Harry good night or thank him for letting her steal his money. She slept tucked on her side at the other side of the bed.

THREE DAYS PASSED. Sam was getting up earlier now. She would put on jeans and a ratty jacket and head right to the barn. Wouldn't come back till dusk. Told Harry she was hand-walking the horse every day. Harry couldn't figure out how it took close to ten hours to hand-walk a horse. But he was glad that, as far as he could tell, Sam wasn't drinking. Which wasn't to say she was warming to Harry or dragging him repeatedly into the sack to work off whatever excess energy she had from not drinking. No. All she did was go to the barn, and even that didn't seem to give her much joy. When Harry asked after the horse, she would answer monosyllabically.

At night, Samantha would put on her big fuzzy robe and vegetate in front of the TV for several hours before going to bed and sleeping at the far edge of the mattress.

Five days after Sam claimed Sherpa Guide, Harry went into Manhattan to have lunch with his cousin, also named Sam, short for Samuel. Cousin Sam asked about Harry's Sam. Harry just shrugged. Cousin Sam left it alone.

Harry took the subway home, got back to his building, and found the front door to his apartment open, McCormick Two standing in the doorway holding a suitcase.

"Harry." McCormick Two nodded with his chin.

"What are you doing here?"

"Helping Sam."

"Helping Sam what?"

"Move her shit into my car."

"You have a car?"

"Yeah," McCormick Two drawled.

Samantha emerged from the bedroom. She had an enormous backpack slung over one shoulder and was dragging a wheelie suitcase. She had cut bangs into her hair.

"Sam?" Harry said helplessly.

"Sorry." Sam shrugged. "You had to know it was coming."

"I did?"

"You did, Harry," she said almost tenderly. "Here," she said, thrusting a thick envelope at Harry, "you'll need these."

Harry stared at the envelope without opening it.

"It's Sherpa Guide's papers. You'll look after him now, right?"

"I will?"

Sam sounded exasperated, "You need a companion."

Harry wanted to punch her.

"I'm sorry, Harry," Sam said, then turned toward McCormick Two. The creep didn't even offer to help her with the massive backpack.

Harry went to the window. He watched Sam loading her stuff into the trunk of an ancient Chevy Caprice Classic. She didn't look up even though Harry knew she could feel him watching her.

HARRY WENT TO SIT ON THE COUCH. He thought about turning on channel 71 but didn't have the strength to. Flipper jumped into his lap.

At some point, the phone rang.

"Yes?" Harry said, even though the answer to almost anything anyone asked him would be no.

It was Ferdinand Hollow. He expressed his thanks. Then

told Harry he had his eye on some gynecological tools in the Old Operating Theatre Museum in London. Harry told Ferdinand he didn't do transcontinental work. The truth was, he didn't have the heart for any work.

"That's a shame, Mr. Sparrow. You're very gifted."

"Thanks," Harry said.

"Call if you change your mind," Ferdinand Hollow said.

"I will," Harry said.

Harry rested the phone back in its cradle.

He sat on the couch for four hours. When dusk came, he got up and put his coat on. He walked the six blocks to Windsor Stables.

There were two little girls out front grooming a pony. Woody was pushing a wheelbarrow full of manure down the barn aisle.

"Hello," Harry said.

Woody put the wheelbarrow down and scratched his head.

"So the horse is yours now?"

"Sam told you?"

"Said she was moving and that you'd take care of the horse. Weird girl."

"I know," Harry said.

"You gonna keep the horse?" Woody arched one eyebrow.

Harry hadn't even considered the possibility of selling the horse. Just hadn't occurred to him. He realized this would be the sane course of action—to sell the horse, or even give the horse away to someone who knew something about horses. But Harry had no desire to sell the horse.

"Of course," Harry said.

"Good," Woody said. He picked his wheelbarrow back up. "He's in that same stall."

"Thanks."

Harry walked back to Sherpa Guide's stall. The horse was pulling hay from his net. As Harry came closer, Sherpa Guide stopped what he was doing, stared at Harry, and put one ear forward. There were pieces of hay sticking out the sides of his mouth. He didn't chew, didn't even seem to breathe, just stared at Harry, evaluating him.

"Hey, horse," Harry said. He slowly reached one hand into the horse's stall, palm up.

Sherpa Guide tentatively sniffed at Harry's hand, his nostrils expanding and contracting, the bits of hay still sticking out of his mouth. When he'd thoroughly investigated Harry's hand, he chewed his mouthful of hay, then put his head out over his stall guard and nudged Harry's shoulder.

Harry smiled.

WISE CROWDS AND FOOLISH BETTORS

Why It's Hard to Beat the Track

James Surowiecki

DAMON RUNYON FAMOUSLY SUMMED UP the truth about racetrack betting in a single sentence: "All horseplayers die broke." Like all rules, this one has its exceptions—Andrew Beyer, for instance, the man who invented speed figures and who in 1991 hit two double triples for $330,000, seems unlikely to die penniless—but it has always struck me as a pretty good description of the fate of most bettors. This hasn't, of course, ever stopped me from doggedly trekking to the betting windows before each race. It just means that I'm always surprised whenever I leave the track with more cash than I had when I arrived. And while I am not a good bettor—my knowledge is limited, and my money management is poor—it's clear that even smart handicappers often struggle to end up ahead.

This is, on the face of it, a strange state of affairs. Betting on horses, after all, is not like betting on casino games. In the casino, with the possible exception of blackjack, the house has an ineradicable mathematical edge. So over time it's effectively inevitable that you will lose. At the track—at least in the United States, where betting is done on a pari-mutuel system—the situation is completely different. There, you're competing not against the house, but against every other bettor. So to make money, you just need to be smarter than other bettors. To be sure, you have to be quite a bit smarter, since the state takes 15 to 20 percent of every bet off the top. But when you look around at the track and consider the number of people who, even today, bet while barely perusing the *Daily Racing Form,* or who rely on outmoded assumptions or dubious tips, it doesn't seem like it should be all that hard to outthink them.

But it is. The real challenge for any bettor at the track is not the fact that you have to pay 15 percent vigorish on every bet (though that doesn't help). The real challenge is that, no matter what track you find yourself betting at, you can be sure that the crowd of bettors in the stands (no matter how motley in appearance, or seemingly reckless in temperament) will be, as a group, remarkably intelligent. No one individual, as it turns out—not even the smartest handicapper—does a better job of picking winners than the crowd does. Even more important, no one does a better job of forecasting how likely it is that a given horse is going to win (which is to say, no one does a better job of calculating a horse's true odds) or the order in which the horses will finish than the crowd does. Stand in the betting-window lines in the minutes just before a race, in fact, and you'll find yourself in the middle of one of the most successful and powerful methods of predicting the future ever invented.

Consider, for a moment, the story of Smarty Jones, who won the Kentucky Derby and the Preakness in 2004 before coming up short in the Belmont Stakes. Smarty Jones was impressive as a two-year-old. He was undefeated and his Beyer speed numbers were very good. His performances as a three-year-old in the months leading up to the Derby were also solid—again, he was not beaten. But Smarty Jones was a horse from Philadelphia, not New York or California, which meant that he didn't have much credibility in the eyes of horse racing world pundits. So when the time came to pick the winner of the Derby, the experts paid Smarty Jones little attention. The *Daily Racing Form*, for instance, asked twenty professional handicappers and pundits to predict the Derby's order of finish. Remarkably, only one picked Smarty Jones to win, and most had him finishing out of the money.

There was, though, one group of people that actually did like Smarty's chances of winning: the bettors. By post time, he was the clear favorite. Now, because this was the Kentucky Derby, there were lots of people betting who were, in track parlance, "suckers," so that there was a lot of seemingly dumb money in the pool. Received wisdom at the track, in fact, says that the odds in high-profile races are far more likely to be off than in smaller races, precisely because high-profile races attract so many people who have no real idea of how to bet. And given the resounding dismissal of Smarty by the experts, his chances of victory looked slim at best. Instead, he dominated the field, and made a lot of that dumb money look very smart.

Now, this is just an anecdote, but it's a useful one because the contrast between the judgment of bettors as a whole and the judgment of the pundits was so extreme, and because it was an almost perfect example of the phenomenon I call the wisdom of crowds. The idea of the wisdom of crowds is a simple one: under the right circumstances, groups (like the motley collection of bettors at a racetrack) are remarkably intelligent, and are often smarter than even the smartest people in them. As a result, when you're faced with problems that have a right answer—like which horse is most likely to win a race—a diverse group of people, even if many of them are not especially well informed, will consistently offer better solutions than even the smartest expert.

There is, you'll be glad to hear, a lot more evidence for this than just the performance of Smarty Jones. (In fact, Smarty's status as an overwhelming favorite at the Belmont, where the crowd got caught up in Triple Crown hysteria and overbet him, was an excellent example of the unwisdom of crowds.) Most of that evidence, oddly enough, has been collected not by horseplayers but by economists. Economists are fascinated by the racetrack because it gives them a chance to evaluate how well markets work. (A pari-mutuel betting pool is simply a kind of market, different from the stock market in the way prices get set but otherwise very similar.) If the odds on a horse are generally good predictors of how that horse will do in a race, then that's a sign that the market is working. (And if they're not good predictors, then that's a sign that the market isn't.) So economists have scrutinized results from racetracks across the country, measuring just how accurate a forecast of the future odds offer.

The answer, you won't be surprised to hear, is "remarkably accurate." In the early seventies, for instance, two men named

Arthur Hoerl and Herbert Fallin looked at every race that
had been run at Belmont Park and Aqueduct in 1970. They
wanted to know two things: Were the odds good predictors of
the frequency with which horses won, and was the market's
ranking of the horses' chances a good predictor of the order
in which horses finished?

Here's what they found: With only a few exceptions, bettors predicted almost perfectly the order in which horses finished. This was true no matter how many horses were in a
given race (the sizes of the fields varied that year from five
horses to twelve). Over the season as a whole, the favorite finished first most often, the second-favored horse finished first,
second most often, and so on.

Even more startling, there was an amazingly close match
between the odds on horses and how frequently they won.
Take, for instance, the 312 races run that year in which seven
horses ran. In those races, the favorite was predicted to win
33 percent of the time. It actually won 34 percent of the time.
The second-place horse was predicted to win 22 percent of
the time, and it won 21 percent of the time, while the third-
place horse was predicted to win 16 percent of the time and,
in fact, won 16 percent of the time. This doesn't mean that
the betting crowd was right in every race, but it means that it
was almost literally impossible to do a better job than the
crowd of evaluating the horses' chances of winning.

It's worth pausing for a moment just to be amazed by this.
After all, what the crowd of bettors is effectively doing is collectively predicting the future, at least in probabilistic terms.
And it's doing so even though the future it's trying to predict
is genuinely uncertain and depends entirely on notoriously
high-strung animals. If you're a bettor trying to make money,

it can be hard to admire the crowd's prescience—since it's precisely this collective intelligence that makes it so hard to clear a profit. But it's fair to say that anyone interested in doing a better job of forecasting the future—and I mean anyone from corporate bigwigs to people in military intelligence to weathermen—should be paying a lot more attention to what horseplayers are doing, and should be trying their best to emulate it.

This doesn't mean that you could just drag a random bunch of people off the street and trust that they'll give you some good picks for the fourth race at Aqueduct. Bettors as a group are collectively brilliant because the crowd at the track includes so many different kinds of people—some suckers, some brilliant handicappers, and lots of mediocre bettors who occasionally see something that other people have missed—with so many different and distinct pieces of information. And when you add up all those pieces of information, they create a kind of mosaic that maps uncannily well onto the real world. It is, of course, true that lots of bettors at the track are making bad mistakes—betting on the wrong horses, betting too much or too little money, and just trying to figure out what horse is going to win the race rather than trying to figure out if the odds on the horse are fair. But the important thing is that as long as the mistakes they make are their own—that is, as long as they're not spending a lot of time imitating what those around them are doing—the errors end up not mattering, because they effectively cancel themselves out. This sounds improbable, but you can see the exact same phenomenon at work if you ask a group of people to guess how many jellybeans are in a jar. The vast majority of people will be way off the mark with their guesses. Some people guess too high, and others guess too low. But the group's average guess will almost invariably be very close to the real number.

In the face of this, it seems logical to say that bettors should just pack up their bags and go home. (Of course, if they did, then the betting crowd would no longer be smart—which is a real paradox.) But while it's difficult to do better than the crowd, it's not impossible. All the numbers I've mentioned, after all, are averages. They tell you that over eighteen hundred races, the betting public is brilliant. But if you're a bettor, you don't have to bet on eighteen hundred races. In fact, you don't have to bet on ten races. Some of your best bets, in other words, are the ones you don't make. You get to pick and choose the time and place when you put down your money, which means—at least in theory—that you can bet only when you're convinced that you have a real edge. And there are undoubtedly times when you do, times when the public has gotten overly smitten with a horse—as happened with Smarty Jones at the Belmont Stakes—or overly down on a horse. Those are the times when serious overlays are possible, which is when serious money can be made. Recognizing that the wisdom of crowds exists doesn't mean always deferring to the judgment of the mass. But it does mean approaching betting with a certain measure of humility. And it means understanding that you can't win by outguessing the crowd race after race. You can make money only by taking advantage—by putting down big bets—when the crowd is really wrong. Going for bigger scores, rather than trying to grind out steady victories, turns out to be a smart play. Which is, when you think about it, as it should be, since as Andrew Beyer puts it, one of the great things about the track is that it's still one of the few places where you can start out with very little capital and end up with a whole lot of money.

The ironic thing about all of this is that the thing that has always made racing less than respectable—betting—is the very thing that is, in some ways, the most remarkable thing about it. As the racing writer Joe Palmer wrote many years ago, "Thoroughbred racing is an unusual sport in that anyone who goes past a racetrack feels privileged to throw a rock or two over the fence. There are quite possibly persons . . . who are not entertained by football or basketball. But it does not therefore occur to them to oppose these sports, or to say unpleasant things about these sports." Racing has always been different, because betting has always been so integral to the sport. One answer for racing fans—and this was the answer that Palmer chose—is effectively to ignore the betting and to focus solely on the "athletic contest among horses." That's a good answer in many ways, since Secretariat's run at the Belmont would not have been any more beautiful or more moving if he had gone off at one to five instead of one to ten. But I've come to think that what bettors do at the racetrack every day, when they produce that amazingly accurate picture of the future, has its own beauty as well, and that in a way it is as surprising, and as impressive, as anything that happens on the track.

GURRIERS

Bill Barich

MOONEY AND I WERE TALKING about the Hennessy Gold Cup on one of those Dublin nights when you fear the dawn will never come. The rain lashed down in sheets, and the Dodder River began to rise. We heard the thump of sandbags lodged against doors and the fierce howls of knacker lads playing at theft in the floodtide, here an apple from the corner shop and there a shiny hubcap to fling into the sea. Through the dire blackness, the lights of Shelbourne Park dog track still glowed. God help us all, I thought.

"There's no stopping the hounds," Mooney said. "They'll run through all eternity."

"It's a power they have."

"The power to harbor human greed. To attract it, and to nourish it."

"Where's the beauty in it?" I wanted to know.

"No beauty at all!" Mooney slapped the table. "And those poor animals! My sister adopted a retired hound, and the sorry thing just lies on the floor and whimpers."

"Nice for the children," I said. "A lovely pet."

"They take it for walks, but it can't go far. Down the street and back, whimpering all the way."

"Ah, well, I'm a man for the horses myself." I called for two more pints, though when they'd arrive was anybody's guess. Our new barman was on the slow side. Polishing up a glass, that came as a challenge to him. "Give me the jump races any day. There's no finer sight than a strappy gelding sailing over a steeplechase fence."

"Will you join me for the Hennessy at Leopardstown, then?" Mooney asked. "The craic will be mighty."

"Wouldn't it be grand?" I sighed, and that was true. Grand it would be, but I was enduring a small bout of financial trauma. I'm too excitable to hold a steady job—inclined to disagree with the boss, like—and though it's a handicap, don't waste any prayers on Johnny Boy. I manage fine, except when the cannabis in town is of a very low standard and I'm obliged to advise my regulars against a substantial purchase, which was the case just then and no Colombian rescue ship on the horizon. Hence, my means were humble. I lacked the price of a Gold Cup ticket.

Though I wouldn't admit it to Niall Mooney. Might as well go on talk radio and blab about your problems to the whole universe. But he has a good heart, Mooney does. When our postmistress stuck her head in the door, all wet and shivery, he shouted, "Come in here and sit by the fire, you old dear!" And he even bought the old dear a hot brandy.

"You're an odd one," I teased him. "You'd put your own

mum in the poorhouse, but you can't do enough for Mrs. Grady."

It's a fact that Mooney still lives at home, even though he qualifies for straight-up, honest-type jobs. But he has his handicaps, too. He's stone clumsy, for example. Only a week ago, he tripped while he was carrying a bag of cement to a customer's car and broke his big toe on the left side. This was at Woody's Do It Yourself, where supposedly respectable citizens spend a fortune fixing up the house and garden, never mind the starving African children, thank you very much.

Anyway, Mooney was mooching off his mum's sympathy while the toe healed and he waited to hear about the lawsuit he'd filed via a dodgy solicitor. The mum doled out bits and bobs of cash, so he could afford to buy drinks for wet old ladies and treat himself to the luxury of the Gold Cup.

Well, we couldn't complain despite our setbacks, could we? We had it nice and cozy there in our Ringsend local, and when I set off for the gents I had a stroke of superior luck and found a *Racing Post* in nearly perfect condition. There's a sign for you, Johnny Boy, I said to myself. The shape that *Post* was in, you could return it to the newsagent, claim you bought it by mistake, and pick up a bit of change.

"Take a look here," I said to Mooney, after a good long flush of a pee.

He let out a low whistle of admiration. "How often do you find a *Post* like that?" he asked.

"Once in a blue moon, my son. It's a sign."

"They'll be jumping at Thurles tomorrow," he said, checking the entries at a lowly track in Tipperary. "Tara's Reward, now there's a horse I fancy. Almost won last time out at Gowran Park, but it fell at the last fence."

The name rang several bells in my own head. Hadn't I heard a rumble about Tara's Reward from Tim Flynn? True, Tim's a gurrier and has no respect for the law, always in and out of court. He spreads around the hot tips like manure, too, but you have to listen anyway because he has a barber uncle who cuts the hair of a famous jockey, so the tips are legitimate sometimes. "Who's riding?" I asked.

"Barry Ryan."

Barry Ryan! That was the very jockey himself! The signs were multiplying like rats. "We ought to go to Thurles," I said, casting about. A sort of plan had formed in my head. "As a warm-up for the Gold Cup, like."

"You're joking me!" Mooney laughed and signaled for another round. "In this monsoon?"

"The sky will be clear in the morning. All the world's tears will be shed by then, as my grannie used to say."

"Your grannie said no such thing."

He had me there. My grannie could neither read nor write, and she often spoke in tongues. "It must be from a poem."

"A poem farted from the nether regions. A very greyhound of a poem."

"I try to elevate the conversation, and you apply the old jackboot."

"We'll watch the races at Brady's Bookmakers," Mooney sniffed. "Same as ever, Johnny Boy."

Same as ever! What good was that to me! Old Mrs. Mooney was a soft touch, you see, and Niall was her darling baby boy, the last of seven children, so she indulged his every whim. If he told her I wanted to take him racing at Thurles to cheer him up after his accident, she'd dig deep into the

purse she hides under her mattress, and the funds could be
used for a massive wager on Tara's Reward. The profit would
buy my Gold Cup ticket. But an expedition to Brady's around
the corner? The old gal wouldn't cough up a penny for that.

"Seriously, Niall," I insisted, and I almost meant it. "That
toe is turning you into an invalid. You're like some old loony
on a park bench. You're ancient before your time."

That caught him off guard. His eyes twirled in his head.
"Where the fuck are those pints?" he shouted to the barman,
trying to change the subject.

"Am I not your good and old friend?" I pressed on. "You
need a change of scenery. It will lift your tortured spirit. All
that fresh air, the wonders of the countryside . . ."

"Have a gape at my toe, Johnny Boy. It's in a bleedin' cast.
How am I going to drive?"

The self-pity of this geezer! I had an urge to lop off that
toe with the old pruning shears. "Why not let me handle the
wheel?"

"You lost your license."

"Ah, but that was years ago! It's since been remedied. Case
of mistaken identity."

"Bollocks."

"All right!" I cried. Now I was the one banging about.
"Let's not make a hash of it, Niall. I have a plan." And I spelled
it out for him, simply and carefully, in basic words he could
understand.

"She'd be good for the money," Mooney agreed. He was
deep in thought, his face twisted up in a painful way. "What
if we lie to her? We could say we were going to Thurles, then
park the car at Brady's. It's only a short drive. You couldn't do
much harm, and there'd be no trouble with the coppers."

"Oh, that's superstar!" Good old Mooney, he'd prefer to be a decent fella, but he isn't, not really. He's as rotten as they come. "That is absolutely superstar! Full marks to you, Niall Mooney."

So the next morning I put on my clean shirt and knocked at the Mooneys' cottage bright and early. The rain was still lashing down, but I was all sunshine and roses, and there was Mrs. Mooney in her church dress congratulating me for being so kind to her baby boy, blah, blah. I jollied it up some more and even said, "What are friends for if not to help in difficult times?" And the old gal gripped my elbow and replied, "Bless you, Johnny Boy." Then she gave me the car keys and put a hundred-euro note in Mooney's paw. "Enjoy yourselves, lads."

Well, how could we not? Her car was fucking brilliant. A top-of-the-line Toyota with gauges and dials everywhere. You don't expect such style from an aged person, do you?

And that Toyota could fly! Being out of practice, I skidded a bit in the damp, and there was a slight visual problem until I mastered the wiper blades, but only a psycho would accuse me of speeding and showing off.

Mooney was that psycho, though. He had regrets about ripping off his mother. Guilt oozed from every pore, stinking like the plague. "It'll be on my head forever," he whined.

"I'd better rush you to a therapist, then. Or maybe a few hours in the old confession box would do the trick?"

"Fuck's sake!" he shrieked. "Look where you're going, Johnny Boy!"

We made it across town in record time. Brady's didn't open till ten thirty, so we ingested a sociable breakfast at a café nearby. The food killed off Mooney's guilt, and he was normal again, somewhat. Together we consulted the magical *Post* and reviewed the card at Thurles. There were six races in all, three each over hurdles and fences.

Tara's Reward was in the fifth race, a three-mile chase. The *Post*'s expert rated the horse's chances as "limited at best," but I had no fear in my heart, not with Barry Ryan in the saddle. Ryan would replace the apprentice rider who'd fallen at Gowran Park, and he was a master at getting a horse to relax and jump well. When I pictured Barry in the barber chair whispering the tip to Tim Flynn's uncle, I felt almost holy.

So I was well fed and ready for action, but Mooney had to read the whole paper. It was remarkable, really. In our school days, when the teachers used to beat us senseless for various crimes, he rarely passed an exam, but if you handed him a racing paper, he scanned it like a human X-ray machine, studying all the angles. Only when the bill arrived did he interrupt his concentration.

"My treat," he said, and that was noble and splendid, but when the waiter brought his change from the hundred-euro note, he only passed me a twenty.

"What's this for?" I asked, puzzled.

"It's your share."

"My share?" I was shocked. As the plan's instigator, its very architect, I deserved much more. "Are you daft, man? I expect half."

"Expect away. It's me mum's money. It belongs to me."

I stomped on his bad toe and seized my rightful portion.

"Bastard!" he yelped. Tears flowed from his eyes. "You low, cunning fuck!"

On our stroll to the bookie's he affected a limp, very exaggerated in my opinion, and bored the bejesus out of the clerks with his tale of the mayhem I'd committed. Unprovoked attack? As if cheating a friend was as natural as drawing a breath! Fortunately, I'm not the sort who's easily offended. Grave would be the consequences for Niall Mooney if that were the case.

Brady's was in its usual stellar condition. You won't find a cleaner betting shop in Dublin. The clerks all wear ties and call you "sir," even if you're known to the police. If you care to enjoy a can of Dutch Gold lager on the premises, they look the other way. As for the TVs that show the races, they're flat and plasmatic, state-of-the-art. The tellies flash the odds, too, and I noticed the early price on Tara's Reward was nine to one. That was welcome news, indeed, for it meant most punters hadn't caught wind of the caper.

I settled into a chair in front of a giant plasmatic, and there before me was Thurles Racecourse in all its glory. The track appeared so pretty and green amid the rolling hills of Tipperary I wished I could join the crowd, but then I heard the rain pounding down on Brady's roof and retracted the wish immediately.

"Come have a seat, Niall," I called to Mooney. He's not one to hold a grudge, so he limped over, and we watched the first race together. There were sixteen maidens entered, with nine hurdles to jump. Those animals were suited to the barnyard, really. You'd want to be counting their legs. Angel of Clonmel was still a virgin after a dozen runs. Who'd bet on such a loser? Mooney, that's who. He was even proud of it and showed me the slip with his bet written on it, all neat and tidy, ten euros to win at twelve to one.

"I wouldn't admit it in public," I warned. "You'll be taken for a mental deficient."

For once, though, he had the last laugh. The other horses

were so desperate that Angel of Clonmel actually won. Mooney leaped up from his chair and created a mighty ruckus. "Shake hands with a genius," he said, sticking out a paw. "It's the brainpower that does it. You have to study the form, Johnny Boy. You can't just drink and guess."

"Will you quit it, please? You're disturbing the other patrons."

"That horse was steadily improving. Check the *Post*— eighth, fifth, and then third." He put an arm around my shoulders, and his big, smelly face was far too close to mine. "You want some advice from a mental deficient? It's Bold Bandit in the next race."

Genius, my arse, I said to myself. I'll save my money for Tara's Reward.

Has it ever occurred to you how unfair life can be? How for no reason related to your morals or personal hygiene it can turn on you like a bloody cur and sink its fangs into your leg? That was my experience when Bold Bandit crossed the finish in front. Hateful Niall Mooney! Again he did his demented little dance and sang his own praises, all for backing the favorite. Anybody can back a favorite! Oh, you are a right fool, Mooney! I knew fate would soon slap him down. Why? On account of his fucking hubris.

I slipped out to the car for a smoke. Quality cannabis might be in short supply, but I always have an emergency stash of high-grade material. Probably if I weren't so excitable, I wouldn't need the drugs, but how many supercalm people are there in the world? About three. The pope, Nelson Mandela, and somebody else. The Dalai Lama, maybe. I wondered if they had any horse racing in Tibet, or if the Buddhists would be too good at picking winners. Did they race camels over there, or was that in Egypt? When I was a wee lad, I had a picture book about the pyramids and used to pretend I lived inside one like old King Tut, and all of a sudden I could feel the cool walls of a pyramid around me, and it was then I realized I was well and truly stoned.

THE WALK BACK TO BRADY'S took forever, but I still made it with time to spare. I checked the odds on Tara's Reward and saw that the horse had dropped to eight to one. I had to act right away, even though I was shaky. Soaked to the bone, I filled out my betting slip with trembly fingers. The little pen slipped a bit due to the amount of water pouring off me, but I managed to write both words. *Tara's Reward, fifty euros to win.*

I looked around. The shop was packed now with gurriers newly awakened from the nasty stunts they'd pulled the night before, and there among them was Tim Flynn, his nose flat against a racing page tacked to a wall. Omen of omens, sign above all other signs! Tim was ready to collect on his tip, so I gave him a wink and a nod. "Old Tim Flynn!" I greeted him. "Just happened to be in the neighborhood, did you?"

"Blasted again, Johnny Boy?" he asked.

"Most unkind, old Tim. I'm only dossing off for the day, like. Taking a break from the hard labor. What do you hear about this Tara's Reward?"

Well, the look on his face! He tried to play it dumb, as if he'd never tipped me in the first place. "Where's the horse running?"

"Why, I believe he's to run at Thurles, old Tim. With Barry Ryan as his jockey."

Now an honorable fella would have dropped the charade, but not Tim Flynn. No, the gurrier had to see it through to the bitter end. He wanted to throw me off the scent, so I wouldn't pass along the tip and lower the odds further. What an insult! Once I'm in on a scam, my lips are sealed.

He put his nose to the racing paper again. "The horse hasn't a chance," he said finally. "The conditions aren't in his favor."

"Are they not? He almost won at Roscommon last time."

"That was on firm ground. Thurles is a bog this afternoon."

Well, I'd had enough, so I called his bluff. "Funny then, isn't it, old Tim, that you tipped me on Tara's Reward yourself the other day?"

"Sorry, mate. You've got it wrong. It wasn't me."

"Got it wrong, did I?" I stopped to consider. It's true I get confused at times, and also suffer panic attacks, and if Tim weren't so dishonest, I might have believed him. But I knew better. "Ah, yes, it all comes back to me," I told him, closing my eyes. "Forgive me, Tim. A shrunken little barber gave me that tip."

"Think rehab, Johnny Boy," he said, shoving off.

The cheek of him! I was forced to seek out Mooney's company. In light of Flynn's manure flinging, his value as a friend had increased.

"How goes it?" I asked, clapping him on the thigh.

"I lost the third and fourth, but I'm still alive in the placepot."

"Good on you!" The placepot's serious business. You pick a horse to place in every race, and if they all come in, you win big. "We'll both be rich men soon."

"I don't fancy Tara's Reward anymore," he said glumly.

"The ground's gone against the horse. It's too muddy. I'm after Pins and Needles."

What? I could scarcely believe my ears. Had Tim Flynn gotten to Mooney? I searched the shop for Tim, but he'd scarpered. He'd gone elsewhere to bet, hoping to keep the other punters in the dark. It was no use, though. The word was out. "Jaysus, Niall, you must back the horse!" I scolded. "It's down to five to one."

But Mooney wouldn't budge. He was too much of a genius with his headful of statistics. Your funeral, mate, I thought as the horses circled before the start, only six of them because of the slop. Yielding turf? I'd call it *swallowing* turf. It was about to open up like a black hole and send the jockeys on a terrible journey to the center of the earth.

Pins and Needles was the favorite, of course. Mooney's in-bred caution, his babyness, had returned. He elbowed me happily when his horse shot to the front, a handsome chestnut with a white blaze, while Tara's Reward dawdled at the rear and traveled sweetly for the first mile or so, never off the bridle. Barry Ryan was working his magic. He massaged the horse until it hadn't a care in the world. There was no energy wasted, and Tara's Reward never struggled despite the hideous ground.

Pins and Needles jumped like a bloody stag, though, and put the fear of God into me. I had to remind myself that Ryan often played a waiting game, and wait he did until the third-last fence, when he asked his horse for a mighty jump and moved up to join the leader. He took full command at the second-last and put five lengths between himself and Pins and Needles. As he approached the last fence at a good gallop, I prayed Tara's Reward wouldn't hit the birch and fall again, and when my prayer was answered, I felt a cloud lift, as if all my sins had been forgiven.

I did not brag; I did not dance. I didn't even poke fun at Mooney, though the temptation was severe. Instead, I waited patiently for the result to be official, and then marched up to collect, already thinking about the new pin-striped suit I'd be wearing to the Gold Cup. Hector, the head clerk, he's a nice lad from Poland, but he gave me a queer look when I passed over my betting slip.

"Can't pay out on this, Johnny Boy," he said, pushing it back to me.

"No jokes today, Hector," I told him. "I'll just have my money now."

"Can't pay out. Look there what you wrote."

"Tara's Reward, isn't it?" I asked. I picked up the slip and fucking hell! I could barely read the words. I'd written something like Tut Rewind. "Ah, the pen was a little wet from the rain, Hector," I said, thinking fast. "Happens all the time. Occupational hazard." And I pushed the slip toward him again.

He pushed it right back. "Can't pay. It's all scribbly."

"Maybe you're not the best judge, Hector." I controlled my violent urges, but I had a knife pain in my stomach and rued the day I'd inhaled my first toke. "English isn't exactly your native tongue, is it? I'd better speak to the manager."

Now the manager at Brady's has a reputation. He isn't known for granting mercy or saving souls. He's a mug, and Brady hired him to quash the last hopes of the bitterly disappointed.

"I admit it looks bad," I explained to him. "The writing's hard to read, but that's because of the weather. See those two capital letters? The *T* and the *R*? They stand for Tara's Reward. What else could they stand for? Isn't that right, Niall?"

Mooney shrugged. "I couldn't say."

"You couldn't say?" I asked him.

"I didn't see you write it out."

"You were blind, like?"

"Minding my own business."

Well, you know the rest. Plea denied, case closed. My sins had not been forgiven, and my life was still a misery. Probably I shouldn't have nicked the stereo from Mrs. Mooney's car and sold it down by the Liffey, and definitely I shouldn't have drunk seven pints of cider and tried to break into the cottage to strangle Niall while he slept, but when you're miserable, you want everybody else to be miserable, too. I had learned my lesson, though. I understood as never before that gurriers rule the world. Injustice would be my lot forever after.

THE HORSE
IN OUR HISTORY

Daniel Woodrell

THE BODY FELL WITHIN A SHOUT of a house that still
stands. A house shown up rudely in morning brightness, a dull
small box gone shabby along the roof edge, with tar shingles
hanging frayed over a gutter that had parted from the eaves
and rolled under like a slackened lip. The yard between the
house and the railroad tracks has become an undistinguished
green, the old oaks have grown fatter with the decades, and
new neighbors have been built closer. At the bottom of the
yard near the tracks there are burnished little stumps where
elms that likely witnessed everything had been culled in the
1960s, probably, after the Dutch blight moved into our town
and caught them all.

The body fell within a shout and surely those in the house

must have heard something. Shouts, pleas, cries or brute laughter carrying loudly on that summer night before the war, here in the town this was then of lulled hearts and wincing spirits, a democratic mess of abashed citizenry hard to rouse toward anything but winked eyes and tut-tuts on "Negro matters." A Saturday in summer, the town square bunched with folks in for trading from the hills and hollers, hauling okra, tomatoes, chickens, goats, and alfalfa honey. Saturday crowds closed the streets around the square to traffic and it became a huge veranda of massed amblers. Long hellos and nodded good-byes. Farmers in bib overalls with dirty seats, sporting dusted and crestfallen hats, raising pocket hankies already made stiff and angular with salt dried from sweat wiped during the hot wagon ride to town. In the shops and shade there are others, wearing creased town clothes, with the white hankies of gentlefolk folded to peek above breast pockets in a perfect suggestion of gentility and standing. The citizenry mingles—Howdy, Hello, Good gracious, is that you? The hardware store is busy all day and the bench seats outside become heavy with squatting men who spit brown splotches toward the gutter. Boys and girls hefted baskets of produce, ate penny candy and screamed, begged nickels so they could catch the cowboy matinee at the Avenue Theater. Automobiles and trucks park east of the square; wagons and mules rest north in the field below the stockyard pens. Toward evening the drinking and gambling men would gather to cheer or curse or wave weapons when local horses were raced on the flat beaten track that circled the pens.

It was a man named Blue who fell on a night that followed such a day, a man and a falling I knew only from whispers, and the whispering had it that Blue tended horses here and

there and was the only jockey around who could get the very
best from a spectacular dun gelding named Greenvoe.

Mrs. E. H. Chambliss, in conversation outside Otto and
Belle's Barbecue, probably in June of 1976: "That horse had
a grandeur like no man and few beasts. He'd fly if he wanted
to go slow."

Mr. Todd Pilkington, smoking in the men's room just before the funeral of a classmate he'd served beside at Anzio,
spring 1984: "I've heard that horse mentioned—but wasn't
that from you? Askin' me at some other funeral?"

Mr. Edward H. Chambliss, during a phone call in winter
of 1994: "That nigra Blue was the best rider and hand here-
abouts in them days, and him'n your granddaddy trained that
horse up together real well. Real well."

My father, as the whistling breaths from his oxygen tubes
kept the cat scared, and after the dog had smelled the near
future on his master and run into the woods, never to return,
the week of his death, 1993: "Son, I heard the water pump
squeakin' in the yard late that night. That old pump, gushin'
water for quite a spell, so late, and voices."

Black families had been recruited in Oxford, Mississippi,
and brought to town by Dr. Brumleigh in 1910. The doctor
owned vast fruit orchards just east of town, several hundred
acres, and brought fourteen complete families north to work
them for him. A bare clutch of rudimentary houses were built
for the families on a gullied slope out of view from the square
in the still largely forsaken northeastern reaches of town. The
orchard failed within a decade. The blacks remained in homes
that were soon too small, unsnug and uneven against the sky.
New rooms were made of what was easily found: wood scraps
from backyards and trash piles, sheets of crumpled metal

blown free by storms, chicken wire, river stones, with foundation stumps of almost the right size tipping the floors slightly this way and that. There were no romantic entryways or cozy embellishments. Windows cracked at angles as the houses relaxed farther into the dirt.

Mr. Micah Kerr, beside Howl Creek, holding a cane pole while watching his bobber not bob, around 1969: "Them days, boy, furniture'd really start a-fallin' of a Saturday night over on Nigger Hill, there. Somebody'd a-get to fussin' with somebody else 'til furniture started flyin' and a-fallin', and that fussin'd go on and on 'til the makin' up started, which was usually louder."

My oldest living relative, who had, with great single-mindedness, remarried in less than a year, at her spacious new home, late 1993: "Don't write that. Why write that? There wasn't any murder like that. It *never* happened. Never happened. And please listen good to me for once—they're not *all* dead yet."

The horse was, in most versions of the story, a bangtail grown powerful from running the sand bottoms of the Jacks Fork. Sometimes the horse had been stolen out of Sallisaw by one of the Grieve brothers, or a sly stranger who gave a false name on sale day and promptly left town. The horse was always dun, a bitter gelding, with a crisp stride and endless stamina. A horse worth fighting over.

Mr. Willie Johnstone, bourbon in hand, at a fish fry of red-ear perch on the Eleven Point, 1995: "I guess your granddaddy and ol' Blue was with the horse most days in them years. The lunch whistle'd blow at the mill 'n' lots of times you'd pretty quick see William Sidney walkin' the path yonder above Eccleston's, the path that's gone now but used to be the nigh cut through those woods that were there and came out into a backyard on the Hill. Fetchin' ol' Blue, I guess, to work that horse for the lunch hour in a field somewhere over there. I can still see him in my head, his shape goin' up that path—your granddaddy walked about like you do, kid, sort of hunched, like he was halfway duckin' from somethin' all the time."

Mrs. E. H. Chambliss, with her eyes closed and her hands clasped, on a porch swing in July 1995: "Oh, them two loved that horse. Which is sad, 'cause I think the horse is what killed him, really. The heartbreak, don't you know?"

Mr. Tom Finney, after my father's funeral, while carving a ham: "Shit, boy, his name wasn't Greenvoe—wherever'd you get that from? And he wasn't much of a horse, neither, if I'm rememberin' the horse you mean. Used to stop on the far half of the track and drop horse apples in the midst of a goddamn race—that sound like a great champ to you?"

Mr. Ronnie Thigpen, at his daughter's home near Egypt Grove, with the television blaring world news and a rack of medicine bottles on the table at his side, 1994: "There had been a drunk hobo run over by a train 'n' broken apart a month or so earlier, so when I seen all this blood 'n' splintered wood 'n' stuff, I thought, 'Uh-oh, another drunk hobo forgot to jump.' Then I seen it was a nigger, a nigger from town, there, that had forgot to jump. So I told the man at the train depot there was a sort of familiar-lookin' nigger dead in the weeds over by the tracks, and I guess he flagged a deputy."

My oldest living relative, while picking cherries from her yard trees, 1996: "That's 'cause you got the name wrong. His name wasn't Blue—it was *Ballou*. Folks misheard his last name and thought it was his first name, so that's what he got called. His wife used to be around, did housework and the like, and her name was Ballou. Look for him under Ballou."

Summer had its fangs out sharp and long that year, sucking the joy from every sunny hour. The heat led to erupting meannesses between intimates, bursts of spite that bubbled the truth up top to be hurled from one sweated, sopping side of the bed to the other, never to be truly forgotten or gotten over. Howl Creek, a rumpled, dissolute puddling of water, became the nearest splashing place, and many folks of both sexes took small relief in the darkness there. A fainting quiet fell over the darkened town, and headaches ebbed in the silence, until an approaching train would release a rallying moan into the night. The railroad tracks ran beside the creek and the moan stirred sleep all across town.

Sheriff Solomon Combs, in a ledger found under a basement staircase at the courthouse, dated August 4, 1938: *Ballou. Colored. First name not sure. Drunk and hit by a train hauling timber. Deceased. Accident.*

Mrs. E. H. Chambliss, waiting for hot rolls at the Ramada Inn buffet, on Easter Sunday 1996: "The horse. I'm sure anything that might've happened, or maybe didn't, was about that horse."

Mr. Tom Finney, in the parking lot outside Bobby's Walleye Restaurant, summer 1996: "That worthless pony is probably still lollygaggin' on the far turn to spread horse apples, Danny. Hurry 'n' you can maybe still catch a glimpse of 'im yet, dawdling along the rail with his ass to the finish line and his tail in the air."

Someone official must've carried the news to the Hill. Knocking on doors to raised houses made of things not meant to be nailed together, but that stood for years, invalid structures

patched further with odds and ends as passing seasons brought
rot to the wood and old nails fell away. In the shade and fine
dust beneath the houses, dogs have belly-dragged in and out
until belly-shaped draws have been wiggled into the dirt. Kids
follow dogs, and on the Sundays of most seasons muffled playing voices rise from the shaded crawl spaces and catch the
wind to fly. Knock, knock—you Blue's wife? These li'l girls his
kids? Well, he won't be home no more. Jumped in front of a
timber train. Must've been drunk. You can bury the boy over
at Sadie's.

Mr. Edward H. Chambliss, with his chin in the air and his
ancient fists balled, on his front porch, early 1997: "William
Sidney always was my best friend, goddamn you, Danny. And
best friend don't mean nothin' if you won't stand for each other
when the bad time comes. You might oughta keep clear of me.
You might oughta do that. And don't call my wife, neither."

My oldest living relative, on the phone, early 1997: "These
were not men lamed by any sorts of doubts about anything
they did. Or *might do yet*—hear me?"

An uncle who'd had two ships blown wide and sunk beneath him in the Pacific, and came home with what they
called "shell shock," a cracked and occasionally cascading
state of mind that was accompanied by a delicate lacing of
public shame, on the phone from Australia, where he'd emi-
grated in 1955: "I knew Blue from when I ran errands for the
men out at Cozy Grove, the bar there. I never saw him with
a horse. He wasn't much higher'n a belt buckle, but he was
stronger'n Limburger cheese. He'd carry feed sacks from
town for a nickel. I never heard of Dad doin' much of anything with horses, neither, but go broke bettin' on 'em. You
knew Dad was born well-to-do, didn't you? Had all that land

once out by JJ Highway. Lost everything before I was born on moonshine and ladies in red and mighty slow horses, and never even said sorry, either."

So it's written down for an accident by the law, and the Ballou kids from that homesawn house on the Hill come along fatherless into the war years, years that were hard on everybody, those wrinkling years of rubber rations, gas rations, meat rations, and unlimited worry, worry, every day the worry and the wrinkling and another supper leeched from the same ham bone and more navy beans. See them waiting for dark before touring the square during the holiday season, heavy wet misting clouds between the tall lamps and their feet, pausing before the keenly garish shop windows, dampening scarves molding to their heads, wearing the uncertain slanting gaze of children who've been scalded other times for acting too familiar. A damp virtuosity of misshapen reflections on the street, the windows, the eyeglasses of the few walkers passing by, and two girls noting to each other the presents they most favored from shops they'd never go inside.

My father, drinking the whiskey he loved in the shadowed garage, with meddlers out of sight, fall 1992: "We each of us get dealt a lot of cards by our old ones, son, but you don't want to play them all."

The Hill as it was is vanished now, finished off by high heels and humiliated scolds, flattened to nothing and the scraps carted away, in 1956. The sound of her high heels clicking on sidewalk cement brought water to the mouths of men within ear of her sashay, moist and listening as she came along so avid and fluid, with fluctuating mounds, the clicks entering their heads with the rhythm of dreams. A blooming of taffeta and a sweet woozy smell. Her voice was rich and round and rolled on and on, seducing with each spin, and the voice gave her a fresh name—Dyna Flo. A smitten car dealer used her in local radio spots and she said the tagline so it held within it the promise of everything craved: "It's the Dyna Flo that makes it magic, folks. Come on out to Yount's Buick 'n' see for yourselves." Mr. Yount fell her way, his wallet held open and his mind helplessly made up. He swung by on Saturday nights with bottles of hooch and sporting friends, and the friends soon fell her way, too, and dripped dollar bills to her floor. Dyna Flo Ballou, her first name lost just as her father's had been, walked tall and flush and brought stray bits of finery to the Hill; curtains of bright yellow, brittle champagne glasses, expensive dresses from St. Louis in the wrong color for my skin, honey, that were soon worn by young girls mopping the floors of town.

My oldest living relative, during a warm winter, while her husband cleaned fish near Mammoth Spring: "She was dropdead gorgeous. That gal got prettier every time I saw her, and she stopped traffic the *first* time I saw her. And, lordy, that voice—that Dyna Flo voice! No, no, she wasn't the kind of beauty you could ever miss—had eyes 'bout as blue as yours, Danny. We used to run into her sometimes when you were tiny. She always wanted to touch you. Touch your nose, tickle your cheek. Just touch you."

A schedule was arranged between the men with money, and Dyna Flo laughed low and golden from her porch steps until heard by wives who couldn't stand the sound nor the fact of her. The men were shamed but would not give her up, and marriages split in spots that never healed. Humiliated, the wives gathered uncles, brothers, friends from church with white robes and sticks and during a rainy spell went to Dyna

Flo's house, kicked the door aside and threw everything she had into the yard mud. Get out of town, tonight, or the same train'll hit you that hit your daddy. A week later every household on the Hill received a letter from the city, telling them to vacate the premises while water lines and sewers were put in and the streets were paved. We'll let you know when you can come back.

Mr. Tom Finney: "Most likely St. Louis. That's what I heard. Folks was rough on colored people then, and black was the main one of them colors."

Mr. Ronnie Thigpen, Egypt Grove, 1994: "I went back by once the sheriff come along for a look. There was a bunch of two-by-fours that was splintered a little bit, and had bloody places on 'em. Five or six, I guess. I seen the sheriff sort of kick those two-by-fours away from the tracks, down into the creek, there. That's when he said, 'Looks to me like ol' Blue jumped in front of a timber train. Amen.'"

Mrs. E. H. Chambliss, accosted and held by the wrist outside the Front Street Church of Christ in 1998, a month after her husband's death: "They was all brought together by love, Danny. The love of that horse. Your granddaddy doted on that thing, him 'n' Blue; then somethin' soured and Blue got drunk 'n' died. That horse was *magnificent,* hear? Beautiful to see, he was. Would've won any race he could've been got to— just that special. He was just so special."

My oldest living relative, sitting in a shaded parlor, upon reading my notes and turning the last page, folded her old hands and closed her eyes: "There never was a horse. The rest is true."

HEART

Wallace Stroby

MORGAN RAN OUT OF MUSIC just outside Trenton. He'd only brought two cassettes with him for the drive down from Newark—Harold Melvin and the Blue Notes and O. V. Wright—and he'd played both twice through already. Now he had the radio on, was fishing for something he could stand to listen to. He tuned past gangsta rap, a talk station, a baseball game. Then he turned the radio off, drove in silence.

He took the Trenton exit on the Turnpike, followed the directions he'd been given, steering the big Monte Carlo past rows of crumbling brownstones with plywood windows, cracked sidewalks, BEWARE OF DOG signs. Middle of the summer and no one on the street.

It took him ten minutes to find the address. He parked a

block away, locked the car, and walked back. Small overgrown yards here, weeds coming up through the buckled sidewalk, single-family homes long ago converted to low-rent apartments. Broken glass and crack vials crunched beneath his boots.

He'd grown up in a neighborhood like this. They were all the same. Even in the sixties and seventies, before crack and the mad money that followed it. Before the riots even. Except for the time he'd spent in the foster home—and then later in Rahway—he'd walked a street like this every day of his life until he was thirty.

On the porch he started to cough, the pain coming up in him without warning, steel wool in his lungs. He coughed hard and deep, blood and phlegm filling his mouth. He gagged, spit, waited for the dizziness to pass. After a moment he straightened, breathed deep, took a handkerchief from the pocket of his army field jacket. He wiped his lips, put the handkerchief away, the material blotted with blood.

The windows were barred but open. All the money Lewis was bringing in and he wouldn't spring for air-conditioning. Morgan could hear a television on inside, smell the sweet, sickly odor of marijuana. He knocked twice on the heavy door, stepped back, the porch boards groaning under him.

Movement inside. Morgan knocked again.

"Who is it?" Lewis's voice.

"Open the damn door."

"Morgan?"

The sound of locks being undone. Two dead bolts, a chain, a police bar that fed into the floor. The door swung in and Lewis stood there in a stained white undershirt and sweatpants, barefoot. There were bits of lint in his natural. Barely noon and he already had his smoke on.

"Morgan, yo. What up?"

Morgan stepped past him into the foyer. Lewis closed and locked the door.

"Mikey-Mike told me he was sending somebody," he said. "But I didn't think it be you. You slummin', nigga."

To the right was the living room. A big flat-screen TV in a wall unit, a black leather couch facing it. A woman was curled on one end of the couch, feet tucked under her, watching a basketball game. She was white, chubby, with dyed blond hair, roots showing. She looked at Morgan without interest, then back at the TV, players racing across the court.

"Hey, baby," Lewis said. "This Morgan, from up north. Morgan, this Sheila. Have a seat, man. Got the Nets game from last night. This TiVo is the shit."

There was a haze of smoke in the room, cigarettes and pot, the open windows not helping. The woman wore a XXXL T-shirt that reached to her knees, with a silk screen on it of some rapper Morgan didn't recognize. Her skin was pale, acne scars on her cheekbones. On the coffee table in front of her was an ashtray full of roaches and cigarette butts, a plastic lighter, half-empty containers of Chinese food. She ignored him, sleepy or stoned or both.

"Get you a beer," Lewis said, and went through a narrow hallway into the kitchen.

Morgan sat on the other end of the couch, felt it sink under him, air hiss out. The woman picked up a loose cigarette from the table, lit it with the plastic lighter.

Lewis came back with two open bottles of Heineken.

"Here you go, man." He put one on the table in front of Morgan, settled into a recliner to the left of the couch. The chair's arms were scarred with cigarette burns.

"Jason kicking ass," he said. "Twenty points so far and it only the second quarter."

"I don't follow the game," Morgan said. He picked up the Heineken.

"Must be the only nigga in the wide world don't," Lewis said. The girl laughed without turning.

Morgan picked up the beer, sipped it. It was lukewarm. He put it back down.

"I got the cheddar for you," Lewis said. "But it's a little shy. Shit been crazy lately. That last package a little weak. Everybody know it, too."

On the screen, two players collided midcourt, fell.

"Now that was a motherfucking foul," Lewis said. "Ref blind not to see that."

The woman leaned over, tapped ash into the tray, and Morgan drew the Glock out of his right jacket pocket and shot her in the side of the head.

Even with the suppressor, the shot was loud. Blood spattered the wall behind the couch.

"What the fuck, man!" Lewis leaped from the recliner. Morgan pointed the Glock at him. The woman slumped as if falling asleep, slid halfway off the couch.

"What the fuck . . ."

"Sit down," Morgan said.

"You didn't have to do that, man. She didn't mean nothing by it."

The woman trembled, was still. Her T-shirt had ridden up to show heavy thighs.

"It was just a joke, man. You didn't have to do that."

"Sit down," Morgan said again, and Lewis lowered himself back into the recliner. The sharp tang of cordite drifted in the air. Morgan picked up the shell casing from the floor, put it in his left pocket.

Lewis was looking at the woman, tears in his eyes.

"Why?" Almost a child's voice now. "Why you have to go do that?"

"Get your attention. You know why Mikey-Mike sent me?"

"Man, I got the money. I told you."

"Where is it?"

"In the kitchen."

"Let's go."

Morgan followed him in. The sink was full of dishes. The money was in a Tupperware container on the bottom shelf of the refrigerator. Banded twenties and hundreds.

"Put that shit in a bag or something," Morgan said.

"I told Mikey. I told him I had it. Why you have to go and do that?"

Morgan watched as Lewis rooted through the cabinets, found a plastic garbage bag. Lewis took the money out of the container, put it in the bag.

"Wrap that up," Morgan said. When Lewis was done, the package was no larger than a football.

Morgan nodded back at the living room. Lewis went first.

"I told Mikey-Mike," he said. "I told him I had the mother-fucking money."

The woman had fallen all the way to the floor, was lying on her right side. Blood soaked the carpet around her head.

"Oh, man," Lewis moaned when he saw her again. "Oh, man."

"Put the bag on the floor and sit your ass down in that chair."

Lewis did as he was told. Morgan stood behind him.

"Mikey-Mike don't care about the money," he said. "You should know that by now, brother. How many times you shorted him in the past? It's about respect. It happens too often; he feels like you don't respect him anymore."

Morgan looked at the screen. Players were lining up at the foul line. One of the Nets took the ball, dribbled it in place, looked up at the basket.

"Can you freeze-frame that?" Morgan said.

"What?"

"Freeze-frame it? Stop it where it is?"

"Yeah."

"Go on."

Lewis took a remote from the table, tried not to look at the woman. The Net was poised to throw, the ball held high. Lewis pushed a button and the image froze.

"Who is that?" Morgan said. "The player. Trying to make the shot."

"Jason Kidd."

"He good?"

"What do you mean?"

"He a good player?"

Lewis was looking at him, confused.

"Yeah, he good."

"You watch this game before?"

"No, man. Like I said. It was on last night. I TiVoed it."

"You read the paper today, listen to the radio?"

"What? No, man, we just got up."

"Okay, then," Morgan said. "Here's the deal. Mikey-Mike wants you gone, but he left it to my discretion. You know what that means?"

"Yeah, I know what that means."

"Don't look at me; look at the screen."

Lewis turned back to the TV, Kidd still frozen, the ball on his fingertips.

"So I'll make you a bet. A real one. He makes that shot, sinks that ball, I turn around and walk out of here and you get yourself gone. Out of Jersey. I'll give you that chance. You understand?"

"I understand."

"Good. Now start that up again."

Morgan took a step back, held the Glock out, the suppressor a few inches from the back of Lewis's head.

Lewis lifted the remote, his hand shaking. He pointed it at the TV.

"Go ahead," Morgan said.

The image lived again. Kidd raised the ball, rose onto his toes, lobbed it. It made a perfect arc through the air, all the players watching. It hit the rim, rolled around, hung there for an instant. Dropped off the rim to the floor.

Morgan squeezed the trigger. Blood hit the television. He fired twice more. On the dripping screen, Kidd stood at the foul line again, caught the ball as it was tossed to him, got ready for another throw.

Morgan picked up the shell casings. He tucked the bag with the money under his arm, got the Heineken bottle, poured the contents on the floor, put the empty bottle in his left-hand pocket. On the screen, he saw the ball drop neatly through the net, hit the floor, and bounce, the players galvanizing into action around it.

Not touching anything, he let himself out the front door, walked back to the car.

TERRY LAY ON THE BED, looked up at the ceiling fan turning softly, barely moving the air. All the windows in the house open, but no breeze outside. Joette moved against him, half-asleep, her head on his chest, her skin cool against his. Both of them were slick with sweat, the sheets pushed aside. He looked up at the turning fan and thought about the money.

In the next room, Ricky began to cry. Joette stirred, raised her head, listened for a moment, and then slid quickly out of bed, her feet finding slippers. He watched as she took her robe from a chair, pulled it on. There was a single candle burning on the dresser and it threw her shadow huge against the wall. She tied the belt, went out, left the door ajar. A line of light from the hall stretched across the bedroom floor.

He heard her go into Ricky's room, her voice calm, steady, soothing. The crying slowed, then stopped. She was singing now, low and soft, a tune Terry didn't know.

He swung his feet off the bed, looked at the nightstand clock—two A.M. He had to get some sleep soon, be ready for tomorrow. He stood, knees aching, legs unsteady, found his jeans on the floor, pulled them on.

Barefoot, he went into the hall. Ricky's door was slightly open and he could see Joette in there on the bed, holding him, rocking him slowly, her singing almost a whisper now. Terry walked to the bathroom, shut the door behind him, turned on the light. In the mirror, his skin had a yellowish cast. There were dark circles beneath his eyes.

He urinated for a long time, flushed, washed his hands in the sink, splashed water in his face. Then he went down the hall to the dark kitchen, opened the refrigerator. There were three Budweisers in the bottom rack of the door. He got one out, hipped the door shut, twisted the top off, drank.

There was a single light on in the living room, a three-way bulb turned to low. He carried the beer in, padded across the carpet, looked at the photos atop the TV. Gerald in his dress blues and cap, a Marine Corps flag behind him. Gerald with Ricky, an infant then, cradled in the crook of his arm. Gerald and Joette dressed up, at a wedding somewhere, at a table with another couple, chairs crowded together, smiling for the camera.

He heard footsteps in the hall, the bathroom door closing. He sipped beer, picked up the dress-blues picture. For all the sternness in the pose, the fixed gaze, he guessed Gerald had been only a couple years out of high school when the photo was taken. He thought about the folded flag wrapped in tissue paper that Joette kept in the bottom drawer of her dresser, her wedding ring in a box beside it. That and Ricky and these photos—all she had left of him now.

He heard a toilet flush, water running. He set the photo down, adjusted it to the same position as before. He went back into the kitchen, was leaning against the counter when she came in.

"Nightmares," she said. "He's getting them more and more now. Dr. Calvin says it might be from the chemo. When he starts the next round he wants to try some different combinations, see if it helps. Hopefully the HMO will still pay for it."

She'd tied her long black hair back, her face and neck still slightly flushed from their lovemaking. She took the beer from him, sipped, and handed it back. He put it on the counter and she slipped her arms around him, hugged him tight, her head against his chest.

"Are you going to stay?" she said.

"I don't think it's a good idea."

She looked up at him.

"Why not?"

"I've got to be up early."

"I can set the alarm for whenever you want."

He didn't answer. She pulled away from him.

"You're going to the track again, aren't you?" she said.

"I have to. I told you."

"It's no good for you, Terry, going back there."

"Jo, we talked about this. I fucked up. I know I did. But there's only one way I can get out from under. And this tip from Dominic . . ."

"Dominic? That guy? Jesus, Terry, he's a bookie, I mean . . . don't tell me you borrowed money from Dominic."

"Not this time. He won't lend it to me anymore."

"He knows you have a problem."

"Maybe, but he didn't exactly forgive my debts either. He left me out there hanging. I owed him $20K from the Derby."

"Terry, don't tell me this."

"It's okay. I paid him."

"How?"

"How do you think? I borrowed it from someone else. A guy up in Newark. C-Love put me in touch with him."

"C-Love? At the track? Curtis?"

"Yeah."

"Oh, Terry. What have you done?"

"What I had to."

"You should call that FBI agent. The one that gave you his card."

"You kidding?"

"Maybe he can help."

"He's fishing, Jo. That's all. He hit some other rollers at the track, Len Fisher and Lefty Rosales too. He's looking for something on Dominic and the people he works for. He's hoping to find someone so far in the hole they'll rat somebody out. I wouldn't go near the guy. No one will."

"I worry, Terry."

"I want to make this work, Jo. You and me and Ricky. But I can't do it like this. I start the meetings next week. I've already talked to the counselor. He's going to set me up with a sponsor. But I have to pay these guys off or I'll never get them off my back. Dominic knows the situation I'm in. He wants to help me get out of it."

"All of a sudden he's your friend?"

"He's a businessman. People like me, the state I'm in, we're bad for business."

"This is insane, Terry. With everything you owe already, you're going to bet again, on a tip some bookie gave you?"

"It's the only way. And I have a good feeling about this, Jo. I do."

She leaned against the counter to his left, a foot of space between them. She tucked a stray strand of hair behind her right ear, crossed her arms, looked away. He saw the wetness in her eyes.

"I should go," he said.

"Maybe you should."

He went back down the hall. Through the half-open door, he saw Ricky asleep in NASCAR sheets, face turned toward the wall, his arms wrapped around a stuffed dinosaur. He was small for a six-year-old, and all that was left of his hair was ragged patches of down. Terry watched him, the rise and fall of the boy's breathing almost imperceptible.

He moved quietly into the room, sat on the edge of the bed. Ricky didn't stir. Terry leaned close, kissed him lightly on the forehead. When he stood up, he saw Joette in the doorway. Tears streaked her face. She stood aside to let him through.

In the bedroom, he found his T-shirt, work boots, dressed by candlelight. When he was done he went back into the kitchen. She was leaning against the counter again, arms folded, looking out the window into the side yard. He got his keys from the counter.

"I'll call you tomorrow, when I get back," he said.

She nodded without looking at him. He went out the door and into the night.

The pickup was slow to start, and he let it run a little, smoke coughing out behind. He saw her standing at the lighted kitchen window, watching him. Then she turned away from the window and the light went out.

MORGAN STEERED THE MONTE CARLO into the lot at Monmouth Park, drove past endless lines of cars gleaming in the afternoon sun. He found a spot against the back fence, parked and locked the car, joined the stream of people crossing Oceanport Avenue, queuing up at the track entrance. He paid the two-dollar admission fee, pushed through the turnstile and onto the grounds.

It took him a few minutes to get his bearings. Ahead of him the grandstand rose, with breezeways leading to the track area. There was a separate entrance for the clubhouse, a woman checking tickets at the door. People everywhere, a Saturday-afternoon crowd.

Morgan scanned faces, bought a *Daily Racing Form.* Over the PA, the track announcer was calling the results of the last race. Morgan folded the *Racing Form* under his left arm, made his way toward the grandstand.

Inside was a betting and concession area, a bank of closed-circuit televisions on one wall. The big room smelled of popcorn, stale cigar smoke, sweat. Torn betting tickets littered the floor.

He wandered through the breezeway that led out to the track, heard the call to post being played. There were people lined up five deep at the track rail. As he watched, horses were led out onto the track and into the starting gate.

He stood there for a while, watching the crowd, thinking it through. Then he went back inside.

TERRY COUNTED THE MONEY a final time in a men's room stall. Ten thousand dollars in twenties and fifties, wrapped with denomination bands he'd gotten from the bank the day before. The cash was old and he'd had to straighten the bills out before banding them. It was the way Mikey-Mike's man had given him the money. Thirty-five thousand in all, loose in a Nike shoebox.

He'd used twenty-three of it to pay Dominic back with interest, two thousand for immediate expenses—rent, truck insurance, groceries. And now the last ten for the next race, the Select Stakes, and Dominic's tip. It hadn't been easy, but he'd resisted the temptation to bet on any of the earlier races. Trusting Dominic, what he'd said. The horse was ready for the big win, the jockey and trainer holding him back in his last three races, waiting for today. For the money to be right.

He'd worn his lucky jacket, a thin black leather car coat with deep pockets for carrying the cash. When he was through counting, he put the money back, went out into the empty men's room. From the speakers mounted on the walls, he could hear the eleventh race being called. The Select was next.

He looked at himself in the mirror, ran water in his hands and passed it over his face, then yanked paper towels from the dispenser, dried off. He tossed the towels away, tried to control his breathing, slow it down. It was then he heard his name over the PA, calling him to the phone.

MORGAN HELD HIS CELL PHONE to his ear, watched the information booth on the other side of the big room, the heavy-set black woman behind the counter. Outside, the noise of the crowd rose. Over the indoor PA, the announcer's staccato voice became more excited, the words running together, and Morgan got it in stereo, coming through the phone as well. Was ready to hang up when he saw the white boy in the leather jacket head toward the information booth.

TERRY PICKED UP THE PHONE, said "Hello?", heard nothing. A click and then the dial tone was back. He looked at the woman behind the counter who'd handed it to him.

"No one there," he said.

She shrugged.

"There was. They asked me to page you and that's what I did."

Outside, the crowd noise was peaking, the race almost over. He handed the receiver back, dug his cell out. No calls. If it had been Joette, she would have tried him that way first. And then the fear hit him that it had been Dominic, not remembering his cell number, calling to tell him something had changed, the tip no longer valid. Not to bet.

The crowd noise grew and then dropped off abruptly, the race over. He scanned the speed-dial numbers on his cell, realized he'd taken Dominic's off three weeks ago, a gesture to Jo. He felt the panic setting in.

The announcer was back on, talking up the Select, but Terry couldn't register what he was saying. He felt the sudden need to urinate. He started back to the men's room, nearly bumped into a middle-aged black man in a green army jacket looking up at one of the screens, a simulcast from another track. Terry said, "Excuse me," moved around him.

When he was done, he came out to find bettors already lined up at the windows, some ten deep. He went to the $200-and-up window, the line shorter here, only four people in front of him. When he reached the window, he smiled at the blond woman behind it, slowly pulled the money from his pockets, and laid the bundles side by side in the gap beneath the bulletproof glass. She looked at them without expression.

"That's ten thousand," he said. "On number twelve. To win."

MORGAN WATCHED THE WHITE BOY place his bet. Had him now, wouldn't lose him in the crowd. The high-roller window, so he had cash to spend. Mikey-Mike's cash. Morgan knew the story. The white boy was into Mikey for thirty-five large, but the FBI had been sniffing around and Mikey had gotten nervous. He'd decided to eat the thirty-five, cut his losses, eliminate the risk. It would be an example too, for others. Don't fuck with Mikey-Mike. White or black or yellow.

Morgan saw the logic, agreed with it. But everyone else that Morgan had done for Mikey-Mike was in the game. When they stole, when they went behind Mikey-Mike's back, they knew they were gambling with their lives. But this white boy was different. He had no clue what he'd gotten into. He was oblivious to his surroundings, the danger.

Morgan watched him walk out into the sunlight, start to wade into the crowd toward the rail. He slipped the Glock out of his jacket pocket, fit it into the fold of the *Racing Form,* tucked it under his left arm, followed in the white boy's wake.

TERRY MOVED OUT INTO THE CROWD, brushing elbows, shoulders, the smell of hot dogs and popcorn from the grandstand mixed with the faint odor of sweat. The sky was a hard blue.

On the track, they'd moved the starting gate into place for the six-furlong Select course. Terry found a spot five people in from the rail, to the right of the finish line. Others filled in around him.

He heard the call to post and the horses were led out onto the track one by one, all three-year-olds. Here was the favorite, Storm Warning, number six, dark copper with white stockings, heavily muscled, four to five, even money. The jockey was leaning forward, whispering into the horse's ear. Behind them, Virgil's Dream, number ten, a deep brown, looking compact and powerful, seven to five.

Four more horses and then finally number twelve, Byzantium, a dark bay, smaller than the others, maybe fifteen hands from withers to the ground. The long shot at twelve to one. Terry could tell why. The horse was out of place, outclassed in looks and size. He seemed skittish as he was led out, backpedaled for a moment until the jockey gentled him. As if the horse himself knew he didn't belong. His eyes were wide and yellow; his glance ranged across the crowd as he moved toward the gate.

The fear crept back. Was this Dominic's idea of a joke? Getting him to bet everything on a horse that had no chance of winning? Too late now. Too late for anything.

He felt the acid in the pit of his stomach, and something

else too. The first stirrings of the adrenaline that always took him before a race he had big money on. It was the sense of being alive, that this was something that mattered. He hadn't lied to Jo; he would start the counseling next week. But he would miss this and he knew it. There was nothing like it in the world. It was better than sex, better than anything.

The crowd was tightening around him as the starting gate crew helped load the horses into their stalls. He felt someone press up against his back, shifted to give them room. The pressure stayed. Irritated, he looked over his left shoulder, saw the black man he'd almost bumped into inside. Something hard poked him just below the left shoulder blade.

"Easy," the man said. "Eyes forward."

Terry looked at him, not understanding.

"Face forward." Enough above a whisper to be heard over the crowd. Terry saw the folded *Racing Form,* something inside it. Knew then what it was.

"Forward," the man said again, and Terry obeyed. He watched the last of the horses being led into the starting gate. The crowd chattered around him, oblivious. Some shouted to the jockeys. He felt the strength drain from his legs.

The black man coughed, once, twice, the second time violently, and the pressure on Terry's back eased. He started to turn again, was prodded hard, faced forward.

After a moment, he said, "I can pay it back. I have the money."

"If you had the money, would you be here?"

"I can get it."

"Shut up. Watch the horses."

The pressure below Terry's shoulder blade was steady again. The barrel of the gun—that was what it was, what it had to be—dug into him slightly. There was some muscle there, he knew, then his heart. At this range there was no way he would survive. He was aware of these things almost coldly, realizing them, evaluating the odds. He was going to die. He knew that now. Over a stupid thirty-five grand.

The horses were all in the gate, the crowd growing almost quiet, a prerace hush. Terry wondered what the man was waiting for. Realized then. He would wait until the crowd noise was at its peak, just as the horses reached the finish line. And then he would shoot Terry through the heart.

MORGAN WIPED BLOOD FROM HIS LIP, tasted copper. He wanted to spit but the people were packed in too close; there was nowhere to do it. He swallowed blood, pressed up closer to the white boy, screwed the suppressor into his back, thumbed the hammer to full cock. The boy wouldn't even be able to fall—the crowd would hold him up. Morgan could turn and work his way back through the crowd to the grandstand and the exits before anyone even knew what had happened.

His index finger slid across the curve of the trigger. And then the horses broke from the gate.

TERRY'S VISION SEEMED TO BLUR. He saw the gates snap open, the horses charge out. People around him began to yell. He forced himself to watch the race. Storm Warning was already in the lead, two other horses behind him, then Virgil's Dream, and finally Byzantium in fifth. They neared the first turn, Byzantium on the inside, the other horses crowding him, keeping him from moving up. Storm Warning stayed ahead, Virgil's Dream gaining on the right. Byzantium tried to move forward, couldn't. The horses came out of the turn and Byzantium was in sixth place, no room to maneuver, no holes to push through. Terry watched, realized it didn't matter now. And then the black man leaned forward, inches from Terry's left ear.

"Which horse you bet on?"

Terry could feel the pulse in his own neck, the beat of his heart. He'd heard the faint snick of the gun being cocked before the horses broke.

"I asked you a question."

He went blank for a moment. The gun pushed against him.

"Number twelve," he said. "Byzantium."

The horses were in the second turn, Virgil's Dream leading, Storm Warning in second, four other horses behind him. Byzantium was still in sixth place.

"You bet to win?"

Terry nodded.

Out of the turn and the positions the same. Byzantium struggling up on the inside, getting cut off.

"Doesn't look good," the man said, the crowd noise rising as the horses headed toward the next turn. Soon it would be loud enough, Terry knew.

"I'll make you a bet," the man said.

Terry half turned.

"Don't look at me; look at the horses."

Terry did as he was told.

"Here's the bet," the man said. "Your horse wins, I let you live."

Byzantium was still crowded on the inside, nowhere to go,

the field leaving him behind. Then the last turn, the horses surging forward, and Byzantium maneuvered away from the inside rail, found a spot between the two horses that had blocked him, moved through them. The announcer was calling it, Virgil's Dream in the lead, Storm Warning second.

Into the stretch and Byzantium moved into a hole straight up the center, pouring on the speed, the jockey bent forward to reduce wind resistance. A surge went through the crowd. Byzantium gained ground, moved into fourth unopposed. The third-place horse veered to his left, closing the gap, steering across Byzantium's path. Byzantium hung back, let the horse pass in front of him, and then moved to the right, filled the space the other horse had left.

The announcer's voice was more excited now, breathless, the crowd noise almost drowning it out. Halfway through the stretch and Storm Warning had taken the lead again, Virgil's Dream just behind it, Byzantium in third. Terry felt his heart leap like a flag in the wind, the black man forgotten, the gun forgotten. There was nothing but the horses and the track, the speed, the race.

MORGAN WATCHED THE HORSES, not believing what he was seeing. The jockey on Virgil's Dream turned to look at Byzantium coming up behind him, and the smaller horse powered past, eating up the track. Byzantium's head was now abreast and to the left of Storm Warning's haunches. Virgil's Dream fell back as if the air had been let out of him, his energy diffused. The two lead horses charged toward the finish line, almost neck and neck, the crowd in the grandstand on its feet, screaming.

The horse had been near dead last, and here he was, moving up, giving it all he had, looking for the opportunities and taking them, not slowing, showing Morgan something he hadn't seen before, hadn't expected to see. Smaller than the other horses, the odds against him, but something driving him, something that left circumstance and handicap behind. Something Morgan understood.

NECK AND NECK, the finish line straight ahead, the crowd louder than Terry had ever heard it before, louder than anything, drowning out the announcer. He felt the sound coming up through the ground, the vibrations of it filling the air, filling him, and then Storm Warning shot forward, gained speed and strength as if from some divine source, pulled ahead and plunged over the finish line, Byzantium behind it. Virgil's Dream third.

The crowd noise swelled and Terry closed his eyes, waiting for the bullet. Then realized the pressure was no longer there. He opened his eyes, turned his head to the left slightly. The black man met his glance, held it.

"I lost," Terry said.

The man shook his head.

"Not today," he said. And then he turned back into the crowd and was gone.

DRIVING BACK TO NEWARK, Morgan wondered what he would tell Mikey-Mike. Fuck it, he wouldn't tell him anything. And what could he say anyway? Just that he didn't do it, but that the white boy had seen him. If Mikey-Mike still wanted him taken out, he'd have to send someone else.

When he hit the Garden State Parkway, he headed north, turned on the radio, fiddled with the tuner until he found an R & B station out of New York. It was Old-School Hour, the deejay affecting that smooth seventies FM voice between songs. Morgan knew the songs, something he almost never did when he listened to the radio. The Chi-Lites' "Have You Seen Her?" now—smooth and easy and soothing. Then the 5 Stairsteps and "Ooh Child." He smiled when he heard the familiar drum and horn intro. By the time he reached the Turnpike, he was humming along.

ALL HORSES HAVE BEAUTIFUL EYES AND A BIG COCK

Jonathan Ames

MY WHOLE SEX LIFE has been one big cry for help. It also costs a lot of money.

So, a couple of weeks ago, as usual, I was low on cash. I called Lou to try to fix the situation.

"Lou here," he said, his typical greeting.

"Minimus, the two horse, in the Fifth at Belmont on Friday," I said. It was Wednesday. Lou knew my voice. He liked my voice.

"Are you nuts?" he said.

"Yeah," I said.

"Oh, yeah, that's right, I forgot," he said. "Are you good for it this time?"

"Of course not," I said. But then I quickly added, "I'm only joking."

"You're not joking. You won't have the money; you never do," he said. "But my sickness is thinking you're going to change. Your sickness is you don't change."

"All right, forget the bet on Minimus. Let's book a flight for Minneapolis and check into the Mayo Clinic for what ails us."

"That's it, be a wise guy. You know, with you I broke the number one bookie rule—don't get personal. But that's what I get for being an old queer. I couldn't resist you. All right, I'll put three hundred on that skeleton with a tail."

"Don't jinx him. I think this Minimus is a winner. I went out to Belmont. He's got a big cock and beautiful eyes. Real long feminine eyelashes. He's going to win for me."

"All horses have big cocks and beautiful eyes, you idiot! The males, anyway."

"I know, but his cock was extra big and his eyes were extra beautiful. I think this will make him extra fast."

"Whatever . . . The bottom line is this: I'm not protecting you this time. The Gioni brothers know I pay off your bets and they don't like it. I told them I wouldn't do it anymore. You're going to have to deal with them directly if you don't pay on time, and with them if you're late they're going to take a crowbar to your shins and a hammer to your elbows."

"What about my kneecaps?"

"Okay, you're very funny," he said, resigned, not wanting to play around with me. With Lou I always enjoyed trying to sound snappy and full of tough-guy banter. "Listen," he continued, "I gotta bring it up. I hate to, but I have to. You owe me three thousand bucks. The brothers think you're all paid up. I lied to them. If they find out that you owe me, it may be more than broken bones. They'll think they're doing it to help me."

"Don't worry. Just make the bet on Friday and I'll pay you, and I'm gonna win," I said. "And if I lose, I'll let you spoon me. I liked it when you spooned me that time. Your belly felt good against my back."

"Listen, kid, you got to get over this camp-counselor problem. It's all right that you like men and women."

"You know I don't like men."

"I know. I wish your damn therapy would set you straight."

"Is that pun intentional?"

"What pun?"

Then Lou had another call and so we rang off. I don't think he intended the pun. I never got to ask him again. Lou died on Thursday. He was a sweet guy, very good to me. It was a massive heart attack. He was sixty-one years old and weighed at least 220 pounds, and he was a short guy, maybe five-foot-eight, so all that weight was no good for his heart. He had a big Italian face, and he was mostly bald with a white fringe around the sides, which he kept trim and neat. He dressed simply, nothing flashy. He didn't look gay but he was. He lived in Carroll Gardens with his mother. She was eighty-six and had to bury her only child. I didn't go to the funeral. I sent her flowers. They cost forty-five dollars. Hardly a dent in the three thousand I owed him.

I met Lou in the neighborhood at the barbershop. I live in Carroll Gardens, too. It's a half-Italian, half-artist neighborhood. I heard him talking about horses—we were getting our hair cut at the same time. Then we left together and I politely inquired, "Would you know how I could place bets on horses?" I'd always been interested in gambling and horses, but I had never known how to get started. I had never wanted to go to OTB. I always just wanted to do it illegally with a bookie; it seemed more romantic. And Lou, incredibly, was a bookie. He was the first person I asked about horses and I unknowingly went right to the source.

Well, that's how our friendship began. Three years ago. Now he's dead and my debt went into the grave with him. So I think this will be the end of my betting days. It's a sign. It's a chance to start clean.

I wish I could give up sex as easy as gambling but I can't. My problem is that I was molested when I was thirteen and away at summer camp. It was the head counselor—no pun intended, not really anyway—who messed with me and a few summers later he was arrested for doing what he had done to me, but I never told anybody. It's such a cliché by now—sex abuse—but what can I do? I came out of the whole thing half-gay and it's a real pain in the ass, literally and metaphorically. Since I'm only half-gay, and maybe even less than that, I go to male prostitutes. Lou was an odd exception—I think I wanted to make him happy, so one time we lay down together. It seemed to please him, which is good, that I could give him *something*.

But you see, I don't want a relationship. I don't want to kiss anybody. I don't want any kind of real closeness to a man. I just want to re-create what happened with the counselor, which is why I go to prostitutes. With them I can control the situation. Keep it safe. I go maybe one or two times a month. It's sick. I'm stuck in a loop. It's what happens to people. So it costs me money. Money, I don't have, which is part of the reason why I got into horses. I'm a freelance illustrator and I'm my own boss, I work at home, but I don't have a big income.

I don't think you're supposed to be happy in life—the Declaration of Independence talks about the "*pursuit* of happiness"; they probably realized that's all there is, that you never actually attain it—but I also don't think I should be as miserable as I am, which is about 90 percent of the time. I

think 90 percent of the time a person should be neutral—
getting by without too much complaint. But that's not me.
Most of the time I live with this nervous, uncomfortable feeling that I'm about to be caught and punished. But caught at
what? Punished for what? Of course, every now and then
there's the light and happy moment, but I have to say it's
pretty rare. I never feel fully at ease. I almost never feel right
in my own skin.

I do have a few simple pleasures. I like coffee in the morning and I like sleeping. The whole world is a mess, but at least
you can still sleep. I did like going to the track once in a
while—the pageantry, the beauty of the horses, the noise, the
risk of the bet—and I liked calling Lou and acting like a tough
guy. But I'm done with all of that now. If I pick it up again, I
won't find a Lou this time. I won't find somebody who will
look after me, who will be kind to me.

So my problem makes it difficult for me to get close to a
woman. The last girl I dated, I did try to open up to her. This
was about a year ago. I really liked her. She was smart, dark-
haired, petite, sweet little breasts, gorgeous mouth, beautiful
big clear eyes, only twenty-one. She was going to cooking
school—her dream was to make it as a chef in the world of
high-powered restaurants, which isn't easy for women. We met
at a bar here in Carroll Gardens. After sleeping together for
about a month, we were lying in bed one night, fooling around,
and she started to mess with my ass. I asked her to stop.

"Why?" she said.

"I don't like it," I said, which was true. When I'm with a girl
I don't want to be reminded of my other life, my secret life.

"Really? Most guys act like they don't like it but they really
do." For a twenty-one-year-old she had a lot of experience;

she'd been working just about full-time in restaurants since she was fifteen, which meant that she had known a lot of older guys—waiters, cooks, managers. She was from Seattle and had been in New York for a year going to school.

"I'm not like most guys," I said, which sounded tougher than I meant it.

So she let it drop. Then a month later, she tried again to put her finger in my ass. We had been sleeping together for about two months at this point and I hadn't done any of my bad stuff that whole time. I had wanted to but I didn't want to taint what I had going on with her. And, too, there was always the risk of disease. Thankfully, in the past, I had been neurotically careful, but still, you never know.

"Please don't," I said as she probed. "It's not my thing."

"Let me do it," she said. "It turns me on. I think you'll like it."

I closed my legs tight like a schoolgirl.

Then I made that very human mistake: "Listen, can I tell you something about myself?"

"Of course," she said. "But it sounds scary."

I hadn't said anything yet and she was already scared. Intuition.

I gave her the R-rated version. When I talked about the counselor it went well. She was sympathetic—like most cute girls she had been touched inappropriately quite a lot while growing up. Then I hinted at how sometimes I had this compulsion to have guys hold me the same way I had been held as a kid, but I quickly added, which was true, that I felt no attraction to men. She didn't believe that, but it is true. I never notice guys and I don't care at all what they look like, which is why I was willing to lie down with Lou.

Anyway, it was too much for her. She was a mature twenty-one-year-old but not that mature. Or maybe she *was* mature and knew enough to get out—she stopped seeing me after that night. She gently suggested that I should get therapy, and I told her I had tried counseling in the past but would look into it again. Since that relationship ended, I haven't gone out with any girls, but I did go back into therapy at this clinic that gives a discount to artists. Mostly, I'm hoping to just get over the damn thing and then I'll never have to mention it ever again to anybody, especially to a girl I like.

Well, Minimus won that Friday. As a way to mourn Lou, I went to the OTB on Jay Street, near the Manhattan Bridge. There were about twenty scraggly old guys there, the kind of men who someday will be pushed out of New York. Well, they won't exactly be pushed out; they're just going to die, but no new ones will grow up to replace them. Who can afford this city anymore? Where do all these rich people in New York actually work? Anyway, I stood next to this one fifty-something, slouched-over fellow whose face was sliding off his face, if you know what I mean. It was all slack and the skin was gray. He was skinny but he had two chins and his lip jutted out with sadness. The strangest thing about him was that his thinning black hair was actually pulled into a ponytail. He was a weird mixture of an old hippie crossed with an old OTB addict. His hands trembled and his sneakers had Velcro straps. While we waited for the race to start, I studied him pretty closely. I thought I'd do a cartoon of him. Then the starting gate opened and all heads in the OTB shot up to the televisions mounted in the corners.

Minimus broke slow from the gate, but I still had hopes—it was just the start. But then he stumbled and it looked like the jockey almost fell off. I was thinking, in a very selfish way, that it was a good thing Lou had died. But then I immediately canceled that thought and apologized to God.

A minute and a half into the race, Minimus trailed the field by about ten lengths. I looked at the ponytailed guy next to me and his sad lip was really trembling. I didn't ask him what his bet was, but I was sure it wasn't on Minimus. Nobody had bet on that horse. They were all too smart. Then out of nowhere, with one furlong to go, Minimus flattened himself low to the ground, the way a horse will, like an arrow with these impossibly beautiful legs, and he passed the whole damn field and nailed the front runner at the wire at odds of twenty to one! I had been right about his big cock and beautiful eyes! If Lou had lived and placed my bet I would have won six thousand dollars!

I left the place feeling exuberant, even though I hadn't actually won any money. I kept thinking that I had to call Lou, see Lou, boast to Lou, but then I had to keep telling myself that he was dead, though I didn't really believe it. By the time I got home, about a twenty-minute walk, my good mood had worn down.

It's been a couple of weeks now and I still don't believe Lou had a heart attack. It's that old weird thing about death— you just feel like you haven't seen the person for a while, that they can't be gone.

So I don't have the horses anymore. I haven't looked in the papers to see who's racing, I haven't gone out to Belmont, and I haven't returned to the OTB. I'm down to coffee in the morning and sleeping at night. I've got to find something to go in between, besides drawing. I imagine something will turn up. I hope I haven't sounded like I feel sorry for myself.

Wait a second; I take that back. I do feel sorry for myself, so I imagine that's the way I sound. But I don't think the world owes me anything. I don't blame the world. It's my own fault that I'm wasting my life being miserable most of the time. I do like, though, that first moment when I lie down with a prostitute. Then I'm calm. I'm like a horse that's quit—I'm not running from the problem. The problem has caught me, and there's a relief in just giving up. Must be why I keep doing it. I feel terrible when it's over, but that first minute is pretty good.

THE CYNICAL BREED

Charlie Stella

"YOU DRESS LIKE A FAGGOT," Abe Goldman told young
Teddy Stone.

"Excuse me?" Teddy said. He looked across the table at
the seventy-six-year-old bookmaker and frowned when he noticed liver spots on the back of the old man's hands.

"Those clothes," Abe said. "You look like a yuppie, faggot,
quinella queen, cocksucker."

"Sorry you disapprove," said Teddy, staring now.

"It's none of my business," Abe said. "Just saying, is all."

Teddy was twenty-two years old and had recently gradu-
ated with an economics degree from Hofstra University. He
was at the diner this morning to discuss the bookmaking business. His aunt had arranged the meeting from Florida. She
had dated Abe more than thirty years ago.

A thin waitress with short red hair stood alongside their table with pen and order pad in hand.

"Bran muffin?" she asked Abe.

"Make it corn," he said, "toasted, no butter."

"And you?" she asked Teddy.

"Fruit salad and coffee."

She wrote Teddy's order as she walked away.

"How's your aunt?" Abe asked.

"Good," Teddy said. "She said to say hello."

"She still with the guy she married?"

"Few years now, yeah."

"He okay? She deserves a good guy."

"He's a little too boring for me, doesn't like to get out much, but he treats her good."

Abe nodded his approval. "I wasn't involved this life, I would've married her. She mention it?"

The waitress was back with coffee. She poured and was gone again. Abe added sugar, stirred, and sipped his. Teddy added cream, then let it settle.

Teddy said, "She said it was bookmaking ruined the relationship."

"It did," Abe said. "Ruined a few more after her, too."

"But here you are still at it."

"The fuck else I'm gonna do, sell umbrellas?"

Teddy raised his hands. "I'm just saying."

Abe sipped his coffee a few times before setting the cup down. He said, "You went to college, right? You finish?"

"Last month. Economics."

"What's that, like, business?"

"Something like that."

"You wanted to be an economist? The fuck is that, fancy way to say teacher?"

"To some people, yeah, I guess."

Abe pointed at Teddy's coffee. "You drink a lot of that?"

"Fair amount," Teddy said. "Probably too much."

"You get into this business, you'll drink two pots a day. Pro'lly start smokin', too, you don't already."

"I can understand the coffee, but I won't start smoking. I watched my old man die from it."

Abe stared into Teddy's eyes. "You're sure about that, huh?"

"Pretty sure, yeah."

"You're a smug cocksucker. Think you know it all?"

"Nope," Teddy said.

"Yeah, you are," Abe said. "Most college kids are smug cocksuckers."

Teddy was about to sip his coffee. He set the cup down instead. "What's with the hard-on routine?" he asked. "My aunt said I should come talk to you, so here I am, but I don't need to get jerked around either. You wanna show me the ropes, I'm willing to pay for the lessons, but I'm not here to get abused."

Abe smirked.

"I say something funny?" Teddy asked.

"What do you know about it, the business?" Abe said.

"I took some action at school," Teddy said. "I ran a small book there."

Abe smirked again. "How small?"

"I paid most my tuition," Teddy said. "I don't have student loans to pay off."

"You got start-up cash?"

"I have some money put away."

"How much is some?"

"Enough, I think."

Abe sipped his coffee. He spoke from behind the cup. "Stop being smug. How much cash you got?"

Teddy took his time answering. "Close to fifty grand," he finally said.

"That's piss," Abe said. "Unless you're gonna take sucker bets, ignore the real money."

Now Teddy smirked. "It worked in college."

The waitress brought their food, refilled both cups, and left them alone.

Abe pointed at his *Racing Form*. "You gonna take horses?"

"I don't know," Teddy said. "What do you think?"

"They're essentially sucker bets, but they're a lot of work, too. Sometimes too much, all the crap you gotta take into consideration, the different tracks and all. You limit it to New York, Jersey, maybe Philly down there, Baltimore, you use Pimlico, Laurel Park, you can handle it. You gotta set limits, shave the long shots down to something affordable. Then there's the harness tracks and past posting, and don't think it don't happen, because it does. The computers today, the level of sophistication and all, the sharp guys'll come in out the sky on an inquiry, say, your office is still doing the work. You can get fucked six ways to Sunday like that. And they don't need somebody on the inside; they're good at it. You'll make mistakes same as everybody else, but you can't make the big ones and survive. It's an unforgiving business, bookmaking, you get in over your head. Nobody gives a fuck you got problems when you owe them. Nobody rushes to pay you when they owe you."

"I did pretty well with the Derby at college," Teddy said. "I did better with the Belmont when horses that won the Derby and Preakness lost there."

Abe said, "Because they were long shots, those horses, they won the Derby at ridiculous odds and the smug assholes at the college all thought they were handicappers betting the chalk. Then they all go with the one wins the Derby in the Preakness, and the original favorites usually win there, and now they got new chalk going in the Belmont, and there they get buried. Last few years it went like that, the long shot Derby, a Preakness favorite, and another long shot the Belmont."

"Like Birdstone last year," Teddy said. "Returned seventy-four at the track. I had one winner, a five-dollar bet, but I had that hedged with OTB. I wound up paying the guy won a hundred twenty-seven bucks while I picked up almost four and a half. Paid for the rest of my hedges, too."

Abe stopped eating his muffin. "You laid them off the OTB?"

"I put down ten bucks on everything in the race to win and place," Teddy said. "That was my hedge. I didn't have anyplace else to lay it off."

"Faggot move, the OTB."

"Faggot, but it worked."

Abe shrugged. "I'll give you that," he said. "At least you were thinking. You had nowhere else to lay it off, it was smart. I was thinking Lemon Drop Kid, the mess that thing caused a few years back. Lot of wise-guy money on that horse the last minute. Guys couldn't lay it off took a bath."

"When Charismatic broke a leg, right?"

"Had nothing to do with it, that leg," Abe said. "Happened after the wire. Lemon Drop Kid come off the stretch turn like a slingshot, would've won it anyways."

"Sixty-one fifty at the track," said Teddy proudly.

"You keep the stats, think that makes you a BM, a book-maker?"

"I didn't say that."

"I don't know a fuckin' guy the Mets lineup besides the

good-looking kid behind the plate, Pizza, whatever his name is. I don't give a fuck either, he's good or not. He fucks up and helps them lose when I need them to lose, I'm a big fan. He does good and helps them win when I need them to win, I'm still a big fan. Any other scenario, I don't give a fuck he's a walkin' AIDS case. Understand?"

"I think so."

Abe took his time sipping his coffee. When he set the cup down again, he launched back into the point he was making earlier. "I had the horse hedged across the board, Lemon Drop Kid, same as you did."

"With OTB?"

Abe shook his head. "Vegas office. I'm with them forever."

Teddy said, "You take horses all the time or just the big races?"

"Just the big ones," Abe said. "Had a horse room over the west side, but it didn't pay after the OTB. Now, the offshore bullshit, the sports book at the casinos, it's not worth it. Your basic horse bettor, the ones you can count on, are degenerates. Now they can bet a dollar a race, can even call the OTB, they got an account. I take the Derby, Preakness, and Belmont. I used to take the Wood and Travers, but they don't pay either anymore. More work'n I need. Besides, a guy calls in a bet, the Wood say, the other degenerates, the ones with money, they'll wanna play Hialeah, Delaware, and Santa Anita the same time. I can't do that. Offshore can."

"Can I work with your guy out in Vegas?" Teddy asked. "Laying off, I mean."

"Maybe, we'll see. You'll have to prove yourself first. I don't vouch for people I don't know."

Abe was finishing up the first half of his muffin now. He

wiped his hands on a paper napkin a few times before the waitress brought him a *Daily News.*

"Thanks, hon," he told her.

"Your routine?" Teddy asked. "You read for scores now?"

Abe had opened the first page of the newspaper. He glanced at something and set the paper down.

"That's almost cute," he said. "Any BM tells you they go to bed without they know the scores the night before, they'll full of shit. Remember that."

"I used to go to sleep before the West Coast games came in," Teddy said. "Sometimes it was too late."

"Only on nights you didn't need them, my friend," Abe said. "You think about it. Only on nights you didn't need them."

Teddy shook his head side to side. "Maybe, come to think of it."

"We're a cynical breed, BMs," Abe said. "We think the world is out to fuck us and it is. We think everybody is taking a shot, and they would, they could. It's a day-to-day existence, no matter what your bankroll, and everybody puts something in, you're their best friend you're taking the bet, you hate their guts next day, they win. It's the nature of the beast to think like that. If you don't yet, you will."

"I hope it don't get that ugly," Teddy said.

"Oh, it will, my young, green, dresses-like-a-yuppie, faggot, cocksucker friend. It will indeed."

Teddy was tired of catching the old man's flak. He pointed at the *Racing Form.*

"So, what about that?" he said. "I thought that was rule one, never make a bet."

"It's my pleasure this life, doping horses," Abe said. "I read the thing, circle what I like, and take a look-see the next morning, see how I did, only it don't cost me nothing. I hope you're more careful taking action than passing judgment. That's yesterday's *Racing Form.* Other guys go to whores get their knob polished, or jerk off to dirty magazines or porn flicks. I read the *Form,* pick horses I'll never bet, and go see an occasional play. I like theater. Didn't your aunt tell you that?"

"Yeah, come to think of it, she did. You used to go a lot when you were dating."

"Musicals, mostly," Abe said. "Both loved it. I never go anymore, but I listen to the old ones on the CD."

"She said it all ended when you expanded the business," Teddy said. "That true?"

"'Fifty-nine, I think it was," Abe said, "Year the Big A opened. Maybe it was sixty. Guy could make a living running numbers off the track handle and booking horses. People played cards and bet horses back then, the average blue-collar types. Some BMs didn't even need the other stuff. It was all gravy, the sports. Baseball, baskets, and so on. I didn't take anything more than hundred'olla action until sixty-three, the year of Koufax, that beautiful man; what he did for my bankroll, LA swept the Yankees. That's when I expanded, after Koufax. Kept the wire room until OTB, 1971 that was. Mayor fuckin' Lindsay. Couldn't find enough ways to ruin this city, he brought the OTB."

"I'm thinking I can do it," Teddy said. "Horses, I mean. I'm thinking I can take small action, the campuses, just sucker bettors, so I don't get hurt."

"Guy finds enough small action, he can stay healthy," Abe said. "I'd be careful about the colleges, though. You were a kid making tuition, it's one thing. You're a guy on the outside hawking some school, you're a predator. You get bagged, you could go away. I don't know you're ready for that, the prison experience."

Teddy blushed.

Abe used a thumb to point at himself. "Eight months on a year-and-change bid," he said. "But they don't give those good-time deals anymore. It's eighty-five percent now, no matter how good you play with the other fellas inside. I did mine up Buffalo, back in seventy-nine. Opened a Brooklyn office that year and that old prick DA, whatever his name is, he won't die already, he was on one of his crusades. They put you away now, they can."

Teddy said, "I figured if I kept it small, enough to make a living, I could avoid going away."

"Nobody goes in this business just to make a living. It's gambling, same as any other business. Guys taking the layoff action are the real bookmakers. You're gonna do this, take the risks, you're gonna wanna earn more than a living. This business is way too much work, never mind the risk, to just earn a living."

"I wasn't going to take more than nickel bets the first year," Teddy said. "I didn't take that in college."

"Yeah, well, you can't avoid a pinch, they want you," Abe said. "Getting arrested comes with the territory. You have to use tapes to record bets. Some guys use computers. Either way, you're fucked. If they're watching, they get a warrant, they have you."

"What if I keep the bets under a nickel?"

"Under the radar works most times, but you hawk action on some campus after a kid goes bad, you gotta send somebody to collect, bust him up a little, he runs to the law, it won't make a difference you're small or not. They come out the woodwork and give you up, the other kids the campus there, you're cooked, my young economist friend. And those threads you're wearing now won't do it inside. You walk into Rikers that outfit you'll come out a swish, guaranteed."

"Maybe I could start with you," Teddy suggested. "I'll run a sheet at the colleges, just horse action, turn it in end of each day. For a trial period, say. Couple months, if you want. See how we do. Give me a fifty sheet until I'm ready to go it alone."

"And then what, you walk with the customers I'm funding? I look that fuckin' stupid? Is it my shirt, I'm not wearing khakis?"

"I'll be bringing you action you don't have now," Teddy reasoned. "If I'm with you six months, it's six months of freebies on your end. Money you never saw before."

"Unless they win."

"I'll be on a sheet. I go red, I stay until it's clean or I buy it out."

"And then I did it for what, some new fuckin' thrill? I'm in this business almost fifty years, kid. I don't need any new thrills."

"What would make you happy?" Teddy asked.

"A nice, slow blow job," Abe said. "Still interested?"

"Be serious."

Abe said, "You got moxie, I'll give you that."

Teddy glanced at his watch. "Look, I was hoping to get this thing started today, to be honest."

"But, what, you need money to back it?"

"I have the money to back it. I need connections down the road. That guy in Vegas, for instance. I can use an office to lay it off."

"My office or Vegas?"

"Don't take offense, but I'd rather have your guy in Vegas."

Abe sat back in the booth. He looked at Teddy and said, "There's a hole in a great black pit filled with people who are filled with shit."

"The fuck is that?" Teddy asked.

"My pleasant thought for the day. My motto most days, while we're being honest and all."

"Excuse me?"

"You must think I'm one uncultured fuck, huh? A real low-life piece of shit from Canarsie doesn't have any the social graces they taught you that faggot school you went."

"I didn't say that."

"I saw you look the *Form* before," Abe said. "Like I'm some degenerate in the business just so I can bet."

"You're way off here," said Teddy defensively. "You're wrong."

Abe leaned forward. "Go to theater much?"

"What? No."

"*Sweeney Todd.* Ever see it?"

"No."

"No, you didn't. Those were my favorite couple lines from that particular musical, what I quoted a moment ago."

Teddy was confused. "What is this? The fuck is your problem?"

"It ain't my problem, sonny, it's yours; you need an office to lay off bets. Me, I got a few of those."

"Look," Teddy said, "my aunt said you were—"

"Your aunt told you come see me, you wanna be a book-maker. You decided you'd come take a shot because what the fuck could I do, I used to date her, I gotta be an old man and all. You come take a shot at me, see you can hook into my office, and what? You gonna feed me *fugazi* names on a sheet don't pay they lose? You think I went in the business last night?"

Teddy pointed at Abe. "You're fuckin' paranoid is what you are."

"Think so, huh?"

"Yeah, I know so, if you think that. I'm not looking to take a shot at anybody. What the fuck, Abe, we just met."

"What happened to that fifty grand you have on the side? Why you wanna come to me with a sheet if you're booking your own action out the colleges? You want my hook in Vegas for what? They won't let you run a fifty sheet. Besides, I don't give a fifty sheet to no fucking body. Those days are long gone, fifty sheets."

Teddy tried to stare the old man down. Abe didn't flinch.

"Hey, I'm sorry you feel this way," Teddy finally said. "I wasn't looking to burn you. I'm trying to learn the business is all. I figure somebody with your experience can teach me. My aunt thought so, too. She isn't happy I'm doing this, especially because of my mother, but it's what I wanna do."

Abe held up his empty coffee cup for the waitress to see. She wasn't busy and hustled over to the table. "Gimme another muffin, bran this time," he told her.

"You?" she asked Teddy.

"Just another coffee," he said.

Abe waited until she was gone again. He pointed at her back and toward the cash register. "Her and him," he said. "And a couple more people I got nothing to do with except I pay for their services, those are the only people I trust, my friend, and only as far as I can throw them, which isn't very far, I'm an old man. I don't know you're looking to take a shot or not, tell you the truth, but it won't work for you, you are, and it's good to warn you up front, you're just being nosy."

"I'm just here to learn," Teddy said.

"Then shut up and listen," Abe said. "You say you'll start small and be content with that, but you won't. Like I said, it's too much work to settle for making a living. You open up your book to money guys, first thing the sharp bettors out there will find you and maul you with late action you can't lay off. Then the wise guys'll find you and eat you alive you're not wired with somebody. You open up to other tracks, same thing. You don't have a wire room, you better stick to nickel-diming college kids. And you better be careful which college kids, because I read someplace where a bunch of them took down some casinos for heavy gelt. Anybody smart enough to take down casinos, you definitely want to avoid."

"Why I'd keep it small," Teddy said, "keep the sharks away."

"How small? How many players you figure you got betting horses?"

"Hundred or so," Teddy said. "About half that are fairly steady, bet a couple races every day."

"Small is one thing. That's fuckin' Mickey Mouse. What's the average bet?"

"Twenty bucks."

"Times fifty is a grand," Abe said. "You do realize how small that is, right? It's piss is what it is."

"Why I need to get out there and tap into some more suckers," Teddy said. "I'm only dealing with the tip of the iceberg here. I know I can quadruple the number of players with just a little hustle on my end. It's the time factor involved. I need to be with somebody else to take the action, somebody I can trust, so I can drum it up."

Abe counted off the fingers of his left hand. "Quarter sheet, for starters," he said. "Based on one hundred new players, what you said you had."

Teddy nodded.

"Twenty of whom I get to keep, we go our separate ways."

"Twenty? That's a little steep."

"Only if you're looking up, my young khaki-wearing friend."

Teddy reluctantly nodded. "Anything else?"

"You don't fuck up. You don't call it in before post time each race, it's over. No bet."

"Fair enough," Teddy said. "I'm not looking to past post here."

Abe chuckled. "You ever do something that stupid, they'll find you floating in those khakis."

"Not to worry," Teddy said. "We have a deal?"

"What about muscle?"

"What about it?"

"You got any?"

"I haven't really needed it so far," Teddy said. "Just a few times with slow payers, but I cut them off until they came across."

Abe smiled. "You telling me you're the one BM's never been burned?"

"I didn't say that," Teddy said. "I said I haven't had to use violence yet."

"What happened?"

"Couple guys putting in something for somebody else, didn't have it when they lost. I make my steady players vouch for new ones, so I took it back when they won."

"Okay, but it won't work that way you go off the campus. Or when some wise guy's kid gets word you're taking action, gets your number. They'll come after you like a pack of wolves then."

Teddy swallowed hard.

Abe said, "It's the nature of the beast, khaki man. The state of nature on the street is no different than it was the beginning of civilization, except for cell phones. People will fuck you at every turn. The wise guys, what's left of them, and the ones operating with protection from the feds, they'll take your money and crawl over your sister to fuck your mother."

Teddy sighed. "What'll that cost me?"

"Nothing until you need it. I had my brother, rest in peace, when he was around. He was hooked up the West Side there, except they're all gone now. Now I gotta pay same as everybody else, unless you got a big scary-looking friend will do it for a steak dinner or tickets the Mets game."

Teddy nodded.

"Anything else?" Abe asked.

Teddy motioned toward the *Racing Form* with his head. "Who'd you like first race Belmont yesterday?"

"The one I picked, I didn't play."

"You really don't play? Ever?"

"Just once the last few years," Abe said. "Lemon Drop Kid. I sent it in like Mack the fuckin' Knife. Had a friend put it in down the track that day. He said the president was there. First lady, too. All in yellow, like a big fat canary."

Teddy was curious. "You knew something about the race?"

"I knew dick. Was pure hunch, that play."

"You get the exacta? That was huge that day."

"Fifteen hundred dollars," Abe said.

"What the offices pay?"

"Whatever they could get away with," said Abe, waving it off. "I know a guy got twenny to one on his ten dollars. Robbed is what he got. Sometimes offices have to do that, 'specially when they get dumped on all of a sudden like."

"I won't even ask how much you bet," Teddy said.

"Good, because I wouldn't tell you. But it was enough to start me playing the *Form* only. Haven't made a bet since."

Teddy finished what was left of his coffee. "So, we're good then. I can start today?"

"After you pay for breakfast," Abe said. "I don't give class for the exercise."

Teddy pulled his wallet out and fingered a ten-dollar bill. "That cover it?"

"Only if you're stiffing the kid brought the coffee," Abe said. "Show some class."

Teddy fingered another ten from his wallet and dropped it on the table.

"Give me your number and I'll call whatever I get before the first race," Teddy said.

Abe tore off a piece of the *Racing Form* and wrote down two telephone numbers. "You're late, we're done," he told Teddy. "No second chances."

"No problem," Teddy said. He slid out of the booth and extended his right hand.

Abe shook it without looking.

"I appreciate this," Teddy said.

"Just don't fuck up."

"I won't. I'll call later."

"Right," Abe said. He watched the kid leave the diner and cross Second Avenue to a BMW at the curb alongside St. Vartan Park. Abe waited for the kid to pull away before he used his cell phone to call Florida. A woman answered on the third ring.

"Hello?" she said.

"The kid says your old man is boring," Abe said into the phone. "You need a little action, it's been a while for me."

"My old man is just fine," the woman said. "We move at a different pace down here."

"Yeah, your nephew said. Boring, he called it."

"Never mind him; what does he know?" the woman joked. "You talked to him?"

"Just now, yeah."

"And?"

"He's a putz."

"His mother is going crazy."

"She should. He don't have a clue what he's in for."

"Can you talk him out of it?"

"I did better'n that, I think."

"What you do?"

Abe stopped to laugh.

"What's so funny?" she asked.

"I give him two precinct numbers to call me back at," Abe said. "He'll spend a few minutes cursing me out, but he won't wanna do business with me afterward."

"You sure?"

"Unless he's a bigger putz than he looked."

"I hope you're right, Abe. My sister is so upset. He has a college degree."

"Hey, at least he's ambitious. Lotta kids today, they get calluses on their asses from sitting around doing nothing. Sort of like your old man there."

"Never mind him. Jerry is a good guy. He's not flashy, but he's a good guy."

"When's the last musical you saw?"

"I haven't, a long time now."

"You still listen, the records, CDs?"

"Not really. The radio, when they play show tunes. That's all."

"Shame."

"It's been so long."

"You still got family here; look me up when you come up to visit."

"For what? A date at the track?"

"Why not? I'll take you back the trees there, Belmont, ruffle your undergarments."

"You wish."

"I do indeed."

The woman giggled. "It's not 1978 anymore. I don't look like I did back then."

"What, I do?"

She giggled again. "Yeah, but you weren't very handsome to begin with."

"You're gonna insult me now?"

"I'm just saying."

"But I was flashy, right?"

"You had a certain amount of class back then, yeah."

"I was the badass made your heart beat faster is what I was."

"For a while, I guess so," she said, then laughed again. "Thank God I came to my senses."

"He around now, the boring one?"

"He's sleeping."

"Oh, Jesus."

"Never you mind. He played a round of golf already this morning."

"What, the miniature game there?"

"No, at the club he belongs to."

"Oh, big shot, huh?"

"What about Teddy? You sure he'll be okay? I don't want him involved in that business. For my sister's sake."

"He'll play with himself a little before he figures out it ain't worth it," Abe said. "He's just ambitious is all. Like I said, you should be happy he's not content taking naps."

"Again with the nap?" she joked. "Meantime he's here re-laxing and you gotta run all over the place taking bets, and then worry you don't get arrested again in your old age. What kind of life is that?"

Abe smiled on his end of the phone. "It ain't a boring one, I'll tell you that much."

"It's dangerous is what it is," she said. "It's crazy, a man of your age still doing that."

"You're a regular cynic, you know that, Jean?"

"Me? You're the one doesn't trust anybody."

"Hey, I did something for you; now you do something back."

"Yeah, right. What? And keep it clean."

"Go wake the old man up with a hummer."

"Oh, my God! You haven't changed at all."

"Go 'head, unzipper him, let me listen."

"You're crazy."

"Can't he get it up?"

"Never mind him. He does fine."

"Remember that time, Aqueduct, the afternoon I hit the triple there?"

"You're disgusting. Don't bring that up now."

"That was the best head I ever had my life that day. Right the middle of the grandstand, under the blanket there on the bench."

"I have to go now."

Abe was seeing it in his head. He felt excited as he smiled.

"Good-bye, Abe," the woman told him, and then hung up.

"Christ, I can almost feel it again," Abe said before he realized she was gone.

"Jean?"

Abe shrugged it off, then slid out of the booth. He palmed one of the two tens on the table and pointed to the other one for the waitress.

"Thanks, hon," he told her on his way out.

THE DERBY

Laura Hillenbrand

THE HILLS OF KENTUCKY have a tempered roundness to them, as if cupped in the hollow of God's palm. In the century before last, a man named Meriwether Lewis Clark, Jr., played out his life among them. In 1875, on a coil of land just south of Louisville, he christened the Kentucky Derby, a race that would dominate his life and ultimately consume him. When he died in 1899, friends laid his body in this soil, under a blanket of bluegrass.

More than a century later, on the first Saturday of every May, 150,000 people venture over the backs of Clark's hills to animate his dream. They come to witness a race that has exercised a pull on the American imagination for more than 125 years. Perhaps they come in reverence for a creature whose form, like a bicycle or a baseball diamond, is intrinsically, viscerally pleasing. Maybe the appeal is the elegance of the test, demanding that man and horse, in a single motion, press the limits of strength, speed, endurance, daring, resolve. Perhaps the lure is the rush of emotion that attends the winnowing of the great from the merely good, distilled into two minutes.

The Derby is the supreme hour of a supreme creature, a moment in which most falter and one transcends. It is not the richest race, not the longest, nor the fastest, but for many, it is the only race. Wrote Steinbeck: "This Kentucky Derby, whatever it is—a race, an emotion, a turbulence, an explosion—is one of the most beautiful and violent and satisfying things I have ever experienced."

AMONG WHITE MEN, Daniel Boone walked here first. From the far side of the Cumberland Gap, he saw Kentucky spilling out beneath him and believed that he had found a "second paradise." Next came the Virginians, castoffs of primogeniture and masters of horsemanship, the twin legacies of their royalist ancestors. They gazed over the rippling landscape and saw an Eden for their blooded horses. With them came Pennsylvanian Amish and Mennonites, bearing in wooden casks the seeds of Kentucky's future, *Poa pratensis,* the nutrient-rich, hearty bluegrass, a manna for horses, that William Penn had imported from the Eurasian steppes. The Virginians brought the Thoroughbred here to be wedded to the land: born with the first shoots of spring, weaned with the turning of leaves, his life ultimately measured by the speed at which he moves over the Kentucky ground.

In Kentucky, wrote the racing editor Joe A. Estes, "It usually takes a horse race to settle an argument." Within a few years of the Thoroughbred's arrival, reckless match races were regular events on Louisville streets. Dodging speeding horses became a routine hazard of pedestrian life; on at least one occasion races were run concurrently, in opposite directions, on the same road. In 1793, terrorized locals finally banned street racing. Undaunted, horsemen built a series of racetracks, running horses in sets of marathon heats. Under this system, Kentucky racing and breeding flourished for decades. But the Civil War brought armies that ransacked stud farms and destroyed tracks. By 1872, Louisville's last track had failed.

Salvation came in the guise of a former bank teller named Meriwether Lewis Clark, Jr. A grandson of the explorer William Clark, M. L. Clark was an avid racegoer who was distressed over the failure of Kentucky tracks. In 1872, at the age of twenty-six, he set off on a tour of Europe, scrutinizing the thriving tracks abroad in search of lessons on reviving Kentucky racing. Britain proved the best teacher. The nation had abandoned endurance races and multiple heats in favor of single-event, shorter contests. Its Epsom Derby had grown into England's racing championship.

Upon his return, Clark presented an ambitious plan to Louisville's gentry: Build an opulent track, create a championship race on the model of Epsom, cater to high-society racegoers, and the world would beat a path to Kentucky. The marquee event, the Kentucky Derby, would be restricted to elite three-year-old horses running a single mile-and-a-half contest. The idea appealed to 320 Louisvillians, who put up one hundred dollars each. On eighty acres leased from his uncles, the Churchill brothers, Clark built an extravagant racecourse and named it Churchill Downs. He then embarked on extensive personal tours of Louisville to cajole citizens into coming to the Derby.

The first Derby Day, May 17, 1875, drew twelve thousand spectators. Horses raced around an infield brimming with picnicking fans, and the winning riders dismounted to snatch ornate silk bags, stuffed with purse money, hanging by the finish line. Ladies were seated in a special section discreetly out of view of betting pools. In Clark's clubhouse, spectators sipped mint juleps and enjoyed the races from rockers on a veranda while Strauss waltzes played.

These pampered racegoers were treated to a race whose unpredictability, drama, and display of superb horsemanship set the standard for the Derby. The favorite was Chesapeake, a closer trained by the profoundly gifted Ansel Williamson, a former slave. To ensure that the front-runners would exhaust themselves early in the race, Williamson had honed the speed of Chesapeake's stablemate, Aristides, then entered him as a rabbit. The strategy worked, but not as Williamson anticipated. Aristides set a blistering pace, fought off his challengers, then was eased up to wait for his stablemate. But Chesapeake, compromised by a poor start, never came. Aristides had something left. Urged on again, he repelled the closers and won. His time was an American record, and the Derby was off to a rousing start.

For the next several years, the Derby was a success, attracting huge crowds and the nation's best horses. Clark dedicated himself to crafting dazzling fetes for his wealthy patrons, and his track became the place to be for high society. The moneyed set warmed to the attention, but at a cost. Clark reportedly focused entirely on his well-heeled patrons, leaving critical details of track operations to bumbling subordinates. Churchill Downs never turned a profit.

In 1886, a petty squabble nearly ended the Derby. It began when bookmakers refused to pay the track their operating fees, prompting track management to bar them from the track on Derby Day. James Ben Ali Haggin, a high-rolling New York gambler and influential owner, had brought a large string of horses to Churchill Downs for the season. Though he was upset at the absence of bookmaking, he ran his namesake, Ben Ali, in the Derby and watched him win it. He then announced that if bookies didn't return, he would pack up his horses and leave. The threat carried considerable weight; without Haggin's fine horses, the 1886 Churchill Downs season, as well as the 1887 Derby, would be seriously diminished.

Within hours, the crisis seemed to be averted when the bookies reached a settlement with the track. But the triumph was undercut by a track official, who told listeners in no uncertain terms where Haggin could go. Word of the statement reached Haggin that night. By dawn, his barn was empty.

HAGGIN MEANT BUSINESS. Back in New York, he persuaded Eastern horsemen, whose runners dominated racing, to join a boycott of Churchill Downs. The impact was staggering. Kentucky's horses were not yet the cream of the industry they would later become, and they couldn't carry the track or the Derby. Interest in the race plummeted, and its fields shrank to three or four woeful entries. Clark struggled on, waiving his salary and emptying his own pockets to cover his track's huge debts. It was no use. Churchill Downs drifted deep into the red. The Derby declined with it; by early 1894 the *Louisville Commercial* was referring to the race as "a contest of dogs." That August, the track went bankrupt, and Clark, utterly despondent, left its helm. He never recovered. Five years later, he was found dead in a hotel room, the pistol still in his hand.

A group of investors bought Churchill Downs in hopes of reviving it to its former glory. They renovated the grandstand, installed the now-signature twin spires, cut the Derby distance to a mile and a quarter—a particularly formidable distance requiring both speed and stamina—and began draping the winner in roses, a tradition that later inspired the race's nickname, Run for the Roses. But the boycott continued, and management was forced to slash purses. Trainers took their better animals away in search of bigger purses, attendance sank further, and Derby fields remained an embarrassment. In 1902, the managers gave up and began hunting for someone on whom to dump their white elephant.

The man they found was an unlikely deliverer, a merchant tailor named Colonel Matt J. Winn. At the age of thirteen, Winn had seen Aristides' Derby triumph from his father's grocery wagon. Utterly smitten, he had witnessed every running since. He had no experience managing a track, but he was endowed with irresistible charm and uncanny business sense. Taking over as vice president and later as general manager, Winn began by making personal appeals to Louisvillians who had once frequented the track, offering them choice seats at the 1903 Derby. The campaign worked. Returning fans brought loads of friends to the race, and Winn entertained them so well that they kept coming back. For the first time, Churchill Downs made a profit. It continued to run in the black in succeeding years, and though the Derby couldn't seem to draw more than six modest, locally based horses, things looked promising.

Soon, though, the race was in trouble again. Just after the turn of the century, the nation was swept up in an antigambling "reform" movement. In 1907, reformers won the Louisville mayorship and promptly banned bookmaking, the only form of wagering at Churchill Downs. Winn was left with two alternatives: a complicated, antiquated system called "auction pool" wagering, or the French pari-mutuel machine, which automatically calculated the winners' rewards based on what they had wagered, dividing up the total pool of money bet.

The former was a poor option, excluding low-stakes bettors, but the latter seemed ideal, eliminating the famous corruption of bookmaking while allowing bets as low as one dollar. But pari-mutuels had had a disappointing history in America; Clark had imported four machines, and like other track operators, he had failed to lure bettors to them. Still, pari-mutuels were the better choice, so Winn opted to use them. City Hall responded by citing an ancient law banning machine betting. Winn was left only with auction pools, which would surely be banned also. The Derby and Churchill Downs appeared doomed.

PONDERING THE LOOMING FAILURE of their race, Winn and the track president, Charlie Grainger, began to wonder how Clark had gained legal authority to use pari-mutuels. They scoured law books and found the answer. Buried deep in the legal code was an amendment excluding pari-mutuels from the antimachine gambling law. "We were jubilant," Winn later wrote.

With little time before the Derby, he had no pari-mutuels to use. Importation would take too long, and no one knew what had become of Clark's four machines. Winn recruited an army of Louisvillians to hunt for them, and urged them to hurry; he suspected that City Hall was also searching for the pari-mutuels in hopes of destroying them. Proracing hunters found all four, and Winn persuaded a New York track to ship in two abandoned machines. Every one of them was in deplorable condition. Mechanics, working frantically, rebuilt all six.

The crisis still wasn't over. Learning that Winn had obtained pari-mutuels, City Hall vowed to summon the police to arrest everyone connected to wagering. Winn took the issue to court and won. The Derby was on. Ironically, by flooding the city with publicity, the clash boosted Derby attendance. Buoyed by the attention and Winn's promotional flyers, the machines were immensely popular; wagering on the 1908 Derby was five times greater than in 1907. "The machines," Winn wrote, "had saved racing in Kentucky."

Reformism was soon dead, but the Derby remained no more than a local function. Winn needed a headliner, something to break into the national consciousness. In 1913, his wish was answered when an impossible long shot named Donerail dropped from out of the clouds to win the Derby in what remains the race's greatest shocker. Donerail paid a stunning $184.90 for a $2 bet, landing the race in the national news. Seizing the opportunity, Winn traveled back East and turned on the charm, trying to end the quarter-century boycott of the race. In 1915 came the breakthrough: Winn convinced the influential New Yorker Harry Payne Whitney to run his mighty filly Regret in his race. Regret annihilated the boys, becoming the first filly to win the race. Whitney was euphoric. "I do not care if she wins another race, or if she never starts in another race," he said. "She has won the greatest race in America, and I am satisfied."

With the statement, "the Derby was thus 'made' as an American institution," wrote Winn. Regret "put us over the top."

The boycott was over, and the Derby prospered, drawing as many as twenty or more world-class horses each year. Winn began wooing influential journalists, treating them to every possible luxury during Derby week. Drawn by the glowing news coverage, Americans focused on the race each May; by the mid-1920s eighty thousand people were cramming into the track for the race. In 1925, the Derby's first radio broadcast drew an estimated five to six million listeners, believed to be the largest audience ever generated for a broadcast of any kind. By 1931, half the nation was tuning in for the race. With the onset of the Depression, state legislatures across the nation looked at Winn's success and saw a means to raise desperately needed revenue. Ten states soon authorized pari-mutuel betting and began taxing the winnings. Racing quickly became the most heavily attended sport in the nation, and the Derby became its crowning moment.

AS THE DERBY BASKED in its newfound fame, two other spring races for top three-year-olds, Maryland's Preakness Stakes and New York's Belmont Stakes, were also enjoying prominence. In 1935, when a colt named Omaha achieved the fantastically difficult task of winning all three, writer Charles Hatton coined the term *Triple Crown*. What is arguably the most formidable challenge in sports had been born. The two horses that had won all three races in earlier years, Sir Barton and Gallant Fox, were retroactively named Triple Crown winners. In 1937, War Admiral became the fourth horse to sweep. The Derby now marked the start of a nationally celebrated, weeks-long rite of spring. Winn's race, hamstrung for so long by political and financial problems, would from now on be defined solely by its spectacular competitors.

In 1941 came Whirlaway. The chestnut horse with the exceptionally long tail was the most eccentric personality to make his mark on the Derby. He was, said his trainer, Ben Jones, as "nervous as a cat in a room full of rocking chairs." He was known to make sudden turns toward the crowd in midrace, zigzag drunkenly, and run entire races along the outside rail, losing massive amounts of ground as he blew past the grandstand inches from the amazed fans. His jockey, Eddie Arcaro, admitted that he was terrified of the colt. Yet even as he invariably took the scenic route around the track, Whirlaway could unleash a closing rally that was absolutely scorching. Arcaro described him as a "blinding tornado . . . What a horse! What a horse!"

Whirlaway's kick was so extraordinary that against lesser horses, he could career all over the course and still win, but Jones knew that against the top-caliber horses of the Derby, the colt couldn't afford to indulge his erratic habits. In training hours, Jones tried everything to reform him, including ordering an intimidated Arcaro to charge Whirlaway through a razor-thin gap between a standing lead pony and the rail. Before the Derby, Jones walked Whirlaway along the inside rail, then took him to the outer rail in hopes of satisfying his insatiable curiosity about spectators. Then, minutes before the race, Jones cut away the left eye cup on the colt's blinkers, hoping that opening the horse's vision to the inside would help him resist the urge to buzz the crowd.

Leaving the gate, Whirlaway and Arcaro dropped behind the field. On the far turn, a hole leading into the pack opened before them. Arcaro had a weighty decision to make: Dive into the hole and risk being blocked while moving at terrific speed, or lose ground circling the pack and face the possibility that Whirlaway would pay the crowd a visit. Arcaro chose the former and gunned Whirlaway into the hole. In a moment of supreme drama, Whirlaway darted into the back of the pack and disappeared from view. A second later, he came roaring out the other side, pouncing forward with such force that Arcaro nearly tumbled backward out of the saddle. "I felt as if I were flying through the air," the jockey later wrote. Whirlaway hit the lead and kept rolling, arrow straight, to an eight-length victory. His record time of 2:01 2/5 would stand for twenty-one years. Whirlaway went on to win the Triple Crown.

In his eighties but vigorous as ever, Matt Winn guided the Derby through the 1940s. Perched in an infield tower, he watched a remarkable procession of gifted horses, including eventual Triple Crown winners Count Fleet and Assault, sail to Derby victories. In 1948, with the emphatic victory of soon-to-be Triple Crown champ Citation, he hosted his greatest runner yet. Winn's job was done. In 1949 the man who compared his seventy-five Derbies to rosary beads, "always before me, always vivid, with every detail silhouetted in the light of the vanished years," died.

With Winn's death, the Derby reached an odd turning point. Year after year, great horses had paraded through

Louisville and emerged as champions. A single generation had seen eight horses sweep the Triple Crown; one arrived every few years with clockwork regularity. But in the 1950s, the unexpected became the rule.

It began in 1953, when the wildly popular, wonderfully telegenic Native Dancer, the Derby's first television star, was bumped, checked, and blocked into a heartbreaking head loss, the only race in which he was ever beaten. The unthinkable recurred in 1955, when the seemingly unbeatable Nashua was hoodwinked by Swaps, a California speedball whose owner slept in the stall to be near him. Two years later, the unexpected gave way to the truly bizarre. A few days before the Derby, the owner of the great Gallant Man dreamed that he saw his colt leading the Derby down the stretch. The dream then became a nightmare. Just before the wire, Gallant Man's jockey inexplicably pulled up, slowing the horse and costing him the race. Sure enough, on Derby day, Gallant Man rocketed down the Derby stretch, looking like a winner until his jockey, Bill Shoemaker, misjudged the sixteenth pole as the finish, stopped urging his mount momentarily, and lost by a nose.

In April 1971, a colt named Canonero II stepped aboard a cargo plane in Caracas, en route to the Derby. The race he was set to contest was in turmoil. Three years earlier, Derby winner Dancer's Image had been disqualified after traces of Butazolidin, a non-performance-affecting anti-inflammatory drug similar to aspirin, were found in his system. Many suspected that outsiders seeking to discredit the horse's owner, Peter Fuller, had tampered with his horse; Fuller had been receiving racist hate mail since donating some of the colt's earnings to the widowed Coretta King. But no one ever de-

termined who gave the colt the drug, which, most frustrat-
ingly, was later legalized. As Canonero embarked for Miami
on the first leg of his journey, the Derby remained mired in a
wrenching court battle as a devastated Fuller fought in vain
for vindication for his "doped" horse. A pall hung over the
Derby; the race needed redemption.

Canonero's only escorts were the teenage son of his owner,
Pedro Baptista, and several crates of ducks and chickens. No
one in the United States had ever heard of him; when a rep-
resentative called to nominate him to the Triple Crown, racing official Chick Lang thought it was a practical joke. He had
good reason. Thanks to an ugly, backward-bending foreleg,
the colt had been given away, then sold to a Venezuelan for a
pittance, then given away again, a questionable gift to the
Venezuelan's son-in-law. He had been shipped all over the
Western hemisphere to run in cheap races, logging enough
airtime, wrote Joseph Challmes in *The Preakness: A History,*
"to qualify as a pilot." But the colt, named for Latin American
street musicians, had a taste for distance running, and the
Derby's mile and a quarter looked about right.

Canonero's first flight turned back when the plane's engine
caught fire. The second returned with mechanical problems.
When he finally got to Miami, he was at wit's end from the in-
cessant clucking of his fellow passengers. Someone had forgotten the customs papers, so he spent four days locked in
quarantine. After clearing customs, he was loaded into a van,
which broke down. By the time he finally made it to the track,
Canonero had lost between seventy and eighty pounds. His
trainer, Juan Arias, feared he would have to be scratched. He
sent the colt out to exercise with a rope around his neck
and a boy riding him bareback, to the ridicule of onlookers.

Canonero clocked preposterously slow times. But as Derby day approached, the colt began coming around. Arias decided to run him.

Leaving the starting gate, Canonero dropped back to sixteenth. By the half-mile pole, he was eighteenth. Everybody expected him to stay there. But what hadn't occurred to anyone was that in Venezuela the colt had been racing in thin air three thousand feet above sea level; in the oxygen-rich Kentucky air, he had virtually infinite stamina. As the front-runners faded, Canonero was just getting going.

"There was no such animal at the head of the stretch," Lang told Challmes. "You couldn't find him. He was back there sucking up all the grit. . . . And then—*pffsst*, out like a grapefruit seed—here he came."

The Venezuelan disgrace caught the field, then buried it behind him. The crowd was dead silent. In the press box, a reporter muttered, "Canonero II? Who the hell was Canonero I?" As the horse loped back to the grandstand, his jockey, Gustavo Avila, began waving his arms wildly, and the crowd finally raised a cheer. Down in Venezuela, his owner received a call from someone telling him he had won. "That's a sick joke!" Baptista shouted, hanging up. When more calls came in, he realized what his colt had done. In Caracas, they danced and sang for Canonero all night long.

The "Caracas Cannonball" won the Preakness and drew a cult following, but like every Derby winner in the long, strange years since Citation, he failed to win the Triple Crown. Pressure was building for a superstar to emerge. Racing, and the Derby, needed a Triple Crown winner, but after twenty-five years of mishaps, scandal, outrageous fortune, and near misses, many racegoers believed that they would never see another one.

On May 5, 1973, a sleek black colt named Sham leaned out of the final turn in the lead in the ninety-ninth Kentucky Derby. The front-runners were finished, and though he had blood spraying from his chin after ripping two teeth loose in the starting gate, Sham was staging an epic performance. When he hit the wire seconds later, he would register a time fast enough to win every Derby in history with ease.

But Sham lost.

As he shot to the lead, an enormous red colt hurtled up behind him, running with fearsome, predatory lunges. He may have been the most awesome racing engine ever crafted. In his massive chest, which measured well over six feet around, beat a heart weighing some twenty-two pounds; at nearly three times the normal size, it was the largest healthy heart known to equine medicine. He pushed his 1,160-pound body over the earth with a twenty-four-foot, three-inch stride that, when analyzed by Professor George W. Pratt at MIT, proved to be the most efficient ever studied. According to Pratt, the colt was so fast that at the breed's rate of improvement, elite horses wouldn't catch up to him until 2064, ninety-one years later. He ran with a geometry of straight lines, precise turns, relentless, unflagging rhythm; the race caller Chick Anderson would call him "a tremendous machine." His name was Secretariat.

He closed on Sham with a terrible inevitability, seeming to feed off each grueling furlong; he was running each quarter mile faster than the one before, an unprecedented feat. Sham fought like a tiger; Secretariat overwhelmed him. He hit the wire traveling more than fifty-seven feet per second, halting the clock at 1:59 2/5, a Derby time that has never been approached, before or since.

The spell that had hung over the Derby had been shattered. Secretariat, with Sham pushing him all the way, won the Triple Crown, a feat repeated by Seattle Slew in 1977 and Affirmed in 1978.

AFTER MORE THAN A CENTURY, it seemed that the Derby had displayed to the utmost every virtue of the communion between horses and men, and that runnings to follow would not find a fresh answer to the glories of the past. But the genius of the Derby is that it reaches for the hard, hidden places in its competitors and invariably finds there something singular, something to surprise and dazzle and astonish. Thus it was in 1987.

In the starting gate, jockey Chris McCarron crouched low over the neck of an exuberant colt named Alysheba, bracing himself for a race that had become his life's obsession. He had no idea that the contest about to unfold would be one of the roughest major races in history. Shocked spectators would call the race chilling. One jockey would liken it to a rodeo, while another would be too shaken to talk about it. For McCarron and Alysheba, it would be a two-minute horror show.

It began the instant the gate doors crashed open. From stall three, McCarron gunned Alysheba forward with three other colts, trying to gain forward position. In a chaotic headlong charge, the horses to their outside angled inward, compressing them into a high-speed bottleneck. Alysheba was slammed into the horse to his left, who shouldered another horse into the rail. Ahead of them, horses crushed inward, their legs nearly tangling with the horses behind. For a dozen strides, Alysheba and three rivals were pinned together between seven tons of horseflesh and an unforgiving strip of metal. There was nowhere to go but back.

McCarron snatched up the reins. Alysheba threw his head up in protest, knocking McCarron backward. Regaining his balance, the jockey hauled his colt out of the vise and dropped back to fourteenth. Though he had narrowly escaped falling, McCarron now found himself straggling ten lengths behind the leaders. His game plan, and possibly his chance of winning, were dashed just seconds into the race.

Hugging the rail into the first turn, McCarron watched the pack of horses ahead surge inward again. Those to the outside cut in much too fast, causing another chain-reaction collision. A few feet in front of him, McCarron remembers, "there were about three horses where there was room for one." One of them, a colt named War, was rammed into the rail. Desperate to escape, he lunged up and hung partway over the barrier for an awful moment, a millimeter from flipping into the infield. Thinking a pileup was coming, McCarron sacrificed his ground-saving rail position and yanked Alysheba out from behind War, bouncing hard off another horse but staying on his feet.

Safely outside as the horses to his inside recovered, McCarron waited until the far turn. There, he turned Alysheba loose. The response was electrifying; while nearly every other horse that had been buffeted in the traffic jams retreated, Alysheba was crying out to run. He swooped around the field, and turning into the stretch, McCarron recalls, "I had one horse ahead of me and I thought I had a dynamite chance to win."

That horse was Bet Twice, and he was laboring, his stride deteriorating into lazy, irregular footfalls. Alysheba drove at him from the grandstand side, his nose lapping Bet Twice's tail. Suddenly, Bet Twice ducked sharply outward. McCarron saw the churning hindquarters veering into him and knew what was coming.

Alysheba reached out just as Bet Twice's hind legs pushed out behind him. McCarron felt Alysheba's forelegs being kicked out from under him. The colt's front end dropped like a hammer. McCarron saw his colt's head and neck fall away as the ground heaved up. His hands, clutching the reins, were jerked forward. With fifteen horses behind him, Alysheba was dragging McCarron into a forty-mile-per-hour somersault. "I thought," the jockey told *Sports Illustrated,* "I was gone."

McCarron threw himself backward and gripped the reins in a hammerlock, taking weight off Alysheba's sinking front end. Alysheba, his knees nearly on the ground, whirled his legs forward in one lithe motion. He landed violently on one foreleg, catching himself just in time.

McCarron expected his mount, like virtually every other horse in his experience, to be intimidated by the mishap that easily could have resulted in a horse and rider being trampled to death. He was wrong. Alysheba pinned his ears and took off after Bet Twice. He was spoiling for a fight.

Alysheba and McCarron charged down the stretch in pursuit of Bet Twice. Again Bet Twice veered outward. McCarron swerved his colt out sharply just in time to miss a second collision, then had to dodge right again as Bet Twice veered out a third time. With McCarron shouting him home, Alysheba stretched for the finish. The Kentucky ground shivered with the roar of 140,000 voices as man and animal took the lead and hurled themselves under the wire.

THE VICTOR IS LED over the infield bluegrass, walking down a gauntlet of men to the winner's circle. He treads a path ennobled by Secretariat, Citation, Arcaro, Smarty Jones, Regret, and Aristides. His hooves rest on earth cultivated by Winn, shaped by the visions of Clark, touched by Boone. They wreathe his shoulders in a rush of roses and the weight of tradition, his name forever amended with the grand words *Derby winner.*

"This is the moment, the peak, the pinnacle," wrote Faulkner, "after this, all is ebb."

WHITE MULE, SPOTTED PIG

Joe R. Lansdale

FRANK'S PAPA, THE SUMMER of nineteen hundred and nine, told him right before he died that he had a good chance to win the annual Camp Rapture mule race. He told Frank this 'cause he needed money to keep getting drunk, and he wasn't about to ride no mule himself, fat as he was. If the old man had known he was about to die, Frank figured he would have saved his breath on the race talk and asked for whiskey instead, maybe a chaw. But as it was, he said it, and it planted in Frank's head the desire to ride and win.

Frank hated that about himself. Once a thing got into his head he couldn't derail it. He was on the track then, and had to see it to the end. 'Course, that could be a good trait, but problem was, and Frank knew it, the only things that normally caught up in his head like that and pushed him were bad ideas. Even if he could sense their badness, he couldn't seem to stop their running forward and dragging him with them. He also thought his mama had been right when she told him once that their family was like shit on shoes; the stink of it followed them wherever they went.

But this idea. Winning a mule race. Well, that had some good sides to it. Mainly money.

He thought about what his papa said, and how he said it, and then how, within a few moments, the old man grabbed the bedsheets, moaned once, dribbled some drool, and was gone to wherever it was he was supposed to go, probably a stool next to the devil at fireside.

He didn't leave Frank nothing but an old run-down place with a bit of dried-out corn crop, a mule, a horse with one foot in the grave and the other on a slick spot. And his very own shit to clean out of the sheets, 'cause when the old man let go and departed, he left Frank that present, which was the only kind he had ever given. Something dirty. Something painful. Something shitty.

Frank had to burn the mattress and set fire to the bed-clothes, so there really wasn't any cleaning about it. Then he dug a big hole, and cut roots to do it. Next he had to wrap the old man's naked body in a dirty canvas and put him down and cover him up. It took some work, 'cause the old man must have weighed three hundred pounds, and he wasn't one inch taller than five-three if he was wearing boots with dried cow shit on the heels and paper tucked inside them to jack his height. Dragging him along on his dead ass from the house had damn near caused one of Frank's balls to swell up and pop out.

Finished with the burying, Frank leaned against a sickly
sweet gum tree and rolled himself a smoke, and thought:
Shit, I should have dragged the old man over here on the
tarp. Or maybe hitched him up to the mule and dragged his
naked ass facedown through the dirt. That would have been
the way to go, not pulling my guts out.

But it was done now, and as always, he had used his brain
late in the game.

Frank scratched a match on a thumbnail, smoked and considered. It wasn't that he was all that fond of his old man, but
damn if he still didn't in some way want to make him proud.
He thought: Funny, him not being worth a damn, and me still
wanting to please him. Funnier yet, considering the old man
used to beat him like a tom-tom. Frank had seen him knock
Mama down once and put his foot on the back of her neck
and use his belt to beat her ass while he cussed her for having burned the corn bread. It wasn't the only beating she got,
but it was damn sure the champion.

It was shortly after that she decamped with the good
horse, a bag of cornmeal, some dried meat, and a butcher
knife. She also managed, with what Frank thought must have
been incredible aim, to piss in one of his old man's liquor
jugs. This was discovered by the old man after he took a good
strong jolt of refreshment.

Papa had ridden out after her on the mule but hadn't
found her, which wasn't a surprise, because the only thing
Papa had been good at tracking was a whiskey bottle or some
whore, provided she was practically tied down and didn't cost
much. He probably tracked the whores he messed with by
their stench.

Back from the hunt, drunk and pissed and empty-handed,

Papa had said it was bad enough Frank's mama was a horse and meal thief, but at least she hadn't taken the mule, and frankly, she wasn't that good a cook anyhow.

The mule's name was Rupert, and he could run like his tail was on fire. Papa had actually thought about the mule as a contender for a while, and had put out a little money to have him trained by Leroy, who, though short in many departments, and known for having been caught fucking a goat by a half-dozen hunters, was pretty good with mules and horses.

The night after Frank buried his pa, he got in some corn squeezings and got drunk enough to imagine weasels crawling out from under the floorboards. To clear his head and to relieve his bladder, he went out to do something on his father's grave that would never pass for prayers. He stood there watering, thinking about the prize money and what he would do with it. He looked at the house and the barn and the lot, out to where he could see the dead corn standing in rows like dehydrated soldiers. The house leaned to the left, and one of the windowsills was near on the ground. When he slept at night, he slept on a bed with one side jacked up with flat rocks so that it was high enough and even enough he wouldn't roll out of bed. The barn had one side missing and the land was all rutted from run-off.

With the exception of the hill where they grazed their bit of stock, the place was void of grass, and all it brought to mind was brown things and dead things, though there were a few bedraggled chickens who wandered the yard like wild Indians, taking what they could find, even eating one another should one of them keel over dead from starvation or exhaustion. Frank, on more than one occasion, had seen a half-dozen chickens go at a weak one lying on the ground, tearing him apart like miners at a free lunch table.

Frank smoked his cigarette and thought that if he could win that race, he would move away from this shit pile. Sell it to some fool. Move into town and get a job that would keep him. Never again would he look up a mule's ass or fit his hands around the handles on a plow. He was thinking on this while looking up the hill at his mule, Rupert.

The hill was surrounded by a rickety rail fence within which the mule resided primarily on the honor system. At the top of the hill were a bunch of oaks and pines and assorted survivor trees. As Frank watched the sun fall down behind the hill, it seemed as if the limbs of the trees wadded together into a crawling shadow. Rupert was clearly outlined near a pathetic persimmon tree from which the mule had stripped the persimmons and much of the leaves.

Frank thought Rupert looked quite noble up there, his mule ears standing high in outline against the redness of the sun behind the dark trees. The world seemed strange and beautiful, as if just created. In that moment Frank felt much older than his years and not so fresh as the world seemed, but ancient and worn like the old Indian pottery he had found while plowing through what had once been great Indian mounds. And now, even as he watched, he noted the sun seemed to darken, as if it were a hot wound turning black from infection. The wind cooled and began to whistle. Frank turned his head to the north and watched as clouds pushed across the fading sky. In an instant, all the light was gone and there were just shadows, spitting and twisting in the heavens and filling the hard-blowing wind with the aroma of wet dirt.

When Frank turned again to note Rupert, the mule was still there, but was now little more than a peculiar shape next to the ragged persimmon tree. Had Frank not known it was the mule, he might well have mistaken it for a peculiar rise in the terrain, or a fallen tree lying at an odd angle.

The storm was from the north and blowing west. Thunder boomed and lightning cracked in the dirty sky, popped and fizzled like a doused campfire. In that moment, the shadow Frank knew to be Rupert lifted its head and pointed its dark muzzle toward the sky, as if in defiance. A bolt of lightning, crooked as a dog's hind leg, jumped from the heavens and dove for the mule, striking him a perfect white-hot blow on the tip of his nose, making him glow, causing Frank to think that he had in fact seen the inside of the mule light up with all its bones in a row. Then Rupert's head exploded, his body blazed, the persimmon tree leaped to flames, and the mule fell over in a swirl of heavenly fire and a cannon shot of flying mule shit. The corpse caught a patch of dried grass ablaze. The flames burned in a perfect circle around the corpse and blinked out, leaving a circle of smoke rising skyward.

"Goddamn," Frank said. "Shit."

The clouds split open and pissed all over the hillside, and not a drop, not one goddamn drop, was thrown away from the hill. The rain just covered that spot, put out the mule and the persimmon tree with a sizzling sound, then passed on, taking darkness, rain, and cool wind with it.

Frank stood there for a long time, looking up the hill, watching his hundred dollars crackle and smoke. Pretty soon the smell from the grilled mule floated down the hill and filled his nostrils.

"Shit," Frank said. "Shit. Shit. Shit."

LATE MORNING, WHEN FRANK could finally drag himself out of bed, he went out and caught the horse, Dobbin, hitched him to a singletree and fastened on some chains and drove him out to where the mule lay. He hooked one of the mule's hind legs to the rigging, and Dobbin dragged the corpse up the hill, between the trees, to the other side. Frank figured he'd just let the body rot there, on the other side of the hill where there was less chance of the wind carrying the smell.

After that, Frank moped around for a few days, drank enough to see weasels again, and then had an idea. His idea was to seek out Leroy, who had been Rupert's trainer. See if he could work a deal with him.

Frank rode Dobbin over to Leroy's place, which was even nastier than his own due to the yard being full not only of chickens and goats, but children. Leroy had five of them, and when Frank rode up, he saw them right away, running about, raising hell in the yard, one of them minus pants, his little johnson flopping about like a grub worm on a hot griddle. Leroy's old lady was on the porch, fat and greasy with her hair tied up. She was yelling at the kids and telling them how she was going to kill them and feed them to the chickens. One of the boys, the ten-year-old, ran by the porch whooping, and the missus, moving deftly for such a big woman, scrambled to the edge of the porch, stuck her foot out, caught him one just above the waist and sent him tumbling. He went down hard. She laughed like a lunatic. The boy got up with a bloody nose and ran off across the yard and into the woods, screaming.

Frank climbed down from Dobbin and went over to Leroy who was sitting on a bucket in the front yard whittling a green limb with a knife big enough to sword-fight. Leroy was watching his son retreat into the greenery. As Frank came up, leading Dobbin, Leroy said, "Does that all the time. Sometimes, though, she'll throw something at him. Good thing wasn't nothing lying about. She's got a pretty good throwin' arm on her. Seen her hit a seed salesman with a tossed frying pan from the porch there to about where the road meets the property. Knocked him down and knocked his hat off. Scattered his seed samples, which the chickens ate. Must have laid there for an hour afore he got up and wandered off. Forgot his hat. Got it on my head right now, though I had to put me some newspaper in the band to make it fit."

Wasn't nothing Frank could say to that, so he said, " Leroy, Rupert got hit by lightning. Right in the head."

"The head?"

"Wouldn't have mattered had it been the ass. It killed him deader than a post and burned him up."

"Damn. That there is a shame," Leroy said, and stopped whittling. He pushed the seed salesman's hat up on his forehead to reveal some forks of greasy brown hair. Leroy studied Frank. "Is there something I can do for you? Or you come around to visit?"

"I'm thinking you might could help me get a mule and get back in the race."

"Mules cost."

"I know. Thought we might could come up with something. And if we could, and we won, I'd give you a quarter of the prize money."

"I get a quarter for grooming folks' critters in town."

"I mean a quarter of a hundred. Twenty-five dollars."

"I see. Well, I am your man for animals. I got a knack. I

can talk to them like I was one of them. Except for chickens. Ain't no one can talk to chickens."

"They're birds."

"That there is the problem. They ain't animal enough."

"I know you run in the circles of them that own or know about mules,.." Frank said. "Why I thought you maybe could help me."

Leroy took off the seed salesman's hat, put it on his knee, threw his knife in the dirt, let the whittling stick fall from his hand. "I could sneak up on an idea or two. Old man Torrence, he's got a mule he's looking to sell. And by his claim, it's a runner. He ain't never ridden it himself, but he's had it ridden. Says it can run."

"There's that buying stuff again. I ain't got no real money."

"Takes money to make money."

"Takes money to have money."

Leroy put the seed salesman's hat back on. "You know, we might could ask him if he'd rent out his mule. Race is a ways off yet, so we could get some good practice in. You being about a hundred and twenty-five pounds, you're light enough to make a good rider."

"I've ridden a lot. I was ready on Rupert, reckon I can get ready on another mule."

"Deal we might have to make is, we win the race, we buy the mule afterwards. That might be the way he'd do it."

"Buy the mule?"

"At a fair price."

"How fair?"

"Say twenty-five dollars."

"That's a big slice of the prize money. And a mule for twenty-five, that's cheap."

"I know Torrence got the mule cheap. Fella that owed him made a deal. Besides, times is hard. So they're selling cheap. Cost more, we can make extra money on side bets. Bet on ourselves. Or if we don't think we got a chance, we bet against ourselves."

"I don't know. We lose, it could be said we did it on purpose."

"I can get someone to bet for us."

"Only if we bet to win. I ain't never won nothing or done nothing right in my life, and I figure this here might be my chance."

"You gettin' Jesus?"

"I'm gettin' tired," Frank said.

THERE ARE NO REAL MOUNTAINS IN EAST TEXAS, and only a few hills of consequence, but Old Man Torrence lived at the top of a big hill that was called, with a kind of braggart's lie, Barrow Dog Mountain. Frank had no idea who Barrow or Dog were, but that was what the big hill had been called for as long as he remembered, probably well before he was born. There was a ridge at the top of it that overlooked the road below. Frank found it an impressive sight as he and Leroy rode in on Dobbin, he at the reins, Leroy riding double behind him.

It was pretty on top of the hill too. The air smelled good, and flowers grew all about in red, blue, and yellow blooms, and the cloudless sky was so blue you felt as if a great lake were falling down from the heavens. Trees fanned out bright green on either side of the path, and near the top, on a flat section, was Old Man Torrence's place. It was made of cured logs, and he had a fine chicken coop that was built straight and true. There were hog pens and a nice barn of thick cured logs with a roof that had all of its roofing slats. There was a sizable garden that rolled along the top of the hill, full of tall bright green cornstalks, so tall they shaded the rows between them. There was no grass between the rows, and the dirt there looked freshly laid by. Squash and all manner of vegetables exploded out of the ground alongside the corn, and there were little clumps of beans and peas growing in long, pretty rows.

In a large pen next to the barn was a fifteen-hands-high chocolate-colored mule, prettiest thing Frank had ever seen in the muleflesh department. Its ears stood up straight, and it gave Frank and Leroy a snort as they rode in.

"He's a big one," Leroy said.

"Won't he be slow, being that big?" Frank asked.

"Big mule's also got big muscles, he's worked right. And he looks to have been worked right. Got enough muscles, he can haul some freight. Might be fast as Rupert."

"Sure faster right now," Frank said.

As they rode up, they saw Old Man Torrence on the front porch with his wife and three kids, two boys and a girl. Torrence was a fat, ruddy-faced man. His wife was a little plump, but pretty. His kids were all nice-looking, and they, unlike Leroy's kids, had their hair combed and looked clean. Coming closer, Frank could see that none of the kids looked whacked on. They were laughing at something the mother was saying. It certainly was different from his own upbringing, different from Leroy's place. Wasn't anyone tripping anyone, cussing, tossing frying pans, threatening to cripple one another or put out an eye. Thinking on this, Frank felt something twist around inside of him like some kind of serpent looking for a rock to slide under.

He and Leroy got off Dobbin and tied him to a little hitching post that was built out front of the house, took off their hats, and walked up to the steps.

After they were offered lemonade, which they turned down, Old Man Torrence came off the porch, ruffling one of his kids' hair as he did. He smiled back at his wife, and then walked with Frank and Leroy out toward the mule pen, Leroy explaining what they had in mind.

"You want to rent my mule? What if I wanted to run him?"

"Well, I don't know," Leroy said. "It hadn't occurred to me you might. You ain't never before, though I heard tell he was a mule could be run."

"It's a good mule," Torrence said. "Real fast."

"You've ridden him?" Frank asked.

"No. I haven't had the pleasure. But my brother and his boys have. They borrow him from time to time, and they thought on running him this year. Nothing serious. Just a thought. They say he can really cover ground."

"Frank here," Leroy said, "plans on entering the mule race, and we would like to rent your mule. If we win, we could give you a bit of the prize money. What say we rent him for ten, and if he wins, we give you another fifteen. That way you pick up twenty-five dollars."

Frank was listening to all this, thinking: This purse I haven't won yet is getting smaller and smaller.

"And if he don't win?" Torrence asked.

"You've made ten dollars," Leroy said.

"And I got to take the chance my mule might go lame or get hurt or some such. I don't know. Ten dollars, that's not a lot of money for what you're asking. It ain't even your mule."

"Which is why we're offering the ten dollars," Leroy said.

They went over and leaned on the fence and looked at the

great mule, watched his muscles roll beneath his chocolate flesh as he trotted nervously about the pen.

"He looks excitable," Frank said.

"Robert E. Lee has just got a lot of energy is all," Torrence said.

"He's named Robert E. Lee?" Frank asked.

"Best damn general ever lived. Tell you boys what. You give me twenty-five, and another twenty-five if he wins, and you got a deal."

"But I give you that, and Leroy his share, I don't have nothing hardly left."

"You ain't got nothing at all right now," Torrence said.

"How's about," Leroy said, "we do it this way. We give you fifteen, and another fifteen if he wins. That's thirty. Now that's fair for a rented mule. Hell, we might could go shopping, buy a mule for twenty-five, and even if he don't win, we got a mule. He don't race worth a damn, we could put him to plow."

Old Man Torrence pursed his lips. "That sounds good. All right," he said, sticking out his hand. "Deal."

"Well, now," Frank said, not taking the hand. "Before I shake on that, I'd like to make sure he can run. Let me ride him."

Old Man Torrence withdrew his hand and wiped it on his pants as if something had gotten on his palm. "I reckon I could do that, but seeing how we don't have a deal yet, and ain't no fifteen dollars has changed hands, how's about I ride him for you. So you can see."

Frank and Leroy agreed, and watched from the fence as Torrence got the equipment and saddled up Robert E. Lee. Torrence walked Robert E. Lee out of the lot and onto a pasture atop the hill, where the overhang was. The pasture was huge and the grass was as green as Ireland. It was all fenced in with barbwire strung tight between deeply planted posts.

"I'll ride him around in a loop. Once slow, and then real fast toward the edge of the overhang there, then cut back before we get there. I ain't got a pocket watch, so you'll have to be your own judge."

Torrence swung into the saddle. "You boys ready?"

"Let 'er rip," Leroy said.

Old Man Torrence gave Robert E. Lee his heels. The mule shot off so fast that Old Man Torrence's hat flew off, and Leroy, in sympathy, took hold of the brim of the seed salesman's hat, as if Robert E. Lee's lunge might blow it off his head.

"Goddamn," Leroy said. "Look how low that mule is to the ground. He's goin' have the grass touching his belly."

And so the mule ran, and as it neared the barbwire fence, Old Man Torrence gave the mule a tug, to turn him. But Robert E. Lee wasn't having any. The critter's speed picked up, and the barbwire fence came closer.

Leroy said, "Uh-oh."

Robert E. Lee hit the fence hard. So hard it caused his head to dip over the top wire and his ass to rise up as if he might be planning a headstand. Over the mule flipped, tearing loose the fence, causing a strand of wire to snap and strike Old Man Torrence just as he was thrown ahead of the tumbling mule. Over the overhang. Out of sight. The mule did in fact do a headstand, landed hard that way, its hind legs high in the air, wiggling. For a moment it seemed as if he might hang there, and then Robert E. Lee lost his headstand and went over after his owner.

"Damn," Leroy said.

"Damn," Frank said.

They both ran toward the broken fence. When they got there Frank hesitated, not able to look. He glanced away, back across the bright green field.

Leroy scooted up to the cliff's edge and took a gander, studied what he saw for a long time.

"Well?" Frank said, finally turning his head back to Leroy.

"Robert E. Lee just met his Gettysburg. And Old Man Torrence is somewhere between Gettysburg and Robert E. Lee. . . . Actually, you can't tell which is which. Mule, Gettysburg, or Old Man Torrence. It's all kind of bunched up."

WHEN FRANK AND LEROY GOT DOWN THERE, which took some considerable time, as they worked their way down a little trail on foot, they discovered that Old Man Torrence had been lucky in a fashion. He had landed in sand, and the force of Robert E. Lee's body had driven him down deep into it, his nose poking up and out enough to take in air. Robert E. Lee was as dead as a threepenny nail, and his tail was stuck up in the air and bent over like a flag that had been broken at the staff. The wind moved the hairs on it a little.

Frank and Leroy went about digging Old Man Torrence out, starting first with his head so he could breathe better. When Torrence had spit enough sand out of his mouth, he looked up and said, "You sons a' bitches. This is your fault."

"Our fault?" Leroy said. "You was riding him."

"You goat-fucking bastard child, get me out of here."

Leroy's body sagged a little. "I knew that was gonna get around good. Ain't nobody keeps a secret. There was only that one time too, and them hunters had to come up on me."

They dug Torrence out from under the mule, and Frank went up the trail and got old Dobbin and rode to the doctor. When Frank got back with the sawbones, Torrence was none the happier to see him. Leroy had gone off to the side to sit by himself, which made Frank think maybe the business about the goat had come up.

Old Man Torrence was mostly all right, but he blamed Frank and Leroy, especially Leroy, from then on. And he walked in a way that when he stepped with his right leg, it always looked as if he were about to bend over and tie his shoe. Even in later years, when Frank saw him, he went out of his way to avoid him, and Leroy dodged him like the smallpox, not wanting to hear reference to the goat.

But in that moment in time, the important thing to Frank was simply that he was still without a mule. And the race was coming closer.

THAT NIGHT, AS FRANK LAY in his sagging bed, looking out from it at the slanted wall of the room, listening to the crickets saw their fiddles both outside and inside the house, he closed his eyes and remembered how Old Man Torrence's place had looked. He saw himself sitting with the pretty, plump wife and the clean, polite kids. Then he saw himself with the wife inside that pretty house, on the bed, and he imagined that for a long time.

It was a pleasant thought, the wife and the bed, but even more pleasant was imagining Torrence's place as his. All that greenery and high-growing corn and blooming squash and thick pea and bean vines dripping with vegetables. The house and the barn and the pasture. And, in his dream, the big mule, alive, not yet a confusion of bones and flesh and fur, the tail a broken flag.

He thought then of his mother, and the only way he could remember her was with her hair tied back and her face sweaty and both of her eyes blacked. That was how she had looked the last time he had seen her, right before she run off with a horse and some cornmeal and a butcher knife. He wondered where she was, and if she now lived in a place where the buildings were straight and the grass was green and the corn was tall.

After a while he got up and peed out the window, and smelled the aroma of other nights drifting up from the ground he had poisoned with his water, and thought: I am better than Papa. He just peed in the corner of the room and shit out the window, splattering it all down the side of the house. I don't do that. I pee out the window, but I don't shit, and I don't pee in the corner. That's a step up. I go outside for the messy business. And if I had a good house I'd use the slop jar. I'd go to the privy.

Thinking on all this didn't stop him from finishing his pee. Peeing was the one thing he was really good at. He could piss like a horse and from a goodly distance. He had even won money on his ability. It was the one thing his father had been proud of. "My son, Frank. He can piss like a goddamn horse. Get it out, Frank. Show them."

And he would.

But compared to what he wanted out of life, his ability to throw water from his johnson didn't seem all that wonderful right then.

FRANK THOUGHT HE OUGHT to call a halt to his racing plans, but like so many of his ideas, he couldn't let it go. It blossomed inside of him until he was filled with it. Then he was obsessed with an even wilder plan. A story he had heard came back to him, and ran around inside his head like a greased pig.

He would find the white mule and capture it and run it. It was a mule he could have for free, and it was known to be fast, if wild. And, of course, he would have to capture its companion, the spotted pig. Though he figured, by now, the pig was no longer a pig, but a hog, and the mule would be three, maybe four years old.

If they really existed.

It was a story he had heard for the last three years or so, and it was told for the truth by them who told him, his papa among them. But if drinking made him see weasels oozing out of the floorboards, it might have made Papa see white mules and spotted pigs on parade. But the story wasn't just Papa's story. He had heard it from others and it went like this:

Once upon a time, there was this pretty white mule with pink eyes, and the mule was fine and strong and set to the plow early on, but he didn't take to it. Not at all. But the odder part of the story was that the mule took up with a farm pig, and they became friends. There was no explaining it. It happened now and then, a horse or mule adopting their own pet, and that was what had happened with the white mule and the spotted pig.

When Frank had asked his papa why would a mule take up with a pig, his father had said: "Ain't no explaining. Why the hell did I take up with your mother?"

Frank thought the question went the other way, but the tale fascinated him, and that night his papa was just drunk enough to be in a good mood. Another pint swallowed, he'd be kicking Frank's ass or his mama's. But he pushed while he could, trying to get the goods on the tale, since outside of worrying about dying corn and sagging barns, there wasn't that much in life that excited him.

The story his papa told him was that the farmer who owned the mule—and no one could ever put a name to who that farmer was—had supposedly found the mule wouldn't work if the pig wasn't around, leading him between the rows. The pig was in front, the mule plowed fine. The pig wasn't there, the mule wouldn't plow.

This caused the farmer to come up with an even better idea. What would the mule do if the pig was made to run? The farmer got the mule all tacked up, then had one of his boys put the pig out front of the mule and swat it with a knotted plow line, and away went the pig and away went the white mule. The pig pretty soon veered off, but the mule, once set to run, couldn't stop, and would race so fast that the only way it halted was when it was tuckered out. Then it would go back to the start and look for its pig. Never failed.

One night the mule broke loose, kicked the pig's pen down, and he and the pig, like they was Jesse and Frank James, headed for the hills. Went into the East Texas greenery and wound in amongst the trees, and were lost to the farmer, only to be seen after that in glimpses and in stories that might or might not be true. Stories about how they raided cornfields and ate the corn and how the mule kicked down pens and let hogs and goats and cattle go free.

The white mule and the spotted pig. Out there. On the run. Doing whatever it was that white mules and spotted pigs did when they weren't raiding crops and freeing critters.

Frank thought on this for a long time, saddled up Dobbin, and rode over to Leroy's place. When Frank arrived, Leroy was out in the yard on his back, unconscious, the seed salesman hat spun off to the side and being moved around by a curious chicken. Finding Leroy like this didn't frighten Frank any. He often found Leroy that way, cold as a wedge from drink, or unconscious from the missus having snuck up behind him with a stick of stove wood. They were rowdy, Leroy's bunch.

The missus came out on the porch and shook her fist at Frank, and, not knowing anything else to do, he waved. She spit a stream of brown tobacco off the porch in his direction and went inside. A moment later, one of the kids bellowed from being whapped, and there was a sound like someone slamming a big fish on flat ground. Then silence.

Frank bent down and shook Leroy awake. Leroy cursed, and Frank dragged him to an overturned bucket and sat him up on it, asked him, "What happened?"

"Missus come up behind me. I've got so I don't watch my back enough."

"Why'd she do it?"

"Just her way. She has spells."

"You all right?"

"I got a headache."

Frank went straight to business. "I come to say maybe we ain't out of the mule business."

"What you mean?"

Frank told him about the mule and the pig, about his idea.

"Oh, yeah. Mule and pig are real. I've seen 'em once myself. Out hunting. I looked up, and there they were at the end of a trail, just watching. I was so startled, I just stood there looking at them."

"What did they do?"

"Well, Frank, they ran off. What do you think? But it was kind of funny. They didn't get in no hurry, just turned and went around the trail, showing me their ass, the pig's tail curled up and a little swishy, and the mule swatting his like at flies. They just went around that curve in the trail, behind some oaks and blackberry vines, and they was gone. I tracked them a bit, but they got down in a stream and walked it. I could find their tracks in the stream with my hands, but pretty soon the whole stream was brown with mud, and they come out of it somewhere I didn't find, and they was gone like a swamp fog come noon."

"Was the mule really white?"

"Dirty a bit, but white. Even from where I was standing, just bits of light coming in through the trees, I could see he had pink eyes. Story is, that's why he don't like to come out in day much, likes to stay in the trees and do his crop raiding at night. Say the sun hurts his skin."

"That could be a drawback."

"You act like you got him in a pen somewhere."

"I'd like to see if I could get hold of him. Story is he can run, and he needs the pig to do it."

"That's the story. But stories ain't always true. I even heard stories about how the pig rides the mule. I've heard all manner of tale, and ain't maybe none of it got so much as a nut of truth in it. Still, it's one of them ideas that kind of appeals to me. 'Course, you know, we might catch that mule and he might not can run at all. Maybe all he can do is sneak around in the woods and eat corn crops."

"Well, it's all the idea I got, " Frank said, and the thought of that worried Frank more than a little. He considered on his knack for clinging to bad notions like a rutting dog hanging onto a fella's leg. But, like the dog, he was determined to finish what he started.

"So what you're saying here," Leroy said, "is you want to

capture the mule and the pig, so the mule has got his help-mate. And you want to ride the mule in the race?"

"That's what I said."

Leroy paused for a moment, rubbed the knot on the back of his noggin. "I think we should get Nigger Joe to help us track him. We want that mule, that's the way we do it. Nigger Joe catches him, and we'll break him, and you can ride him."

NIGGER JOE WAS PART INDIAN and part Irish and part Negro. His skin was somewhere between brown and red and he had a red cast to his kinky hair and strawberry freckles and bright green eyes. But the black blood named him, and he himself went by the name Nigger Joe.

He was supposed to be able to track a bird across the sky, a fart across the yard. He had two women who lived with him and he called them his wives. One of them was a Negro, and the other one was part Negro and Cherokee. He called the black one Sweetie, the red-and-black one Pie.

When Frank and Leroy rode up double on Dobbin and stopped in Nigger Joe's yard, a rooster was fucking one of the hens. It was a quick matter, and a moment later the rooster was strutting across the yard like he was ten foot tall and bulletproof.

They got off Dobbin, and no sooner had they hit the ground than Nigger Joe was beside them, tall and broad shouldered with his freckled face.

"Damn, man," Frank said, "where did you come from?"

Nigger Joe pointed in an easterly direction.

"Shit," Leroy said, "coming up on a man like that could make him bust a heart."

"Want something?" Nigger Joe asked.

"Yeah," Leroy said. "We want you to help track the white mule and the spotted pig, 'cause Frank here, he's going to race him."

"Pig or mule?" Nigger Joe asked.

"The mule," Leroy said. "He's gonna ride the mule."

"Eat the pig?"

"Well," Leroy said, continuing his role as spokesman, "not right away. But there could come a point."

"He eats the pig, I get half of pig," Nigger Joe said.

"If he eats it, yeah," Leroy said. "Shit, he eats the mule, he'll give you half of that."

"My women like mule meat," Nigger Joe said. "I've eat it, but it don't agree with me. Horse is better." And to strengthen his statement, he gave Dobbin a look-over.

"We was thinking," Leroy said, "we could hire you to find the mule and the pig, capture them with us."

"What was you thinking of giving me, besides half the critters if you eat them?"

"How about ten dollars?"

"How about twelve?"

"Eleven."

"Eleven fifty."

Leroy looked at Frank. Frank sighed and nodded, stuck out his hand. Nigger Joe shook it, then shook Leroy's hand.

Nigger Joe said, "Now, mule runs like the rock, ain't my fault. I get the eleven fifty anyway."

Frank nodded.

"Okay, tomorrow morning," Nigger Joe said, "just before light, we'll go look for him real serious and then some."

"Thing does come to me," Frank said, "is haven't other folks tried to get hold of this mule and pig before? Why are you so confident?"

Nigger Joe nodded. "They not Nigger Joe."

"You could have tracked them before on your own," Frank said. "Why now?"

Nigger Joe looked at Frank. "Eleven fifty."

IN THE PREDAWN LIGHT, down in the swamp, the fog moved through the trees like someone slow-pulling strands of cotton from cotton bolls. It wound its way amongst the limbs that were low down, along the ground. There were wisps of it on the water, right near the bank, and as Frank and Leroy and Nigger Joe stood there, they saw what looked like dozens of sticks rise up in the swamp water and move along briskly.

Nigger Joe said, "Cottonmouth snakes. They going with they heads up, looking for anything foolish enough to get out there. You swimming out there now, pretty quick you be bit good and plenty and swole up like old tick. Only you burst all over and spill green poison and die. Seen it happen."

"Ain't planning on swimming," Frank said.

"Watch your feet," Nigger Joe said. "Them snakes is thick this year. Them cottons and them copperheads. Cottons, they always mad."

"We've seen snakes," Leroy said.

"I know it," Nigger Joe said, "but where we go, they are more than a few, that's what I'm trying to tell you. Back there where mule and pig hides, it's thick in snakes and blackberry vines. And the trees thick like the wool on a sheep. It a goat or a sheep you fucked?"

"For Christ sakes," Leroy said. "You heard that too?"

"Wives talk about it when they see you yesterday. There the man who fuck a sheep, or a goat, or some such. Say you ain't a man can get pussy."

"Oh, hell," Leroy said.

"So, tell me some," Nigger Joe said. "Which was it, now?"

"Goat," Leroy said.

"That is big nasty," Nigger Joe said, and started walking, leading them along a narrow trail by the water. Frank watched the cottonmouth snakes swim onward, their evil heads sticking up like some sort of water-devil erections.

The day grew hot and the trees held the hot and made it hotter and hard to breathe, like sucking down wool and chunks of flannel. Frank and Leroy sweated their clothes through, and their hair turned to wet strings. Nigger Joe, though sweaty, appeared as fresh as a virgin in spring.

"Where you get your hat?" Nigger Joe asked Leroy suddenly, when they stopped for a swig from canteens.

"Seed salesman. My wife knocked him out and I kept the hat."

"Huh, no shit?" Nigger Joe took off his big old hat and waved around. "Bible salesman. He told me I was gonna go to hell, so I beat him up, kept his hat. I shit in his Bible case."

"Wow, that's mean," Frank said.

"Him telling me I'm going to hell, that make me real mad. I tell you that to tell you not to forget my eleven fifty. I'm big on payment."

"You can count on us, we win," Frank said.

"No. You owe me eleven fifty win or lose." Nigger Joe said this, putting his hat back carefully on his head, looking at the two smaller men like a man about to pick a hen for neck wringing and Sunday dinner.

"Sure," Frank said. "Eleven fifty, win or lose. Eleven fifty when we get the pig and the mule."

"Now that's the deal as I see it," Nigger Joe said. "I tell

women it's eight dollars, that way I make some whiskey money. Nigger Joe didn't get up yesterday. No, he didn't. And when he gets up, he's got Bible salesman's hat on."

Frank thought: What? What the hell does that mean?

THEY WADED THROUGH THE SWAMP and through the woods for some time, and just before dark, Nigger Joe picked up on the mule's unshod tracks. He bent down and looked at them. He said, "We catch him, he's gonna need trimming and shoes. Not enough rock to wear them down. Soft sand and swamp. And here's the pig's tracks. Hell, he's big. Tracks say three hundred pounds. Maybe more."

"That's no pig," Leroy said. "That's a full-blown hog."

"Damn," Frank said. "They're real."

"But can he race?" Leroy said. "And will the pig cooperate?"

They followed the tracks until it turned dark. They threw up a camp, made a fire, and made it big so the smoke was strong, as the mosquitoes were everywhere and hungry and the smoke kept them off a little. They sat there in the night before the fire, the smoke making them cough, watching it churn up above them, through the trees. And up there, as if resting on a limb, was a piece of the moon.

They built the fire up big one last time, turned in to their covers, and tried to sleep. Finally, they did, but before morning Frank awoke, his bladder full, his mind as sharp as if he had slept well. He got up and stoked up the fire, and walked out a few paces in the dark and let it fly. When he looked up to button his pants, he saw through the trees, across a stretch of swamp water, something moving.

He looked carefully, because whatever it was had stopped.

He stood very still for a long time, and finally what he had seen moved again. He thought at first it was a deer, but no. There was enough light from the early rising sun shining through the trees that he could now see clearly what it was.

The white mule. It stood between two large trees, just looking at him, its head held high, its tall ears alert. The mule was big. Fifteen hands high, like Robert E. Lee, and it was big-chested, and its legs were long. Something moved beside it.

The spotted pig. It was big and ugly, with one ear turned up and one ear turned down. It grunted once, and the mule snorted, but neither moved.

Frank wasn't sure what to do. He couldn't go tearing across the stretch of swamp after them, since he didn't know how deep it was and what might be waiting for him. Gators, snakes, and sinkholes. And by the time he woke up the others, the mule and hog would be gone. He just stood there instead, staring at them. This went on for a long time, and finally the hog turned and started moving away, behind a thicket. The mule tossed its head, turned, and followed.

My God, thought Frank. The mule is beautiful. And the hog, he's a pistol. He could tell that from the way it had grunted at him. Frank had some strange feelings inside of him that he couldn't explain. Some sensation of having had a moment that was greater than any moment he had had before.

He walked back to the fire and lay down on his blankets, tried to figure the reason behind the feeling, but only came up with a headache and more mosquito bites. He closed his eyes and slept a little while longer, thinking of the mule and the hog, and the way they were free and beautiful. Then he was awakened by the toe of Nigger Joe's boot in his ribs.

"Time to do it," Nigger Joe said.

Frank sat up. "I saw them."

"What?" Leroy said, stirring out of his blankets.

Frank told them what he had seen, and how there was nothing he could do then. Told them all this, but didn't tell them how the mule and the hog had made him feel.

"Shit," Leroy said. "You should have woke us."

Nigger Joe shook his head. "No matter. We see over there where they stood. See what tracks they leave us. Then we do the sneak on them."

THEY WORKED THEIR WAY to the other side of the swamp, swatting mosquitoes and killing a cottonmouth in the process, and when they got to where the mule and the hog had stood, they found tracks and mule droppings.

"You not full of shit, like Nigger Joe thinking," Nigger Joe said. "You really see them."

"Yep," Frank said.

Nigger Joe bent down and rubbed some of the mule shit between his fingers and smelled it. "Not more than a couple hours old."

"Should have got us up," Leroy said.

"Easier to track in the day," Nigger Joe said. "They got their place they stay. They got some hideout."

The mosquitoes were not so bad now, and finally they came to some clear areas, marshy, but clear, and they lost the tracks there, but Nigger Joe said, "The two of them, they probably cross here. It's a good spot. Pick their tracks up in the trees over there, on the soft ground."

When they crossed the marshy stretch, they came to a

batch of willows and looked around there. Nigger Joe was the one who found their tracks.

"Here they go," he said. "Here they go."

They traveled through woods and more swamp, and from time to time they lost the tracks, but Nigger Joe always found them again. Sometimes Frank couldn't even see what Nigger Joe saw. But Nigger Joe saw something, because he kept looking at the ground, stopping to stretch out on the earth, his face close to it. Sometimes he would pinch the earth between finger and thumb, rub it about. Frank wasn't sure why he did that, and he didn't ask. Like Leroy, he just followed.

Midday, they came to a place that amazed Frank. Out there in the middle of what should have been swamp, there was a great clear area, at least a hundred acres. They found it when they came out of a stretch of shady oaks. The air was sweeter there, in the trees, and the shadows were cooling, and at the far edge was a drop of about fifty feet. Down below was a great and natural pasture. A fire, brought on by heat or lightning, might have cleared the place at some point in time. It had grown back without trees, just tall green grass amongst a few rotting, ant-infested stumps. It was surrounded by the oaks, high up on their side, and low down on the other. The oaks on the far side stretched out and blended with sweet gums and blackjack and hickory and bursts of pines. From their vantage point they could see all of this, and see the cool shadow on the other side amongst the trees.

A hawk sailed over it all, and Frank saw there was a snake in its beak. Something stirred again inside of Frank, and he was sure it wasn't his last meal. "You're part Indian," Frank said to Nigger Joe. "That hawk and that snake, does it mean something?"

"Means that snake is gonna get et," Nigger Joe said. "Damn trees. Don't you know that make a lot of good hard lumber. . . . Go quiet. Look there."

Coming out of the trees into the great pasture was the mule and the hog. The hog led the way, and the mule followed close behind. They came out into the sunlight, and pretty soon the hog began to root and the mule began to graze.

"Got their own paradise," Frank said.

"We'll fix that," Leroy said.

They waited there, sitting amongst the oaks, watching, and late in the day the hog and the mule wandered off into the trees across the way.

"Ain't we gonna do something besides watch?" Leroy said.

"They leave, tomorrow they come back," Nigger Joe said. "Got their spot. Be back tomorrow. We'll be ready for them."

JUST BEFORE DARK THEY CAME DOWN from their hiding place on a little trail, crossed the pasture, and walked over to where the mule and the hog had come out of the trees. Nigger Joe looked around for some time, said, "Got a path. Worked it out. Always the same. Same spot. Come through here, out into the pasture. What we do is we get up in a tree. Or I get in tree with my rope. I rope the mule and tie him off and let him wear himself down."

"He could kill himself, thrashing," Frank said.

"Could kill myself, him thrashing. I think it best tie him to a tree, folks."

Frank translated Nigger Joe's strange way of talking in his head, said, "He dies, you don't get the eleven fifty."

"Not how I understand it," Nigger Joe said.

"That's how it is," Frank said, feeling as if he might be asking for a knife in his belly, his guts spilled. Out here, no one would ever know. Nigger Joe might think he could do that, kill Leroy too, take their money. Course, they didn't have any money. Not here. There was fifteen dollars buried in a jar out back of the house, eleven fifty of which would go to Nigger Joe, if he didn't kill them.

Nigger Joe studied Frank for a long moment. Frank shifted from one foot to the other, trying not to do it, but unable to stop. "Okay," Nigger Joe said. "That will work up good enough."

"What about Mr. Porky?" Leroy asked.

"That gonna be you two's job. I rope damn mule, and you two, you gonna rope damn pig. First, we got to smell like dirt."

"What?" Frank said.

NIGGER JOE RUBBED HIMSELF down with dark soil. He had Frank and Leroy rub themselves down with it. Leroy hated it and complained, but Frank found the earth smelled like incoming rain, and he thought it pleasant. It felt good on his skin, and he had a sudden strange thought that when he died, he would become one and the same as the earth, and he wondered how many dead animals, maybe people, made up the dirt he had rubbed onto himself. He felt odd thinking that way. He felt odd thinking in any way.

They slept for a while, then Nigger Joe kicked him and Leroy awake. It was still dark when they rolled dirty out of their bedclothes.

"Couldn't we have waited on the dirt?" Leroy said, climbing out of his blankets. "It's all in my bedroll."

"Need time for dirt to like you good, so you smell like it,"
Nigger Joe said. "We put some more on now, rub in the hair
good, then get ready."

"It's still dark," Frank said. "They gonna come in the dark?
How you know when they're gonna come?"

"They come. But we gotta be ready. They have a good night
in farmers' cornfields, they might come real soon, full bellies.
Way ground reads, they come here to stand and to wallow.
Hog wallows all time, way ground looks. And they shit all over.
This their spot. They don't get corn and peas and such, they'll
be back here. Water not far from spot, and they got good
grass. Under the trees, hog has some acorns. Hogs like acorns.
Wife Sweetie makes sometimes coffee from acorns."

"How about I make some regular coffee, made from coffee?" Leroy said.

"Nope. We don't want a smoke smell. Don't want our
smell. Need to piss or shit, don't let free here. Go across pasture there. Far side. Dump over there. Piss over there. Use
the heel of your shoe to cover it all. Give it lots of dirt."

"Walk all the way across?" Leroy said.

"Want hog and mule," Nigger Joe said, "walk all the way
across. Now, eat some jerky, do your shit over on other side.
Put more dirt on. And wait."

THE SUN ROSE UP and it got hot, and the dirt on their skins
itched, or at least Frank itched, and he could tell Leroy itched,
but Nigger Joe, he didn't seem to. Sat silent. And when the
early morning was eaten up by the heat, Nigger Joe showed
them places to be. He had them lie down in trenches they
scooped in the dirt, and Nigger Joe covered them with leaves

and dirt and bits of hog and mule shit. It was terrible. They lay
there with their ropes and waited. Nigger Joe, with his lasso,
climbed up into an oak and sat on a fat limb, his feet stretched
along it, his back against the trunk, the rope in his lap.

The day crawled forward and so did the worms. They were
all around Frank, and it was all he could do not to jump up
screaming. It wasn't that he was afraid of them. He had put a
many of them on hooks for fishing. But to just lie there and
have them squirm against your arm, your neck. And there was
something that bit. Something in the hog shit was Frank's
thought.

Frank heard a sound. A different sound. It was the slow,
careful plodding of the mule's hooves, and another sound.
The hog, maybe.

They listened and waited and the sounds came closer, and
then Frank, lying there, trying not to tremble with anticipation, heard a whizzing sound. The rope. And then there was
a bray, and a scuffling sound.

Frank lifted his head slightly.

Not ten feet from him was the great white mule, the rope
around its neck, the length of it stretching up into the tree.
Frank could see Nigger Joe. He had wrapped the rope
around the limb and was holding on to it, tugging, waiting for
the mule to wear itself out.

The hog was bounding about near the mule, as if it might
jump up and grab the rope and chew it in two. It actually
went up on its hind legs once.

Frank knew it was time. He burst out of his hiding place,
and Leroy came out of his. The hog went straight for Leroy.
Frank darted in front of the leaping mule and threw his rope
and caught the hog around the neck. It turned instantly and
went for him.

Leroy dove and grabbed the hog's hind leg. The hog kicked him in the face, but Leroy hung on. The hog dragged Leroy across the ground, going for Frank, and as his rope become more slack, Frank darted for a tree.

By the time Frank arrived at the tree trunk, Leroy had managed to put his rope around the hog's hind leg, and now Frank and Leroy had the hog in a kind of tug-of-war.

"Don't hurt him now some," Nigger Joe yelled from the tree. "Got to keep him up for it. He's the mule leader. Makes him run."

"What the hell did he say?" Frank said.

"Don't hurt the goddamn pig," Leroy said.

"Ha," Frank said, tying off his end of the rope to a tree trunk. Leroy stretched his end, giving the hog a little slack, and tied off to another tree. Nearby the mule bucked and kicked.

Leroy made a move to try to grab the rope on the mule, pull him up short, but the mule whipped as if on a Yankee dollar, and kicked Leroy smooth in the chest, launching him over the hog and into the brush. The hog would have had him then, but the rope around its neck and back leg held it just short of Leroy, but close enough a string of hog spittle and snot was flung across Leroy's face.

"Goddamn," Leroy said, as he inched farther away from the hog.

For a long while, they watched the mule kick and buck and snort and snap its large teeth.

It was near nightfall when the mule, exhausted, settled down on its front knees first, then rolled over on its side. The hog scooted across the dirt and came to rest near the great mule, its snout resting on the mule's flank.

"I'll be damned," Leroy said. "The hog's girlie or something."

IT TOOK THREE DAYS TO GET BACK, because the mule wasn't cooperating, and the hog was no pushover either. They tied logs on either side of the hog, so that he had to drag them. It wore the hog down, but it wore the men down too, because the logs would tangle in vines and roughs, and constantly had to be untangled. The mule was hobbled loosely, so that it could walk, but couldn't bolt. The mule was led by Nigger Joe, and fastened around the mule's waist was a rope with two rope lines leading off to the rear. They were in turn fastened to a heavy log that kept the mule from bolting forward to have a taste of Nigger Joe, and to keep him, like the hog, worn down.

At night they left the logs on the critters, and built make-do corrals of vines and limbs and bits of leather straps.

By the time they were out of the woods and the swamp, the mule and the hog were covered in dirt and mud and such. The animals heaved as they walked, and Frank feared they might keel over and die.

They made it though, and they took the mule up to Nigger Joe's. He had a corral there. It wasn't much, but it was solid and it held the mule in. The hog they put in a small pen. There was hardly room for the hog to turn around. Now that the hog was well-placed, Frank stood by the pen and studied the animal. The beast looked at him with a feral eye. This wasn't a hog who had been slopped and watered. This was an animal who early on had escaped into the wild, as a pig, and had made his way to adulthood. The hog's spotted hide was covered in scars, and though he had a coating of fat on him, his body was long and muscular, and when the critter flexed its shoulders to startle a fly, muscles rolled beneath its skin like snakes beneath a tight-stretched blanket.

The mule, after the first day, began to perk up. But he didn't do much. Stood around mostly, and when they walked away for a distance, he began to trot the corral, stopping often to look out at his friend in the hog pen. The mule made a sound, and the hog made a sound back.

"Damn if I don't think they're talking to one another," Leroy said.

"Oh, yeah. You can bet. They do that, all right," Nigger Joe said.

THE RACE WAS COMING CLOSER and, within the week, Leroy and Nigger Joe had the mule's hooves trimmed, but no shoes. Decided he didn't need them, as the ground was soft this time of year. They got him saddled. Leroy got bucked off and kicked and bitten once, a big plug out of his right elbow.

"Mean one," Nigger Joe said. "Real bastard, this mule. Strong. He got the time, he eat Leroy."

"Do you think he can run?" Frank asked.

"Time to see soon," Nigger Joe said.

That night, when the saddling and bucking was done, the mule began to wear down, let Nigger Joe stay on his back. As a reward, Nigger Joe fed the mule well on grain, but gave him only a little water. He fed the hog some pulled-up weeds, a bit of corn, watered him.

"Want mule strong, but hog weak," Nigger Joe said. "Don't want hog strong enough to do digging out of pen, that's for some sure."

Frank listened to this, wondering where Nigger Joe had learned his American.

Nigger Joe went in for the night, his two wives calling him

to supper. Leroy walked home. Frank saddled up Dobbin, but before he left, he led the horse out to the corral and stared at the mule. There in the starlight, the beams settled around the mule's head and made it very white. The mud was gone now, the mule had been groomed, cleaned of briars and burrs from the woods, and the beast looked magnificent. Once Frank had seen a book. It was the only book he had ever seen other than the Bible, which his mother owned. But he had seen this one in the window of the general store downtown. He hadn't opened the book, just looked at it through the window. There on the cover was a white horse with wings on its back. Well, the mule didn't look like a horse, and it didn't have wings on its back, but it certainly had the bearing of the beast on the book's cover. Like maybe it was from somewhere other than here, like the sky had ripped open and the mule had ridden into this world through the tear.

Frank led Dobbin over to the hog pen. There was nothing beautiful about the spotted hog. It stared up at him, and the starlight filled its eyes and made them sharp and bright as shrapnel.

As Frank was riding away, he heard the mule make a sound, then the hog. They did it more than once, and were still doing it when he rode out of earshot.

IT TOOK SOME DOING, and it took some time, and Frank, though he did little but watch, felt as if he were going to work every day. It was a new feeling for him. His old man often made him work, but as he grew older he had quit, just like his father. The fields rarely got attention, and being drunk became more important than hoeing corn and digging taters. But here he was not only showing up early, but staying all day,

handing harness and such to Nigger Joe and Leroy, bringing
out feed and pouring water.

In time Nigger Joe was able to saddle up the mule with no
more than a snort from the beast, and he could ride about the
pen without the mule turning to try and bite him or buck
him. He even stopped kicking at Nigger Joe and Leroy, whom
he hated, when they first entered the pen.

The hog watched all of this through the slats of his pen, his
beady eyes slanting tight, his battle-torn ears flicking at flies, his
curly tail curled even tighter. Frank wondered what the hog
was thinking. He was certain, whatever it was, it was not good.

Soon enough, Nigger Joe had Frank enter the pen, climb
up in the saddle. Sensing a new rider, the mule threw him.
But the second time he was on board, the mule trotted him
around the corral, running lightly with that kind of rolling
barrel run mules have.

"He's about ready for a real run, he is," Nigger Joe said.

FRANK LED THE MULE OUT of the pen and out to the road,
Leroy following. Nigger Joe led Dobbin. "See he'll run that
way. Not so fast at first," Nigger Joe said. "Me and this almost
dead horse, we follow and find you, you ain't neck-broke in
some ditch somewheres."

Cautiously, Frank climbed on the white mule's back. He
took a deep breath, then settling himself in the saddle, he
gave the mule a kick.

The mule didn't move.

He kicked again.

The mule trotted down the road about twenty feet, then
turned, dipped his head into the grass that grew alongside the
red-clay road, and took a mouthful.

Frank kicked at the mule some more, but the mule wasn't having any. He only moved a few feet down the road, then across the road and into the grass, amongst the trees, biting leaves off of them with a sharp snap of his head, a smack of his teeth.

Nigger Joe trotted up on Dobbin.

"You ain't going so fast."

"Way I see it too," Frank said. "He ain't worth a shit."

"We not bring the hog in on some business yet."

"How's that gonna work? I mean, how's he gonna stay around and not run off?"

"Maybe hog run off in goddamn woods and not see again, how it may work. But, nothing else, hitch mule to plow or sell. You done paid me eleven fifty."

"Your job isn't done," Frank said.

"You say, and may be right, but we got the one card, the hog, you see. He don't deal out with an ace, we got to call him a joker, and call us assholes, and the mule, we got to make what we can. We have to shoot and eat the hog. Best, keep him up a few more days, put some corn in him, make him better than what he is. Fatter. The mule, I told you ideas. Hell, eat mule too if nothing other works out."

THEY LET THE HOG OUT OF THE PEN.

Or rather Leroy did. Just picked up the gate, and out came the hog. The hog didn't bolt. It bounded over to the mule, on which Frank was mounted. The mule dipped its head, touched noses with the hog.

"I'll be damn," Frank said, thinking he had never had a friend like that. Leroy was as close as it got, and he had to watch Leroy. He'd cheat you. And if you had a goat, he might fuck it. Leroy was no real friend. Frank thought Leroy was like most things in his life, just something to make do till the real thing came along, and so far, he was still waiting. It made Frank feel lonesome.

Nigger Joe took the mule's reins and led Frank and the mule out to the road. The hog trotted beside the mule.

"Now, story is, hog likes to run," Nigger Joe said. "And when he run, mule follows. And then hog, he falls off, not keeping up, and mule, he got the arrow sight then, run like someone put turpentine on his nut sac. Or that the story as I hear it. You?"

"Pretty close," Frank said.

Frank took the reins back, and the hog stood beside the mule. Nothing happened.

"Gonna say go, is what I'm to do here now. And when I say, you kick mule real goddamn hard. Me, I'm gonna stick boot in hog's big ass. Hear me now, Frank?"

"I do."

"Signal will be me shouting when kick the hog's ass, okay?"

"Okay."

"Ready some."

"Ready."

Nigger Joe yelled, "Git, hog," and kicked the hog in the ass with all his might. The hog did a kind of hop and bolted. A hog can move quick for its size for a short distance, haul some serious freight, and the old spotted hog, he was really fast, hauling the whole freight line. Frank expected the hog to dart into the woods and be long gone. But it didn't. The hog bounded down the road, running for all it was worth, and before Frank could put his heels to the mule, the mule leaped. That was the only way to describe it. The mule did not seem cocked to fire, but suddenly it was a white bullet, shooting forward so fast Frank nearly flew out of the saddle. But he clung, and the mule ran, and the hog ran, and after a bit, the mule ducked its head and the hog began to fade. But the mule was no longer following the hog. Not even close. It snorted, and its nose appeared to get long and the ears laid back flat. The mule jetted by the fat porker and stretched its legs longer, and Frank could feel the wind whipping cool on his face. The body of the mule rolled like a barrel. But man, my God, thought Frank, this son of a bitch can run.

There was one problem. Frank couldn't turn him. When he felt the mule had gone far enough, it just kept running, and no amount of tugging led to response. That booger was gone. Frank just leaned forward over the mule's neck, hung on, and let it run.

Eventually the mule quit, just stopped, dipped his head to the ground, then looked left and right. Trying to find the hog, Frank figured. It was like the mule had gone into a kind of spell, and now he was out of it and wanted his friend.

He could turn the mule then. He trotted it back down the road, not trying to get it to run anymore, just letting it trot, and when it came upon Nigger Joe and Leroy, standing in the road, the hog came out of the woods and moseyed up beside the mule.

As Nigger Joe reached up and took the mule's reins, he said, "See that there. Hog and him are buddies. He stays around. He don't want to run off. Wants to be with mule. Hog a goddamn fool. Could be long gone, out in the woods. Find some other wild hog and fuck it. Eat acorns. Die of old age. Now he gonna get et sometime."

"Dumb-shit hog," Leroy said.

The mule tugged at the reins, dipped its head. The hog's

and the mule's noses came together. The mule snorted. The hog made a kind of squealing sound.

THEY TRAINED FOR SEVERAL DAYS the same way. The hog would start, and then the mule would run. Fast. They put the mule up at night in the corral, hobbled, and the hog, they didn't have to pen him anymore. He stayed with the mule by choice.

One day, after practice, Frank said, "He seems pretty fast."

"Never have seen so fast," Nigger Joe said. "He's moving way good."

"Do you think he can win?" Leroy said.

"He can win, they let us bring hog in. No hog, not much on the run. Got to have hog. But there's one mule give him trouble. Dynamite. He runs fast too. Might can run faster."

"You think?"

"Could be. I hear he can go lickety-split. Tomorrow, we find out, hey?"

THE WORLD WAS MADE of men and mules and dogs and one hog. There were women too, most of them with parasols. Some sitting in the rows of chairs at the starting line, their legs tucked together primly, their dresses pulled down tight to the ankles. The air smelled of early summer morning and hot mule shit, sweat, perfume, cigar smoke, beer, and farts. Down from it all, in tents, were other women who smelled different and wore fewer clothes. The women with parasols would not catch their eyes, but some of the men would, many when their wives or girls were not looking.

Frank was not interested. He couldn't think of anything but the race. Leroy was with him, and of course, Nigger Joe. They brought the mule in, Nigger Joe leading him. Frank on old Dobbin, Leroy riding double. And the hog, loose, on his own, strutting as if he were the one throwing the whole damn shindig.

The mules at the gathering were not getting along. There were bites and snorts and kicks. The mules could kick backward, and they could kick out sideways like cattle. You had to watch them.

White Mule was surprisingly docile. It was as if his balls had been clipped. He walked with his head down, the pig trotting beside him.

As they neared the forming line of mules, Frank looked at them. Most were smaller than the white mule, but there was one that was bigger, jet-black, and had a roaming eye, as if he might be searching for victims. He had a big hard-on and it was throbbing in the sunlight like a fat cottonmouth.

"That mule there, big-dicked one," Nigger Joe said. "He the kind get a hard-on he gonna race or fight, maybe quicker than the fuck, you see. He's the one to watch. Anything that like the running or fighting better than pussy, him the one you got to keep the eye on."

"That's Dynamite," Leroy said. "Got all kinds of mule muscle, that's for sure."

White Mule saw Dynamite, lifted his head high, threw back his ears, and snorted.

"Oh, yeah," said Leroy. "There's some shit between them already."

"Somebody gonna outrun somebody or fuck other in ass, that's what I tell you for sure. Maybe they fight some too. Whole big blanket of business here."

White Mule wanted to trot, and Nigger Joe had to run a little to keep up with him. They went right through a clutch of mules about to be lined up, and moved quickly so that White Mule was standing beside Dynamite. The two mules looked at one another and snorted. In that moment, the owner of Dynamite slipped blinders and a bridle onto Dynamite's head, tossing off the halter to a partner.

The spotted hog slid in between the feet of his mule, stood with his head poking out beneath his buddy's legs, looking up with his ugly face, flaring his nostrils, narrowing his cave-dark eyes.

Dynamite's owner was Levi Crone, one big gent in a dirty white shirt with the sleeves ripped out. He had a big red face and big fat muscles and a belly like a big iron washpot. He wore a hat you could have bathed in. He was as tall as Nigger Joe, six foot two or more. Hands like hams, feet like boats. He looked at the White Mule, said, "That ain't the story mule, is it?"

"One and the same," Frank said, as if he had raised the white mule from a colt.

"I heard someone had him. That he had been caught. Catch and train him?"

"Me and my partners."

"You mean Leroy and the nigger?"

"Yeah."

"That the hog in the stories, too, I guess?"

"Yep," Frank said.

"What's he for? A step stool?"

"He runs with the mule. For a ways."

"That ain't allowed."

"Where say can't do it, huh?" Nigger Joe asked.

Crone thought. "Nowhere, but it stands to reason."

"What about rule can't run with the dick hard," Nigger Joe said, pointing at Dynamite's member.

"Ain't no rule like that," Crone said. "Mule can't help that."

"Ain't no rule about goddamn hog none either," Nigger Joe said.

"It don't matter," Crone said. "You got this mule from hell, given to you by the goddamn red-assed devil his own self, and you got the pork chop there too from the same place, it ain't gonna matter. Dynamite here, he's gonna outrun him. Gets finished, he'll fuck your mule in the ass and shit a turd on him."

"Care to make a bet on the side some?" Nigger Joe said.

"Sure," Crone said. "I'll bet you all till my money runs out. That ain't good enough, I'll arm-wrestle you or body-wrestle you or see which of us can shoot jack-off the farthest. You name it, speckled nigger."

Nigger Joe studied Crone as if he might be thinking about where to make all the prime cuts, but he finally just grinned, got out ten of the eleven fifty he had been paid. "There mine. You got some holders?"

"Ten dollars. I got sight of it, and I got your word, which better be good," Crone said.

"Where's your money?" Leroy said.

Crone pulled out a wad from his front pocket, presenting it with open palm, as if he might be giving a teacher an apple. He looked at Leroy, said, "You gonna trade a goat? I hear you like goats."

"Okay," Leroy said. "Okay. I fucked a goddamn goat. What of it?"

Crone laughed at him. He shook the money at Nigger Joe. "Good enough?"

"Okay," Nigger Joe said.

"Here's three dollars," Frank said. He dug in his pocket, held it so Crone could see.

Crone nodded.

Frank slipped the money back in his pocket.

"Well," Leroy said. "I ain't got shit, so I just throw out my best wishes."

"You boys could bet the mule," Crone said.

"That could be an idea," Leroy said.

"No," Frank said. "We won't do that."

"Ain't we partners?" Leroy said, taking off his seed salesman hat.

"We got a deal," Frank said, "but I'm the one paid Nigger Joe for catching and training. So, I decide. And that's about as partner as we get."

Leroy shrugged, put the seed salesman's hat back on.

THE MULES LINED UP and it was difficult to make them stay the line. Dynamite, still toting serious business on the undercarriage, lined up by White Mule, stood at least a shoulder above him. Both wore blinders now, but they turned their heads and looked at one another. Dynamite snapped at the white mule, who moved quickly, nearly throwing Frank from the saddle. White Mule snapped back at Dynamite's nose, grazing him. He threw a little kick sideways that made Dynamite shuffle to his right.

There was yelling from the judges, threats of disqualification, though no one expected that. The crowd had already figured this race out. White Mule, the forest legend, and Dynamite, of the swinging big dick, they were the two to watch.

Leroy and Nigger Joe had pulled the hog back with a rope, but now they brought him out and let him stand in front of his mule. They had to talk to the judges on the matter, explain. There wasn't any rule for or against it. One judge said he didn't like the idea. One said the hog would get trampled to death anyway. Another said, Shit, why not. Final decision, they let the hog stay in the race.

SO THE MULES and the hog and the riders lined up, the hog just slightly to the side of the white mule. The hog looked over its shoulder at Nigger Joe standing behind him. By now the hog knew what was coming. A swift kick in the ass.

Frank climbed up on the white mule, and a little guy with a face like a timber ax climbed up on Crone's mule, Dynamite.

Out front of the line was a little bald man in a loose shirt and suspenders holding up his high-water pants, showing his scuffed and broken-laced boots. He had a pistol in his hand. He had a voice loud as Nestor on the Greek line.

"Now, we got us a mule race today, ladies and gentlemen. And there will be no cheatin', or there will be disqualification, and a butt beating you can count on to be remembered by everyone, 'specially the cheater. What I want now, line of mules and riders, is a clean race. This here path is wide enough for all twenty of you, and you can't fan too much to the right or left, as we got folks all along the run watching. You got to keep up pretty tight. Now, there might be some biting and kicking, and that's to be expected. From the mules. You riders got to be civil. Or mostly. A little out of line is all right, but no knives or guns or such. Everyone understand and ain't got no questions, let up a shout."

A shout came from the line. The mules stirred, stepped back, stepped forward.

"Anybody don't understand what I just said? Anyone not speak Texan or Meskin here that's gonna race?"

No response.

"All right, then. Watch women and children, and try not to run over the men or the whores neither. I'm gonna step over there to the side, and I'm gonna raise this pistol, and when you hear the shot, there you go. May the best mule and the best rider win. Oh, yeah. We got a hog in the race too. He ain't supposed to stay long. Just kind of lead. No problems with that from anybody, is there?"

There were no complaints.

"All right, then."

The judge stepped briskly to the side of the road and raised his old worn .36 Navy at the sky and got an important look on his face. Nigger Joe removed the rope from the pig's neck and found a solid position between mules and behind the hog. He cocked his foot back.

The judge fired his pistol. Nigger Joe kicked the hog in the ass. The mule line charged forward.

The hog, running for all it was worth, surged forward as well, taking the lead. White Mule and Dynamite ran dead even. The mules ran so hard a cloud of dust was thrown up. The mules and the men and the hog were swallowed by it. Frank, seeing nothing but dust, coughed and cursed and lay tight against the white mule's neck, and squinted his eyes. He feared, without the white mule being able to see the hog, he might bolt. Maybe run into another mule, throw him into a stampede, get him stomped flat. But as they ran the cloud moved behind them, and when Frank came coughing out of the cloud, he was amazed to see the hog was well out in front, running as if he could go like that all the way to Mexico.

To his right, Frank saw Dynamite and his little ax-faced rider. The rider looked at him and smiled with gritty teeth. "You gonna get run into a hole, shit breath."

"Shit ass," Frank said. It was the best he could come up with, but he threw it out with meaning.

Dynamite was leading the pack now, leaving the white mule and the others behind, throwing dust in their faces. White Mule saw Dynamite start to straighten out in front of him, and he moved left, nearly knocking against a mule on that side. Frank figured it was so he could see the hog. The hog was moving his spotted ass on down the line.

"Git him, White Mule," Frank said, leaning close to the mule's left ear, resting his head against the mule's mane. The white mule focused on the hog and started hauling some ass. He went lower and his strides got longer and the barrel back and belly rolled. When Frank looked up, the hog was bolting left, across the path of a dozen mules, just making it off the trail before taking a tumble under hooves. He fell, rolled over and over in the grass.

Frank thought: Shit, White Mule, he's gonna bolt, gonna go after the hog. But, nope, he was true to the trail, and closing on Dynamite. The spell was on. And now the other mules were moving up too, taking a whipping, getting their sides slapped hard enough Frank could hear it, thinking it sounded like Papa's belt on his back.

"Come on, White Mule. You don't need no hittin', don't need no hard heels. You got to outrun that hard dick for your own sake."

It was as if White Mule understood him. White Mule

dropped lower and his strides got longer yet. Frank clung for all he was worth, fearing the saddle might twist and lose him.

But no, Leroy, for all his goat fucking and seed salesman hat stealing, could fasten harnesses and belly bands better than anyone who walked.

The trail became shady as they moved into a line of oaks on either side of the road. For a long moment the shadows were so thick they ran in near darkness. Then there were patches of light through the leaves and the dust was lying closer to the ground and the road was sunbaked and harder and showing clay the color of a poison-ivy rash.

Scattered here and there along the road were viewers. A few in chairs. Most standing.

Frank ventured a look over his shoulder. The other mules and riders were way back, and some of them were already starting to falter. He noticed a couple of the mules were riderless, and one had broken rank with its rider and was off trail, cutting across the grass, heading toward the creek that twisted down amongst a line of willow trees.

As White Mule closed on Dynamite, he took a snapping bite at Dynamite's tail, jerking his head back with teeth full of tail hair.

Dynamite tried to turn and look, but his rider pulled his head back into line. White Mule lunged forward, going even lower than before. Lower than Frank had ever seen him go. Lower than he thought he could go. Now White Mule was pulling up on Dynamite's left. Dynamite's rider jerked Dynamite back into the path in front of White Mule. Frank wheeled his mount to the right side of Dynamite. In midrun, Dynamite wheeled and kicked, hit White Mule in the side hard enough there was an explosion of breath that made Frank think his mule would go down.

Dynamite pulled ahead.

White Mule was not so low now. He was even staggering a little as he ran.

"Easy, boy," Frank said. "You can do it. You're the best goddamn mule ever ran a road."

White Mule began to run evenly again, or as even as a mule can run. He began to stretch out, going low. Frank was surprised to see they were closing on Dynamite again.

Frank looked back.

No one was in sight. Just a few twists of dust, a ripple of heat waves. It was White Mule and Dynamite all the way.

As Frank and White Mule passed Dynamite, Frank noted Dynamite didn't run with a hard-on anymore. Dynamite's rider let the mule turn its head and snap at White Mule. Frank, without really thinking about it, slipped his foot from the saddle and kicked the mule in the jaw.

"Hey," yelled Dynamite's rider. "Stop that."

"Hey, shit ass," Frank said. "You better watch . . . that limb."

Dynamite and his rider had let White Mule push them to the right side of the road, near the trees, and a low-hanging hickory limb was right in line with them. The rider ducked it by a half inch, losing only his cap.

Shouldn't have told him, thought Frank. What he was hoping was to say something smart just as the limb caught the bastard. That would have made it choice, seeing the little ax-faced shit take it in the teeth. But he had outsmarted his own self.

"Fuck," Frank said.

Now they were thundering around a bend, and there were lots of people there, along both sides. There had been a spot of people here and there along the way, but now they were everywhere.

Must be getting to the end of it, thought Frank.

Dynamite had lost a step for a moment, allowing White Mule to move ahead, but now he was closing again. Frank looked up. He could see that a long red ribbon was stretched across in front of them. It was almost the end.

Dynamite lit a fuse.

He came up hard on the left and began to pass. The ax-faced rider slapped out with the long reins and caught Frank across the face.

"You goddamn turd," Frank said, and slashed out with his own reins, missing by six inches. Dynamite and Ax-face pulled ahead.

Frank turned his attention back to the finish line. Thought: This is it. White Mule was any lower to the ground he'd have a bellyful of gravel, stretched out any farther, he'd come apart. He's gonna be second. And no prize.

"You done what you could," Frank said, putting his mouth close to the bobbing head of the mule, rubbing the side of his neck with the tips of his fingers.

White Mule brought out the reinforcements. He was low and he was stretched, but now his legs were moving even faster, and for a long, strange moment, Frank thought the mule had sprung wings, like that horse he had seen on that book so long ago. It was as if he and White Mule were floating on air.

Frank couldn't believe it. Dynamite was falling behind, snorting and blowing, his body lathering up as if he were soaped.

White Mule leaped through the red ribbon a full three lengths ahead to win.

Frank let White Mule run past the watchers, on until he slowed and began to trot, and then walk. He let the mule go on like that for some time, then he gently pulled the reins and got out of the saddle. He walked the mule awhile. Then he stopped and unbuttoned the belly band. He slid the saddle into the dirt. He pulled the bridle off of the mule's head.

The mule turned and looked at him.

"You done your part," Frank said, and swung the bridle gently against the mule's ass. "Go on."

White Mule sort of skipped forward and began running down the road, then turned into the trees. And was gone.

FRANK WALKED ALL THE WAY BACK to the beginning of the race, the viewers amazed he was without his mule.

But he was still the winner.

"You let him go?" Leroy said. "After all we went through, you let him go?"

"Yep," Frank said.

Nigger Joe shook his head. "Could have run him again. Plowed him. Ate him."

Frank took his prize money from the judges and a side bet from Crone, paid Leroy his money, watched Nigger Joe follow Crone away from the race's starting line, on out to Crone's horse and wagon. Dynamite, his head down, was being led to the wagon by Ax-face.

Frank knew what was coming. Nigger Joe had not been paid, and on top of that, he was ill-tempered and grudge-minded. As Frank watched, Nigger Joe hit Crone and knocked him flat. No one did anything.

Black man or not, you didn't mess with Nigger Joe.

Nigger Joe took his money from Crone's wallet, punched the ax-faced rider in the nose for the hell of it, and walked back in their direction.

Frank didn't wait. He went over to where the hog lay on the grass. His front and back legs had been tied and a kid about thirteen was poking him with a stick. Frank slapped the kid in the back of the head, knocking his hat off. The kid bolted like a deer.

Frank got Dobbin and called Nigger Joe over. "Help me."

Nigger Joe and Frank loaded the hog across the back of Dobbin as if he were a sack of potatoes. Heavy as the porker was, it was accomplished with some difficulty, the hog's head hanging down on one side, his feet on the other. The hog seemed defeated. He hardly even squirmed.

"Misses that mule," Nigger Joe said.

"You and me got our business done, Joe," Frank asked.

Nigger Joe nodded.

Frank took Dobbin's reins and started leading him away.

"Wait," Leroy said.

Frank turned on him. "No. I'm through with you. You and me. We're quits."

"What?" Leroy said.

Frank pulled at the reins and kept walking. He glanced back once to see Leroy standing where they had last spoke, standing in the road looking at him, wearing the seed salesman's hat.

FRANK PUT THE HOG IN THE OLD HOG PEN at his place and fed him good. Then he ate and poured out all the liquor he had, and waited until dark. When it came he sat on a large rock out back of the house. The wind carried the urine smell of all those out-the-window pees to his nostrils. He kept his place.

The moon was near full that night and it had risen high above the world and its light was bright and silver. Even the old ugly place looked good under that light.

Frank sat there for a long time, finally dozed. He was awakened by the sound of wood cracking. He snapped his head up and looked out at the hog pen. The mule was there. He was kicking at the slats of the pen, trying to free his friend.

Frank got up and walked out there. The mule saw him, ran back a few paces, stared at him.

"Knew you'd show," Frank said. "Just wanted to see you one more time. Today, buddy, you had wings."

The mule turned its head and snorted.

Frank lifted the gate to the pen and the hog ran out. The hog stopped beside the mule and they both looked at Frank.

"It's all right," Frank said. "I ain't gonna try and stop you."

The mule dipped its nose to the hog's snout and they pressed them together. Frank smiled. The mule and the hog wheeled suddenly, as if by agreed signal, and raced toward the rickety rail fence near the hill.

The mule, with one beautiful leap, jumped the fence, seemed pinned in the air for a long time, held there by the rays of the moon. The way the rays fell, for a strange short instant, it seemed as if he were sprouting gossamer wings.

The hog wiggled under the bottom rail and the two of them ran across the pasture, between the trees and out of sight. Frank didn't have to go look to know that the mule had jumped the other side of the fence as well, that the hog had worked his way under. And that they were gone.

WHEN THE SUN CAME UP and Frank was sure there was no wind, he put a match to a broom's straw and used it to start the house afire, then the barn and the rotten outbuildings. He kicked the slats on the hog pen until one side of it fell down.

He went out to where Dobbin was tied to a tree, saddled and ready to go. He mounted him and turned his head toward the rail fence and the hill. He looked at it for a long time. He gave a gentle nudge to Dobbin with his heels and started out of there, on down toward the road and town.

AUGUST OF 1959

William Nack

IN THE SUMMER OF 1959, not far from that old wooden bandbox known as Arlington Park, I awoke early one morning in my bunk in Barn 4A, descended the rickety staircase from my room, and there at once found myself living out the oldest and fondest of my youthful dreams. Arlington was a prosperous gambling hell northwest of Chicago, and I had already misspent a good deal of my boyhood prowling its grounds, first as a young horseplayer, later as a track photographer, and in the last few weeks as a stablehand working for the powerful Kerr Stables, cooling down the horses by walking them in circles after their morning workouts. Now it was the final week of July, and just the night before, in an unexpected turn of events, I had been promoted from hotwalker to groom—a

change that instantly threw me into the job of feeding, grazing, rubbing, and otherwise doting on four Thoroughbred
racehorses.

There were no Swapsian luminaries in this quartet. One,
named Vienna Doll, was a doe-eyed filly with long lashes who
had yet to show much interest in her work. Another, a once
brilliantly fast sprinter, was convalescing from a bowed tendon
and suffering a kind of long-faced melancholy brought on by
his idleness. The third, an English bred, as I recall, has long
since vanished traceless in the moors of memory. But then, of
course, there was the fourth halter hanging on my little string—
that princess of the blood, that mystery in fur, that elegant
zephyr of my summer known as Queen of Turf. Queenie, as I
called her then, was a leggy chestnut filly with a white blaze
down her tapered nose, a pedigree that waved the flags of
three Triple Crown winners, and a gusting turn of foot that
gave me hope that one day, perhaps, she might take me to that
one place I'd always wanted to go, to that charmed circle re-
served for all who came home winners at Arlington Park.

All that said, though, there was one disturbing thing:
Queenie had what old Doc Peters, the stable vet, once called
"a troublesome left knee." It was a flat but knobby gourd of
bone and gristle that had kept her in the barn through all
of her two-year-old year and was threatening now, as the end
of her third summer drew near, to keep her unraced and
untested to the end, a maiden forever in waiting. Everybody
who worked in that shed knew she was among the favorites of
her owner, Oklahoma oilman Travis M. Kerr, who was always
dropping by Queenie's stall whenever he came to town to
watch his horses run. At age fifty-seven, he was a droll, avun-
cular chap with noticeable jowls and eyes that twinkled when

he laughed. So far as I know, he had never missed a performance by the unrivaled pride of his racing life, the center of his string of well-bred Thoroughbreds—that smallish, homely, hickory-boned bay who swept tirelessly around the courses in a low, smooth, rhythmic stride that had become his hallmark as a racehorse, thrumming out a pace as neat and steady as the tick-tock needle on a metronome.

He was Round Table, the undisputed king of the Kerr Stables, Travis's simple nom de course, and by then a racing immortal heading for the sport's Hall of Fame.

We hired hands all called him RT. The horse's groom was a dark-skinned Argentine who looked like one of those wavy-haired Spanish dancers who kept time with castanets. Juan Alaniz barely spoke English and muttered oaths in Spanish while he worked, stomping around the dirt ring of the shed in front of the horse's stall and pausing only now and then to smoke a cigarette. He drank beer by the quart at night but he was up by five A.M. sharp and never missed a day at work. He would later become even better known as the groom of the 1978 Triple Crown winner, Affirmed, but Round Table was his first great horse, a monster already known by then as the best grass horse ever bred in America, the nation's Horse of the Year in 1958 and, through the summer of fifty-nine, the winner of a world-record $1.7 million in purses . . . and climbing; Juan was his corner man, his head cheerleader and caretaker, his feed man, his scold. The dark bay used to stand in his stall with his head out the door and sway back and forth like a zoo elephant, shifting his weight from the left leg to the right and back again, his neck and head swinging to and fro, until Juan would growl, in his fractured Pampas accent, "Stop eet, Roun' Tale!" The horse would freeze and almost sneer at

Juan through bared teeth, thrust from his mouth the thick, pink sausage of his tongue—here we hotwalkers would all stop and laugh—and then draw slowly back into the lampless cool of his stall.

Kerr usually showed up on mornings of the days that RT raced. Leaning slightly forward as he walked, his hands joined behind his back, he greeted trainer Bill Molter and the stable help with a nod and a merry smile; he gave the appearance of a shy Midwestern gentleman who liked nothing more than to trundle behind his lathered steeds as they swirled and snorted into winner's circles from California to Chicago, floating in their wakes and handing out, one by one, $50 tickets to win on his victorious charges. He doled them out by the fistful to all who happened to be around—to the ushers and grooms, to the hotwalkers and clerks, to the agents and their winning jocks, who wore like ancient heraldry his dirt-spattered silks. It was a bright and colorful world that encircled him with outstretched hands. Travis liked the racing and the roars of crowds but clearly he loved, too, the intoxicating smells of the liniments and lotions that wafted of a morning through the barns. He liked the reassuring sight of men at work—his men working on his horses. Loved watching the grooms on bended knees as they swabbed the healing unguents on his horses' legs. Liked it too when his little army of grays and bays and chestnuts and roans, all standing at attention at the doors of their stalls and waiting for him like a troop of cavalry, pricked their ears and stretched their necks and tried to hustle him for one more slice of apple. We hired help stepped out of his way when he came by. He was the reason that we all had work. So of course the whole shed folded into a burlap silence one morning in early August when Ray

Diaz, the stable's tough Hispanic exercise rider and jockey, called out to him: "Hey, Mr. Kerr! If I had your money, I'd be in bed with a two-hundred-dollar hooker every night!"

The old man turned away, red-faced as he pivoted, har-rumphing as he stepped into the feed room across from the rows of stalls. Molter, as proper and reserved as Kerr, barely managed to mount that half-crooked smile of his, finally look-ing up and shaking his head at Diaz, who was dancing by on a gifted, floppy-eared bay mare named Milly K.

"Enough of that, Ray," Molter said quietly. "Just watch what you're doin' with her."

All along the shed the grooms and hotwalkers slipped into their stalls to laugh at what Ray had said to Travis. "What the fuck is wrong with Diaz?" groom Paul Parker said up around the corner of the shed. "Is he nuts talkin' like that to the old man?" He swung the muck sack over his shoulders and car-ried it, wavering, to the manure bin out back. Jockey Bill Shoemaker sometimes came by, usually to ride a horse or visit with Molter, and always stopped long enough to slip a sugar cube to Round Table. That summer, as usual, he was the na-tion's leading rider in races and money won and he was riding RT in the Equipoise Mile a few days later.

The Shoe was nearing the milestone mark of 3,500 wins and there had been a flurry of notes about it in the papers. "When are you gettin' to that mark?" Paul Parker asked. "I'm gettin' tired of readin' about it."

"Not long now," said the Shoe. "Next week maybe."

Many jocks came by the Kerr Stables that year, hustling mounts from Molter. His barn was filled with fast horses, Round Table and Milly K aside, with flyers named Top Charger and Grey Eagle, Prince Blessed and Fightin' Indian

and Tall Chief II, a gangly gray router who had a displaced
cowboy as a groom. We swipes and hotwalkers used to head
to the races together in the afternoons and then return after
the ninth to gather at twilight outside the shed and graze the
horses on the patches of grass between barns. And at night
we'd sit in those little rooms above the shed, sprawling on
cots and chairs, and drink beer and smoke our Viceroys and
brag about our charges.

It was the greatest of all summers, by far, though touched
as it was by the darksome passage of the times, by the evanes-
cence of that familiar ghost called youth. I was spending it
where I'd decided to spend it months before—around the
most generous and seductive of all the planet's horses. I had
grown up around saddlebreds at a riding stable in a little town
called Morton Grove, fifteen miles southeast of Arlington, and
had passed my teens in the company of many of the world's
flashiest show horses, at venues from northern Indiana to
Kansas City to Chicago's South Side; in fact, I can say in truth
that I witnessed the final triumphant performance of the undefeated Wing Commander, the greatest of all five-gaited
saddle horses, in the Chicago Amphitheatre, December of
1955—the night he stormed past Bo Jangles and Tommy
Moore in front of a packed house that howled them round
and round again.

Those echoes linger yet today. As stunningly beautiful as
Wing Commander was, though, with his luminous dark coat
supplely shifting over great packs of muscle, he and his kind
had already become by then a thing of memory for me: Just
that summer past I had seen the chestnut beast that truly
kindled dreams. Sitting in the stands at old Washington Park,
I had watched Kentucky Derby winner Swaps hang it on

Traffic Judge in the fifty-five American Derby, and the sur-
passing finality of that performance—with Swaps plunging
home in the late-afternoon gloaming, his ears pricked forward and the sunlight playing off his golden coat, galloping
on to a new course record—had won me to the sport forever.

Now here I was, four years later, out of the grandstand and
in the show. I had toiled the first six weeks walking hots for
Molter, cooling them out in the wake of their morning works
and gallops, and ended up grooming a set of four only after
the stable had lost one of its most prized grooms, Rafael de
Coco Cortes, one morning in late July, when a squad of zeal-
ous federal agents swept through the racetrack grounds and
carried off all unpapered aliens. Among them was the artful
Rafael, Queenie's groom, a sad-eyed *mejicano* who left the
shed in cuffs and tears, glancing back at her and his three
other charges as he climbed into the government car, his rub
rags dangling from his pocket and his pitchfork still leaning
against the green-and-yellow webbing of Queenie's stall.

The stable foreman, a Luxembourgian immigrant known
to all as Mr. Hack, approached me at once. "You want dem
four horses?" he asked. "Better get over dere now. Two hundred and fifty dollars a month. Gotta be down here by five
thirty. Muck dem stalls and work dem rags. I want dem slick
as seals when dey go to the track. Now get to work dere, son."

So that is how, on a summer morning in 1959, I came to
take over the care and feeding of Queen of Turf and three of
her closest friends, none remotely as promising as she. I had
already been accepted as a freshman at the University of
Illinois, but now I wasn't sure what I wanted to do or where
I wanted to go. My father sensed that I was wavering. He
knew I loved the races and the horses and the footloose way

of life. He and my mother used to drive out to Arlington every weekend to play the horses and sit on wooden benches in the sun. She sat and knitted Christmas sweaters. Or read Agatha Christie. He hung on paddock fences and chewed the ends of half-smoked cigars. I joined them one afternoon. It was already early August and growing late. I told them I was thinking of taking off a year, of heading east with the outfit to New Jersey and New York.

"Round Table is going to Atlantic City for the United Nations Handicap and then to Aqueduct," I told them. "They're talking about running him in the Woodward again. Maybe the Manhattan Handicap. I was thinking I might tag along."

My mother set down her needles and closed her eyes. She pursed her lips and sighed heavily, arranging all the familiar wrinkles of her discontent. She had been a professional dancer and a ballet teacher when she was young and she had traveled east, too, and I reminded her of that: "Didn't you go to New York when you were young and dance in vaudeville with Pat Rooney? How old were you?"

"Don't give me that," she said. "My situation was very different from yours. My father died in that fire when I was thirteen and Nonnie never remarried. You know the story." I'd been hearing it for years. How he was run over by horses fleeing in a panic from a fire. How his body was laid out in the living room of their small, wood-framed house on Orchard Street in Chicago. How all the firemen in his engine company showed up in uniform to pay their respects. Joe Feeney left his widow and four kids to live on a fireman's pension. Ten dollars a month. Nonnie went to work packing dried fruit in a factory off Halsted Street. My mother, the oldest of the

four, went to New York to dance for a living. She was billed
as the Atlantic City Peach.

"I was making sixty bucks a week dancing with Rooney in
that troupe," she said. "I was living off Times Square with a
girlfriend and sending most of it home. That was big dough
in those days."

My father listened in silence. They were Chicago born.
Dollars were bucks and money was dough. She was Irish and
quick to fire, a wizard in the kitchen making stroganoff and
pies, a gardener of clinging roses and clematis vines. He was
German and Alsatian, by nature generous and kind, an elec-
trical engineer who had learned to make and read blueprints
by age eighteen. He was spare with words, never veering far
from the point. "Why don't you just join the circus and get it
over with?" he said.

"Can we talk about this?" I said.

"I thought we were," she said.

"I mean later . . ."

"So what's this new job you have?" he asked. "You say
you're a groom?"

The change of subject came as a relief. "Yeah. I got four
horses now," I said. "I don't just walk 'em anymore. Now I've
got four of my own. I clean 'em and feed 'em and put the
bandages on 'em."

He lit his cigar. "Got anything good coming up?" he said.

I smiled at my feet. My father never learned to read the
Daily Racing Form. The numbers were as arcane to him as
the stone drawings in a cave, a mystery of swirls and glyphs.
He divined his choices by the music of their names and by
how strapping they looked in the paddock and the post parade. He devoutly admired all tip sheets and touts. He knew

them all by name. He used to stop and cadge tips from an old blind man named Peaches who sat by the back entrance at Arlington and passed out the overnights to the horsemen scurrying to and from the barns and the paddock. Since June, through roaming the sheds and befriending stable boys, I'd already plugged my father into a few hot and buzzing wires of my own.

Let's see . . .

One night, a week after Round Table won the Citation Handicap at old Washington Park, Arlington's sister track south of Chicago, Juan Alaniz got into the beer with us and we drank late. Juan started talking about this filly that he rubbed, Our Special Jet, a daughter of the 1947 Kentucky Derby winner, Jet Pilot. She had won going three furlongs at Santa Anita in March but had twice run so poorly going five-eighths in May at Washington Park, fading both times after flashing early speed, that she looked hopeless going any distance beyond that. It was the night of Sunday, June 21, and she had been entered to run in the fourth race the next day, a five-and-a-half-furlong pop for three-year-olds.

Wrapped around yet another bottle of Pabst Blue Ribbon, Juan announced that she had lost eighty pounds since coming to Chicago, that the baby fat was gone and now she was fit. She had just worked five-eighths in a blistering fifty-eight seconds, Juan said quietly, and the clockers had missed it. "A good *feely!*" he said. "She *ween!*"

I was on the phone with my father early the next morning. He listened as I rhapsodized. "What's her name again?" he asked.

"Our Special Jet. Now don't go nuts betting on her. She's not a young Round Table."

"Thanks, kid," he said.

Of course he unloaded on her, at least for him, betting $50 to win across the board, and told his favorite bookie—a bartender named Vinnie who worked at the Metropole Hotel—that the little bay was a very good thing.

"My kid works in the Molter barn at Arlington," he recalled telling the bookie. "He said the same guy who takes care of Round Table also takes care of this filly. My kid and this guy Juan, they work together. Juan tells my kid that she's lost eighty pounds since coming from California and she'll run good today. She's worked a lot faster than the tab shows. He says she'll win."

Every boy should be his father's hero at least once, and that day belonged to me. The Calumet Farm entry of Desert Dream and Dasheen were odds-on, and the Jet got away at almost fifteen to one. What a race it was! Under Cowboy Jimmy Nichols, Our Special Jet was off slowly and bounding along in seventh around the far turn, six lengths off the lead, when Nichols cracked her hard and she took off. She was racing to the eighth pole when a hole on the rail began to close in front of her. For an instant she seemed to hesitate. I was hanging on the fence and gasped as her head came up. "Noooo!" I yelled. As though hearing my bellow, Nichols raised his whip and popped her once between the ears. Startled, she dropped her chocolate nose and thrust it flat into the breach. Nichols rode the hide off her the final two hundred yards. She wore down Miss Frio and Johnny Rotz in the closing yards and drew off to win it by a half length.

My mother and brother had come to the races together, just to watch her run, and as the filly hit the line we all clasped arms and danced along the grandstand apron to the winner's circle. Moments later, the lights on the tote board shouted their glorious message: $31 to win, $12.40 to place, $7.60 to show.

Next day, Vinnie greeted my father with a ten-pound ham, a quart of Wild Turkey, and a Metropole envelope filled with $1,125 in cash, the biggest score of his life. And with words that my father, filled with pride, repeated for a week: "That's a heck of a kid you got out there, Gordon. He pays attention. Tell him thanks from me. I was down for two bills. Your kid got me even for the year."

And then, glancing furtively about, Vinnie said, "Does he like anything out there today?"

Now, nearly two months later, we were straddling a bench in the grandstand and it was starting to rain again and he was asking about the horses I was rubbing.

I got up to leave. "I think I've got one that can run," I said.

"You think?"

"Well, Dad, she's never started, so you never know. But the word around the barn is she can run. She also has a problem. But I'll let you know."

"What's her name?" he asked.

"I'll call you when she's in."

"What's her problem?" he said.

"Minor, I think . . . I'll call you."

Over the next few days, the world around Queenie's stall grew busier. Mr. Hack, tugging on a pipe, seemed to drift past by the hour, like a watchman with a key, looking in on us as I dosed her with liniments and fussed around her feet and legs. Molter seemed to come by more frequently, too, running his hands up and down her knees and legs. Even Diaz hung around her cubicle one morning, watching me paint her shins and fluff her tail. Word around the barn was that Molter thought he'd found a spot for her a few days later, a tough six-furlong sprint for maiden colts and fillies, but he never said anything to me. I left Barn 4A only to sit in the stands and watch the races by myself, or eat alone at the backstretch kitchen—a sad fluorescence of scrambled eggs and hominy grits afloat on plastic trays and coffee dark as Oklahoma crude. Mostly, though, I rubbed and curried and shined my horses' coats, changed their buckets of water and beds of straw, lifted and picked their sixteen feet with a steel-pointed hook, wrapped their legs in bolts of protective cotton and elastic Ace bandages—and finally, as the late-afternoon sun fell in yellow curtains on the shed-row eaves, I took them from their stalls and marched them, one by one, to the lusher ribbons of grass outside the shed and grazed them there, thirty minutes each, tethered to them only by a shank of chain and leather clipped to the rings on their halters.

One morning, as the work wound down, I was gathering a pile of wet straw and droppings on a rug of burlap in front of Queenie's stall when I saw them at the end of the shed, in front of Round Table's place, the big three—Molter, Shoe-maker, and Kerr. Juan led the big horse out of the barn and they all followed him into the sun. It was Sunday, August 8, and the barn was in what can only be described as a state of mourning. Round Table had just suffered one of the most shocking losses of his career—a listless third-place finish in Saturday's Equipoise Mile, five lengths astern of a workaday animal named Better Bee. As important as the Equipoise Mile was, though, that race was but a prelude to the two big hundred granders, the Arlington and Washington Park hand-icaps, that loomed for RT over the next four weeks.

Things had not been going well in Barn 4A. A week ear-

lier, the stable's two most promising two-year-olds, Prince
Blessed and Grey Eagle, had finished fifteenth and nine-
teenth, with tongues hanging out, in the $100,000 Arlington
Futurity, far behind thirty-three-to-one shot T. V. Lark's hys-
terical neck victory over favored Bally Ache. But it was
Round Table's crushing defeat in the Equipoise that troubled
Kerr. And now the three men were walking up the shed
toward my four charges, and Molter was telling Kerr and the
Shoe what he had just told the *Morning Telegraph*'s estimable
Chicago correspondent, Joe Hirsch. I could hear them speak-
ing in hushed tones.

"Travis, I just can't say the way he ran was totally unexpected," Molter said. "He needed the race. I've got to get him
ready for those two big handicaps coming up here, and I had
to run him somewhere."

"He got off sluggish and never really got into it," said the
Shoe.

Kerr listened and walked on, silent and leaning like a
tower, his fingers twined behind his back. I slipped inside
Queenie's stall and drew a rub rag down her neck and shoulders. She was a twitchy bitch when you rubbed her, and she
started fidgeting and stepped left and tried to push me into
the wooden wall until I growled at her. I could hear the three
men coming closer. The cloth was damp. I wanted her to
shine. I began moving around her too fast and I could feel her
stiffen as she raised her head and threw a cow kick at me. I
saw it coming and slipped it like a fighter and ran the rub rag
from her stifle to her hock.

"Be careful of her," a voice said. "She'll kick hell out of
you." It was Molter at the door, his arms over the webbing,
Kerr and the Shoe standing next to him.

"Who is this?" asked the Shoe.

"Queen of Turf," said Kerr. "My baby. I bought her to breed to Round Table."

I had been studying Throughbred history and bloodlines since I was a kid, as a kind of hobby, and I fairly jumped at what he said. "She's sure got the pedigree," I said. "With those three Triple Crown winners hanging in her tree."

Kerr looked at me curiously. "Three?" he said. "I was looking at her papers just last week and I saw only one. She's out of a Count Fleet mare. . . ."

I could feel the line tighten and I loved playing it. "Yes, sir, three," I said. "Count Fleet won the American Triple Crown in 1943, and don't forget her sire, Alibhai, descends from two English Triple Crown winners. One, Gainsborough, won the English Triple in 1918. Rock Sand, a great-grandsire, won it back in 1903."

The silence was delicious. "Young man, how do you happen to know that?" Kerr asked.

"I been studying it since I was a kid."

"What are you now?"

"Eighteen."

"Are you going to college?"

"I think so, sir. This fall . . . unless I head east with the outfit."

Molter was not listening. "How's she doing?" he said.

"She's okay," I said. "A little nervous but she eats up every day and I graze her in the afternooons. That seems to settle her a little."

"Good," said Molter. "Hold her a minute." Ducking into the stall, the trainer dropped to his knees and ran a hand down her left front leg, starting along the forearm and then down over the knee, slowly, then back up to the forearm and over the knee again, feeling for any telltale signs of heat.

"The knee's been cool every morning," I said.

"Can she run?" said Shoemaker.

Molter nodded. "She's got speed but she's always had a knee, and I can't do much with her. Went three-quarters in eighteen and two out of the gate the other day. But a nice filly."

"I'd like to get her maiden broke before she kisses the groom," Kerr said.

Molter grinned and ducked out of the stall. He slapped his hands together. "I've got her in day after tomorrow," he said.

Stunned, I thought I may not have heard him right. "She's in? Tuesday?" Molter was silent.

"Am I ridin' her?" asked Shoemaker. The Shoe had no clue. His agent, Harry Silbert, made all his bookings.

"Harry says you're riding some Dixiana colt. Spy something? She just got beat here a head with Brooks on her. You'll be the favorite. Ray Diaz is on this filly."

The three men had started toward Round Table's corner when Molter turned around and came back.

"Where are you from, son?"

"Not far from here. A place called Skokie . . . I was around show horses most of my life. I groomed them and rode them too. . . ." The trainer said nothing and I went on: "And by the way, sir, while I'm at it, I'm supposed to go to school this fall, but now I'm actually thinking of heading east with the outfit . . . if that's all right with you."

Queen of Turf was listening at her door. Molter reached over and picked a hay briar from her whiskers. "We can talk about that later," Molter said. "Keep an eye on this filly. Watch that knee. Be careful when you wrap her bandages. The vet will come by to see her on Tuesday morning."

The whole gang, the hotwalkers and grooms, all went to the Loop on Monday night to see a movie, but I did not want to leave the filly and stayed close to the barn. I sat on a bale of straw in front of Queenie's stall and read the *Daily Racing Form*. I studied her race, the sixth, a competitive sprint over the dirt. Some of the pedigrees leaped off the page. Cuzin' Leslie Combs owned one filly, named Spinosa, who was by Count Fleet out of Crepe Myrtle, a daughter of the immortal Equipose and one of history's greatest broodmares, Myrtlewood. Another filly, named Swooner, was out of Swoon, the dam of Swoon's Son, the most brilliant racehorse of all the Thoroughbreds born in fifty-three. And then there was Shoemaker's horse, Spy Hope, a son of the nimble-footed Spy Song and heavily favored to win it. By nine P.M. I had moved to my room and was still reading when the Molter gang came home from the Loop. They rapped boozily on my door.

"You missed a great movie, man!" Jimmy Cooper cried. "*North by Northwest*. Cary Grant and . . . who was that blonde? Oh, yeah. Eva Marie Saint. They ended up climbin' all over Mount Rushmore! Damn, she's fuckin' gorgeous!"

Juan poked his head in the door. I had not spoken to him since Round Table had lost the Equipoise.

"Is RT okay?" I asked.

"Verry good!" he said. "He ween next time."

I told him I was running Queen of Turf tomorrow and asked him if he knew anything about her, if Molter had told him anything, if there was any scuttlebutt I didn't know. "Feely have a knee! Knee not good. She need more work. Maybe ween . . . maybe lose!"

Paul Parker knew nothing. He was a burly former airline mechanic who had migrated to the racetrack with aspirations to train his own string one day. He knew the filly had had her problems. "She's a three-year-old and has never started!" he said that night. "What the hell does that tell ya? Anyway, this outfit wouldn't tell ya a fuckin' thing anyway. She could be Count Fleet and you'd never know it. Ya look up at the end of the day and they'll all be cashin' bets."

A young veterinarian came by on Tuesday morning and went over her, one hock and knee at a time, but left before I had a chance to talk to him. She was cool all over. I called my father at ten A.M.

"Remember that filly I told you about? Well, she's in the sixth today. Her name is Queen of Turf."

"She any good?" he said.

"I told you she can run. And she seems fit. But the *Tribune* has her at six to one and she's in against colts. The thing also is that she has—"

He cut me off and I could hear the excitement in his voice. "I'm coming out there! I'll meet you where Peaches sits by the paddock gate."

I had never taken a horse to the paddock before, and Mr. Hack hovered over me from the moment I started to get her ready for the races. I took from the tack trunk my set of brushes and combs and picks and methodically, moving deliberately, I cleaned her from forehead to fetlocks, carefully removing all strands of straw from her mane and tail. She hardly turned a hair. She took the bit quite easily, and I slipped the bridle over the head and fastened the leather straps. I wet her forelock and her mane.

"Take her dere for a walk," Mr. Hack said. I unfastened the webbing on the door of her stall and led her into the aisle of the shed.

"Keep movin' dere," he said. I had barely finished one circuit of the barn when the announcement boomed over the loudspeaker: "Horsemen! Bring your horses to the paddock for the sixth race! The sixth race!"

The rest of that fateful hour has since graded into a kind of vaporous blur. Queenie was a princess walking over there, at least until she entered the paddock gate and saw the hundreds of people milling at the fence. She spun in circles and scattered the crowds. I spotted my father standing next to Peaches, the blind tout who had just tilted back his head and was blinking furiously at the black sky as my father whispered the good and welcome news to him. In the reverse order of things, my father had become like him, a guy on the inside, in the know. He loved getting the skinny and he loved giving it away. Glancing up now, he waved and smiled at me. In the paddock, under the elms, I walked my filly in a tight circle around a tree while Molter huddled with Diaz. Molter was a recovering jockey and he was mimicking a rider's hands as he gave Diaz instructions. He boosted the rider aboard and they were gone—out through the tunnel to the track.

My father had already had himself a day. He had bet $5 on a daily double that had paid off at the rate of $45 for $2— he fancied the winners' names, Leap Year Maid and Rash Statement—so he came to the sixth with more than $100 charring a hole in his baggy brown pants. I do not know the moment that it happened, the transfixing instant in space and time, but somewhere between the barn and the paddock— was it the fear of being wrong, the phantom clicking I heard in the knee, the surreal sense that I was only living a dream?—I was seized by a sudden loss of faith, by doubts that the filly had any chance at all.

"How much should I go for?" my father asked me.

"Don't bet her!" I said. "She won't win. She can't win!"

"But Bill, I—"

"Dad, she's got a bum knee. What can I tell ya? That's why she hasn't had a single start. The problem is, he can't train her hard enough to get her ready. Her last work—look at it here—was six furlongs in one eighteen and two. That's trotting horse time . . ."

His eyes widened. "I wish the hell you'd have told me!"

"I just did!"

"I mean this morning! Damn it, I called Vinnie and told him that you were her groom and you said she could run."

I was beginning to feel a bit light-headed. "Dad, who's this guy Vinnie?"

"The bartender at the place where I have lunch every day. He gave me the ham for giving him Our Special Jet. He makes book on the side."

"Is Vinnie connected to . . . ?"

He did not answer.

"Christ!" I said. "I gotta go."

It was three minutes to post. I left my father by the paddock fence and dashed out to the track. I could see the horses moving in file to the three-quarters pole on the backstretch. It was five thirty-four P.M. I slung the lead shank over my shoulder and stubbed out a smoke as they stepped into the gate. I looked over my left shoulder and saw hundreds of people standing at the grandstand rail with their arms draped over the fence. I was scanning the faces looking for my father's when the doors banged open and I dropped my head. I heard like a bark of thunder the caller's rising voice: "And they're off! Swooner is going to the front. . . . Queen of Turf is moving quickly into second!"

Good God! She's running! I thought.

I clambered to the top of the outside fence along the finish line and stared across the infield toward the backstretch. It was a blur of light. Swooner was leading by a length and a half as they raced for the turn. Diaz had Queenie under a snugging hold. She was bounding like a doe across an open field. And then, as they neared the far turn, Diaz clucked to her and struck her once with the whip. Queen of Turf charged forward in a rush and swept past Swooner easily. She quickly opened a daylight lead—one, two, three lengths. I held a pole with my left hand and punched the air with my right fist. Diaz glanced back and took another hold of her, steadying her around the turn and waiting for the straight. I could see the other jockeys in a panic, moving their hands and arms and asking their mounts for speed.

She was bounding along on her own, her motion clean and fluid as she skipped along. Nothing could get near her. Swooner could not keep up. Spy Hope and the Shoe were going nowhere. Crepe Myrtle's daughter Spinosa drifted rearward. Only Queenie was running now as they spun the turn. She turned for home in front by three. She picked up the beat again, extending the lead to four as they neared the eighth pole in midstretch. I leaped down from the fence as Diaz, crouched and pumping his hands, drove her through the straight.

She swept under the wire in front by three and a half lengths. In 1:11 flat for six furlongs. Easily. "Won in hand," said the chart.

Head down, listening for my father's voice, hoping he had ignored my pleas and bet her anyway, I strode quickly to the center of the racetrack, near the mouth of the winner's circle, and waited for her return. Moments later she came bouncing home to me. A beaming Diaz, breathing hard, pulled her up.

He waved his whip in the air, the high sign for the stewards, and then that unforgettable roar went up among the crowds, ringing up and down the grandstand.

The tote board was flashing her message to the winning $2 players: $27.40 to win, $14.40 to place, $7.80 to show.

I was beginning to feel vaguely wiggy. I heard the crowds shouting and the late-afternoon sun was beating down, and so I leaned on a fence by the gap of the tunnel leading back to the paddock and I heard a voice. It was Bill Shoemaker. He stopped next to me. A ring of dirt encrusted his mouth. He was only one shy of that thirty-five hundredth victory and going winless the rest of the day. He looked at Queen of Turf as she pulled up. "That's a nice filly," he said. "Is Molter around?"

"I haven't seen him," I said.

Diaz turned and stared at the board and slapped the filly on the neck. "Attagirl!" he said.

I led them into the circle to have our pictures taken. Almost fifty years have passed since that day, but I still have that winning photo—a frayed, fading black-and-white that shows an earnest-looking Diaz astride the horse and the assistant trainer, Larry Larkin, holding a half-smoked cigarette and smiling thinly for the camera. And there I am, at the filly's head, mouth dropped open and gaping at the camera like a dumb man, in a state akin to shock. You look more closely and right over there, barely visible beyond my shoulder, is my father, standing by himself in the distant crowd, wearing his flat-brimmed straw hat and looking at all the commotion surrounding a filly I'd just assured him could not win. After the winner's circle ceremonies had ended, I tried to lead her straight on home, but she was so hot and on the muscle that I had to keep stopping and turning her in small circles to rest my arms. We had just passed through the tunnel and we were spinning in circles through the paddock when I heard my father's voice. I glanced over. He was in a crowd, his angry pumpkin face aglow on the paddock fence, looking as hot and nearly on the muscle as Queenie herself. It was too late to take evasive action. Naturally, he came straight to the point.

"Thanks a hell of a lot, Bill! I think you better go to college. You'll go broke in this game!"

Back at the shed, Parker was madder than two hornets. Figuring he'd been frozen out of a nifty betting coup, he lumbered around the barn kicking buckets and bellowing in a rage that was almost comic: "What kind of a fuckin' outfit is this?! We're all left to eat that crap in the kitchen and they're toddlin' around Rush Street eatin' lobster fuckin' Newburg! Goddamn cheap, thieving bastards! You'd think they'd throw us a bone every once in a while." Paul got to cursing and yelling so loud that poor Mr. Hack hid in his room, Juan put on a white shirt and evaporated into the night, and Molter, well . . . he didn't come around until late the next morning.

Paul even figured I was in on it. I was doing her up in the stall that evening and he looked in. "Did you know about her?" he asked.

"No more than you knew. You said yourself she had problems. Hell, I even touted my father off her. He was yellin' at me to go to college when I was walkin' her back through the paddock. We all knew she had a knee! Molter was feeling it every day."

"Knee my ass," he said. "She run like fuckin' Count Fleet today."

He started to leave but then turned back. "Why the hell do you think they had Diaz on her instead of Shoemaker? Compared to Shoemaker, who the fuck is Diaz, anyway? Does that tell ya anything?"

"I heard Molter tell Shoemaker one day, they were standing right here, that he wasn't riding my filly because he had a call on that Dixiana filly."

"Bullshit! They wanted a price on her, and you don't put Shoemaker on a horse if you want a price on her. Don't you see that? They pulled a fast one today."

No one ever fessed up about any betting coup that afternoon, but it didn't matter in the end. Juan had it right. Round Table came back to win three big hundred granders that summer, the two handicaps at Arlington and the United Nations in Atlantic City, and two months later he was off to the breeding grounds of central Kentucky, retiring as the richest racehorse in history. Queen of Turf remains today the only horse I ever took to the races, and I never lost track of most of the characters who roamed that landscape in 'fifty-nine. Nineteen years later, as a racing writer, I shook Juan's hand just minutes after Affirmed won the Triple Crown at Belmont Park. Shoemaker finally did scale 3,500 wins that August; actually, he kept on riding for thirty-one more years, until 1990, finally riding to a record 8,833 victories.

Parker also got what he came looking for. When Molter died of a massive heart attack in 1960, a few months after taking over the training of T. V. Lark—that long shot who had whipped Bally Ache in the 'fifty-nine Arlington Futurity—the colt's handlers passed him right on to Parker, the Lark's groom. So Paul got his chance to train at last. He quietly turned the Lark into a grass runner extraordinaire—into America's 1961 turf champion, winning the title on the day he outran the mighty Kelso in the $100,000 Washington D.C. International. Travis Kerr eventually did breed Queen of Turf to Round Table, and from that union came two colts, Turf Table and Turfland, but neither ever amounted to much.

Travis died on June 8, 1970, of a cerebral hemorrhage, in Beverly Hills, and I always thought of him as having written much of the epitaph for that glorious summer.

A few days after Queenie broke her maiden, Mr. Hack came by my stalls and handed me a blank envelope. Inside was a $50 win ticket on Queen of Turf, worth $685. It was wrapped in a note that read, in longhand: "Three Triple Crown winners indeed! Keep up the good work and thanks for taking care of her. T. M. Kerr." That very night my father called to pass along a message. I could hear my mother laughing in the background. "Vinnie says he made the score of his life and wants to thank you," my father said. "Then he gives me another ham and this time a case of booze. He buys me a drink. Then he calls a hack to drive me home. The driver gets out and helps me carry the case to the door. Then he hands me an envelope and says, 'From Vinnie.' I open it up. Two hundred bucks in there!"

"So you had her after all and didn't know it," I said.

"Yeah, I had her after all," he said. "Sorry I got so hot out there. I saw that big payoff and, you know . . ."

"How do you think I felt?" I said. I told him about my envelope from Kerr. "I'll need that for school," I said. "I'm enrolling this fall."

"That's good to hear," he said. "It's the smart move. Your mother'll be happy to hear that."

"Sunday is my last day," I said. "I better go. Gotta graze that filly."

"Hey, Bill," he said.

"Yeah, Dad," I said.

"Got anything good this week?"

THE SELECTOR

Jerry Stahl

SCOWLING AT A SLOVENLY *schvartze* breast-feeding her baby in the betting line, Joseph Mengele stepped up to the cage and shoved a pile of quarters toward the blinking clerk. Hollywood Park was definitely a nest of bottom-feeders. But the bus stop to the track was three blocks from his condo in Reseda. Plus which, there was a barmaid at the Tack 'n' Tap who reminded him of Kristy Soderbaum, *Reichwasserleiche*— screen heartthrob during his lonely days in the Race and Resettlement Bureau, measuring Hungarian nationals' skulls to see if they had some Aryan in them. Should one of his selections turn out to be a thieving syphilitic, a doctor of race science would have to answer for it. Even then, he had a gift for picking winners.

"Number three, Humble Girlfriend. Twenty on the nose."

Mengele had managed, since moving to the Valley, to modify his Bavarian accent to something more akin to a speech impediment. Better to arouse pity than curiosity, even now. If anyone asked, he told them he burned his mouth on a hot coal as a child, like baby Moses.

On the overhead monitor, Carlo "Candy" Canero beamed from the winner's circle. The handsome Dominican patted his horse and stood on his toes to kiss a blue-eyed blonde. The blonde owned breasts that could feed an army. A perfect breeder. All she needed was a dirndl and milk pail, and she could have stepped out of a German Girls League poster. Mengele stared up at the mismatched couple, and what he saw was the future: her pure Nordic blood curdled in the veins of Canero's half-breed jockey spawn.

He brushed a speck of filth from the razor crease of his Perma Prest pants and waited for the man to count his quarters.

"Fifty cents short, bud."

Bud!

Three decades in America, and he still couldn't get used to the heinous familiarity of the lower classes.

Mengele thumbed a pair of quarters from the polished coin dispenser on his belt and hurled them in the metal scoop.

"Have a nice day," mumbled the little bureaucrat, sliding the former SS *Hauptsturmführer* his ticket.

"YOU LOOK HAPPY," said Rombach.

The flabby old Nazi's face was spidered with gin blossoms. Mengele wished he'd had him as a subject at Auschwitz, just so he could peel his skin off and study it. A durable fabric might be developed in the same pattern as Rombach's spray of exploded veins, the red zigzags glowing in his jowls like lava in concrete. With so many freezing to death on the Russian front—

"*Herr Doktor!*" Rombach teased, bringing Mengele back to the present. "*Herr Doktor,* you are smiling like a man with a secret. . . ."

"So I am," said Mengele, just to sound like he was paying attention.

In a man's last years, his mind flew all over, even if his body went nowhere. The tote board over the Bud Light poster said fifteen minutes to post time. Girlsintheoffice was three to two, Enchanted Evening four to one, Himbo Cutie hanging in at seven to one. According to Mengele's calculations, Humble Girlfriend—pegged by George Drakulas in the *Morning Line* at eighteen to one, and still there—was the sure winner. The doctor's handicapping was slanted toward standards of genetic purity. Blood.

"I *do* have a secret," Mengele said.

"Ho, ho! Do tell."

Rombach raised two fat fingers and signaled the barmaid—the same busty Aryan gal who made Mengele feel boyish. The doctor was glad he'd dabbed on lavender, a scent he favored when he'd made his selections on the Auschwitz ramp. Even later, naked and doomed, the women swooned. He didn't miss the power; he missed having somewhere to be charming in spite of it. Where was the harm in giving a lady a lift at the end? Did that make him evil?

Mengele smoothed his mustache in his hand mirror, then allowed himself an eyeful of the Racetrack Rhinemaiden as she approached. He almost told her how much she resembled the belle of National Socialist Cinema, but reason prevailed. Last week he'd asked her to the movies, and she'd laughed at him. Nevertheless, he gave her a tip on a Trifecta that won her $85. Today her sneer was almost friendly. *You big creamy* bitch, Mengele said with his eyes.

He looked at his watch and calculated. At eighteen to one, his twenty-dollar bet could net him $360. Maybe he would take Lisel—that's what he'd call her, whatever her name was—to a restaurant. A hotel, even. Live a little! After all those decades spent in cramped and stinking farmhouses in places like Asunción and São Paulo, why not?

He was ninety-two. They could sentence him to life, and it might be only fifteen minutes. He'd won.

Mengele closed his eyes. Imagined the crack of whip on rump as his pony broke from the pack and galloped over the finish line. He lightly tongued the tuft of mustache wedged in the gap between his front teeth. Visualizing a perfect tomorrow . . . until his countryman trampled on his fantasies for a second time with his grating whine.

"*Herr Doktor,* are you with us? I said do tell!"

Mengele sighed. "I will tell you, Heinrich, because with your short legs, you'll never make it to the window in time to place a bet. Are you sure your parents weren't *giftzwerg*?"

"I assure you. Mother was no picnic, but she wasn't a poison dwarf."

With that, Rombach looked slyly left and right, opened his *Racing Form,* and made a great show of "reading"—as if to throw off anyone watching. Everything was espionage with Rombach. He had, so he claimed, served as attaché to Rudolf Hess. Until Hess took it in his head to fly to Scotland on a one-man secret mission to meet with the Royal Family and secure peace. After which he was derided by the führer as a man in the grips of psychotic delusions.

Post-Hess, as Rombach admitted when he was in his cups, things went south. He was reassigned to Berlin and put in charge of securing jigsaw puzzles for Eva Braun. For now, he seemed to have forgotten that shameful admission. He cast his eyes about the nearby track rats with the grotesque entitlement of boy-toy SS men with their fingers on their triggers and a pleading mother at their feet.

In Mengele's experience, the real heroes of the Reich went to great lengths to play down their involvement; the pretenders preened as if they'd personally wiped Hitler's lips when he belched.

Kristy Soderbaum's doppelgänger handed him his drink—a glass of rosé wine from a box—and Mengele resigned himself to talking with his bumptious compatriot. At least he was able to speak German.

"Are you going to tell me how you know what you know, or do I have to beg?"

Mengele touched his lip, chewing the tips of his mustache despite doctors' warnings. "If you must know, I bribed a hotwalker. She's about nineteen. Lives in my building. I pay her sometimes. . . . This morning, she let me pretend I was her grandfather."

"Why, you old disciplinarian!"

"Not like that, you idiot. At the stables."

Rombach waggled his orange eyebrows. Why he chose that clownish color to paint over his salt-and-pepper pompadour was his own little mystery. Mengele found so much about him annoying, he tried not to dwell.

"She introduced me as Grandpa Hans," he went on. "Track security is lax. Like everything else in this country. I could walk in and shoot the horses up with oven cleaner, for all they know. When I was close enough I fed Girlsintheoffice a handful of ants."

"Ants?" Rombach dropped his paper and looked up. Forgetting, for the moment, that he was supposed to be throwing off Nazi hunters, defying the sons of Wiesenthal by appearing to do the jumble in the paper. "Did you say *ants*?"

"Something I learned from a Berlin horse trainer." Mengele plucked a hair from the gap in his front teeth and examined it. "He was also an amateur entolomologist. Felix Uttenstein. Fifth most successful ever at Hoppengarten."

"And he won because he fed his horses ants?"

"Of course not. Sometimes he used wasp venom. The man had a theory that cockroaches were, ultimately, the most superior species. Because they could adapt to Apocalypse. He published a paper saying Gregor Samsa was a genetic precursor. For that he got his own cot at Buchenwald."

Rombach's face flushed. "Sorry, *Doktor*, you lost me on the last curve. . . ."

Mengele put the hair in his pocket and sighed. "Let me tell you a story."

"Now? But *Herr Doktor*, the next race—"

"Shush! Listen and you might learn something."

Rombach swallowed guiltily and Mengele began.

"In 1936, as a joke, Henry Ford asked der führer if he wanted him to place a bet for him in the Kentucky Derby. Der führer, who didn't understand jokes, felt he had to pick the right horse, to show the superiority of German intellect. In crisis, he turned to Otmar von Verschuer, my mentor at the Kaiser Wilhelm Institute of Human Genetics and Eugenics, to determine the winner on the basis of probability. Von Verschuer asked yours truly, an up-and-coming racial hygiene ace, to do the heavy lifting."

Mengele paused, drawing in a full breath. It was a glorious thing to relive one's life. Though tragic to have no one to relive it with. His own son, Rolf, had pretended Mengele'd dialed a wrong number when he called to tell him he wasn't dead. But still . . .

Rombach cleared his throat. "Pardon me, *Herr Doktor,* can you tell your story and walk? Call me old-fashioned, but I hate watching the race on TV when I'm at the track."

Mengele, slightly stung, nodded and held out his arm. Rombach yanked him up and he stood unsteadily as a trio of green-blazered track security guards squeezed by into the bar. One of the no-necks apologized to Mengele for brushing against him. That was the difference between Germany and America, right there. In America, authority wants to look benevolent. The Nazis wanted it to look godlike. A joke, if you ever saw a picture of Göring.

"Here's the kicker!" Mengele shouted in Rombach's ear as they made their way down the crowded ramp to the stands. "At the same time the führer was consulting the party's top racial scientists, he'd also asked Hanussen, his personal clairvoyant, to give *his* pick for the Derby. Hanussen's prognostications depended heavily on Nostradamus, who, apparently, could predict the fiery chariots of the millennium and the winner in Kentucky with equal alacrity."

"Equal what?"

Rombach cupped a hand over one cauliflower ear, trying to listen and dodge what seemed like legions of lumpen souls headed in the other direction. No doubt all the rich whites were up in the clubhouse or in private boxes.

"Not important," Mengele shouted back, fighting deep indignation. "The point is, der führer staged the bet as challenge between the supernatural and the scientific. On my shoulders, as von Verschuer took no pains to spare reminding me, was der führer's future allegiance: Would he cleave to reason, or would he, like Himmler, succumb completely to the occult?"

Without realizing, Mengele fondled his uneven lip hair again.

"It was during this period," he confided, barely dodging a blue-hair bent double over a wire garbage bin, "I began the habit of mustache-chewing. Inevitably I would swallow a few follicles, which, over time, assembled themselves like plucky ghetto resistors into a single, deadly mass and nearly killed me."

No memory of wartime atrocity burned with as much hot misery as that moment, in Valley General, when the smarmy MD—not knowing that he was treating a historical figure— smirked at him and said, "I'm afraid you have a hairball."

The doctor, he could still recall, smelled like breath mints and rancid salami, and owned the classic elongated nose, furry ears, and back-sloping forehead of the Semite. It was clearly all the ER Jew could do not to laugh in his face as he explained. "I'm sorry, sir, but it appears as if all the hairs you've gulped have formed what the medical books call a bezoar, which is blocking your lower bowel."

Mengele willed his jaws still at the memory and saw a young redhead smiling his way from the row in front of them. Hah! He still knew how to make a woman weak. To this end, he tried to smile back, but his smile would not come. It was more and more disconcerting, the way the past had begun to blend with the present, until both were rendered unpleasant and disorienting.

"You're doing it again!" Rombach snapped. "You're chewing!"

"Thank you." Mengele nodded curtly. "Now, where were we?"

"I'm not sure."

The pair had to watch where they walked. Dozens of drunken, desperate souls had already begun the futile process of sifting through the tickets tossed on the ground after the last race, hoping to find, against all odds, a discarded winner.

"I remember! We were talking about ants," Rombach blurted proudly. "What I want to know is, were they red or black?"

"Are we both senile?" Mengele wondered aloud.

"What?" yelled Rombach.

"Javanese black," said Mengele, feeling a migraine on the horizon. "*Dolichoderus bituberculatus*. What you do, you hollow out an apple, fill it with black ants, and feed it to the horse. In fifteen minutes the animal's digestive juices work through the meat of the fruit, freeing the insects. The first bite will make the horse start moving. The faster it moves, the more they bite."

Rombach was so stunned he stopped moving and just stared. Mengele took his expression as wonder, and his looming despair lifted. He couldn't resist a twinge of pride as he continued.

"I was able to time it, so they started biting at the exact moment Girlsintheoffice took her morning workout. With those pincers in her gut, she had the fastest clock of the day. They thought she was hopped up but she tested clean. So now all the money's on her."

"But who did *you* bet?"

Mengele hesitated, then came out with it. "Humble Girlfriend."

"You're kidding!" Rombach looked like he was going to

wet himself. He consulted the *Racing Form*, then looked up in confusion, "Why?"

"Breeding."

"What? Her mother might as well have pulled a wagon. She's straight off the leaky-roof circuit."

"I'm not talking about the horse," said Mengele, as if addressing someone mildly retarded. "Or not just—I'm talking about the jockey. He was Aryan on three sides. Helmut Schmid."

"I understand," said Rombach, almost pleading now. "But surely you must have checked the filly."

"Of course," said Mengele, "that's why I was trying to tell you about 1936. My research. Whatever the creature—the only hope of survival is genetic purification."

For a strange moment, Mengele's eyes softened. His voice sounded almost gentle. "Sometimes, when I'm shopping at Whole Foods, I look around all the shelves full of pills devoted to 'detoxification' and I think, *'If only der führer could have lived.'* I picture Hitler running his fingers through a barrel of bulgur, nodding with tears in his eyes at these blood purifiers. What were we trying to do, after all, but purify the blood of the fatherland?"

"One man's murder is another man's de-tox."

"Yes! Leave it to the Americans to make it about the individual. The genius of making the process as simple as popping a pill. Of course der führer would have taken one. Hitler, the vegetarian, would have sooner kissed a rabbi on the lips than admit chicken into his system. He worked hard at purity. He had to!

"As with all the dark-haired, dark-eyed fathers of the putatively Nordic fatherland, the blood in all the top Nazis' veins was suspect. None were Thoroughbreds. And yet you couldn't join the SS unless you could prove your purity back to 1750. The führer—and this, to me, is a sign of his greatness—would have been hard-pressed to vouch far beyond half a century. Goebbels declared Germany der führer's bride. But the marriage would not have been allowed under his own laws of Aryan family hygiene.

"Can we not assume that horses, too, have a master race?"

THEY FOUND SEATS ON THE METAL SLATS of the grandstand, where Rombach instantly began to sweat. The sky shone a painful blue. A clown entertained children at the rail. What kind of parents thought bringing children to see them gamble away rent money was an uplifting outing? These were the breeds that made eugenics necessary. Hitler understood: For the state to maintain greatness, it had to breed its own citizens. When had the clown become part of the races?

The sun pounded down with what felt like hatred.

"*Gott,* this heat," moaned Rombach.

"The runic foundation of Nazism, according to Himmler, is sun worship."

"Don't go highfalutin on me. I saw you giving the eye to Fräulein Big Tits in the bar."

Mengele cringed. "If you act like a pig, people will think all Germans are pigs. Did you ever think of that?"

Rombach held up his pink hands.

"Bend me over and spank me, *Kommandant.* After wiping out six million and change, we wouldn't want them to think we don't mind our manners."

"Easy on the beer, comrade. I am simply saying, despite the Aryans' esteemed ancestors in the Nordic isles, when is the last time you heard of a high-level Nazi going anywhere but south? Not a single one tried to hide in Iceland."

Rombach belched, and Mengele decided he had ample reason to kill Mrs. Hitler's ex–puzzle procurer if he had the chance. The man's behavior was appalling.

"Do you want to hear about 1936 or not?"

"Absolutely," said Rombach, with no enthusiasm whatsoever.

"Fine. So there I am," resumed Mengele, "three weeks to pick a winner, and—"

"Wait! There she is!"

Rombach gawked at the jockeys angling their horses into the starting gate. Humble Girlfriend, the roan three-year-old ridden by Schmid (green and white, green cap) eased into her spot on the outside as easily as a coin in a slot. Then Rombach looked up and gave a start.

"Oops-la!" he exclaimed. "Looks like Girlsintheoffice has been scratched."

Mengele felt the other man's eyes on him as he checked the board.

"To think"—sighed Rombach—"all those ants died in vain."

Mengele shrugged. "Go ahead and mock. There is no sacrifice too great or too small for perfection of the species. Humble Girlfriend is going to win going away. She's got the blood. And so does her jockey."

"You studied all this, and you *still* couldn't me give me a tip?"

"I'm noticing an edge, Rombach. Do we need to talk?"

Something in the way Mengele said this made Rombach lean backward, as if to get as far away as he could without overtly moving. Out of fang range. He snuck a short dog of schnapps out of his pocket and knocked some back. Booze made him voluble.

"The problem is, you're not heartwarming, *Herr Doktor.* I respect you, but you make me feel uneducated. Perhaps that's genetic. The jealousy of the unwashed for the elite. Did you study a lot of winners?"

"You learn more from losers," said Mengele, eyeing Rombach with undisguised disgust. "Winners are not as expendable. What you want are anomalies. Things I learned researching horseflesh for the Derby stood me well later, at Auschwitz/Birkenau."

"Ah, der Zwillings!"

"No twins on the farm. In this way human breeding differs from horses. Twin foals are one in ten thousand. During the third trimester the placenta can't cope. The mare births four weeks early. But there are other conditions, hundreds when you really delve into it, the study of which could pave the way for development of a superhorse. Just as I did in the camp, I studied nature's mistakes."

"You mean you sifted through the trash." Rombach snickered, then caught himself. "Forgive me, *Herr Doktor.* I'm nervous. I've lost a lot of money already. One more dog and I'll be a *financial* anomaly."

Mengele waved away the apology with his program. "You want to talk finances? Our money came from John D. Rockefeller. He'd already poured trainloads of cash into eugenics research and implementation all over America. By 1930, twenty-seven U.S. states had compulsory sterilization for 'inferior races.' Hitler was just playing catch-up!"

"I like Ike," said Rombach inanely, but Mengele was too involved to notice. His eyes fixed on some middle distance over the infield as he rhapsodized, oblivious to the adrenalized buzz of bettors all around him. "With all those dollars, I was able to turn an old stud farm into a working horse laboratory. In one month I rounded up a corral of genetic head defects: aniridia, parrot mouth, wryneck. Then I expanded to skin and reproductive deformities. Curlycoat, mallenders. Atresia coli and cryptorchidism."

"Crypto-what? They're going to be running in a minute."

"Cryptorchidism. Abnormally small testicles. Are you blushing, Herr Rombach?"

"No, yes . . . It's just . . . You had a concentration camp for ponies?"

"I prefer the term 'mutant rodeo.' " Mengele ran his tongue over his mustache and winced. "I thought it would be wonderful for local children. Then one boy came down with hysterics at the sight of a goitered colt. He thought it had two heads. After that, word spread. . . ." Suddenly his mood shifted, and he stared at his own hands with wet eyes. "During the years when I did not see my son, Rolf, I wrote him a little children's book called *Daddy Beppo, The Funny Horse Farmer*, and mailed it to him in Günzburg. I never knew if he received it."

But Rombach wasn't listening. The array of horseflesh before him was too enticing. "Stella by Starlight is having a little trouble," he announced, as fans up on the rail roared approval at the skittish chestnut.

"That filly's not letting anybody put her in a box, even temporarily."

Finally, the bugle sounded. Vic Stauffer let out his nasal "And . . . they're off. . . . Enchanted Evening to the lead followed by Pillowbiter, with Tallulah's Bag at the rail and Himbo Cutie caught four wide."

"Oh, God," groaned Rombach. He sat with his head

bowed, pressing a ticket to his forehead, as if praying to whatever God held sway over Inglewood. But Mengele stared past him. At the clubhouse turn, Humble Girlfriend, in semi-respectable fifth, looked to be flattening out. Her strides were shortening, as if she were already exhausted at the quarter.

Rombach came out of his prayerlike stupor. Mengele noticed that he'd vomited on his shoes while praying.

"Who won?" he hollered over the trackside roar.

"Ask me in a minute," Mengele yelled back.

"I mean the Derby."

The doctor stared at him, as if gauging his interest. Seeing his earnest look, Mengele produced a red felt-tip.

"I ruled out all the Jewish jockeys immediately," he explained, repeating a formula as he jotted it down on a mustard-streaked napkin. "Percentage of Heritability for Training equals V due to Heredity over V due to Heredity and Environment times a hundred."

"And it's Bottoms Up, Himbo Cutie, and Enchanted Evening down the stretch."

"What happened?" shouted Rombach.

The horses thundered toward the wire. Humble Girlfriend, now at the rear, seemed to be looking for flowers in the dust as she galloped. "It was a fluke." Mengele sighed, showing no emotion at the photo finish in the making. "It was a Jewish sweep. Bold Venture was the winner. Owned by Morton Schwartz. Trained by Max Hirsch. Ridden by Ira Hanford. All bar mitzvah boys. Never happened before. Never since. Certainly not in Germany—where the führer banned Jews as jockeys in 1933."

"So you fucked up. I'm surprised you're still alive. And the clairvoyant?"

"Hanussen picked the winner." Mengele allowed himself a rare smile. "For this triumph, der führer had him shot. Hitler already suspected his magician was a Jew. But this clinched it."

"How?"

"Himmler, that master spiritualist, had a premonition that Hanussen had made the sweep happen, to humiliate the fatherland."

"But that's insane!"

"True. But just in case, two in the head."

"And it's Enchanted Evening by a nose!"

Amidst general roars of disbelief and delight, Rombach looked desperately around and tore up his ticket. "Typical," he said as he reached in his pocket. "I saw you circle her name, so I put all my money on Humble goddamn Girlfriend. She might as well have waited for a taxi."

Mengele kept his eyes on Rombach's hand in his pocket. He knew at once that he had a gun.

"You're going to shoot me because I lost you a bet?"

"In a manner of speaking. But not because of the bet. Because I'm a Jew."

"*Rombach?*"

"Is dead. I'm Hi Steiner. Mossad. My grandmother's maiden name was Shulvitz. She was a twin. Maybe you remember. Heidi and Sheila Shulvitz. You sewed them together back-to-back. Grandma Heidi's spine looked like it took short-range machine gun fire."

"I was researching skin grafts."

The man now called Steiner spit on him.

"Bush has faith-based science. You had faith-based sadism."

Mengele made no effort to wipe the saliva from his shirt. "So this is how it ends?"

"Please. You Nazis are all are so fucking operatic."

Looking around, the man now called Steiner saw that all the other racegoers were preoccupied with cashing or tearing up their tickets. He discreetly bit the top off a full syringe, created a screen with his sports jacket, and jammed the needle into Mengele's neck. The doctor didn't flinch. Steiner had missed the jugular. He pulled the needle out, then tried again, this time hitting the vein.

"And you Jews are all so predictable," Mengele said, his voice disturbingly steady. "AIDS-tainted blood? I'll be dead before I ever have a symptom."

"It's not tainted. At least not to me. It's my blood. One hundred percent *Judenblutt*. Now running in your veins."

Mengele's face grew pale. Then began to purple. For perhaps the first time in his life, he felt helpless.

But Steiner wasn't done. Fishing through his pockets, he produced a tube of superglue. He doused the doctor's bald spot, then slapped on a yarmulke.

"What was that?" Mengele hissed, managing to sound testy and petrified the same time.

"Yarmulke," Steiner replied. "Superglued to your scalp. I was thinking yellow star on your arm, but that's so old-fashioned. This way folks'll think you're one of the tribe."

Mengele's face betrayed a twitch. "What do you want to me do?"

A batch of smiley Enchanted Evening bettors shimmied by. Steiner kept his voice low. "There's always suicide."

"I call that cowardice."

"You could call it extermination. Technically, you are now part Jew."

"My own Final Solution. Elegant."

Steiner just patted his pockets to make sure he had everything. "Death or degradation. Even money. Same choice you gave us."

He stepped past Mengele, toward the throng heading up the ramp to the bars and betting windows. But at the last second, he leaned down and whispered, "Now you know what we know. When you get out of the camp, you still can't get out of the camp."

Then he disappeared into the crowd.

A HALF HOUR AFTER THE LAST RACE, track security got a call: An old man was still in the stands, babbling about how he'd made his selections.

Lots of times guys who lost their shirts couldn't bring themselves to leave. The world of brokeness was out there. But this was different.

The uniformed guard loomed over him and cackled into his walkie-talkie. "It's some old Jew. Hurry up. Looks like the rabbi pissed himself."

RACING GODS AND WILD THINGS

John Schaefer

When Worlds Collide

One of the things I've liked about the track since becoming an alleged grown-up is that it's a completely different world from the one I've inhabited professionally. The world of public radio—which in the 1980s at least seemed full of earnest, sensitive men with beards—was my musical home. But I felt like a changeling, inserted into that nest by some bizarre cigar-chomping, *Form*-slapping cuckoo. I suspected I had more in common with the denizens of Aqueduct and Belmont, who wouldn't know what to make of a Mahler symphony but could yell, "Come on with that six!" at orchestral volume. My profession and my obsession were light-years apart. Over the years, though, I've found that the worlds of music and the track have intersected in some unexpected ways.

First there was Irwin "Bud" Bazelon. A classical composer—and a writer of the sort of ferocious music that scared most classical music fans away—Bud came into the WNYC studios one day in the early nineties to talk about a group of new works he'd recorded. One was a symphony, which he'd subtitled *Sunday Silence*. We got to talking, reminiscing about the epic battles between Easy Goer and Sunday Silence during the Triple Crown chase of 1989. Like most New York racing fans, we shared the opinion that despite ample evidence to the contrary, Easy Goer really was the better horse, and that he was hurt simply by Pat Day's inability to produce a decent ride when it counted. And it turned out that *Sunday Silence* wasn't the first horse-based piece Bud had written. Many years earlier, he had written a Churchill Downs Concerto, for rock band and orchestra. The piece, from the early seventies, now sounded hopelessly dated. Didn't matter, though. *This* was a composer I could deal with.

The story of Bud's career as a composer actually begins at the track. Apparently, Bud had a big score one day in the early 1960s. I mean, really big—like, hire-the-New-York-Philharmonic-to-read-through-one-of-your-pieces big. And that, the legend says, is precisely what Bud did. It jump-started his career, and at a time when most composers (especially of such thorny, dissonant, "modernist" music) had to teach in order to make ends meet, Bud made his living as a composer. It was such a great story that I never had the heart to question him about it. (Though I did wonder how someone could win that much money in the days before most exotic wagers were even available, and how one went about hiring the august NY Phil to read through an unknown composer's music, and how that reading would lead to a career, since the orchestra was too traditional to play any of Bud's newfangled music anyway.) At any rate, Bud Bazelon died in 1995, and I for one am happy to leave the story as is.

A few years after Bud's death, a large manila envelope appeared in the daily mail bin. By 2000, all music submissions came as CDs—even the homemade ones. No one used cassette tapes. But it was clear from the feel of the envelope that there was a cassette inside—a cassette without any case protecting it. This was not the sign of a serious professional musician, and I was about to set it aside when I noticed the name on the return address. Curiously, the sender's name was Ragozin, the same name as the man responsible for the high-tech handicapping tool known as "the Sheets." I opened it, and inside was some of the lowest-tech material I'd seen in years: a hand-labeled cassette, three pages of cramped, old-fashioned typing—and a copy of an old *New Yorker* profile of betting guru Len Ragozin.

His homemade cassette, Ragozin wrote, was full of arrangements and improvisations on traditional folk songs, like "The Drunken Sailor," played on a synthesizer and recorded in his apartment. This was too good to put on a pile for later listening. I put it in the rarely used cassette deck. It was, as expected, a completely amateurish recording. But *amateur* doesn't just mean nonprofessional. The word originally means doing something for the love of it. (Most of us are amateur bettors, for example.) Len Ragozin's synthesizer folk songs were amateur in both senses of the word: low-fi home recordings made with cheap equipment, but also arrangements that were done simply for the love of playing familiar old tunes in a personal way. It was strangely touching.

In his letter, Ragozin explained that he'd been doing this work for years, just for his own enjoyment. He knew the recordings were subpar, and he wasn't asking for airplay anyway.

But he *was* sending the tapes to see if I could suggest any way for this music to find a wider audience—a group that might be interested in playing the arrangements live, perhaps. Or even recording them properly. Maybe, he wrote, I knew of a young female musician who might be interested in his music.

I wasn't sure what to make of this last bit.

We corresponded briefly—I'm afraid I didn't know any musicians, young and female or otherwise, who were itching to play "The Drunken Sailor" in *any* arrangement—and then moved on. What impressed me about Len Ragozin, though, was that this man, who had created some of the most gnomic, mysterious, and (to me) impenetrable handicapping tools ever devised, had managed to keep separate a part of his life where he could indulge in a simple love of music. I had now crossed paths with two men who seemed to be at home in both of the worlds I lived in, and while each was respected within a small circle of friends, I began to wonder if there were someone a bit more widely known who also shared these interests. In early 2005, a routine interview with a successful songwriter took an unexpected detour, and my question was answered with an emphatic yes.

Wild Thing

Even if you don't know Chip Taylor's name, you know his international hit. By the time I was nine, I could sing three different versions of "Wild Thing"—the Troggs' original smash and two novelty versions by the Hardly Worthit Players "sung" by actors pretending to be the leading contenders in the 1968 presidential race (Democrat Robert Kennedy and Republican Senator Everett Dirksen). While I was thus employed, Chip Taylor was beginning to find his way into horse racing. Royalties from "Wild Thing," along with another top-twenty hit called "Angel of the Morning," meant that he had a stake to play with, and he intended to use it. Taylor had already begun his apprenticeship in the art of handicapping the races with his acting teacher. (Chip's brother, Jon Voight, would put those acting lessons to arguably better use.) One weekend he made a spreadsheet, trying to codify the lessons he was learning at the track. "It was the greatest insight I ever had," he recalls. "I was trying to prove something, and ended up proving something else. If you had a horse who raced after being off for three or four weeks, and then he came back ten days later, that was a really powerful tool for certain levels of claiming horses." Blessed with an analytical mind, Chip found early success combing the entries at Belmont and Aqueduct for a single horse worth betting on. He also found that early success meant that most bookies would stop taking his bets after a few months.

But one bookie didn't drop Chip Taylor from his client list. "I was beating this guy almost every month," Chip says. "Twenty-four months out of a twenty-five-month stretch, this guy would come by to pay me. Not only that, he would give me Christmas presents, bottles of champagne, or cognac . . . Finally I said to him, 'I don't understand, I keep beating you but you're always happy to see me.' Well this guy worked for the Meyer Lansky operation, and he says, 'Hey, Chip, we're not dumb over here. After the first two months of you beating us, you became the biggest moneymaker we have. Every time you bet, we bet twenty times as much on the same thing.' They were all real happy that I won."

In the 1970s, the record industry went through a number

of wrenching changes, and Chip Taylor and his record company fought over the direction of his music. They wanted more top-twenty hits; Chip was interested in his own personal form of Yonkers, New York–based country music. If he'd been playing twenty years later, the press would've termed him "alt country" and he'd have had a big following. But in the 1970s, Chip Taylor was too far ahead of the curve. He and his label parted ways, and shortly after that Chip left the music business.

He soon found that picking one horse a day was very different from being at the track all day and staring at nine fields of horses. He started keeping records of track biases, and kept an eye out for races with unusually fast internal fractions. Then in the early 1980s, he joined forces with Ernie Dahlman, the so-called Wizard of Odds and one of the most successful horse racing bettors in the world. Their partnership would last for fifteen years, during which time they were given their own private room and teller at the Long Island OTB branch that served as their office. Dahlman once told the *New York Times,* "My approach is ridiculously rational. I'm looking for the obvious winner. He [Chip] was more of an artist. He'd study everything about a horse looking for the fifty-to-one shot who could get second or third." Like all gamblers, Chip was looking for an edge. In the 1980s, access to speed figures could give you an edge—Ernie Dahlman used the Brown Sheets and the Ragozin Sheets, and even amateurs like me would make our own. But Chip found something less obvious.

He was at Belmont Park, watching the horses in the paddock getting ready for a race, when he noticed that one of them seemed to be walking differently. "I called Ernie and I said, Ernie, there's a horse here wearing these shoes—I don't know what the hell they are, but he looks like he's up on his toes." Bettors would later come to know these shoes as "bends," or more precisely, "quarter-inch bends." The back of the hind shoes are turned down a quarter inch, providing better traction for the horse (think Thoroughbred cleats), especially on wet tracks. But in those days, as Chip recalls, "they were more like half-inch or three-quarter-inch bends. And it became a big factor, knowing who was using those shoes—even when it wasn't wet." For a while, he says, keeping track of shoes was the biggest moneymaker they had.

Eventually, Taylor and Dahlman moved into racing their own horses. They employed Michael Hushion, then just starting out, as their primary trainer—and he used mud caulks and bends on everything. Hushion also used Richard Migliore as his "go-to" jockey—a trainer/jockey combo that would be successful for years. As a horse owner, Chip saw all the chicanery that went on behind the scenes: running horses that weren't ready, holding a horse back, or using a "joint" or buzzer to shock an animal into a final spurt of energy. Sometimes it struck uncomfortably close to home.

"I had a horse out at Turfway Park, in Phoenix," Chip says. "I was touring through the area [though he didn't record, he did still play live gigs occasionally], and I stopped in because my trainer, a guy named Mel, had my horse entered in a race. So I walk into the paddock, and the trainer and the jockey are talking. Mel sees me and I walk over and shake his hand. Then I turn to the jockey, and he just looks at my hand. Then he looks up at Mel, and looks back at my hand. Now Mel is looking at me, and I said, 'Oh, man, Mel, you are *not* using a joint on my horse.'"

Still, a good gambler wants an edge, and being an owner

occasionally provided a legal one. Taylor and Dahlman claimed a horse named Alpine Music for $20,000, and "right away, we realized he was *good*. So we waited a few weeks, and we had Mike [Hushion] drop him into a fifteen-thousand-dollar race and use a different jockey." With their main rider off and a suspicious drop in class, the owners were suggesting that Alpine Music wasn't in peak condition. "All the newspaper writers were saying something must be wrong. So he's going off at three to one, and we're waiting and waiting until the last minute, then Ernie and I bet like crazy. He ended at eight to five, but he won by something like twenty lengths—and nobody claimed him." Then they bumped the horse up to a $30,000 claimer next time, and won that too.

The Racing Gods

The racing gods seem to have smiled on Chip Taylor and Ernie Dahlman. But for the most part, these twisted, sadistic deities delight in finding ever new, ever more creative ways of crushing the souls of their followers. It can't be something as simple as making one's horses run slow—no, there's no sport, no *art* in that. And make no mistake, the racing gods are artists, capable of exquisitely delicious torments. But they do occasionally spare a quick grin for a lucky few. One such person is my brother Jerry. Since he has never had an unexpressed thought in his life, he is a vastly entertaining companion at the track, where he will tout a horse in increasingly ebullient fashion, until his "blue plate special" comes staggering home at the back of the pack. Although good at math, he has never learned to make speed figures. (Why should he, when he could just look at mine or, after the mid-nineties, the *Daily Racing Form*'s?) And he is a veteran ticket ripper.

Some horseplayers save losing tickets. A big score can appear on your income tax, and if you have losing tickets you can offset your winnings. And sometimes at the end of the day it's useful to review your bets to see where your betting strategy went wrong. (That's the theory, anyway. In practice, they end up taking up badly needed space in the underwear drawer.) But other players, denied the thrill of a win, will settle for the smaller satisfaction of ripping their tickets in half and flinging them to the ground. Jerry has always done this with alarming regularity. In short, he will impress no one with his handicapping prowess. But God, can he get lucky sometimes. Take the 1970 Kentucky Derby, for example. I'm eleven, Jerry's ten; we're watching the post parade on TV, and he idly announces the fact that he likes the name Dust Commander. We then watch that horse win the Derby, at something like twenty to one. Fine. But my dad, apparently feeling that this constituted good handicapping technique, gave Jerry *two whole dollars*.

Since this is a racing gods story, it involves a bet that Jerry got wrong. It was winter of 2003–2004, and Jerry had stopped at Aqueduct on his lunch hour. He was not doing well, and had just about run out of cash. With no further appetite for the live fare at Aqueduct, he tried a race at Calder, the Florida track being offered via simulcast. No luck there either. Down to his last buck, Jerry decided that since he couldn't pick a winner, he'd let the machine do it. He went to the automated betting machine, put in a one-dollar voucher, punched in a one-dollar superfecta bet on the next race at Calder, and instead of picking the four required horses himself, hit "Quick Pick."

I was at work when Jerry called. He was clearly agitated as he recounted what happened with his bet. "The ticket had this sixty-to-one shot in the first spot," he said. "So I figured, great, that'll never happen, and I started to leave." He hadn't watched the race, but by the time he got to the grandstand exit, by the last TV screen, the winning numbers were posted. There, in the first position, was Jerry's sixty-to-one shot. "Then I start looking at the rest of the ticket. I've got another long shot in second, and I look up and he's there too! Now I'm looking at the third number, and I've got that too!" There was apparently a photo for fourth place, to round out the superfecta, and Jerry was left with a minute to ponder what he was holding. "All I could think was, I got greedy. I couldn't pick a winner, and now I'm trying to pick a superfecta. If I just stuck to the triple I would have had a huge winner! But no. I had to go for the superfecta. Now I need the three horse—another long shot—to come up. So I'm looking at the screen, and I'm going, 'Come on three, come on three.' And the number comes up. It's four."

At this point, because it was Jerry, I waited for him to say that the INQUIRY sign went on—but no, the results were official. Because he had gone for the home run, Jerry had missed a big triple payoff. Even halving the triple, since he'd only bet a buck, Jerry would've stood to make a couple of thousand dollars. Like any good gambler, Jerry now had to make the torture complete. "So I'm waiting to see what the payoff is on this superfecta," he told me. "And when they come up, the superfecta has my first three numbers, and then instead of the four, it says 'all.' I never saw that before—do you know what it means?" And it was then that I realized, to my horror, where Jerry's story was leading. He had not hit the superfecta—but neither had anyone else. So they were paying out to anyone who had picked the first three horses. Jerry's ticket was a winner . . . but Jerry was a ticket ripper.

"Jerry," I said carefully, "'all' means that no one picked the right combination. Your ticket was a winner." I paused, afraid of what I'd hear next. "Do you still have it?"

"Well, I didn't know what 'all' meant, so I took the ticket to a machine and stuck it in. And it said, 'Take to cashier.' So I brought it to the cashier."

Ah, now this was more like it. "How much?"

"I'm standing here with seventy-five hundred dollars in my pockets," he practically yelled. (I should add that he was still in the grandstand when he made this loud announcement, and that when he said $7,500 in his pockets, he didn't mean something nice and secure, like a cashier's check. He had wads of cash coming out of every available pocket.) The racing gods had smiled, and Jerry had cashed a 7,500-to-one bet. On a ticket that he didn't pick. And that didn't even have the winning numbers on it.

Sometimes I hate this game.

Wild Things Again

June 5, 1999. Belmont Park. Charismatic is going for the Triple Crown. The reformed claimer has captured the attention and the affection of hundreds of thousands of otherwise uninterested Americans, but many veteran bettors are suspicious of the horse's ability to win at the mile-and-a-half distance. Chip Taylor is one; I am another. As I would learn years later, we would both settle on the same alternative: Lemon Drop Kid. But we were about to have two very different experiences of this Belmont Stakes day.

Chip had returned to the music scene in the mid-1990s,

giving up the life of the professional gambler. On that June day, Chip Taylor was in midtour, and his swing through the East had put him back in New York for a short time. He had no intention of playing the races until a couple of friends expressed an interest in trying to hit the Pick-Six and asked him to help with what looked like a contentious series of races. Chip had a history of success with the Pick-Six: He once confidently bet the same Pick-Six ticket three times; six races later, each ticket was worth about $30,000. But his first reaction was to say, "Guys, I'm not doing that anymore. I don't have all my stats and records." His friends were persistent, and soon, looking over the card, Chip found himself liking Lemon Drop Kid in the Belmont Stakes. The horse had flashed potential, but had not yet proven he could win at the top level and was likely to be a long shot. Several of the other races seemed to be reasonable betting propositions, too. Chip constructed a series of bets around Lemon Drop Kid.

Meanwhile, I decided that since I was having trouble picking one, I was not going to try to pick six. This proved to be a good decision as the sequence began with a nine-to-one winner that I did not have. Two short-priced favorites followed. (I was looking for value, and watched my horses run second and then third.) Then it was bombs away: Kashatreya pulled off an unlikely upset over the speedy Artax in the race before the Belmont Stakes, and in the big event itself, Lemon Drop Kid scored a $61 upset, keying some enormous payoffs in the various exotic betting pools and knocking out most of the Pick Six gamblers. When two-to-one East of Easy won the final race, Chip Taylor and his friends were celebrating a good day. The Pick Six payoff was over $282,000, and Chip's share completely paid for his tour.

I, on the other hand, was having a dismal day. Lemon Drop Kid had won, at twenty-nine to one, but I'd bet him only in exactas, none of which contained the even more unlikely Vision and Verse, who finished second. I trudged out of Belmont Park with one or two stray bills left in my pocket and my binoculars weighing heavily around my neck. A train ride later, I was climbing the stairs from the busy terminal at Atlantic and Flatbush avenues, with my binoculars hanging from my wrist, when I felt a tug. A large man wearing a windbreaker and a doo-rag on his head had grabbed the binoculars and had now reached the step I was on.

"Gimme the glasses or I'll blow your head off," he said quietly. A quick glance around showed that the busy staircase was magically empty. Another man climbing past glanced over, quickly glanced back, and hurried up. There was, incredibly, no one else there. I had no real idea whether this guy was carrying a gun or not, but I was not about to find out. Besides, once on the street we'd be in broad daylight on a huge intersection where one could usually find a cop. I gave up the binoculars, and then followed him up the stairs from a safe distance.

Once aboveground, I continued following the thief, thinking that even if he had a gun he wouldn't use it on a crowded street. (I followed from across the street, though, just to be sure.) Once or twice, he turned and made a menacing gesture, and after a block of this I realized I was now close to the local precinct house, just off Flatbush. I turned and went to file a police report. I had forgotten what a long, dreary procedure that is, even when a threat of gunplay is involved, and by the time I left, the sun had set. I resumed walking home. I turned off Flatbush onto Eighth Avenue, dark and tree-lined and almost devoid of traffic, and I was around the corner from my apartment when someone shouted, "Hey!" behind me. I turned, and there, coming toward me, was a dark figure. I could just make out the doo-rag, the bulky windbreaker, and around his neck, my binoculars.

"Hey—was that you?" he said in a challenging voice. I had had a bad day—a long, bad day—and now I did something stupid. I stopped and turned toward him. "Yeah. That was me."

He came right up and said, "What if that was my sister or something?"

Clearly he was up to something, but I had no idea what. "What the hell are you talking about?"

Now it was his turn to be surprised. "Well, what are *you* talking about?"

"Those binoculars—they're mine." I pointed to his neck. He paused momentarily, suddenly realized who I was, and then began to laugh. To make an even longer story short, there followed perhaps the friendliest mugging in the history of Brooklyn, as I was offered the chance to buy back my own binoculars. I explained that I'd had a rough day at the track and had little money left. That was okay, he said; five bucks would do. Actually, now that we were in the middle of the exchange, ten would be better. He needed to buy new shoes, he explained, lifting a sneaker to reveal that it was in fact separating from its sole. I sensed that this could've gone on until I'd lost both my remaining money and the binoculars, so I quickly handed him my ten-dollar bill and grabbed the glasses, advised him to stay off the streets for the rest of the night, since I'd described him to the police, and hurried to the corner as nonchalantly as I could before sprinting home.

My wife said it was a great New York story. And that was

when it occurred to me: I had had a losing day, but I was not coming home a loser. They say that a good day at the track is the only thing better than a bad day at the track, but that's not quite right. If you're not going to win $30,000 in an afternoon, maybe the next-best thing is to come home without the usual whiny tales of hard luck ("my horse got DQ'd" or "I picked the winner but got shut out"), but with that most prized possession of the veteran horseplayer—a good story.

Why I Love This Game

Like most bettors, I am convinced that I have had more than my fair share of tough beats. Meet another horseplayer, and it is a reliable way to get the conversation going. We are a community, but we are a community united by a psychological amusement park of affection, desperation, hope, cynicism, and existential acceptance. A probe of our collective psyche will make some future therapist's reputation someday.

More than just a community, horse racing is a world unto itself. This is by no means an original observation. Anyone walking through the backstretch at a major track, along streets and lanes named after famous horses, watching the steady movement of humans and animals going about their business in a way that is fundamentally unchanged over the past three centuries, might feel that they've stepped into an alternate universe. That feeling is perhaps strongest at Saratoga. Sportswriter Red Smith's famous line on how to get to Saratoga—". . . drive north for about 175 miles, turn left on Union Avenue and go back 100 years"—has the ring of truth to it. In twenty-three years of spending at least some, and often all, of August at Saratoga Race Course, I have seen plenty of evidence that it exists apart from the world around it. Saratoga seems to have its own weather, for one thing. In fact, it took a storm of truly apocalyptic fury there to foil the racing gods and grant me a score that I didn't deserve. It was 1988—my wife and I had decided to spend all of August just outside Saratoga, swimming in Sacandaga Lake and going to the track—and I had played a relative long shot in the race preceding the John A. Morris Handicap. The horse was seven to one or thereabouts, and I'd bet him in two daily doubles, one with Grecian Flight, and the other with Clabber Girl, the two speedy, standout fillies in a small and otherwise nondescript field. When he came home in front, I was certain to win a decent double.

Then a sudden squall blew in. The skies turned black and slightly green. Lightning struck the flagpole in the infield and bent it almost in half. In the backyard, the smell of burning pine indicated that one of the towering trees had also been struck, though not felled, by lightning. Horses whinnied in fear as they were herded off the track. The electricity failed, and anyone who was outside ran into the grandstand in a desperate and unsuccessful attempt to get out of the lashing rain, which was blowing sideways through the grandstand and clubhouse. After twenty minutes the storm passed and the lights came on. But the track had virtually washed away, and for the first time since the Civil War era, races at Saratoga were canceled. Later, on the ride back to Sacandaga Lake, we would see no evidence of a storm. The squall had apparently settled over the track and provided us with our own meteorological display. The real world was largely unaware of it.

It took a while to figure out what was happening with outstanding tickets, but eventually I received two consolation daily double payouts, one for each of the horses I'd bet in the John A. Morris. Each one was a bit under $30, but it was money I felt I'd stolen from the cosmos when the John A. Morris Handicap was run the next day, as an exhibition race, and the only two horses capable of winning it finished last and next to last.

Even more striking was the Great Blackout of 2003. Jerry and I were eyeing the race monitor and a beckoning neon beer sign more or less simultaneously. Suddenly there was no monitor feed. (Although strangely, the neon beer sign stayed on.) Lights and betting machines failed, and the tote board was ominously dark. The PA system never stopped, though, and we were soon informed that there had been a fire in New York City and that electricity throughout the eastern part of the state was out. This was, as it turned out, both inaccurate and unsettling to those of us who were still skittish from the 9/11 attacks. Fortunately, there was a more pressing issue to take our minds off such things: We had horses picked in the next race. They were, it now seemed, mortal locks, absolutely the most certain winners of our lives. When could we bet on them?

After about fifteen or twenty minutes, power came back. The little bubble of racing history that is Saratoga went about its business. But leaving the track dumped us back into the real world, where we found streetlights out, stores closing, and lines forming at supermarkets and convenience stores for ice, canned goods, and anything resembling candles or flashlights. Power would be out until late that evening in some areas, the next day in others. But at Saratoga Race Course, it seemed, the world had intruded for only a brief time before the weight of history and obsession had forced it back out.

Once I became a dad, I found it harder to get away to the track during the other eleven months of the year. But Saratoga has remained a family tradition—in more ways than one: Our older daughter's name is Saratoga. When she was born, this occasioned a blurb in *Sports Illustrated* and a fair amount of local press coverage, especially when she made her first trip to her namesake track at age six months. Now fourteen, she already has a treasure trove of memories: Julie Krone giving her a pair of autographed goggles at Belmont, then recognizing her and coming over to tousle her hair outside the paddock at Saratoga two weeks later; watching the mighty Cigar's final victory, also at Belmont; and of course, the beginnings of her own collection of tough-beat stories.

Our younger daughter, Bella, has begun stockpiling memories too. Getting jockeys' autographs one day, she took a liking to Mark Guidry, who must've said something nice when he signed her program. She came back yelling, "Daddy, I wanna bet on Mark Gidoody! Mark Gidoody, okay?" Well, Gidoody's final mount of the day was almost twenty to one, and wouldn't you know it, he won. Bella now had a stake for her own betting, and she managed that stake for a week and a half, and still had a few bucks left at the end of our vacation. Not bad for a nine-year-old.

Mark Guidry didn't win another race for her, though Bella faithfully bet on him. Of course she was disappointed, but here's the great thing about this game: Both she and her sister are also afflicted with Railbird's Amnesia. This now-familiar phenomenon makes you forget the fact that you left the track hating this game; the next day you remember that one glorious victory, which will inevitably happen again next time, or the gallant near miss that could only be a harbinger of successes to come. As I write this, it is June, and it will be another five weeks before we head upstate, but already the two of them are champing at the bit. They can't wait to hate this game again.

THE GRAVEYARD
OF JIMMY FONTAINE

Jason Starr

WHEN I STEERED MY PIECE-OF-SHIT ninety-six LeBaron
onto the racetrack exit on the Northway I already felt like a
loser. I never won at Saratoga. The races were impossible to
handicap, with horses shipping in from every top track in the
country and long shots winning left and right. I knew I had a
better chance of taking the six hundred and whatever bucks I
had in my pocket and buying scratch-offs or, better yet, tossing the bills out the window, but there I was, ready to blow
the last money I had in the world at the one track where I had
no chance in hell of winning.

I guess you could say I was desperate. All I wanted was to
have one winning day, to have a chance to get my life back on
track, but absolutely nothing was going right for me. Two

weeks ago at Belmont, I bet this horse, Frozen-something. He was eleven to one, had ten lengths at the top of the stretch. *Ten lengths.* John Velazquez had a big hold on the horse, was practically standing up in the saddle, looking back. Meanwhile, I was counting my money. I had it for two hundred across the board and wheeled back and forth in exactas. Not only would it get me out; it would get me *up.* Then, at the eighth pole, the horse starts getting heart failure. I screamed at my TV, "Hold on with him! Hold on with him, JV! Open the reins! Open the reins, baby! Let 'em loose now!" But the whole field was closing in on him like he had a sign taped to his ass: BEAT ME. And they beat him, all right— the goddamn horse couldn't even hold show.

Thinking my luck would have to turn sooner or later, and not wanting to have some bullshit bet down when it did, I stepped it up a few notches, put the pedal to floor. Can you say, bad idea? I bet everything—flats, trots, quarter horses— at tracks in America, England, Australia, South Africa, fucking Dubai, and I got the living shit kicked out of me all over the planet. Yeah, I had a couple of days when I hit cover bets, made a few dollars, but most days I got tattooed. My bank account was long gone, and they'd been turning me down for credit cards for years. My paycheck at the body shop covered food and rent and that's it, and my friends and family had stopped lending to me years ago. I had no choice but to get money off the street, and I was in up to my eyeballs with two loan sharks. I wasn't worried about one of them—my cousin Richie's friend Stevie—but this other one, this crazy Dominican named Jesus, was the problem. Jesus didn't pronounce his name the Spanish way; he pronounced it like the Jesus in Jesus Christ, and I was into him for about twelve Gs, and last week the son of a bitch sent these two goons to my house. They were talking Spanish, so I didn't understand half the shit they said, but I knew what the words *gasolina* and *fuego* and *próxima semana* meant. I'd heard stories how Jesus didn't fuck around, how people who owed him for too long disappeared, but I was still stupid enough to borrow off him.

So I decided I needed to get out of Brooklyn—to clear my head, get a change of scenery. They always say that lame horses sometimes "wake up" and start winning when they get up to Saratoga and start breathing in the fresh country air. Maybe the same thing would happen to me.

"Even," I said out loud as my car crept in traffic toward the racetrack. "Just get me even, God, and I'll never gamble again. I swear on my fucking life I won't."

I wasn't asking for a lot. I didn't want to win a million dollars or buy a Porsche or move to some island in the Caribbean and sip drinks with the little umbrellas in them for the rest of my life. I just wanted to get even—pay off all my debts, clean the slate, start over. And I was serious about quitting gambling. Yeah, I'd said that so many times before that even I was sick of hearing it, but this time I'd actually do it. I was forty-three years old, had been divorced three times, had one kid, was almost flat broke, and lived in an apartment in Sheepshead Bay the size of some people's closets. It was time to take some responsibility. I'd go to Gamblers Anonymous again and this time I'd stick it out. I'd cancel all my betting accounts and get DirecTV to block the fucking racing channel. I'd take it a day, a week, a month at time, and before I knew it I'd have a year of no gambling under my belt. I didn't know what I'd do with my time, but I'd find something. Maybe I'd exercise, jog, fish, hunt, or take up some sport, like tennis or racquet-

ball—do people still play racquetball?—and I'd start spending time with Ella again. I was supposed to get her every
other weekend, but I usually got Diane to keep her so I could
go to the track. What kind of piece-of-shit father was I, blowing off my kid to bet? That definitely had to change; that definitely *would* change if I got my money back. I'd put away for
Ella, start one of those college funds. I wanted her to go to
school someday, to do something with her life. I didn't want
her to wind up like me.

I parked in a backyard across from the track where a kid
with bad acne was holding up a sign: PARKING $5.

"Good luck today," he said when he took my money, and I
said, "Yeah, I'm gonna fuckin' need it," thinking about buying
those scratch-offs again. Who the hell was I kidding anyway,
thinking I had a chance of making my money back at this
gambling hellhole? If I had the money back from all the races
I'd lost at Saratoga during my entire life I could've probably
built another Saratoga. They called Saratoga "the graveyard
of favorites," but they should've called it "the graveyard of
Jimmy Fontaine." I knew I wasn't winning at Saratoga. It
wasn't a matter of how or if I'd lose; it was a matter of when.

As I approached the turnstile, a young girl hawking tout
sheets stuck one of the pink papers out toward me and said,
"Had seven winners yesterday and two triples." And I said,
"Yeah, me too," and kept walking.

People always go on about how nice and pretty Saratoga
is. I guess it is pretty, with all the women in hats and dresses
and all the trees and with all the horses walking around in the
backyard and with the old-style grandstand; but if you wanna
know the truth, I didn't give a shit. If I wanted pretty I'd go
look at paintings at a museum. Like all the other gamblers I

knew, when I went to the track I didn't care if I was at Saratoga or the North Pole, as long as the place had horses and betting windows.

I got the scratches, found a bench somewhere in the grandstand outside a bathroom, and tried to make sense of the first race. As I expected, it was the typical Saratoga crapshoot—a twelve-horse field, and every horse had a shot of winning. The more I looked at the lines in the *Form,* the dizzier I got. With a minute to post I checked out the odds on a TV. The six was nine to one, and I decided to give it a shot. At least the six was speed and would probably make the lead. Maybe if I got lucky a horse would break down behind him and cause a big pileup.

I barely got my action in—two hundred to win on the six and a five-dollar exacta wheel with the six on top. The bets cost me $255, leaving me with about $350 to my name.

I watched the race on a TV monitor in the grandstand. The six didn't leave the gate and was nowhere to be found at the half-mile pole. I hoped they were going fast up front and Chavez was sitting back with my horse to close in the stretch, but they were waltzing, doing the half in a ridiculously slow fifty-one and two for the mile-and-an-eighth race. Chavez tried to make a move, rushing into contention on the far turn, but then he fanned so wide he might as well have been riding the horse on Union Avenue, outside the track, and he flattened out like a pancake in the lane. I have no idea where he finished, because I was too busy cursing, ripping tickets, when the horses crossed the finish line.

A man holding a little girl by the hand came over to me and said, "There're children here, sir."

I realized that during the race I'd been screaming, cursing

at the TV like a maniac, which wasn't a problem at the down-state tracks, where everybody cursed at the TVs like maniacs, but up here it was a big no-no.

"Sorry," I mumbled, walking away.

I sat on the bench again, deciding it was crunch time—I had to make something happen fast. There was no more telling myself, I'll get 'em back tomorrow, no more reloading at the cash machine. This was it—my last shot. I had to bear down, focus, get the job done.

I actually liked something in the second race—the four horse at six to one. She was a filly and had two starts in maiden special fillies and mares, finishing up the track the first time out, but the next time she closed into a slow pace, finishing fourth, and now she was dropping in class, into maiden claiming fillies.

But then as I went up to the SAM machine I started to talk myself out of it.

She was eight to one now, dead on the board, not even getting touched in the betting. Somebody knew something. Maybe the horse was sick or lame and that was why they were dropping her in class. The horse was running today with a big FOR SALE sign around her neck, and only idiots like me were betting her.

I went to the machine, figuring I'd bet the nine horse instead; then at the last second I thought, Fuck it, I'll bet the four. Now you see why I was in the middle of the losing streak from hell? I had no belief in myself; I was lost.

I figured I'd watch the race outside—maybe it would give me luck. Blazing midday sun beat down on my balding head. It was supposed to go up to about ninety today, but it felt like it was at least a hundred already.

The race started but I had no idea what was going on.
Unlike most tracks, the outside of the grandstand at Saratoga
was flat, instead of on a slope, so the view of the horses on the
backstretch was blocked by the odds board. There was a big
monitor on the infield showing the race, but the picture was
too grainy and there was too much glare from the sun to see
anything. I stood on a bench to watch the actual race, but that
didn't help, because everybody was standing on benches. I
thought Tom Durkin called my horse, Jenny's Big Surprise,
sixth on the outside, but I wasn't sure, because the loud-
speakers were echoing. On the odds board they showed the
positions of the first four horses, and mine wasn't one of them.

Then, as the horses approached the far turn, I caught a
glimpse of the field and saw that the horse with the jockey
wearing pink silks was moving up fast from the back of the
pack. I fumbled for my program and it fell to the ground. I
bent down for it and checked and saw that my horse's jockey
was wearing pink silks. When the field reached the top of the
stretch and turned for home it was hard to see again, and I
couldn't hear Durkin's voice at all. But then, midway through
the stretch, I saw the horse with the pink jockey flying on
the outside, and I started screaming, "Yeah, baby! Keep her
going, baby! Yeah, keep her going!" I started counting the
winnings in my head. The four had gone off at eleven to one,
and I had a hundred to win on it. That would get me back
over a grand, and I'd also wheeled the four in exactas for five
dollars, and if I got lucky and a long shot got up for place I
could make another G easy. Then, as the horses passed in
front of me, my heart probably stopped for a couple of seconds when I saw that I'd made a big mistake—there were two
jockeys wearing pink in the race, and mine wasn't the one cel-

ebrating. I had to be the world's biggest moron—screaming my head off, rooting home the wrong horse, thinking I was on my way to even. And the kicker? The other pink jockey was on the nine horse, the horse I almost played before I talked myself back onto the four.

I headed back into the grandstand, wandering toward the far end of the track at the top of the stretch, when I noticed that the third race at Monmouth was going off. I looked at the *Form* quickly, came up with the three horse at nine to one, and it won, wire to wire. I had fifty to win on it, got back five and change. I decided my problem was Saratoga, that I had a better shot of winning at the out-of-town tracks. So I removed the Saratoga pages from my *Form* and flung them into a garbage can. I lost the next race at Monmouth, then caught a nice exacta at Arlington, got my stake up to close to two grand. I thought I was getting hot and I made a couple of wild, stupid bets, stepping out in a few races I should've taken passes on. My stake dipped back below a grand. It went like that for most of the day. I was losing mostly, but hitting cover bets here and there. I had about two grand in my pocket, but decided I'd never make the money I needed this way. I had to slow down and make one big bet, take one shot in a race I really liked. I zeroed in on the ninth race at Monmouth on a seven-year-old gelding named Dinner Party.

I'd seen Dinner Party run many times before. He was a turf specialist out of Dynaformer and he had turf breeding on his mother's side too. When he was a three- and four-year-old he won a couple of big-stakes races, which was why his lifetime earnings were over $750,000. But the last couple of years he'd been running mainly in high-priced claiming company in Florida. His last race was in February, so he was coming off a long six-month layoff, but he'd had a couple of nice works on the turf, and Joe Bravo, the top jockey at Monmouth who'd won on him last winter at Gulfstream, was taking the mount. His best Beyer numbers were as good as any of the likely favorites in the race, and he had a nice post position for the mile-and-a-sixteenth race, right on the rail. Although he'd probably take money, it was a decent-sized field of eight horses, and I figured I'd still get about five to one on him.

I didn't fuck around. I went right up to the window and put a thousand to win on the horse. I played him back and forth in the exactas, investing about another grand, so all the horse had to do was finish first or second and I'd be in super shape.

I got a good position directly in front of the TV. I was staring at the screen as the horses loaded into the starting gate, concentrating harder than a surgeon at an operating table. I remembered seeing something on some talk show about how, if you imagine something happening, if you have a vision of it, the thing will come true. So I closed my eyes and imagined the one horse finishing thirty lengths in front, like Secretariat in the seventy-three Belmont. Then I imagined myself collecting the money and going to the bank on Monday morning and opening that college fund for Ella. It would be great to do something like that for my daughter, to be a good father for a change.

The one horse went into the gate nice and easy, but the four horse, one of the favorites, was acting up, and a couple of guys had to come over and stuff him in. The rest of the field loaded in easily, and my heart was already racing like I was in the middle of a marathon. I didn't care how many kids were around me—I was gonna scream and curse my fucking ass off to get this horse home.

The gate opened and Dinner Party got off to a nice start, protecting his position on the rail, but not working him too hard.

"Way to go, Joe, baby!" I screamed at Joe Bravo. "Nice and easy now, Joe! Nice and easy!"

A few speed horses went to the top, and Bravo settled the one into a good position, fifth on the rail, as the horses hit the clubhouse turn. The four horse, the one that had acted up, was on the lead, but he was being pressured hard on the outside by the two horse, one of the other horses that had taken money. They had two lengths on the six—a bomb I wasn't worried about—and the three. The three was a decent horse, but he was used to being on the lead and he looked like he was laboring. My horse was still sitting chilly, fifth on the rail, and Bravo had a nice hold on him, his hands tight on the reins and his ass high in the air.

"Thataway, Joe! Thataway, Joey, baby!"

The fraction for the half mile flashed on the screen—45.2. The two and the four were going tooth and nail, killing each other on the lead. The six was backing out of the race, and Bravo took over fourth, and the jockey on the three was pumping with his arms, struggling to keep up. Behind Bravo, the five and the seven were trying to rush into contention, but Bravo had definitely worked out the best trip in the race.

As the field hit the far turn I screamed, "Let 'em loose now, Joey, baby! Let 'em loose!" and it was like Bravo could hear me. He let it out a notch and the one started moving up on the two and the four, staying about a length clear of the five and the seven, who looked like they were starting to hang. In a few seconds the one had made up two lengths, and now he was a length off the two leaders, ready to pounce on them in the lane. Then Bravo did something that made me want to run out to my car, drive down to Jersey, and strangle the little midget. He could've taken the one off the rail and gone to the outside and rolled to the top. Yeah, it might've cost him a couple of lengths, but he'd gotten such a perfect trip and the leaders were so cooked up front that he would've made the lead easy. Some horses didn't like to leave the rail, but I'd seen Dinner Party go wide and win before, so I had no idea what the fuck Bravo was doing.

"Joe, what the fuck're you doing?!" I screamed.

The horses hit the stretch and—what a surprise—the two and the four started having heart failure. Bravo, still on the rail, was looking for a seam to run through. He tried to get through on the rail, but there wasn't any room to get in between the two and the four.

"Come on, get him out, Joe! Get him out now!"

He couldn't get around the horses because the five and seven weren't hanging as much as I thought they would. The horses up front were stopping so badly that the five and seven were getting dragged into the race, while my one horse still had no place to run. The five made the lead and the seven was second and my one horse was back in fifth place, boxed in on the rail.

"Jesus Christ!" I screamed, and it seemed hopeless. Then, past the sixteenth pole, a seam finally opened up and the one fought his way through. The five and seven were still running one-two, but the one was flying on the rail. Seventy yards from home the one was a half length behind the seven, but the five was pulling away. The one didn't seem to have any chance to win the race, but the way the seven was swaying, ducking the whip, there was a 100 percent chance that the one would finish second. At least I'd get the exacta, which should pay nice because the five was the longest shot in the field. But just as I finished this thought, the one horse must've taken a bad step or something, because Bravo had to check him, standing up in the saddle for a fraction of a second. He got him going again quickly, but the misstep cost him, and the seven hit the wire with his nose in front and the one finished third.

I was so stunned I couldn't even yell. I was still staring at the TV a couple of minutes after the official sign went up and the prices were posted, and then I wandered through the grandstand, into the backyard. I probably looked like one of those zombies in *Night of the Living Dead.* I had, without a doubt, the best horse in the race. I should've been collecting over ten grand, but instead I was practically broke, with less than a hundred bucks in my pocket.

There was no way I could place another bet. If I couldn't win on that horse I was never gonna win, and the idea of even looking at another horse, or another line of the *Racing Form,* disgusted me. I dropped my *Form* onto the gravel and headed toward the exit.

I was thinking about going right to Diane's place in Queens and begging her for the money for Jesus. I'd tell her about how this Jesus guy was nuts, how he was gonna pour gasoline all over me and set me on fire next week. There was no way that Diane could let anything happen to the father of her daughter. Then I remembered our last fight, Diane telling me that she hoped I died and burned in hell, and I wasn't so sure if she'd give a shit.

I was about to leave the track when I looked at a TV monitor and noticed that there were five minutes to post before the last race at Saratoga. I checked my wallet and counted seventy-six bucks. I knew myself well, and I'd been smart enough to leave fifty bucks—gas money—in the glove compartment of my car so I could afford to lose the seventy-six. Actually, I *wanted* to lose it, because I didn't want to leave this track with a cent in my pocket. If the track was gonna kill me, let it finish the job.

I put the seventy-six on a voucher and went up to a SAM machine and started betting superfectas. I didn't even know what horses were running, so I just started betting random numbers, punching the machine so hard my index finger hurt. In my head I was still reliving that stretch drive at Monmouth, seeing the one horse pinned in on the rail with no place to run. I had a feeling I'd be having nightmares about it for weeks, if I lived that long.

I bet all the money and stuffed the stack of soon-to-be losing tickets into my back pocket. As I headed through the backyard, the race went off. I didn't even bother to go to one of the TV monitors to watch it. The crowd got louder, so I knew the horses were in the stretch, and then there was an even louder roar from the crowd and I knew the horses had hit the wire. I made my way to monitors, squinting to see through the glare, and saw the order of finish: five, twelve, two, six.

I started going through the tickets, tossing the ones that didn't have the five on top. Out of the thirty-eight combinations I'd played I'd played only two tickets with the five horse. One of the tickets went five and nine, so I flung it away. But the next ticket was five, twelve, two, six.

I didn't believe it. I had to be looking at it wrong. I looked at it again—there was a five, a twelve, a two, and a six. I wasn't reading it wrong—those were the numbers. Then I looked at the screen again and the same numbers were there. As impossible as it seemed, I'd actually hit the superfecta.

I hadn't checked the odds for the race, so I figured with my luck the horses were all favorites. I jogged inside the track to a monitor that was showing the odds and couldn't believe it when I saw that the five was forty-seven to one. The twelve was six to one, the two was four to one, and the six was nineteen to one. With the favorite in the race off the board, the payoff was going to be huge.

It seemed like it took forever, but OFFICIAL finally lit up on the tote board. I had to wait for the exacta, daily double, and triple prices to be posted before they put up the superfecta price, and I had to blink a few times to make sure what I was seeing was real: $27,488.60.

I couldn't help screaming my ass off, and, since the grandstand was clearing out and it was getting quiet, it seemed like everyone left was looking at me. Still in shock, I made my way around to the IRS window to cash my ticket.

An old guy came over to me when I was approaching the window and said, "Want me to cash that for you?"

I'd had people over sixty-five cash tickets for me before. Any winner at the track over three hundred to one was considered a "tax number" and you had to give the track your Social Security number and Uncle Sam was your fucking partner, getting 40 percent of your winnings. If I had this old guy cash this ticket for me I could probably save about ten grand on my taxes, but I decided not to chance it. I didn't know if "possession is nine-tenths of the law" was a bullshit saying or not, but this ticket was gonna change my whole life, and I wasn't letting it out of my hands. I figured I'd work it out with an accountant, declare losses against winnings at the end of the year—God knew I had enough losses to declare.

"No, thanks," I told the guy.

"You sure?" he said. "Because—"

"I said no thanks."

I had to wait for two people ahead of me to cash; then it was my turn. I gave the teller—a guy with a grayish yellow mustache—the ticket and watched him stick it into the machine. I expected his eyes to widen, or for him to show some kind of reaction, but unlike most of the Saratoga tellers who were summer employees and barely knew how to put in a two-dollar win bet, this guy must've been a seasoned pro because like a Vegas blackjack dealer at a high-rollers table, he didn't even flinch when he saw the payout number come up. He just said, "You're gonna have to wait a few minutes," and went to talk to his supervisor.

I watched as the supervisor, an older woman, came over. He told her about my ticket and she said, "Wow," and then she said, "Congratulations," to me, and I said, "Thanks."

The supervisor went to get the money from somewhere, maybe a safe. I was still in shock. I wasn't gonna believe this was actually happening until I had the money in my hands and I could smell the ink on the bills.

A few minutes went by and then the supervisor returned with envelopes of money.

"How are you leaving the track today?" the teller asked me.

"What do you mean?"

"I mean, are you driving or walking?"

"Driving."

"Would you like a trooper to escort you to your car? With this kind of money it's probably a good idea."

Figuring this made sense, I said, "Yeah, okay. Why not?"

He started counting the hundreds, putting them in a big stack, and reality was starting to hit home. I'd won $27,000—all my troubles were over. I was gonna pay off Jesus and then

I'd have about fifteen grand left. On Monday I'd open that college fund for Ella and, what the hell, I'd drop a couple thousand off with Diane—I couldn't wait to see her shocked face when I did that. Then I'd take a few days off from work, and then I'd start playing some Pick Sixes, try to turn my stake into fifty or a hundred grand. I knew I'd promised to quit gambling if I got even but, hell, I did more than get even—I hit the jackpot. It would be stupid to quit now, while I was on a roll.

The money wouldn't fit in my wallet. I had to put the rest of it in my other front pocket, and both front pockets were bulging.

"Can you just step aside a second?" the teller asked me.

I moved to my right and then the teller waved over a trooper and said, "Can you escort this gentleman to his car, please?"

"No problem," the trooper, a tall blond guy, said.

I gave the teller a twenty-buck tip and then walked with the trooper through the grandstand out to the backyard. Some people were still milling around, but the track had pretty much emptied out. I still couldn't believe I had all this money in my pockets. I decided that when I got back to Brooklyn, at around nine or nine thirty, I'd go right to Brennan & Carr on Nostrand Avenue and have a big steak dinner.

"So you live around here?" the trooper asked me.

"Nah, I live in the city," I said. "Brooklyn."

"I guess it'll be a nice ride back tonight, huh?"

"Yeah, for a change."

"Why's that?"

"I never win at Saratoga."

"That right?"

"I'm serious. I can't tell you how many times I've left this track without a penny to my name."

"I guess today was your lucky day, huh?"

"You got that right."

We left the track and crossed Union Avenue. The sun looked nice, the way it was shining through the trees. Hell, everything looked nice with that money in my pockets.

We went through a couple of backyards and then got to the one where I'd parked. My car was the only one still there.

"Thanks a lot, man," I said to the trooper.

"Don't mention it," he said, but he stood there, not walking away.

I figured he wanted a tip, so I took out the wad of bills, peeled off a ten, and said, "Here you go."

He didn't take the money, and then I realized why. His right hand was holding a gun, low by his hip. It was pointed up at my chest.

"I guess it's not your lucky day after all, asshole," he said. "Gimme all of it."

I was too shocked to move or say anything.

"Now," he said.

It was still a struggle for my lips to work, but I managed to say, "What the hell?"

"Give me the fucking money, asshole," he said.

My eyes shifted back and forth, looking in every direction, but the closest people nearby were an old man and woman about a hundred yards away.

"Come on," I said. "This is a joke, right?"

"Now," he said, "or I start shooting."

I thought, Would he really shoot me right here in broad daylight? I didn't have time to think it over. All I knew was, there was no way in hell I was giving him this money.

I said, "Hey, who's that?" and when he started to turn to look I tried to get into my car. I found the key right away and got the door open and even got one foot inside before I felt the crash against the top of my head. I fell down onto the grass and looked up at his blurry face. Then he whacked me with the gun again.

I MUST'VE BEEN OUT for only a minute or less, but when I opened my eyes I didn't know where I was or what had happened. Then I found my wallet on the grass with no money it, and I realized that the wads of bills were gone from my pockets too. Then I remembered everything.

I made it to my feet and started running, as fast I could, toward the avenue. I was still very dizzy and I stumbled and fell a few times. Then, as I got closer to the sidewalk, I started screaming, "He stole my money! The trooper stole my money!"

People were giving me weird looks, like I was a freak or something, and then I realized why. My head had gashes in it and blood was streaming down my face.

I went up to a young guy and his girlfriend and said, "Where'd the trooper go? He took my money. Where the hell did he go?"

The guy grabbed his girlfriend's arm and they rushed away from me along the sidewalk.

I went up to other people, saying, "You see the trooper? Where's the trooper?" but they avoided me too.

I spotted another trooper, a woman, who was helping people cross the street at the intersection, and I rushed over to her and said, "A trooper just mugged me! He took all my money—twenty-seven grand!"

"Okay, just wait over there on the corner, sir," the woman said.

"D'you know him? He has blond hair, he's tall."

"Just wait on the corner, sir."

"I can't wait." I grabbed her arm, harder than I meant to.

A trooper, a squat guy, came over, grabbed me, and pushed me up against a lamppost. I tried to tell him about the trooper who'd robbed me, but he kept telling me to shut up. He made a call on his walkie-talkie, and a few minutes later an ambulance showed up and I was taken to the emergency room at Saratoga Hospital. I kept telling the EMS guys about how the trooper had attacked me and stolen all my money, but they kept acting like I was crazy or something and wouldn't listen to me.

At the hospital they put stitches in my forehead and told me I had a mild concussion. A doctor wanted me to stay overnight for observation, but I refused. Finally, near the entrance to the hospital, I found a cop who listened to my story, and he suggested that I go to the police station and file a complaint.

I went to the Saratoga State Police Department and had to wait a couple of hours before a detective would see me. I explained the whole story, and then he said, "So you're saying you were attacked by a state trooper," as if he didn't believe a word I'd said.

I gave him my descriptions of the teller and the trooper and the location of the window where I'd collected the money, and he promised to look into all of it as soon as possible. He asked for a number where I could be reached, and I gave him my cell. The only money I had to my name was the fifty bucks "gas money" in my glove compartment, so there was no way I could afford a hotel. I bought a couple of Big Macs at the McDonald's on Route 9, but I was too nauseous to eat, and then I fell asleep in my car outside the police station.

I slept for only a couple of hours, if that. I kept telling myself that they had to be able to find that guy. He was a trooper; they had background information on him. And the teller at the track would be able to back up my story, so the police would know I wasn't making the whole thing up. I had to just relax, wait for the cops to get to the bottom of it, and I'd get my money back.

In the morning the police had no information for me yet, so I had to hang out, waiting. Finally, at around three o'clock, the same detective I'd spoken to the night before told me he had some information.

"Did you find the guy?" I asked.

"Just come with me, sir," he said with his upstate accent.

I sat across from him at his desk, and then he said, "Well, I'm sorry to say we can't find the man you described, the trooper."

"That's impossible," I said. "The guy escorted me—"

"I believe you. We know who the teller is, the one who cashed your ticket. The trouble is, he died last year."

"The hell're you talking about?"

"The teller falsified his employment history, took the name of a dead man, used his Social and everything. You know, the track does a lot of hiring for the August meet. It looks like a mistake may have been made."

"A mistake? What about my fucking money?"

"Look, we're gonna try to figure all this out, all right? But it looks like these two guys were con men. The teller was waiting for someone to hit for big money and then he got his friend to escort you to your car. We know that the man you described wasn't an actual trooper—he must've just gotten hold of a trooper's uniform somehow."

"But you're looking for the guys, right? I mean, there's a chance you'll find them?"

"A chance, sure. We already put an alert out, but I can't make any guarantees. These guys probably know what they're doing. They planned this whole thing very carefully, and it won't be easy to track them down now. They may've changed their appearances and got to the Canadian border. Who knows? We'll do all we can, but, to be honest, it doesn't look very good."

"This is bullshit," I said. "I'm gonna sue the track. That was my money. It's their fault for hiring that guy."

"You could try to sue, I guess," the detective said. "That's what I'd do if I were you, but I gotta be honest with you. If we don't catch these guys, your story's gonna be hard to prove."

The detective said he'd keep me informed of any progress in the investigation, but I knew that was just to keep me off his back; the chances of these hicks catching those guys was slim to none. Maybe if they started looking for them last night I could've gotten a break, but now they were probably long gone and so was my money. Maybe I could find a cheap lawyer and try to sue the track but what were the chances of me winning that one? They'd probably have a whole team of lawyers going against me.

Figuring there was no point in hanging around Saratoga any longer, I got in my car and headed out of town. I was planning to go right to Diane's. I'd tell her everything that had happened and beg her to give me some money for Jesus. She had to feel sorry for me today, right?

Then, going along Union Avenue, wouldn't you know it, I drove right past the racetrack. I checked my watch and realized I could make the fifth. The gas money could be my ammo. Maybe I could walk in and hit something right away, a nice exacta, and then parlay the winnings, get on a roll.

I was about to make the left, into the official track parking lot, when I thought, Who the hell am I kidding? If I couldn't come out on top at Saratoga yesterday, it sure as hell wasn't happening today. The damn track had my number. Even when I won, I couldn't win.

WHAT I LEARNED FROM THEM AFTER THEY CAME HOME FROM THE TRACK

Jane Smiley

OF COURSE, MY PLAN was that each of the darling foals—Sylvanshine, Hornblower, Waterwheel, Darlin' Corey, Joy Forever, and Dolly—would trundle down to Santa Anita and earn him- or herself a healthy trust fund, say, half a million, to be put in long-term bonds to support that particular Thoroughbred (and me, of course) for the next twenty or thirty years. But that was nothing compared to what they planned for the horse Neil Drysdale gave me (who shall remain nameless) by a $100,000 sire out of a mare who gets bred only to the likes of A. P. Indy. I'm sure they planned for him to be Secretariat, since he's a muscular chestnut with that look of eagles in his eye. I named him Mr. Nice Guy. But, alas, our plans went awry. Sylvanshine pulled a suspensory, twice, without getting to the races. Hornblower had a win and was on the board a few times, but he didn't earn his keep. Darlin' Corey got claimed and vanished. Waterwheel fractured her sesamoids and came home to be a broodmare, Joy Forever got a stress fracture in her right cannon bone and went to the layup farm, and Dolly (by Mr. Expo out of a Northern Baby mare) bowed a tendon. Mr. Nice Guy was sound after half a dozen starts. It appeared he just didn't care to run. It's a good thing they're all good-looking.

Here's a riddle: How many Thoroughbreds does it take to support a $15 billion gambling business at seventy-five race-tracks around the United States every year? Answer: about 75,000 starters. What the bettors like least is short fields, and who can blame them? But when thousands of horses are toiling at the far edge of what horse anatomy was engineered to do, there's a lot of stress failure, and the result of much of it is thousands of horses out of a job and looking for new homes and careers every year. The only difference between me and a lot of owners is I put them to work myself, as dressage horses or jumpers, and in this I consider myself lucky.

The first one home was Sylvanshine, who just couldn't take the breezing. Twice as a three-year-old he got to the track from the training farm and pulled a suspensory in his first timed work. The pulls were mild—no lesions or tears— and he was back in training in four months or so, but what I learned from him was that a certain way of going, with lots of scope and suspension, a way of going that looks great in the dressage arena, doesn't do well for a racehorse. I also learned not to say "what if?" Even though Sylvanshine seems to be mentally the most suited for racing, being big, bold, domi-nant, competitive, and flowing with energy, he had to come home and he did. Like they say, your biggest winner is standing in the barn, eating his hay. Sylvanshine has potential as a dressage horse, but I have to consider his energy level every time we compete. Is he worked down enough and relaxed enough to perform his exercises obediently (or "submissively," as the dressage people say), or is he going to caper down the center line and then buck on his canter circle? A horse with the look of eagles doesn't necessarily excel in submission, though he is quite a riveting sight when he is in the mood.

The next one home was Waterwheel. In some sense, it was good she was injured and we weren't tempted to embark on the heartbreak of training her to be useful. She was small, too small for an adult rider, and beautiful, but she was opinionated and hot. Her jockey likened riding her to driving a Ferrari. She loved to run and loved to slip through the field, sneering at the other fillies as she passed them. She would certainly have been able to jump, and so we would have been tempted to train her as a child's hunter, and she would have learned quickly, but that fiery edge would have always been in there. As a broodmare, she is fat and bossy and she makes good-looking babies. From her I learned not to race two-year-olds, no matter how focused and precocious they seem and no matter how fast they are.

Hornblower was one of those sound gray geldings that win from time to time and always try. My old horse, Mr. T, was the model—on the track until age nine, still running four or five times a year. Hornblower would have done that, but in his last race, when he didn't seem to be working hard, I thought he was burned out and I sent him to the farm. Little did I know. I learned a lot from Hornblower.

The first thing I learned from Hornblower was all about

feet. Yes, his trainer mentioned that he was a little overdue for shoeing, and yes, after a week at home, we pulled his back shoes and reset his front shoes, but that wasn't even the beginning of what I learned about feet. Or, you might say, flippers, because when he came home from the track, his toes were so long that he used his feet like flippers, and was uncomfortable walking, not to mention trotting, which he couldn't do at all. The first thing I learned was that he hadn't been burned out in his last race; he'd been sore. The saga of Hornblower's feet lasted five months, and included a painful bout of laminitis that caused even more painful abscesses in both his front feet. X-rays showed that the soles of his hooves were thin, so the long toes combined with the pounding and the abraded heels inflamed his laminae and made his soles extra tender. One time, I saw him groan and lie down with his legs stretched straight out because he couldn't stand on his sore feet any longer. So, I learned to tell my trainer to watch his or her shoer like a hawk, to make him stand the horse up and not just file him down from side to side and slap the shoes on. I also learned that feet can be fixed. At the end of a year, Hornblower's feet were normal, and they haven't given him any trouble since.

Here's what I thought I knew about Hornblower as a racehorse: He had some speed, but he was a plodder. He had no acceleration, and depended on consistency of stride length and on stamina to stay in the lead and get on the board. He was hard to manage in the paddock and edgy, but easy to load and good out of the gate. He was best at more than a mile but not quite up to a mile and three-eighths. He was a grass horse. Jockeys liked riding him well enough because he did what he was told.

When Hornblower was sound again and ready to go back to work, my cowboy trainer, Ray Berta, got on him. The first thing we learned was that he could change leads at a fast gallop, but he couldn't canter off on his left lead. He nearly fell down the first few times he tried. In three years at the racetrack, it appeared that he had never broken from the gate on his left lead, or transitioned into the gallop on his left lead, though he had, of course, switched leads in many races. Hmm. With Ray, I also learned that he was a twinkletoes over poles on the ground. Walk, trot, canter, he never touched a pole with a front foot or a back foot. It was like he had eyes in his belly, or a sixth sense about where his feet were and where the poles were. It was beautiful and remarkable.

He was affectionate and considerate. When the puppies ran around under his feet, he took care not to step on them. When I brought him food or groomed him or paid attention to him, he was attentive in return, but not pushy. He was obedient without even trying to be. If I opened the gate of his pen, he waited until I held out his halter, and then he stuck his nose into it and let me tie it before he left the pen. He never bucked, reared, bolted, bit, kicked, or even pinned his ears in annoyance. But he was nervous. He hated loud, rhythmic noises and didn't like going on the trail. A particular fallen log that the other horses hardly noticed terrified him, as did birds in the bushes. Even so, he could not be surprised, because he was so alert. Once in a while the other horses really spooked when something unexpected jumped out of the woods, but for Hornblower, nothing was unexpected. He was never tired. He spooked as often at the end of a ride as at the beginning. He almost never worked up a sweat. He seemed quirky and idiosyncratic, but then so did the others. I introduced him to Sylvanshine.

I was skittish about introducing him to Sylvanshine because Sylvanshine considered himself the king of all he surveyed, and watched over his little band of mares the way stallions do, even though he had been gelded at nine months. He had had a cadet whom he oppressed in every way, never allowing him to approach the gate for treats or consort with the mares (unless Sylvanshine was consorting with the more desirable mares; in that case, the cadet could make polite advances toward the less desirable mares). But Hornblower had remained a stallion almost until the age of five, and he seemed to have a strong interest in mares. I wasn't sure he would knuckle under without a fight.

We put them in a hillside paddock together, and within seconds they were all fired up, trotting back and forth with arched necks and lifted tails, both exuding scads of lemme-at-'im energy, but Hornblower never had a chance. Sylvanshine knew just what to do, which was to trot past Hornblower several times without appearing to notice him, inducing Hornblower to do the noticing, which is in itself submissive. Then Sylvanshine would stop and wait for Hornblower to approach, also a submissive act, and then Sylvanshine would curl his neck and touch noses with Hornblower. If Hornblower squealed or struck out, Sylvanshine would squeal louder and give Hornblower a push, trot off proudly, and circle back. He had the body language that said, "I am the boss," and Hornblower did not. After fifteen minutes we put them in a larger space, adding a couple of mares at a time. Hornblower was successfully reduced to second banana with no fighting and minimal kicking or striking; good for me, perhaps bad for him. But then Sylvanshine learned something from Hornblower. One day in the spring, we saw Hornblower off on the far side of the pasture, his member stiff, mounting one of the less desirable mares. On our side of the pasture, by the gate, staring at them, stood Sylvanshine, whose member had never been stiff, as far as we knew. We thought maybe he was putting two and two together.

And of course I couldn't resist the match race. Much against the better judgment of the girl who was helping me, I turned them out together in our big arena, a sandy expanse where, if they wanted to, they could get up some speed. I often turned them out separately. Sylvanshine loved that sort of thing—he would gallop around the outside (eight circuits to the mile), whinnying and digging in, showing me who the racehorse was. Hornblower liked the freedom, too, but was a tad lazier. Together they knew exactly what to do. As soon as we took off their halters, they turned and, in a manner of speaking, broke from the gate, Sylvanshine on the outside, Hornblower on the inside. Sylvanshine was howling with joy, as he always did, and the mares were calling back from up the hill. The girl and I stood in the middle, wondering if we had invited the horses to commit suicide.

There were, after all, plenty of jumps in the arena. But of course, they were Thoroughbreds. They could not only run; they could be smart at the run, and they circled the arena ten or twelve times at top speed, never making a clumsy move or even coming close to hitting a jump. They stayed together, Sylvanshine always in the lead. One time Hornblower tried to cut inside and save ground, but Sylvanshine just lengthened his stride and pulled ahead. Hornblower never got his nose past Sylvanshine's flank. I learned, again, who was the real racehorse, but I also learned that Thoroughbreds can go a mile and a quarter just for the fun of it, on their own.

Hornblower started his jumper training by being sent saddleless and bridleless through a chute with some jumps set across it. They started as poles on the ground and rapidly, in the course of a few days, got larger. He made a few mistakes, but only a few. His form was almost always perfect—knees by his chin, the arc of his back and neck deep and graceful, his back ankles quick over every pole. He jumped four feet as easily as two, and went at it with enthusiasm. For a year after that my trainer brought him along, first riding him over small jumps (about two feet), then over larger ones (about three feet). He learned quickly. Once, my trainer took him through a group of small cross rails, set in a long curve across the arena. Hornblower simply could not turn, even a minimal turn, and jump at the same time. But a few days later he could. Then there were the flying changes. A jumper has to be able to gallop through a twisting course, sometimes turning after every jump or set of jumps. If he can efficiently switch leads on his own, that saves the rider some thought and a second or two on the clock. Hornblower learned to switch leads with more than grace, indeed, with enthusiasm. At one point in his training, for about a week, he would switch leads whether you wanted him to or not, every time you turned your head from one direction to another. It was disconcerting, but he was only practicing. When he had the foot-work down pat, he stopped doing it so often, but as a result, he was always on the proper lead. He took it as his responsibility, and didn't have to be asked. After a year of introducing him to different kinds of jumps in different combinations, we took him to a show.

He was crazy in the trailer and terrified on warm-up day. Flags were flapping, people and horses were everywhere, the rings were full of jumps, and the wider passageways were full of flapping white tents. At the far end of one line of jumps, the mysterious sound of hamburgers sizzling on the grill burst out, while in the middle of another line of jumps, people were sitting in the shadows clicking cameras. Hornblower seemed frantic, and my trainer thought it might take two weeks for him to settle. But he settled by the next day, and never unsettled. He went into his classes and jumped cleanly and quietly; in fact, he seemed more at ease in the ring, doing his courses, than he did elsewhere, and this is what I learned: that it is not so much the human brouhaha that frightens him, but the domination of other horses. His fears shaped his racing style. He broke fast from the gate because he wanted to get out in front of the other horses, and he worked to stay in front of them. Toward the end of the race, the stalkers and closers might overtake him, but by that time he was tired enough not to care. He wanted to do well and stay out of trouble, but he was as a racehorse as he was as a jumper: submissive and eager to please. The aspects of his racing career that I had wondered about fell into place: the nervousness in the paddock, the anxiety about going though the pack, the hyperalertness that forced us to try things like sticking cotton in his ears. And at the track he was a turf horse. When he began jumping on grass he was quicker and more sure-footed than ever.

As Hornblower evolved into a star (at least in our barn), I learned something about Darlin' Corey, his full sister, who went to the racetrack, won some money, got claimed from me, and then won several races, got claimed again, won some more money, and disappeared. Corey was bigger (almost seventeen hands as a three-year-old) and tougher than Hornblower, less sensitive and more a mare. She took a long time to learn how to run—in the head-on, she always looked crooked coming down the stretch, and the jockeys reported that she couldn't change leads easily. If she got interfered with (as she did fairly often, since she was also unlucky) that was that; she couldn't find her stride again. But she loved to run, and nothing daunted her. Watching Hornblower and his other sister (bred by artificial insemination and not eligible for racing) pursue their jumping careers, I learned that jumping ability of the sort they have (absolute confidence and perfect form) is inborn and inherited in certain Thoroughbred lines (in their case, Herbager and Caro).

What I learned about Darlin' Corey was to let her go, not to go searching for her and try to buy her. I learned that you can't own all of them.

Mr. Nice Guy came to me like most ex-racehorses come to their equestrian owners—anonymously. I knew Neil had trained him, I knew who his sire and dam were, but I didn't know anything about his foalhood, his training, or his temperament. He came straight from the track. On the first day, we turned him out in the indoor arena, and I got acquainted by walking over to the fence and presenting myself. He tried to bite me immediately. I came to realize that that was his standard greeting. For a week we kept him in the jumper barn, in a stall. After that we moved him into a pipe corral, then into turnout all day and a pipe corral at night. I did not ride him, leaving that task to my cowboy trainer and his wife. Mr. Nice Guy had his nice days. But he also had his suspicious, resentful, unpredictable, and out-of-control days. He was anomalous. On the one hand he liked to go on the trail and went calmly, though there was no evidence in his biography that he had ever gone on a trail ride in his life. In the arena, he was sometimes sluggish and heavy and sometimes racy and dangerous. He frequently kicked out when asked to do anything at all, but often went forward happily. His relationships with other horses were equally inconsistent and fraught with drama. He sometimes fought through the bars with neighboring geldings; neighboring mares often took issue with him. Thinking he needed a herd, I had the farrier remove his hind shoes, and I turned him out with a group of geldings in a large pasture, but he didn't have time to find his niche—his back feet became so sore that I had to put him back in a stall. But in the stall his back fetlocks were swollen most of the time. Finally I solved the housing problem by putting him in a large paddock, where he could move around, that was next to a pasture containing three or four mares. But that didn't work especially well, either—his feet and his fetlocks were okay, but every time the mares moved away, he ran the fence frantically and worked himself into a sweat. When I arrived at the barn each day, he was literally like an adolescent boy who had to be hosed down and cooled off. He bit and he pinned his ears when the girth was tightened or the brush was too brisk. Finally one day his trainer called me and said that he had intentionally kicked her while she was grooming him, and she had had enough. After that it was up to me.

I tried to be careful while grooming him, and tried to be careful while riding him, but he stayed resentful. I gave up training him as I had trained the others and decided to try something new. I taught him to lunge. Lots of trainers use the lunge line, but I normally prefer the round corral. I like the horse to go away from me and come back, to turn and go in either direction fairly frequently, and to have the opportunity to kick and buck and work out his or her kinks without having to switch the equipment back and forth and get tangled up in the lunge line and the lunge whip. But the round corral wasn't working for Mr. Nice Guy. On the lunge line I taught him voice commands—walk, halt, trot, canter. He picked them up immediately. I worked him on the lunge for about a week, then put him back in the round corral for some more work—"over," meaning to step over behind by crossing the leg near me in front of the outside leg, and "back," meaning, of course, to back up. He was quick learning those, too.

Then I got on him again, and systematically forced myself to announce what he was supposed to do before asking him, with seat, legs, and hands, to do it. He did as he was told. It was then that I learned that an ex-racehorse is an ignorant beast, and the things that an equestrian thinks are natural to him, such as moving forward off the leg (from a squeeze or even a kick), aren't natural at all, but learned. After that, it seemed that all of Mr. Nice Guy's antagonism and resentment were replaced by passionate attachment. When I arrived at the barn, he would carol to me a set of vocalizations that could hardly be called a whinny and sounded more like a conversation. He presented himself for pats and treats even more readily than the others.

His resentments at the girth and the brush began to dissipate. When I moved him to a larger paddock on a hillside, and a grumpy older mare moved in next door, his problems were over. She spent two days pinning her ears, grinding her teeth, and kicking the fence, while he stood back a ways but continued to faithfully and attentively watch her and offer his friendship.

On the third day they were standing companionably over

the water trough they shared like a couple bellied up to the bar, taking a sip every so often and canoodling the rest of the time. Once his worries were over and he had a steady human friend—me—and a steady horse friend—Matty—then I really began to learn from him, and what I learned didn't seem Thoroughbredish at all.

For one thing, he was not going to be a jumper. He could go over a pole or a cross rail twenty times and never twice alike. He seemed not to know or care where the pole was or whether he might hit it. Horses like that can be taught to jump, but when the alternative is a horse like Hornblower, why bother? But Mr. Nice Guy was slow and patient. I could ask him to turn left fifty times in a row, perfecting every movement, and he would enjoy it, then turn right as many times and enjoy that as completely. He liked to get the slow, small things, like turning and stepping over and backing and halting and trotting forward just right before trying out the larger, faster things. He could not really canter. He hated the left lead, and on the right lead he veered uncontrollably to the right, his bulging right shoulder carrying him more and more heavily off the track. So we stuck to the walk and the trot, perfecting them.

I asked my dressage trainer to analyze his gaits. She said that he persistently set his left front foot down underneath his chest rather than underneath his shoulder, simultaneously shifting his front end to the right and burdening his left foot with too much weight. This habit accounted for both the bulge of his right shoulder and the mild damage we had found through X-rays in his left front coffin joint. As I trained him and encouraged him to walk and then trot more squarely, simply by touching him in the side with my right foot between the moment when he lifted his left foot and then set it down, he got sounder, better balanced, and happier. I wondered if his heaviness and lack of balance was what had undermined his racing career. But maybe it was his perfectionist soul. What I learned from Mr. Nice Guy was that not all Thoroughbreds are energetic and nervy, flowing with energy and ready to go, go, go. Some are like warm-bloods—happier getting things right one by one and then building on those things. Whereas making Sylvanshine into a dressage horse was a matter of containing and focusing, making Mr. Nice Guy into a dressage horse was a matter of encouraging and expanding.

As for Joy Forever and Dolly, the lessons are only beginning, but they have what the others have, and, indeed, what almost all Thoroughbreds have: plenty of athletic ability, a pool of talents waiting to be tapped, and many years ahead of them in which to tap them.

WHEN SYLVANSHINE AND HORNBLOWER go to competitions, they are often almost the only Thoroughbreds there. American sport horses now are primarily warm-bloods, that is, European breeds that combine some proportion of Thoroughbred blood with some proportion of draft horse blood. Many of them are nice horses, and the reasons warm-bloods have taken over are numerous. But the fact is, every stall at a horse show that is occupied by a warm-blood is a stall not occupied by a Thoroughbred, by one of the thousands of race-track failures and retirees that the racing industry produces every year. What I learned from all my Thoroughbreds is that Thoroughbreds can do the job, whether it is dressage, or jumping, or trail riding, or three-day eventing (where Thoroughbreds are still common but losing ground).

Individual Thoroughbreds move with all the grace and suspension of individual European dressage horses; individual Thoroughbreds jump with all the power and reliability of individual European jumpers and show hunters.

What I have also learned is that there is almost no connection anymore between the racetrack crowd and the horse show crowd. Equestrians are often suspicious of racing, and may never have been to a race. Racing people don't know any show people, and so don't know to whom they might offer a sound and likely prospect when he (usually a gelding) is ready to retire. Such connections, which used to be routine when I was riding in the sixties, have dissipated over the last generation, and the European sport-horse entrepreneurs, whose methods of breeding, training, and selling show horses are much more systematic than ours, have moved in to fill the gap. One result is that trainers who are adept with Thoroughbreds are older ones.

Younger trainers may never have ridden or trained a horse pin-fired from knees to fetlocks, like Mr. Nice Guy, or willing to run a mile on his own at top speed for sheer joy, like Sylvanshine. In addition, of course, most Thoroughbreds are sensitive, quick, energetic, intelligent, and hardworking. They take a tactful hand and daily discipline, and they reward it with not only good performance but ready affection and strong attachment.

Sylvanshine, Hornblower, Mr. Nice Guy, Joy Forever, and Dolly made no splash at the racetrack. They were thoughtfully but, except for Mr. Nice Guy, not well bred; they qualify as average Thoroughbreds, and there are tens of thousands like them. In the world of equestrian pursuits, I have learned, they and their average Thoroughbred cousins are up to any task. It's a shame, I think, that they can't find homes and trainers while their potential owners and trainers are scouring Europe, planning to spend tens of thousands of dollars shipping horses back to America that are no better than horses we already have. The gambling industry, which owes so much to the horses that make up the fields, should come up with better ways of ensuring the continued well-being and usefulness of as many of the horses they depend upon as possible.

HORSE OF A DIFFERENT COLOR

Ken Bruen

ROMPUM.

Isn't that a great name? You ever see that Oz film, *Romper Stomper*? . . . Reminds me of that flick. I didn't see it, but I know there was lots of stomping on people.

Anyway, Rompum is a horse tranquilizer. Not an easy item to get hold of; you don't exactly find it on the shelf. But there's a vet lives down the road, has a serious coke habit. Puts that crap up his nose at every opportunity; he's under investigation by the Guards and the Board of Veterinary Ethics or whatever the hell them crowd are called. He needs money—who doesn't—but he needs it faster than most of us. I gave him a hundred euro, which I had to borrow.

He wasn't happy to hand over the stuff, said, "This is very dangerous material in the wrong hands."

I stared at him for a moment, then hit with "So is coke."

He gave me a long spiel about dosage, due care, and stuff. I went, "Yeah, *whatever.*"

When Byrne and I finally got around to using it, we had to hold the victim down, his eyes huge when he saw the needle, and then I stuck him. I'm not going to lie to you; it was messy. But the effect, shit, his eyes rolled back in his head and drool came out his mouth. Byrne, in wonderment, said, "You've killed the fooker."

AS THEY SAY IN RACING CIRCLES, I'm getting ahead of meself. Leading from behind, so to speak. Let me back track a bit.

You ever hear the Van Morrison song . . . "Madame George"? . . . From *Astral Weeks,* his first album and his best. That was playing when I won my first big bet. You don't expect to hear music in a betting office, unless it's the dirge of desperation. A fella had his Walkman turned up too loud and the song was leaking out. My horse, White Bay, came in at ten to one . . . I had ten quid on him. This was back in the days when we had punts, before we got into all this euro shite. I'd paid the tax, so I got back a hundred smackers and me tenner.

Fuck, what a night, went out Salthill, our Coney Island, and sank pints like a good'un, flush, I was electric. Used to be a pub there, near the old ballroom, it had a jukebox and sure enough, they had Van the man . . . but not "Madame George" . . . never no mind, I played "Cypress Avenue" till some gobshite complained.

I was drinking Black Bush as backup; that sucker costs, but Jesus, it's smooth, goes down like a rosary and twice as blessed. Met a woman too, named Nora. I was propping the bar, feeding the juke, feeding me face with creamy pints, buying for all and sundry; a hundred green ones paid a lot of freight in those days. I'd bought a new shirt, a Ben Sherman, blue with a nice white stripe, to honor White Bay, and a denim jacket that alas, looked new.

You never want denim to look new, but I knew fuck-all in those days, especially about women, and even less about horses. But standing there, six pints to the wind, a fat wallet, luck in me heart, I was bulletproof. I can still hear her: "Aren't you the gorgeous animal?"

I certainly was.

She was a looker, but at that stage of drink, who wasn't? Shit, I even seemed handsome to me own self. I cringe now at the memory but kind of get off a little too. Strutting me stuff, full of piss and blow, it seems to have lasted for oh, so short a time.

"Horses for courses."

One of my dad's favorite expressions, never tired of it. He tired of everything else, me and my mother most. Drove our old battered Morris Minor into the docks, a full two days before they got it hauled out of there. I got to see what he looked like. My mother was a gentle woman but useless. I was twelve when my dad took his dive and asked her, Why, why did he do it?

Her eyes, those smoky blue ones, full of wonder and bafflement. She was quiet for ages, then said, "He got tired."

At twelve, that's an answer? Hell, at forty-eight, it's not even a question. So I persisted.

"Tired of what, Ma, tired of us?"

She nodded and nothing else. Fuck her, she owed me, and

gentleness is no excuse for evasion—or let's call it what it is . . . cowardice. A friend of mine, Byrne, he often says, "Seamus, come on mate, cut her a bit of slack."

When I get some drinks in, I get to wondering about my heritage, my legacy. Cut her some slack? Christ on a tripod, I'd cut her out of my heart if I could. I blame her for the horses. Every Friday she'd give me a few shillings, say, "Put it on the favorite at Doncaster, the last race, and oh, if the tax isn't too much, buy a bag of sweets for yourself."

Yeah, right.

I'd stand outside the bookies, wait for one of the old lags, get him to place the bet. Became a ritual joke, and of course now I realize the bad bastards kept the money. Candy from a baby?

What the fuck ever.

My lady, the current model, a beaut, and you can take it I'm being sarcastic, says, "You have a filthy mouth."

Like I give a rat's arse. I go, "What'd you expect, I've had a filthy life."

Her name is Brona. . . . In Irish we have the word *bronach.* Doesn't translate so easy but 'tis a blend of melancholy and soul sickness. I don't know if that's her real name. In Ireland we call kids after dead patriots, dead saints, and yeah, dead presidents. After *Dallas,* the country was awash in Crystals, JRs, Sue Ellens. I'm real interested to see what crop *The Sopranos* deeds. I hope they also watched *Deadwood.*

I met Brona in the pub. You don't get too many women in the betting office, which is where I spend most of the day.

It had been a woesome afternoon, lost heavy. February, the bleakest month in the Irish calendar—the days are short and miserable, spring is as likely as a long shot romping home,

the rain lashes down constantly. I had a tiny room near the
Spanish Arch, and, thank Christ, a few months back, I'd been
part of a syndicate that pulled a coup and laid out some
months rent in advance. Forward planning? No, my landlord
met me as I came out of the bookies'. The heating was off, as
I'd neglected to pay the ESB . . . fuckers.

I went into Mc Swiggan's, the only pub with a tree in the
center of the lounge. You think I'm kidding? A full fecking
oak right there. It amuses the tourists, and us, we've seen
stranger things in any of the pubs you care to mention. Down
the docks, there's a rough-trade establishment; a guy sits
there with his own cross, leans it against the counter, and no
one says a word. They've all served time on a cross in one way
or another. I heard an English bloke ask, "Is he barmy?"

The barman, not fond of the Brits in any case, never broke
stride, answered on the hoof: "It's his penance for paying
taxes in the UK."

The English guy waited, sure someone would explain that
statement and learned that rule one in Eire is . . . we never
explain, not out of pigheadedness, though it plays a part, but
because we don't know the answer. Truth is, we've never
been all that sure of the questions.

I digress, as I heard a wanker say on *Sky News.* So I'm in the
tree pub, ordering a Guinness with a Jameson chaser, double,
due to the day I'd had, and not sure if I even had enough to pay
the tab when this woman leans over, says, "Let me buy that."

Stunned? Yeah. I turned to see who the joker was. She was
a bad forty, the years showing in her face, though her body
still had some promise, not much but a hint. A fifty-euro note
was in her hand, so I worked up a smile, asked, "And you're
doing this . . . why?"

I'd moved a little closer, and could see she was well on, the drink showing in her eyes, and not just that day's ration—years of it. She said, "I like the cut of yer jib."

Jaysus, I hadn't heard that line for a long time, and before I could say so, she added, "You're a man who likes the horses."

No argument there. My rep for bad horses and worse judgment was well documented. I let her pay for the round, asked, "You have a name or will I just call you Gorgeous?"

Bad, huh? She bought it and smiled, said, "I'm Brona, and you're Jimmy Reed. I know you, as my ex, Billy Tone, the nasty piece of work, used to frequent the same bookies. He said you were the worst gambler he'd ever met."

I couldn't place who she meant, and I knew most of the regulars, said, "Can't place him."

She was drinking gin; I know the smell, a blend of bitterness and pungency. She drained it, said, "He joined Gamblers Anonymous, though why they call it 'anonymous' when the whole town knows who attends is a mystery."

My pint was ready; the barman had let it sit the requisite time and then creamed the head, perfect. I took a large swallow, hit it with a wallop of the Jameson, felt the glow, and asked, "He's doing good, yeah?"

Like I gave a fuck.

She grimaced, answered, "He's a pain in the arse—he was already that, but now he's a pain with a spiritual content, and it doesn't come any worse."

That's how we started, and six months down the road we were still hanging in there. We have unconditional love . . . that is, the same set of conditions: She needed a man to drink with, keep the bollixes at bay, and me, I had a woman with money. And a drink problem. Matched my gambling problem, kind of canceling out; we weren't about to start outlining each other's faults at any time soon.

The first occasion she came to my room, she did that female thing of wrinkling her nose, said, "You need fresh air in here."

The walls were covered in racing sheets, a photo, framed, of White Bay, and reams of statistics, form figures, trends, tipsters, and other useless shite. She zeroed in on a board in the center of the room, asked, wonder in her voice, "Is that a poem?"

"'At Galway Races'" . . . by the man himself, Yeats.

I don't have a whole lot of book learning. I can tell you who won the Grand National in all the years from 1975 through to 2004, the name of every Gold Cup winner even before then, but formal education, not an iota. That poem, we learned it in school, and for obvious reasons it struck a chord. There's a guy who does calligraphy in the Saturday market, from Lithuania or some just place, and for ten euro he did the poem for me. I know it by heart; why wouldn't I? . . . *Aye, horsemen for companions* . . .

She said, "I'm impressed."

We made love or something like it on the floor, beneath Yeats. I think she muttered on the point of orgasm . . . "Horseman, pass by."

Only later did I find out that's on his gravestone. If I'd have known, it would have told me exactly where she was coming from.

After that first poor encounter, sweaty wrestling, we were bonded. What's the buzz term? We became an item. I introduced her to Byrne, my best mate, and when she'd gone to the ladies' room, I asked him, "What do you think?"

Byrne was as worn as me own self, said, "She surely can put it away."

That's an Irish compliment, not to be analyzed.

I didn't, just took it as acceptance.

Over the next few months, the three of us were joined at the hip. One night we went back to Byrne's place, a fine house on the Shantalla Road, left to him by his mother. He was the proverbial Irish son, lived with his mother and got the house when she passed on. My estate had been a tin Miraculous Medal on a bit of blue string. I flung it in the canal.

We had the Saw Doctors playing, the track "Bless Me Father." I'd asked him if he had any Van Morrison, and he went, "What's the thing with you and Van?"

I told the truth—sometimes it's the only option—said, "He's my lucky mascot."

We'd had a few, shite, a lot, and were ending the evening in traditional form with Jameson shots. One, two, three, down the hatch, grimace and line 'em up again.

Like that.

That's when the crazy plan began. Byrne was saying, "Remember when they stole Shergar?"

The most famous racehorse in these isles, and the paramilitaries grabbed him for ransom. The money was never paid and the horse was never found. Byrne said, "The plan was sound but the execution was flawed."

Brona said, "Wouldn't it be great to have a mountain of money?"

Who'd argue that? I said I'd go to Vegas, have me a time, stay at the Luxor, gamble all night, drink margaritas all day. Somewhere in that muddled, demented chat, Brona said, "I've a notion."

We waited and she paused. The Irish know how to tease the crowd, and she had a showstopper, wanted to time it right—downed a shot, then: "Kidnapping a horse is too complicated. . . ."

We waited; then she added, "Let's grab a jockey."

That's what we did.

Galway Races is the largest meeting in the country. The punters come from all over and for seven days the town is hopping—poker games, hookers, adrenaline, shysters, money, and, of course, the racing. Focal point is the Galway Plate. Every man, woman, and child bets on this. It's the bookie's delight. Odds-on favorite this year was Big Red; he'd cantered home effortlessly at Cheltenham, and, wondrous though the horse was, it was his jockey who made him special. No one else understood the shrill testiness of a real blueblood. The one time he'd been ridden by a different jockey, he lost.

His jockey was the famous Ed McGrath. It was said he could guide a donkey to win. Second-favorite was Morning Dew and he'd have been a shoo-in were it not for McGrath on Big Red.

Brona's scheme was pure simplicity: Kidnap McGrath and bet the mortgage on the second-favorite, ante-post. Get our cash down and then snatch McGrath.

The top guys in any field, football players, rock stars, politicians, business hotshots, all have serious security. Jockeys have never reached the glamour stakes. Maybe it's a height thing. We opened a bottle of Black Bush to celebrate our plan, Brona sang, "When You Were Sweet Sixteen." She had a good voice and quavered in all the right places. Maybe that was the booze, but it sure packed in the sentiment; I swear I saw a tear in Byrne's eye. He followed with, "I Never Will Marry." He wasn't much of a singer, but that time of the morning it doesn't matter. Me, I don't sing, not even when I'm mickey-eyed. I did recite the Yeats poem, twice. Raising my voice for the line, "Sing on; somewhere at some new moon, we'll learn that sleeping is not death." Brona said it was beautiful, that I was beautiful, and me, God help me, I thought there wasn't anything as beautiful as real friends.

Brona said we'd need a drug or something to put McGrath out. I mentioned the dodgy vet I knew and went to see him; that's how we got the dope.

McGrath was staying in the Great Southern, and not as much as one Garda (guard) at his door. Brona got our bets down, and Byrne and I grabbed the jockey. The hotel was chockablock with revelers. Byrne and I knocked on the door, going, "Room service." As I said at the beginning, the effect of the dope was awesome, and Byrne thought I'd killed him. I bent down, took his pulse—no, he was fine-ish.

Carried McGrath out in a bin liner; no one paid us a blind bit of notice. He weighed little more than a sod of turf. Stashed him in Byrne's house.

Tied and gagged, he was stretched in the top room of the house.

The day of the Galway Plate, I went to the track. Byrne was watching McGrath, and Brona was ready to do the rounds of the bookies, collect our takings. Consternation at the meeting—McGrath had simply vanished, and, it emerged, he was fond of a drink, so it was presumed he'd gone on a blinder. I was elated; My day had come; I even bought a ticket to the owners and trainers enclosure, usually reserved for the upper echelons. I was wearing me one suit and drinking champers. It's what the shitheads drink in that space. I eyeballed each and every one of the fucks, wanting to roar, "I'm yer equal now."

I got the best position on the grandstand to watch our victory, and man, it was sweet. The second-favorite, now elevated to favorite since McGrath's nonappearance, won effortlessly.

He was odds-on by then, but we'd backed him at five to one, and in one place got eights! I punched the air with total delight, and a woman beside me smiled, asked, "Did you have much on him?"

I near hugged her, answered, "My life."

Took me three hours to get back into the city center, such were the crowds. I hadn't been much exaggerating when I told the woman I'd bet my life.

I'd borrowed a serious wedge of green from a shady outfit who liked to get their money back and fast; they were not reluctant to sever limbs in the pursuit of that goal.

At Eyre Square, I found a phone that hadn't been vandalized. I hadn't ever got a mobile; my money went on the horses. Tried Brona, Byrne, and no answer. Tried them a lot—nothing.

Slammed the receiver on the cradle, hurting my hand. I was almost penniless, the champagne had cost me the last of my folding money. I had to walk to Shantalla, my heart walloping in my chest. Knocked on Byrne's door, no reply. I was getting a real bad feeling. What the fuck was going on?

So I broke in the back, serious apprehension in my belly.

There was a note on the kitchen table.

Didn't he do well . . . ? God bless his lovely hooves. We'd say you're welcome to the house, except it's already owned by the bank, but we can offer you the jockey. He should be coming 'round by now and is sure to be hungry. Be a sweetheart and get him some grub. In case you're scratching yer little head, Tom and I are in love and, by now, in the money. Are you, as your poem says, "hearing the whole earth change its tune"? You read that so nicely.

We'll place a bet in Vegas for you.
XXXXXXX . . . B 'n' B (Doesn't that have a ring to it?)

Tom! Who the fuck ever called him by his first name?

The three hours it took me to get back to town, Byrne would have been doing the rounds, collecting the winnings.

When I'd asked her one time, "So, what do you think of my mate Byrne?" she'd said he was the type of man who'd look after a woman. I thought she was kidding.

Hatred rose in me like a banshee, hatred of her, hatred of horses, hatred of Tom . . . but mostly, hatred of bloody Yeats.

I'VE UNTIED MCGRATH and he's sitting on the bed, a little befuddled and trying to get his eyes to settle. He's staring at me and I want to ask if he likes poetry—does he know the Yeats poem, or wait . . . what's the deal with Doncaster and the favorite in the last race?

Instead I settle for: "Do you ever listen to Van Morrison?"

I'm thinking, a shot of that Rompum wouldn't be the worst thing for me own self.

MY LIFE AS A CHILDHOOD RACING JUNKIE

Meghan O'Rourke

I BEGAN GOING TO THE TRACK when I was six or so, an accident of geography, I suppose. In the summer of 1980, my family moved from a working-class fishing town in Maine, not far from the Bush family's Kennebunkport compound—where Secret Service motorboats buzzed the blue beaches—to Cobble Hill, in Brooklyn. The neighborhood then was not the hip one it's become today. It was a place of edges that never quite met. The slate sidewalks were cracked and blue, and brown grass sprang through them. Boys carried boom boxes on their shoulders. A girl laced up her roller skates outside our house and skated unsupervised till dark every night. In the lot down the street stickball was played among the shadows. Then there was the track (which I thought at the time was in Brooklyn). On the crisp afternoons of early fall, we began what became a family habit of driving out to Belmont to spend the day watching the horses run, making ourselves thirsty from shouting. We'd leave after the eighth race to beat the traffic, timing our exit so we'd be walking past the far turn as the horses of the ninth race swept past, like a last boom of summer thunder.

Strangely—since all love stories are stories of beginnings—I don't remember the first time my parents took me to the track. What I remember, with a particularity that startles me, is all the time in the middle: the minutes whiled away between post times; leisurely walks to the paddock in sticky August sun; poking my head over the counter at the betting teller as I stood with my father placing his exactas and trifectas; the rush back to our seats to watch the horses loading into the gate. The early eighties were a good time to be introduced to horse racing: There was Spectacular Bid, who had a nine-race winning streak, a perfect season; the inestimable John Henry, a gawky gelding and a latter-day Seabiscuit, who was still trouncing his competition as a six-year-old; the stunning stablemate sons of Seattle Slew, Woody Stephens's Devil's Bag and Swale; and of course, Lady's Secret, the game granddaughter of Secretariat, who liked to set the pace and beat the boys. Or maybe every era is a good one for racing, and it's just the one in which you fall in love that stands in your memory.

I was a childhood horse racing junkie. My father used to like to tell his friends—and later, embarrassingly, my friends—that I could decipher the *Daily Racing Form* before I'd learned to read. Like most of his stories, this was exaggerated for effect—he was an Irishman from a large family—but it wasn't far off the mark. The *Racing Form* is mostly a matter of understanding numbers and shorthand like "Gamely between rivals" or "Failed to menace." This I could do. Like most girls, I read any kind of book I could get my hands on about girls and horses—I loved *Great Heart,* the story of an injured jumper with a large heart, who is healed by a dedicated girl. But it was the racing books that took the top of my head off. I must have lost months reading Walter Farley's Black Stallion series. My favorites were the ones packed with details about racing—like *The Black Stallion's Courage,* which offered a picture of the complexities of handicapping.

In the third grade, I spent much of the time taking notes on my favorite horses. I speculated, in a slim green spiral notebook, on their chances in upcoming stakes races, like the Wood Memorial. I kept a file of statistics clipped from the *Racing Form,* and copies of Steven Crist's latest column in the *New York Times:* lists of the highest earners at stud, the best dams, the top-grossing colts under the age of three. Every few months or so I compared them, to see who was making his way up the earnings ladder, and who down. The *Racing Form* was like a dispatch from a world of pleasure I had only partial glimpses of—it was as delicious to read as Turkish delight is to eat—and on Saturdays I pressed my father to pick it up for me at the newsstand around the corner. The sight of the red logo, with its inset etching of horse and rider walking to the gate, seemed to make the living room bigger. So did the old, esteemed names that cropped up inside: War Admiral, Count Fleet, Citation, Ruffian.

We went to the track nearly a dozen times a year (not that much, really), usually for the Wood Memorial and another day or two at Aqueduct in the spring, and then for the big fall handicappers at Belmont, and my favorites: the Marlboro, the Woodward, and the Jockey Club Gold Cup. As my little brother and I got older and sturdier on our feet, we started going to Saratoga each summer. We drove down from a tiny cottage we rented in the even tinier town of Arlington, Vermont, getting up at five-thirty or six—like the jockeys, I imagined—and made our way south to the old resort town, with its wide sidewalks and tall elms.

I don't know how, exactly, the track became part of our family story, except that my parents took my younger brother and me everywhere—they were schoolteachers, and there wasn't much money in those days. And in Brooklyn my father befriended a man who loved the track and wagered every day on the races (with great success). My mother had grown up riding, in her suburban coastal New Jersey town, and one of her younger sisters owned a neurasthenic claimer named Goldie. Their family had always gone to the track, a place that suited their big, exuberant, talkative style, and the brand of cheerful optimism they practiced, in stark contrast to my father's family. They were genteel, reticent, and anxious in ways I felt sympathetic to.

A day at Saratoga was never an idle summer outing. I was taking notes. After reading William Nack's excellent biography of Secretariat, *Big Red of Meadow Stable* (recently republished as *Secretariat: The Making of a Champion*), I realized that what I really wanted was to be a horse trainer. I began a regimen, in the curious way children do. I woke early (trainers woke early); I ate Raisin Bran for breakfast (horses ate bran mash); I got a stopwatch. I doubt I kept this up for long, but that summer felt to me like a rehearsal for the life I was going to lead. At the time I was paralyzingly shy (the kind of child who wouldn't answer the phone) but also bossy (once I got over the shyness). My vision of myself as a trainer involved a future that, even then, I must have known I wouldn't have: one in which I carried a clipboard and leaped over puddles, and made decisions emphatically and without anxiety. I would be efficient and energetic and closemouthed. I would be working to make the horses into champions. This fantasy that I might become a different person by becoming a trainer was unlikely, only even now I can't help thinking it just might have been true.

For some reason the 1984 season stands out in my memory, maybe because my family seemed on shaky ground that year, and I was, at eight, just becoming aware of myself in the world. Plus, that was the year that Devil's Bag and Swale, Woody Stephens's two stablemate champs, were three years old. They were both sons of Seattle Slew, and the idea that they knew each other somehow—and were trained by the same man—appealed to me. I'd been watching both since they started racing the summer before. We saw Swale break his maiden in late July or early August of eighty-three, after he'd faded on his first try two weeks earlier. And we watched Devil's Bag storm away with a dramatic win. Swale seemed a more reliable horse, hard-driving and kind, but Devil's Bag—a big, dark horse, almost black, with an attitude—had an unearthly wildness and charisma. I fell in love with him the way a seventh-grade girl might fall in love with an eighth-grade boy who has the kind of mercurial temperament that, in the right circumstances, might turn into electric brilliance. As Woody Stephens put it in his phenomenal memoir, *Guess I'm Lucky: My Life in Horseracing*:

> *[Swale] was a sweet-natured horse with the will to win and the promise of greatness in him, yet he stood in the*

shadow of Devil's Bag, who was superior to him in my judgment and everybody else's. The Devil was the grandest-looking horse I'd ever seen . . . .

I was awfully disappointed at Belmont that fall when (as I recall) Devil's Bag let us down. I'd asked my mother to put five dollars to win on him. But he just never took to the race. He didn't quite go after it, for some reason. Funny how a horse can rile you up like that, make you fall in love and break your heart. Months later my parents had a fight at the dinner table over the two horses: My father insisted it was Swale, not Devil's Bag, who'd lost that race. It was an example of how much these things mattered—how strong the attachment one had to one's picture of a given race. The fight ended with a plate being thrown, and my mother and I looking at each other in bewilderment, then saying, "But it *was* Devil's Bag."

We waited all spring for the Devil to show up in the prep races for the Derby. I had a firm belief he would win the Derby; he was *the one.* Then, a week before, Stephens ran him in the Derby Trial Stakes, and he tired after leading. So Stephens decided not to run him, to save him for the shorter Preakness. Swale would represent the Stephens barn in the Run for the Roses. I was crushed, even though I loved Swale too. It was like having your date abandon you and being taken to the prom by your best friend instead. Years later I found out I wasn't alone; Devil's Bag seemed to have that effect on all of us. As Stephens recalls in his memoir, "Right up to the morning of Derby Day, it was Devil's Bag and not Swale that visitors wanted to see in Barn 41, though they were both there, the Devil lazy in stall eleven, Swale acting up some in stall seven."

But Swale won the Derby, and life was a little sweeter for a short time. Until one day he returned from a routine workout and a terrible thing happened. Some witnesses said he reared up, others that he just fell over. Whatever the case, by the time Woody Stephens got there, Swale was twisting in pain on the floor. The doctors pronounced him dead when they arrived. This was a few weeks after death had become real in my own mind for the first time. One afternoon while my parents were away in the Catskills, I'd been playing freeze tag with my brother and my friend Katie when I was caught. Frozen, I leaned on our dining room table, looking down at its pale blond wood, and at my finger just touching the crack between the panels and the lip of the edge, and I realized I was going to die. It was all going to come to an end. No more statistics, no more horses, no more me. When those sudden chills come over me now, Swale and Devil's Bag are all mixed up in it at the edges: the star who died young, and the brilliant meteor who never quite moved into the version of himself I'd—we'd all—imagined for him; he retired early and was a mediocre sire.

NEEDLESS TO SAY, my horse racing infatuation was a pretty lonely one. The girls at my private school could be divided into two groups: those who loved dogs, and those who loved horses. Periodically a classroom-wide debate was staged, and some partisans would cross camp lines like centrist senators. But in these debates "horses" always referred to show horses, another thing altogether. The girls I knew went riding on English saddles in Central Park. There was a girl in my third-grade class, N., whom no one much liked—she was slow to

joke and quick to take offense—but we all admired the seri-
ousness of her horse love: she wore her curly brown hair in a
long horsy braid and came to school wearing her velvet riding
helmet. One day she let the rest of us try it on. Her status
soared that week.

Racehorses, on the other hand, were seedy. One day a friend
told me she thought it was "sad" that the horses were "forced"
to race, which horrified me. She'd missed the point: The best
racehorses weren't just fast; they were game. Or, as one railbird type said in *Sports Illustrated* of Kentucky Derby winner
Smarty Jones, "He was running hard—and he was *likin'* it."
Boys didn't get it either. Preoccupied with Strat-O-Matic
baseball, they wouldn't deign to converse about horses, even
in their own idiom. ("Hey, if you could see one Kentucky
Derby, which would it be, Secretariat's or Citation's?")

It could be that I fell in love with racehorses precisely because I couldn't have any other kind of horse in my life: Since
I lived in New York City and we didn't have enough to pay for
riding lessons, I never learned to ride. But I think the obsession had to do with something else: a model of ambition (the
other great American pastime) and a concrete way of deci-
phering it. Horse racing made the unruly world seem man-
ageable. A fifth of a second equaled a length; a mile was made
up of eight furlongs; when you looked closely at a horse's
bloodlines you could determine, or at least conjecture, where
his burst of speed at the sixteenth pole came from. It was also
breathtaking to watch: to see how much effort is expended
and how fast it is over. The percussive thud of hooves, the
quiet aftermath—and here came a new set of horses into the
paddock, ready to be saddled up, crisp saddlecloths stretched
over their backs, their tails cocked, eyes taking in the crowd.

Even on a bad day there was always a race in which a long shot stalked the pace from behind. We were participants, and it seemed grand. So the thrall of the track was never just about wanting a horse I could call my own. It was about learning how things worked, glimpsing the disappointments of training hard to win a six-furlong stakes race that lasts 1:08 2/5 seconds. In a strange way, it was about wanting to be adult, to read adult newspapers, make adult bets—to feel the consequences of action; but to feel them in a world cradled by a strange, undying romanticism.

Of course there was also something melancholy about it all, and in a sense my friend was right. Today's cautious-parenting columnists would probably hold that a racetrack is not a suitable place for an eight-year-old. But at the time I didn't notice that many of my fellow enthusiasts were ragged around the edges. When I did, I was old enough so that the dilapidated quality of life by the rail made a kind of sense— of course someone who was old or alone or a drunk would come to the track, where every half hour there was the chance of something amazing. Even when the horses were nags, there was the pageantry to keep you going. The bright silks always seemed hopeful, the jockeys and the backstretch hangers-on were right out of Dickens—oversize Jimmy the Greek, digni-fied Charlie Whittingham, and Angel Cordero, Jr., the brusque jockey who simply won, and won, and won one season we spent at Saratoga.

A friend of mine recently pointed out that the crop of books generated in the aftermath of Laura Hillenbrand's best-selling *Seabiscuit* skews more toward memoir than race-track taxonomy. For these writers, he argued, the track is a site of nostalgia: an icon of a lost America, or a lost childhood spent reading *The Black Stallion* or *Misty of Chincoteague.* I suppose that spending all this time talking about my childhood might seem like a yearning for the past. But in those days horse racing seemed to be all about the future. Perhaps that's why I don't remember the beginning of the love affair, and I do remember the intimations of what I thought was its end. It came while watching the 1990 Breeders' Cup, during the Distaff race, for mares. That was the year Go for Wand, the champion filly, broke down in the stretch, right in front of where I sat with my family. A horse had fallen on the far turn earlier that day, and a jockey had been badly injured. It shook the crowd; the white ambulance that carried him off seemed like a harbinger of heartbreak.

But the Distaff was the race the crowd was waiting for, and by the time it went off excitement rippled through the stands. Go for Wand led, I seem to remember, most of the way and was bravely fighting off a late challenge when she took a bad step. She stumbled over herself and fell hard—and then, wildly, got up. Only something had gone terribly wrong. On her next stride, her foreleg went down and bent the wrong way. She picked it up and it flopped back and forth. Someone caught her reins and within what seemed like minutes the track vet had put her down. It was one of the most awful things I've ever seen. There are pictures of it in an old *Sports Illustrated,* and recently I found them online. They were almost unbearable to look at.

IT WAS TEN YEARS or so before I went to the track again. Sometime in 2001 I got on the LIRR and went out to Belmont to watch the Belmont Stakes with a new boyfriend and his friends, who, as it turned out, were horse racing junkies too: one belonged to the family that owned Bold Ruler—the sire of Secretariat, and a great horse in his own right. Another had been a railbird for decades, and built time into his business trips to visit the local tracks. That year, 2001, wasn't a Triple Crown year—Monarchos had won the Derby, and Point Given, the Bob Baffert star, had won the Preakness. But it was exciting to watch the top three-year-olds go after one another in a test of their endurance. (Point Given won.) Something about the day—the bustling crowd, the one exacta I made good on—lit up the track for me again. I felt I could step into a dusty beam of light in the mezzanine and become that other self, an adult I'd envisioned wearing tailored pants and stepping neatly over muddy puddles by the training track, one whose accomplishments were soothingly quantifiable but also, somehow, a little magical.

For a long time I thought that my childhood obsession with the track was a story about me, about the ways in which I was different from other kids. But now I realize that it is not a story about finding myself, which is the kind of story we tend to tell these days. It was a story about losing myself. Those years may have been about an obsession with a world in my head—since we didn't actually get to the track itself all that much—but they were not about the world *of* my head. The love I felt had to do with the kind of effort that couldn't double back on itself and undermine you. And it's a story I go back to, because in some way the particular vision of losing myself I found at the racetrack is one that connects to an older and finer American story, the story of traveling out to a land one has no expectations of, with the one hope of finding something grand, on a journey on which we move with spectacular effort toward a wire that arrives faster than you'd think, navigating moments of great risk, slipping "gamely between foes." No surprise, then, that Woody Stephens writes that after Swale's death he was deluged with poems and cards from children who had loved the dark brown horse for his gameness.

Go for Wand's breakdown was the moment I learned you couldn't always decipher things. Her fall was the messy consequence itself, a tragedy that you were part of simply because you happened to see it. And there was no way to piece together this world, or any other, through information and statistics, just as there was no way any of us were going to be spared simply because we have great hearts. If that were true, Ruffian, who could be seen running in her sleep as she struggled to come to after a failed operation to save her broken leg, would have been saved. So would Ferdinand, the big red champ who pulled away from the pack to win the 1986 Derby, and who was recently reported to have been put down in a Japanese abattoir in 2004. But I still keep a button with a picture of Lady's Secret above my desk, which says, THE LADY IS A CHAMP, and I still like to wear my EASY GOER T-shirt when I go running. It makes me feel faster than I am.

THE CONTRIBUTORS

JONATHAN AMES is the author of six books: *I Pass Like Night, The Extra Man, What's Not to Love?, My Less Than Secret Life, Wake Up, Sir!,* and *I Love You More Than You Know.* He's the winner of a Guggenheim Fellowship, and he has adapted his books for film and television. He divides his time between Monte Carlo and New York City.

BILL BARICH's books include *A Fine Place to Daydream: Racehorses, Romance, and the Irish,* and *Laughing in the Hills,* a classic account of racetrack life first serialized in *The New Yorker.* He lives in Dublin, Ireland.

KEN BRUEN was a finalist for the Edgar, Barry, and Macavity Awards, and the Private Eye Writers of America presented him with the Shamus Award for the Best Novel of 2003 for *The Guards,* the book that introduced Jack Taylor. The second Taylor novel, *The Killing of the Tinkers,* was the 2005 Macavity Award winner for best novel. His first job, at twelve years of age, was serving teas to the jockeys at the Galway races. He lives in Galway, Ireland.

LEE CHILD, previously a television director, trade union organizer, theater lighting designer, stage manager, and law student, has been an author for nine years and has published nine Jack Reacher novels, with the tenth—*The Hard Way*—due out in 2006. Currently his books sell in forty-one countries in twenty-nine languages and have all been international bestsellers. In 2004 in England a well-known racehorse owner named his new three-year-old prospect Jack Reacher after Child's lead character. Child was born in Britain but now lives in New York City and the south of France.

STEVEN CRIST, who covered horse racing for *The New York Times* from 1981 to 1990, is the chairman and publisher of *Daily Racing Form* and the author of the books *Offtrack*, *The Horse Traders*, and *Betting on Myself.* He lives in Hempstead, New York, with his wife, Robin Foster, and two retired racing greyhounds.

LAURA HILLENBRAND is the author of the number one bestseller, *Seabiscuit: An American Legend,* winner of the BookSense Book of the Year and William Hill Sports Book of the Year awards and finalist for the National Book Critics Circle Award and the *Los Angeles Times* Book Prize. Her 2003 *New Yorker* article, "A Sudden Illness," won the National Magazine Award, and she is a two-time winner of the Eclipse Award, the highest journalistic honor in Thoroughbred racing. An alumna of Kenyon College, she lives in Washington, D.C.

JOE R. LANSDALE is the author of several novels, including Edgar Award winner *The Bottoms*, and many short stories. Although he never raced horses, he did own mules at one time. He lives in Nacogdoches, Texas, with his family.

LAURA LIPPMAN's crime novels have won virtually every award given to American writers. Her most recent book is *No Good Deeds*, the ninth installment in her series about private investigator Tess Monaghan. She also is the author of two stand-alones, *Every Secret Thing* and *To the Power of Three*. A former newspaper reporter, she lives in Baltimore.

WILLIAM NACK, longtime racing writer at *Sports Illustrated*, is the author of *Secretariat: The Making of a Champion* and *My Turf: Horses, Boxers, Blood Money and the Sporting Life*. He is a seven-time winner of racing's Eclipse Award for turf writing. Nack is working on a racetrack memoir, of which "August of 1959" is a part. He lives in Washington, D.C.

MEGHAN O'ROURKE is the culture editor at *Slate* and a poetry editor of *The Paris Review*. Her essays and poems have appeared in *Slate*, *The New Yorker*, *The New Republic*, *The New York Times Book Review*, and other magazines. She lives in Brooklyn and still goes to the track.

SCOTT PHILLIPS once saw the great Cash Asmussen win six races of a seven-race card at Longchamp, outside Paris. He is the author of several novels, including *The Ice Harvest* and the forthcoming *The Kind Men Like.* He currently lives in St. Louis, Missouri.

JOHN SCHAEFER is the host of WNYC Radio's culture and talk show *Soundcheck* and the music program *New Sounds.* He has written extensively about music, including the book *New Sounds: A Listener's Guide to New Music, The Cambridge Companion to Singing: World Music*, and the TV program *Bravo Profile: Bobby McFerrin.* A native New Yorker, he grew up within walking distance of Aqueduct Race Track.

JANE SMILEY is the author of *Horse Heaven* and *A Year at the Races.* She lives in California, where she owns and breeds Thoroughbreds who sometimes go to the racetrack but more often eat the bread of idleness at home.

JERRY STAHL is the author of three novels: *Perv, Plainclothes Naked*, and *I, Fatty*, which has been optioned by Johnny Depp. His memoir, *Permanent Midnight*, was made into a movie starring Ben Stiller and Owen Wilson. He has received a Pushcart Prize for short fiction, and his work has appeared in a variety of magazines, including *Details* and *Transatlantic Review.* His journalism and short stories have been anthologized widely. He divides his time between Los Angeles and Vienna.

CHARLIE STELLA started at Roosevelt and Yonkers before moving on to the exciting world of Thoroughbred betting (and doubleheaders). After tearing up enough losing tickets he switched sides and took action. Now he plays drums and lives in Brooklyn.

WALLACE STROBY is an award-winning journalist and author of the novels *The Heartbreak Lounge* and *The Barbed-Wire Kiss*. A Long Branch, New Jersey, native, he worked one long hot summer on a maintenance crew at Monmouth Park, sweeping up losing tickets, cigar butts, and broken dreams. He's now an editor at the *Newark Star-Ledger,* Tony Soprano's hometown paper.

JAMES SUROWIECKI is a financial columnist for *The New Yorker* and writes a regular sports column for *Bookforum*. He's the author of *The Wisdom of Crowds.*

DANIEL WOODRELL lives in the Missouri Ozarks near the Arkansas line. His eighth novel, *Winter's Bone,* will be published by Little, Brown in 2006. Being partially of French descent, whenever Woodrell watches horses gallop in a race, the thoughts that dance in his head are not generally of victory or defeat, but most often romp toward le bistro and the simple request, "Tartare, please, with hard-boiled eggs and the house red."

ACKNOWLEDGMENTS

Jonathan Ames: "All Horses Have Beautiful Eyes and a Big Cock," copyright © 2006 by Jonathan Ames.

Bill Barich: "Gurriers," copyright © 2006 by Bill Barich.

Ken Bruen: "Horse of a Different Color," copyright © 2006 by Ken Bruen.

Lee Child: "The .50 Solution," copyright © 2006 by Lee Child.

Steven Crist: "The Smarty Jones Bubble," copyright © 2006 by Steven Crist.

Maggie Estep: "Beast," copyright © 2006 by Maggie Estep.

Laura Hillenbrand: "The Derby," copyright © 1999 by Laura Hillenbrand. Originally published in *American Heritage* magazine in May/June 1999.

Joe R. Lansdale: "White Mule, Spotted Pig," copyright © 2006 by Joe R. Lansdale.